LILIAN

In 1905, Lilian Rutherford agrees to marry mining office clerk, Bill Robinson, when she becomes pregnant by Johnny Peacock, the mine owner's son. Though aware of his wife's true feelings, Bill never doubts that he is Edward's father. A twist of fate brings prosperity, and a partnership with the Peacocks and their associates, the Fairburns, but when Edward's paternity is unexpectedly revealed, their marriage deteriorates into an empty sham. The four families remain entwined, but it takes the dark shadow of World War I to finally bring true reconciliation to Lilian and Bill.

LILIAN

LILIAN

by

Josephine McCluskey

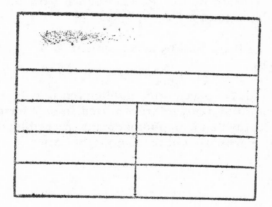

Magna Large Print Books
Long Preston, North Yorkshire,
BD23 4ND, England.

British Library Cataloguing in Publication Data.

McCluskey, Josephine
    Lilian.

    A catalogue record of this book is
    available from the British Library

    ISBN   0-7505-2218-6

First published in Great Britain in 2003 by Heleric Publishing

Copyright © 2003 Josephine McCluskey

Cover illustration © Anthony Monaghan

The right of Josephine McCluskey to be identified as the author of this work has been asserted by her in accordance with the Copyright, Designs and Patents Act, 1988

Published in Large Print 2004 by arrangement with
Mrs M. J. Sanders

Magna Large Print is an imprint of Library Magna Books Ltd.

Printed and bound in Great Britain by
T.J. (International) Ltd., Cornwall, PL28 8RW

'All characters in this book are fictitious and any apparent resemblance to persons living, or dead, is purely accidental.'

CONTENTS

Chapter 1   11
Chapter 2   45
Chapter 3   79
Chapter 4   123
Chapter 5   150
Chapter 6   182
Chapter 7   222
Chapter 8   247
Chapter 9   268
Chapter 10   281
Chapter 11   298
Chapter 12   322
Chapter 13   346
Chapter 14   366
Chapter 15   390
Chapter 16   407
Chapter 17   429
Chapter 18   439

CHAPTER ONE

Gilfell, Cumberland, early August 1905

The evening was grey and shadowy as Lilian crossed the farmyard on light feet, padding soundlessly along the passage from the back door then up the narrow stairs to her room. Earlier in the day she had carefully left everything ready for this moment, and she was panting slightly as she lit the two candles on her dressing table then drew the curtains across the room's single window. Now, safe in her own private haven, she could transform herself in time to see Johnny Peacock again downstairs at the meal her parents were providing for all their harvest helpers.

Pouring water from the jug on the wash stand into its matching china basin she stripped off all her clothes and began to wash herself down, shivering but determined to rinse away every possible trace of the day's hard and sweaty labour, whilst appraising her mirror image as dispassionately as she could. Lilian wondered what Johnny really thought of the tall slim girl with the mane of dark hair and big hazel eyes who viewed him in a manner that was not always flattering, for she sensed that he only continued to pursue her because she had refused to become yet another of his conquests like so many of the girls in the surrounding area whom he had used

11

then left in varying degrees of emotional devastation to move on to pastures new.

When he had unexpectedly arrived to help with the last of the haymaking Lilian had not been the only person to be surprised, for the son of the local lead mine owner was certainly not known for soiling his hands, and while she had felt her heart beat a little faster at the sight of him she had kept her distance.

On the steep field on that sunny afternoon the haymakers had soon become unpleasantly hot at their labours, causing many female glances to be sent in Johnny's direction when he had taken off his shirt to reveal an attractively muscular torso, and although he did not seem to be aware of the flutter he was causing Lilian felt sure that he was really quite conscious of it and deliberately ignored him as she kept her head bent over her rake. Let Marjorie and Mary, the Thompsons' sixteen year old twins, make idiots of themselves and a bigger head for Johnny Peacock if they had no more sense, but she had more self-respect than wear her heart on her sleeve. The moment just before dusk when the last sheaf was lifted onto the cart James Rutherford had urged his daughter to hurry back to the house to lend a hand with supper, and Lilian, glad of the excuse to get out of Johnny's way before he saw just how grimy she was, had run ahead of the Shire horse as he pulled the haycart to the barn for the last time.

Reaching for a large towel off the back of the chair she began to dry herself hastily. He would be downstairs now and she was wasting time daydreaming while already the sounds of loud laughing voices were floating up the stairs making her feel isolated and forgotten. Within minutes Lilian was dressed in her 'second best blue' and sticking the last pin into her loosely piled hair, then with a quick check in the full length mirror she left the room and hurried downstairs, happily aware that she was looking her best. The corridor leading to the kitchen appeared to be deserted when she turned the corner onto the last flight of stairs, but before she reached the bottom the back door opened and Johnny Peacock walked in, stopping short at the sight of her, his brown eyes full of admiration.

'Lilian!'

Moving forward quickly he caught her round the waist and lifted her off the stairs into his arms, kissing her mouth soundly and with a lack of caution that both pleased and alarmed her.

'Not here,' she whispered urgently against his ear as he altered his position briefly to push her back against the wall. 'Someone will catch us.'

'But I want you, Lilian.'

His tone was warm and amused, but if that struck something of a jarring note she had no time to dwell on it before a slight rustle of petticoats and a gasp of disapproval caused them to fall reluctantly apart. Lilian's cousin, Anna, obviously on her way from the kitchen to the dining room with a plate of freshly baked scones, stood watching them with a strange glint in her eye, and after a quick squeeze of her hand Johnny executed a mock bow in Anna's direction before sauntering down the passage and into the room

13

where everyone else was having supper.

Left alone the two young women faced each other in silence for a moment; the tall slender dark-haired girl in the blue dress and her shorter, less impressive, cousin. While falling short of Lilian's beauty, Anna, with her fair hair and freckles, was still a pretty girl though a much more strait-laced one.

'How can you make yourself so cheap with him?' She demanded, not bothering to hide her contempt. 'He's only playing with you the same as all the others he's had, and if you're not careful you'll end up wishing you'd had enough sense not to let him wreck your life.'

'I've no intention of letting anybody wreck my life, as you put it, so don't waste any of your precious time worrying on my account. You know nothing about Johnny and I in any case.'

'I know what I saw, and I saw Johnny Peacock treating you with complete lack of respect. Any of the others could have seen you both, but he didn't care did he? As long as he was being given the chance to maul you about...'

Taking a threatening step towards her Lilian had the satisfaction of seeing Anna move towards the dining room with unseemly haste before she herself entered the large kitchen, where her mother and Aunt Violet were washing dishes and gossiping.

'Oh, there you are at last.' Emily Rutherford pointed towards a large enamel jug steaming on the table. 'Take that tea in for those who want it, will you, then you can give us a hand with the dishes or wait to clear up the tables properly after

14

they've all gone.'

There were no more than ten helpers in total, all eating and talking at the tops of their voices, but in the medium sized room full of tables and chairs from other parts of the house the atmosphere was more suggestive of an over-crowded bar. Anna was leaning her back against the empty hearth, her hair perilously close to the oil lamp on the mantelshelf, as she talked to three workmates of her father's and made a great show of not seeing Lilian as she began to pass from table to table, filling up teacups where necessary. She had glimpsed Johnny on her way into the room but it was only when she reached his table, the last but one, that Lilian realised he had a red-faced giggling Thompson twin on each side hanging on to his every word.

'Tea?' she asked lightly, setting the jug down beside him then raising her eyebrows at the girls in mock enquiry, confident that they would soon know who was, and was not, important to Johnny Peacock. As they both shook their heads Lilian allowed her lips to curve into a slight smile as she looked into Johnny's upturned face. At first the blankness of his expression took her completely by surprise and she frowned a little as she repeated. 'Would you care for some tea?'

'I have ale.'

Just as though she were a stranger the man dropped his head at once and recommenced telling Marjorie and Mary some long-winded story about last year's Dalton Fair, while Lilian, anxious to appear in control of herself, moved on to the last table with as much dignity as she

15

could. Still painfully within earshot of the sound of Johnny's voice as he continued to entertain his admiring audience, she struggled to smile at the two elderly farmers from across the valley who were locked in a heated discussion on the merits of organising a market day for Gilfell as opposed to travelling the five miles to Dalton every week, and the very familiar younger man who was holding out his cup and smiling.

'They're well into their beer Lilian, but I'll have some tea, thanks.'

Hastily pouring the hot liquid into Bill Robinson's cup she was only half aware of the man's eagerness to hold her attention, and looked for the first time directly into his pale blue eyes as he grabbed her free wrist to stop her moving away.

'Sit down a while won't you? It's a week since I last saw you, and that was in chapel so it doesn't count.'

Startled out of her reverie she hesitated just long enough for him to pull her down towards the only empty chair, then, after swiftly considering her situation, she yielded to the pressure of her most persistent suitor and seated herself at his side. Ten years her senior Bill was nothing if not reliable, and had persistently pursued her for three years since moving to Gilfell from Kenhope, a village over the fell. He leaned towards her, the warmth in his regard a balm to her recent humiliation.

'Are you singing again at the service on Sunday?'

Lilian forced a laugh. 'The way things are it will be something of an event when I don't have a solo spot on a Sunday night. I'm singing "The

16

Day Thou Gavest Lord is Ended". Not very cheerful words but I love the tune.'

'Anything you sing sounds wonderful,' he said generously. 'It gives the congregation something to look forward to through some of the more tedious sermons.'

For the first time Lilian felt her interest genuinely aroused as she remembered a very significant detail of the following Sabbath's activities, and she scarcely noticed the sudden watchful silence from Johnny's direction as she teased Bill.

'The chapel will be full to overflowing this Sunday night because your Uncle Jonathan is travelling over from Kenhope to preach, and he is extremely popular isn't he?'

The man's expression changed into one of complete dismay at her words and she watched with amusement as a tide of dull pink worked its way from his open collar to his fair hairline.

'Oh no. The family laughing stock. Why can't he see that they're only there to make fun of him and his ... vernacular style?'

'They enjoy him. He's an interesting speaker Bill, and you must admit he brings the Bible stories to life.'

'Oh, he does that alright.'

Gloomily he drained his cup and wished, for once, that he was not teetotal like the rest of his family. Just a little alcohol at this particular moment might have been quite soothing.

A quick burst of laughter from the back of the room caused Lilian to twist round in her chair to see Johnny Peacock standing by the fireplace

17

with his arm round Anna's waist, obviously having made some joke judging by the broad smiles of those in their area, and she rose to her feet abruptly with the almost empty jug in her hand. Mannerly as always, Bill stood up and followed her to the door after a brief goodbye to his table companions.

'See me to the gate, Lilian.' He pleaded outside in the passage, and she nodded, setting the jug down beside the umbrella stand.

'Alright. I fancy some fresh air.'

If Bill Robinson was aware of Lilian's real reason for leaving the room so suddenly he gave no sign of it, nor did he appear to be at all put out by her air of preoccupation as, tucking her arm firmly into his, he strolled out with the girl into the wide sloping yard of Roughside Farm, steadying her as they made their way over the uneven cobblestones towards the gate. They walked in silence until the five bars stopped their progress and the young man hesitated with his hand on the fastening bar, looking down at her face which was now bathed in the light of the ascending moon. She was staring past his left shoulder down the narrow lane leading to the village, and he felt an unwilling stab of pain at her continued indifference to him as a suitor, for that was what he desperately wished to be despite realising all too well how Johnny Peacock put him in the shade and showed every sign of keeping him there.

'Goodnight Lilian.' He said quietly. 'I'll look forward to hearing you sing again on Sunday.'

With a start she brought her attention back to

the present and smiled faintly as she murmured her thanks before turning away from him to go back to the house, her blue skirts billowing around her as she ran. To Bill she gave no more thought. She was free now to concentrate her mind on Johnny Peacock and how best to bring him into line, being determined that he would see no more of her this night, much as the plan depressed her, but it would be well worth it if he chanced to wonder whether she was romantically lingering with Bill Robinson. Other girls would be vying for his attention all evening, but she was not like other girls as she was now taking pains to point out.

Slipping through the side door she paused for a few seconds to listen, then, satisfied that everything still seemed much as before, sped silently along the passage and on up the stairs to her room.

Walking with measured tread along the uneven surface of the lane, Bill tried hard not to give in to his growing pessimism where Lilian was concerned. He was not normally given to passions but from the moment he had seen her she had proved herself to be the exception. On whatever terms could be arranged he wanted Lilian Rutherford, yet he had so far waited in vain for her obvious infatuation with his employer's son to burn itself out. There had been no need for him to come to Roughside today with the other helpers but when Johnny had breezed into the mining offices, where Bill was Chief Clerk, and announced his intention of assisting the Rutherford family he had made up

19

his mind to come too, if only to keep a protective eye on Lilian. Bleakly he admitted to himself that he had gained nothing more than dirty linen and a weary body from the exercise as the girl was still smitten by the worthless Johnny.

Ahead of him loomed the dark shape of the Assembly Rooms, built to look down on the heart of Gilfell from the first steep slope leading out of the village, and he negotiated the path carefully as it wound in front of the building before the final drop into Hillary Terrace. Had he been a man given to imaginings Bill might well have felt nervous in the eerie white-lit silence, but his basically logical nature allowed for no such follies of the mind and he thought only of Lilian as he approached his home.

All he needed to be happy for the rest of his life was to make Lilian Mrs William Robinson, but if it was not to be he would just have to make do with his interests instead. Everything scientific had always fascinated him, and when he was studying the night sky through his sea-faring grandfather's telescope he felt fulfilled and at peace the way he never did with people, so he would survive even if he did not win Lilian, he told himself as he stepped over the wooden stile at the end of the path. The only trouble with that idea was that he could spend just an hour or two each day on these activities and the rest of the time, without Lilian, he would be utterly wretched.

The midday sun shining down on Louisa's first glimpse of Gilfell should have cheered her up after their two day journey with their belongings stacked on an open cart, but she was too tired of the sound of clanking pots and pans and the sight of the Shire horse's broad back with its endlessly swishing tail to feel anything but weary relief.

'What a sprawling place, and so far from everyone we know.' She sighed, and her husband, Terence Marshall, clicked his tongue encouragingly at the horse as he shook the reins.

'It's halfway between Carlisle and Newcastle, Lou, so it's handy for my work in either town.' He said easily. 'We could have stayed in Carlisle as you suggested, but the living here is much cheaper and I need never be without work now that I can advertise in both towns. Good signwriters are hard to find you know.'

Louisa did not bother to respond. Her husband's reasoning made no sense to her and she was still reeling with shock from the moment just three days ago when he had announced his plan for turning their lives upside down. Aghast, and quite unable to see the benefit in being transported twenty-eight miles away from her family to a remote Pennine village where she knew no one, Louisa had protested in vain to a lightly teasing Terence who kept his good humour by treating her like a tiresome child who could not possibly know what was best. After hours of pleading her cause to deaf ears, the girl finally began to join her husband in the packing process and had bid a tearful farewell to her parents and sisters two days previously, just before the horse and cart were driven down the street by Terence.

At first she could not believe that the local rag and bone man's widow had persuaded him to buy

21

the broken down duo, neither of which would be the slightest use once they arrived at their destination, but the slow journey had passed without either a dislocated wheel, or the untimely demise of the horse. Whatever he planned to do with them now Louisa neither knew nor cared.

The few people along Main Street's short parade of shops paid them surprisingly little attention, and they rounded Chapel Corner onto the rising slope of Hillary Terrace, which lay sandwiched between the street and the Assembly Rooms. The houses were all built on Gilfell's steep right side, stopping abruptly at the Assembly Rooms stile, and the road they were travelling was on almost the same level as the bedroom windows. Louisa looked down from her perch at the next flight of steps from the roadside to the backyard doors of the dwellings. 'Just like tiny caves.' She thought, imagining herself in winter scurrying down into her home out of the rain or snow, and for the first time in hours she smiled.

'Which one is ours, Terry?'

'The very last one ... look! You can see its yard wall just before that stile at the end there. It'll be good here Louie, you'll see.'

When they drew to a halt at the back of number fourteen Hillary Terrace Louisa and Terence sat still for a few seconds, the man simply grateful to have arrived without incident and the woman wondering what kind of rooms lay behind the blank curtainless windows. She was tired, having enjoyed no real comfort since leaving Carlisle, but the thought of getting a proper home together again was already giving her energy. With a quick grin in his wife's direction Terence secured the reins and stepped down from the cart rather more stiffly than he would have wished.

'I'm all tied up with rheumatics like an old man.' He complained. 'Must have been too long in the same position. Hang on till I get to your side Lou, and I'll help you down. There's a lot of work to do before bedtime even though the house is partly furnished.'

Putting his hands on each side of his wife's tiny waist reminded Terence not only why he had been unable to do without this delightful girl with her fair hair and blue eyes, but also why he must never relax his guard to reveal to her the predicament that was his life. Taking her hand in his he produced a bunch of keys from his trouser pocket and began to walk Louisa down the grey stone steps towards the maroon door of the backyard, unaware that from a window in number thirteen a very interested Bill Robinson was watching them.

Bill used his spare bedroom as a study and a rather cramped library for his many books, and from his place at the desk by the window he observed the new tenants' comings and goings for almost half an hour before he was shamed into offering some assistance. It was the sight of such a small girl, ignoring her husband's demands to 'Keep back!' and determinedly trying to take some of the weight of a mahogany chest of drawers, that sent him hurrying down the stairs and across the intervening space between his house and theirs where smiles of relief followed his introduction. Louisa disappeared into the

23

house after shaking hands with Bill, and Terence Marshall grinned as he ran his fingers through his springy auburn hair.

'Good to see you. Quite honestly, I was beginning to despair of ever getting the job finished.'

Bill eyed the contents of the cart and nodded. 'It won't take us long working together.'

The men had just manoeuvred the heavy piece of furniture through the back door of the house when a tall brown-clad figure picked up her skirts and climbed over the Assembly Rooms stile. Having watched the proceedings on her way down the path Lilian had observed Bill helping the strangers to move into number fourteen and occasionally caught a glimpse of a young slightly built girl of around her own age moving about from window to window with a cleaning cloth in her hand. She had not looked up, much to Lilian's annoyance as she liked the look of her and wanted to wave. As she passed by the stationary horse and cart on her way to her practice session at the chapel she could hear the buzz of voices punctuated by sudden bursts of laughter from inside the house and stopped a moment beside the horse, digging into her pocket for the apple she had brought along for later. The poor beast with its wearily drooping head inspired her pity, and she watched it eating the fruit with mingled satisfaction and anger. Surely someone could have taken the trouble to at least give the horse a drink, even if nothing more substantial were available just yet.

With a consoling pat on the animal's broad neck Lilian tucked her music more firmly under her arm and walked on towards the chapel at the end of the terrace. The organist would already be well into her own practice session, and as she regarded Lilian's punctuality as vital to their continuing partnership she took care never to offend her. The intriguing matter of the incoming strangers could now wait until her return journey.

It was Louisa who first met Lilian over an hour later as she walked back along the road. Having seen their few pieces of furniture set into place alongside those already in the house, and lit a cosy fire with coal borrowed from Bill until Monday, she was carrying a pail of dirty scrubbing water to the drain in the yard when a voice asked,

'Are you finished everything now, or is there something I can do to help?'

Looking up Louisa drew the back of her hand across her brow while the warmly smiling hazel eyes regarded the tired girl encouragingly, from her tousled hair to her damp rolled up sleeves.

'Well?' Lilian prompted, taking two or three steps down the slope towards her. 'Do you need some help?'

Louisa's hesitation was barely perceptible before she smiled and nodded. 'I would love it if you would make the tea please. The teapot's ready in the hearth and the kettle's almost boiling. I've just scrubbed the scullery floor and have the things to tidy away now.'

'Right.'

Marching down the steps into the small yard Lilian waited for Louisa to empty her bucket before following her into the house. A good fire was burning in the black-leaded grate and the girl lifted the kettle off the hob with a thick knitted square hanging from a hook on the mantelshelf, feeling that in future she would be repeating this homely task for Louisa quite a lot.

Meanwhile Bill Robinson sat on the cart with Terence, guiding him along the alternative route to Roughside Farm over the wider Back Road out of Gilfell. Leading the new neighbour towards a possible buyer for both cart and animal would not only solve a problem for Terence Marshall but, hopefully, give himself the chance to see Lilian again, and to Bill that was worth every hour of voluntary labour.

Smiling a little at the eccentricity of their arrival he shot Terence a curious look as the farm came into view.

'What made you *buy* a horse and cart? Wouldn't it have been better to hire a proper moving cart where you would, at least, have had two horses instead of this tired old nag, and someone to take them away again?'

Terence flushed. 'The rag and bone man near our street had just died, and his widow was eager to sell at a bargain price that was half the cost of hiring a proper vehicle.'

'Oh, I see.'

But Bill did not see at all. Whichever way he viewed the matter it was still strange behaviour, and he sensed that his questions had annoyed Terence Marshall who was now looking sulkily uncommunicative. Cheerfully, trying to break the mood, he remarked. 'Even if James Rutherford doesn't want the horse he'll probably rent you some grazing until you find someone who does, and that shouldn't take long in this area.'

The other man nodded, searching his mind for something neutral he could say that might help smooth over his show of petulance, and finally decided that deep admiration of the scenery would probably be his best bet. As he had suspected, it was only necessary to comment on the wonderful view down the valley to sidetrack his companion into an enthusiastic monologue on the subject, and he retired into his own thoughts for the rest of the journey, looking attentive whilst not actually listening to anything but the drone of Bill Robinson's voice.

A city dweller all his life, the last thing he had expected to find in this remote Pennine village was a neighbour as mentally alert as this man, and he was beginning to suffer severe misgivings regarding the future. It had seemed such a good idea when he had first heard about the available empty property here in Gilfell, with its Main Street surrounded by scattered cottages and farms spread around the fell sides as though some giant hand had casually thrown them there, but maybe he was worrying unduly. Grimly Terence considered his now depleted finances which, in themselves, prevented him moving on somewhere else. Gilfell was the place he had chosen for Louisa and himself and, for better or worse, Gilfell was where they would have to stay.

'You still haven't answered my question John, so I'll repeat it. When is it your intention to take life

27

seriously? You are twenty one now and it's more than time you applied yourself to the mine with a view to taking over from myself and getting some business ideas of your own.'

With his back to the room Johnny Peacock looked determinedly out of the lounge window of White Court knowing exactly how his father would be twisting round in his fireside chair, and how bullishly angry would be his expression as he squinted through the thick smoke of his cigar.

'I've never known why we have a window here when all we can see through it are those great stinking pines,' he remarked lightly. 'Ever considered cutting them down, father?'

A muscle tightened convulsively in the older man's jaw and he turned his head away from his son, watching fresh smoke curling up from the tip of his Havana.

'We had Gerald and Elisabeth Fairburn to dinner last evening, as I'm sure you were well aware. They brought Constance and Arabella with them and both young ladies appeared to be inordinately disappointed by your absence. I made what excuses I could, but word will doubtless get back to them as to where you actually were ... making hay at the Rutherford farm like a sweaty labourer.'

Johnny made no reply and Thomas Peacock struggled to control his anger for a while longer as he rose to his feet and stood staring at his son's defiant back.

'Luparte is talking about pulling out, John, but Fairburn is showing interest in investing in the mine which will help us expand to find new markets and possibly new ventures, but he will have the upper hand financially which is not good for your longterm future. I want you to apply yourself to the business as never before, and as Fairburn has two unmarried daughters there's one way especially that you can ensure this family's security now, and your own, for the rest of your life.'

The younger man revolved slowly on his heel looking his father straight in the eye, and Thomas flinched slightly at the bitter desperation there. Before he could say any more Johnny walked past him to the door, hands thrust deep into his pockets as he halted briefly in the opening.

'I thought this method of consolidating business mergers had died out last century,' he said bleakly, 'but seeing it's still going strong I'll tell you now that it will have to be Bella. If I must be offered like some prize stallion I'll take the mare who'll be the least trouble.'

Looking down at the polished toes of her best shoes as they rested on a hassock Lilian tried to amass as many sober thoughts as her mind could contain while she fought valiantly with herself not to snigger with the rest of the congregation. Jonathan Robinson's sermon was approaching its conclusion as the preacher showed his usual signs of becoming increasingly carried away by his own enthusiasm. Across the aisle to her right she could see Bill, the only person apart from herself who was not smiling and definitely the only person who did not want to, and could almost feel his embarrassment as Jonathan, short, balding and middle-aged, threw out both arms in a melodramatic gesture.

'...and Jesus looked up into the tree where his servant had climbed to gawk at Him, and He cried "Come down, lad! Come down, before you tear your britches"!'

If Jonathan Robinson was in any way dismayed by the sudden spate of involuntary laughter turned quickly into coughing and nose blowing of epidemic proportions, he gave no hint of it. His homely face shining with fervour he swept on to the end of his sermon, arms still aloft, then slowly lowered them and bent his head waiting for the restlessness to die away before offering the final prayer.

Torn between pity for the ridicule he inspired, and irritation at his blindness to it, Lilian closed her eyes and began the process of mentally preparing herself to sing. During the long service she had concentrated on the ornate railing round the chapel's upper storey and knew that she would fix her gaze upon the flower pattern most directly opposite her as she sang rather than look at the congregation. Familiar faces, even those of her parents sitting close by, disconcerted her, but the railing was beautiful, mostly white but with flower panels painted in delicate pink, green and blue. Pretty to see, and reassuringly impersonal, unlike the faces of Bill Robinson and, nearer the back of the building, Johnny Peacock, who had made no attempt to see her yesterday despite having angered her so deeply at the haymakers' supper.

'...and we ask this in the name of Thy Son,

Jesus Christ, Amen.'

With a silent start Lilian saw Jonathan signal to her to move to the rostrum as he announced her solo, and she got to her feet with her hymn book open at the appropriate page. She was hardly aware of either taking her place at the front of the chapel nor of beginning to sing, but she was sublimely conscious of her own keen sense of fulfilment as her rich mezzo soprano sent the melody out into the air. A girl who had always found the orthodox concept of God hard to accept, Lilian secretly sang to a kinder deity of her own and brought to the hymn a quiet conviction of faith which Bill Robinson found too moving for comfort in such a public place.

A few rows behind him Johnny Peacock watched and listened with grudging admiration. He had not come to bore himself for nearly an hour and a half just to hear Lilian Rutherford sing, but he was impressed in spite of himself. She was lovely to look at and her voice matched her appearance so perfectly that he could almost imagine he loved her.

True to chapel tradition the congregation were allowed to applaud when she had finished her solo, and after the concluding blessings they began to file out in an orderly column, shaking hands with the beaming Jonathan as he stood at his place beside the large double doors, happily ignorant of the fact that he was the butt of their jokes for weeks after each visit. Delighted to see two young men, one of whom was his nephew Bill, stopping just outside the doors as though waiting to speak to him, he was deflated after

31

only a short while to find them surging forward to meet the young soloist who was last to leave. She shook hands with Jonathan, her movements unhurried, waved to her parents who were walking into Hillary Terrace to go home, then turned her attention to her prospective escorts, smiling brilliantly at Johnny before tucking her arm neatly into Bill's.

'How kind of you to wait, Bill. Shall we go for a walk?'

Falling back Johnny stared after them as they walked slowly round the corner into Main Street, linked together and talking to each other in a manner which suggested a newly developed intimacy in their relationship, and with a sigh Jonathan went back into the chapel closing the doors quietly after him. He had done his Sabbath duty and could now take his wife and himself back over the fell in the pony and trap which were tethered to a wooden post round the side of the building. The torturous ways of the young had never really afflicted Jonathan Robinson, and if the scene he had just witnessed were anything to judge by he did not feel he had missed much.

Lilian agreed to walk part of the way up the Kenhope Fell road only because it passed in front of Johnny Peacock's home, White Court, and she wanted to make him really squirm this time. Hoping that he would see them once more when she and Bill made the return journey back into the heart of Gilfell, Lilian deliberately walked as close to her companion as decency would permit, pleased that the hat she was wearing exactly matched her new olive green dress and jacket. Colours were her servants, never dominating her, and she was well aware of how good she looked. Glancing up at Bill as they began the ascent she smiled and wondered how far behind them Johnny Peacock might be, but had she been reckless enough to actually look she would have been surprised to see him striding purposefully away from her along the street that led onto Gilfell's Back Road; the road that eventually passed Roughside Farm.

Stragglers from the evening service ambled up the cobbled slope, exchanging pleasantries and laughing together at the memory of Jonathan's verbal excesses, and Johnny scowled down at the ground as he strode through their midst only half aware of their existence. Parting to make way for him they stared after his well tailored back for a few moments in resentful silence, but his long legs soon carried him round the curve onto the Back Road and out of their sight.

Once free of the wandering inhabitants of Gilfell Johnny slowed his pace to a saunter and tried to relax. Since his father had spelt out his duty earlier in the day he had been in a permanent state of frustrated rage which had eventually led to a desperate wish to see Lilian, although there was no way he could confide his trouble to her, and the fact that she had snubbed him in favour of his father's Chief Clerk did not fool Johnny for one second. He knew that he was temporarily out of her good books for failing to give her the attention she regarded as her due, and this was her way of punishing him. But it would pass. It always did.

Taking out his watch he saw that it was almost eight o'clock, which would leave about two hours of daylight at this time of year. Plenty of time to reach Roughside before Bill and Lilian arrived at the farm gate, and he reckoned to know the girl well enough to be sure that she would not invite him into the house for supper with her family. Lilian was simply using Bill, not encouraging him.

On higher ground now with the road to himself Johnny stopped to look down on the village and surrounding fells. Harsh and bleak in winter, the land lay kinder under the August sun as it moved towards the haze of purple mist at the end of the valley. Hardy moorland sheep with curled horns stared at him over the wall as he leaned his elbows against the top row of loose stones, and many more animals were dotted around the opposite meadows. Peaceful, verging on sleepy, described his home village at this time in the evening, but that was not how Johnny felt.

Reluctantly he turned his thoughts to the Fairburn family and tried to imagine what his life would be like once he had played his part in securing his financial future by marrying Arabella; for there was no doubt in his mind, or his father's, that the Fairburns regarded him as eligible.

Their home, Low Shields, lay midway between Gilfell and Dalton and made an impressive sight placed well back from the road, large and square among the trees through which its Georgian windows could be glimpsed winking in the sun. Easily twice the size of White Court, the house had always appealed to Johnny and he tried now to let the knowledge that it would almost certainly be his one day console him.

Constance, although two years older than Bella, was in his opinion unlikely ever to find a husband. In the past few years she had been engaged twice, the first time to a doctor from Newcastle and the second to a clergyman with private means. Neither man had stayed the course for very long and Johnny could guess why. While Bella was a pretty slightly built blonde with a personality that withered under the disapproval of others, Constance appeared to be some kind of throwback very suggestive of there being Latin blood somewhere in her parents' lineage. Dark-haired, dark-eyed and bold of nature, she frightened men away before reaching the altar yet seemed not to care, treating each defection as a huge joke to be shared with any who would listen. Johnny smiled in spite of his gloom, remembering how her indiscretions at the Fairburns' dinner table embarrassed her family. Infinitely more fun than her sister would ever be, he would have chosen Constance had his decision been made with heart instead of head, but marriage was rather more serious than a dinner party and if he had to take a wife so early she would need to be the sort of woman who melted into the background of his life causing as little disruption to what he considered the normal running of his affairs as possible.

The unmistakable sound of a lark made him turn to look further up the fell where a tiny dot hovered against the backcloth of the sky, its song falling sweetly into the cooling air. Watching it for a few seconds he felt a strange stab of envy at the little creature's freedom, and toyed briefly with the idea of running away before abandoning it with a sigh of regret. It was an attractive thought but impractical for a man with no money of his own.

Squaring his shoulders he began to walk again. There was no way out of his predicament but at least he could comfort himself with as much pleasant distraction as he could arrange, and that, if he was lucky, would recommence very soon with Lilian Rutherford.

'We'd better walk a little faster if I'm to get you home before dark. I don't want to be in disfavour with your parents Lilian.'

She agreed. 'We should have left the dam earlier but it's so lovely up here.'

Quickening her pace as they stepped off the rough path that had led them around Hanson's Dam, Lilian felt relieved that the road plunged steeply downward into the village now that they had to hurry, and Bill cursed himself for having waited too long to speak his mind in comfort. Taking her hand in his, as though to steady her, he glanced down at her face but found no particular pleasure reflected there. If anything, she merely seemed eager to get home now that they were on their way back.

Desperately he stopped walking and pulled her up short beside him.

'I want to talk to you Lilian.' He said quickly. 'It's very important to me ... will you promise to listen?'

Looking up into Bill's anxious face the girl felt a shiver of alarm as she guessed what he was about to say and Bill cleared his throat as he took hold of her other hand, clasping both of them as though afraid she would flee.

'Lilian ... I think you must know how I feel about you, but in case you don't I want to tell you that I've loved you almost from the first day I came to live in Gilfell, and I would be the happiest man in the world if you would agree to marry me!'

As though the effort of declaring himself had drained his strength he broke off, breathing deeply, then hurried on again before she could draw away.

'I'm not expecting you to decide today; I just want you to think about it. I promise I'll do everything I can to make you happy, Lilian, if you'll only say "yes", and you won't want for worldly goods either. I don't intend to be Peacock's Chief Clerk forever, you know, nor do I plan to live the rest of my life in that poky little rabbit hutch on Hillary Terrace. I'd buy a house for us ... a good sized home for a couple with a family ... how about that one at the bottom of the hill that you looked at so long as we passed by?'

'Ivy House? But that foreign family live there ... the Lupartes.'

'Maybe not for much longer. I've heard a rumour that they're thinking of going back to Belgium.'

Fascinated in spite of herself Lilian stared up into his eager face unaware of how her eyes were sparkling, and Bill bent his head suddenly, kissing her on the lips in a way which she found surprisingly pleasant even though it lacked the fiery appeal of Johnny's embraces. His hands moved to her upper arms drawing her to him, and as she felt herself pressed close to his body an alien and disturbing sensation swept through her leaving her flustered when he finally let her go.

Uncertainly Bill studied her expression, noting the spots of high colour on each cheek, and without another word he offered his arm as they briskly resumed their homeward journey.

Preparing for bed at number fourteen Hillary Terrace, Louisa sat before her dressing table at the window brushing her hair and watching her dim reflection in the small mirror stand. Behind her left shoulder she could see Terence propped up against the pillows in bed, smiling as he waited for her, and she smiled back at him through the glass.

'I've just seen Bill and Lilian walking towards the stile,' she remarked. 'They must have been for a long walk because it's getting dark. Shall I light the candle?'

'Why don't you just come to bed?'

He held back the covers invitingly and Louisa put down her hairbrush and got up, laughing softly. Snuggled warmly against Terence in the big bed she forgot all about the way she missed her family, and how tired she felt after the last two days when she had worked every minute to put her new home to rights. Her husband was the most important person in the world to her, and as long as she was with him all was surely right with her life.

Later, lying in his arms, she reached up to kiss him and murmured 'You won't be going away again for a while, will you Terry?'

As the seconds ticked by without a reply of any kind she leaned on one elbow to look at him. There was still enough light in the room for her to see that he was looking back at her.

'Terry?'

'I have to go to Newcastle very soon, Lou. I'm sorry, but it's the way I make my living. I'll be gone three or four days.'

'When are you leaving?'

'Tomorrow.'

Louisa lay down again carefully and closed her eyes as though going to sleep, but her body was stiff and the ever lengthening silence between them remained unbroken.

Darkness was almost total by the time Lilian and Bill reached the farm gate and she felt more than a little anxiety at the thought of her parents' reaction. Bill took her hand again.

'You've hardly spoken to me since I asked you to marry me Lilian, but I hope you'll seriously think it over. I'll make sure you never have cause to regret it if you decide to say "Yes", I promise.'

'I know that, Bill. I'm honoured that you have asked me but I need a little time, that's all.'

He hesitated, looking down at the indistinct shape of her face and wondered if he should risk kissing her again, but as though sensing his thoughts the girl gently pulled her hand away from his and he watched her slip inside the gate and shut it again with the feeling that the barrier of the five bars existed now on all levels of their relationship.

'Goodnight Bill. Thank you for ... everything.'

'Goodnight Lilian.'

He wanted to add 'I love you' but merely tipped his hat and stepped out onto the path again to make his way home as best he could, depressingly certain of the outcome of his proposal. Had he listened to his logic instead of his emotions he realised that he would have given up his quest long ago. Now he had made a fool of himself and still faced the future alone, for if Lilian refused him he was determined never to ask any other girl to be second best. He knew too much about that himself.

Setting her course by the position of the lighted kitchen window Lilian hurried across the yard, and as he waited just inside the haybarn door Johnny Peacock listened with satisfaction to the sound of her rustling skirts coming closer. Enjoying himself hugely he leapt out grabbing her arm, and when she gave a sharp cry of fright he put a hand over her mouth.

'It's me! I've been waiting to see you.'

Recognising Johnny's voice should have reassured her, but knowing herself to be far too late coming home already, and still painfully able to recollect her humiliation at the haymakers' supper, she struggled violently in his grasp, kicking out at his shins and aiming blows towards his face.

'For heaven's sake, what's the matter with you

Lilian? I've waited for hours to see you because I love you. Is that a crime?'

Like magic all turmoil ceased and Johnny pulled her into the darkness of the barn with him. The sweet smell of the newly stored harvest invaded her nostrils as he pushed her up against the high stacked wall of hay, but her temper rose again as he began to unfasten her jacket while kissing her bruisingly on the mouth.

'Get off me you conceited monkey! What makes you imagine that I'm here just to be picked up and put down at your every whim? It's only forty eight hours since we were in a crowded room where you behaved as though you scarcely knew me!'

Drawing back, but still holding her captive, the man shook her a little.

'So? What do you think your parents would have thought if they'd realised we love each other? I'm hardly regarded as a good influence in these parts am I, and I couldn't risk them banning me from seeing you.'

Across the cobbles in the sudden silence the house door opened and the silhouette of her father stood within the rectangle of light. Afraid even to breathe without care, they stood together watching him.

'There's no sign of her, Emily. I'll wait another ten minutes and if she still isn't back I'll get out the pony and trap to look for her.'

'She and Bill went up towards the dam, James. Suppose they've had an accident...'

Her mother's quavering voice was cut off as the door closed again and both Johnny and Lilian felt weak with relief, clinging to each other for a few seconds while the girl let her mind return to what he had said just before the interruption. He loved her! Wild triumphant happiness surged through her while all thoughts of Bill Robinson vanished like bursting bubbles.

'I'll have to go in now,' she whispered, and he tightened his grip convulsively.

'Not yet Lilian, please. I need you to stay a while longer ... I've waited so long ... don't go inside yet.'

Helplessly she stood in his embrace, trying without success not to react to the warmth of his body pressing against her own, or the pleasant clean smell of his skin.

'We can meet again soon, Johnny. We don't have to get ourselves into any worse trouble tonight. I'll meet you tomorrow afternoon at...'

'No!'

Gathering her closer to him Johnny began to whisper urgently in her ear.

'I love you Lilian, you know that. I love you and I need you. Please don't send me away.'

Like a tidal wave his pleading words, spoken with such unusual and deadly tenderness, released all her pent up desire, and when his hands moved to her jacket buttons again she made no move to restrain him. As one they edged further into the barn along the line of hay. The green jacket was discarded now, lying like an old rag on the barn floor, and she hardly noticed when they slowly tumbled into a pile of hay that had fallen from the top of the stack, for his arms were still around her and his kisses made all the sweeter for the words he breathed in between. She was the only girl for him, surely she knew that. Did he not lie awake at nights thinking of her, then when he finally slept it was only to dream about her because he loved her and could never love anyone else.

Aroused beyond any hope of resistance Lilian pulled his body closer to her own and felt at last his hard relentless invasion with shuddering pleasure. Glorying in the strange pain that was unlike any other she had ever known she moved instinctively beneath him as it began to turn into a sensation so delicious that she wondered how much longer she could keep from crying out. Clutching him ever more tightly to her she kissed his cheek, his lips, every part of his face that her mouth could reach in a fever of passion that was rapidly reaching its ultimate height, then suddenly Johnny gave a muffled groan and grew limp in her arms.

Disappointed and disbelieving, she lay staring up into the rafters, visible now like everything else by the light of the newly risen moon, and when after little more than a couple of minutes he pulled away from her to stand up she felt chilled when he neither kissed her nor made any but the most cursory attempt to assist her to her feet.

'Come on! Hurry up! You don't want your father to come out and find us do you?'

Unsteadily she rearranged her skirt, then walked to where her jacket still lay on the ground. Johnny had already adjusted his clothing and was brushing himself down with his palms in an effort to get rid of the many wisps of hay that had become lodged there during their coupling, and she put on her jacket then began to feel frantically in her hair, both to tidy it and remove all traces of hay. Starting at the top of her head she worked her way onto her shoulders then down her body, feeling cheated and cheap in a way she had never done before tonight, and as she saw Johnny walk to the barn door to look cautiously outside she realised how eager he was to leave but felt no surprise any more. When he turned briefly towards her and said 'I'd better go now. Will you be alright?' she replied curtly in the affirmative then remained still for a few seconds staring at the empty space where he had been. Illogically she found herself thinking of Bill Robinson, and had to flick a tear off her cheek with the back of her hand. Why think about Bill when it was still Johnny she wanted, in spite of the way he had made her feel?

Dispiritedly she moved out into the yard. Trouble she now had by the barrow load, and all since this morning when her world had been so delightfully normal. To arrive home as late as this was disgrace enough for a single girl and her parents would soundly blame Bill for it, of that there was no doubt, but it was better than them finding out the truth. Anything had to be better than that.

CHAPTER TWO

Emily Rutherford paused halfway up the stairs with her hand on the banister and her head bent down in an effort to make her breathing easier. The pain in her chest that afflicted her so often now was threatening and depressing, but as long as it remained bearable Emily was determined to keep it a secret from her family and try, as far as possible, to ignore it herself. True to its increasingly familiar pattern the discomfort slowly receded after a time and her breathing became less stressed, but she moved only as far as the last two stairs onto the landing, sitting down on the oak bedding chest by the window with a sigh of relief.

Outside in the yard she could hear James talking to the hired hand and the rhythmic scraping of Lilian's sweeping brush. Thinking of her daughter momentarily brought back the pain, sending an off-shoot across her shoulder and down her left arm, but that too ebbed away after a while and she leaned back against the wall where she could see Lilian at work cleaning up the yard. She had wanted the girl to bake this morning but her request had fallen upon stubbornly deaf ears: Lilian wanted to be outside in the fresh air, and outside she would be.

Watching her now, Emily frowned at the paleness of her face and her very obvious weight loss. She had eaten practically nothing since that Sunday night almost three weeks ago when she had gone walking with Bill Robinson, not returning until after dark, and Emily shuddered at the thought of what might have happened had the outraged James been standing in a position where he could have seen more than just the front of Lilian's clothing when she had finally been dismissed from the room, for although their daughter had appeared perfectly respectable, when she had turned to leave them Emily had seen that the back of her skirt and jacket were strewn with hay. It was painfully hard for her to admit to herself that Lilian must have been lying in the barn with a young man for whom she herself had previously felt a real affection and respect. Out of all the prospective sons-in-law in Gilfell Bill Robinson was the one she would have trusted implicitly to behave like a gentleman, and her disappointment was acute. It was true that he was still attentive to Lilian and had walked her home as far as the gate after chapel these last two Sundays, only ten yards behind James and herself, but their conversation had been practically non-existent leaving the woman to wonder whether Lilian was angrily blaming Bill for proving herself to be no better than the rest when her moment of weakness had come.

As though sensing that she was being watched Lilian abruptly stopped her sweeping and looked up at the window where she sat. James and his worker had disappeared into an outbuilding leaving the two women staring at each other, their faces unsmiling, and as she looked back at

46

her mother the girl wondered just how much of the truth she had guessed. Lifting up the lower sash Emily called to her softly.

'Come in now and I'll brew some tea before you go down to the store. I have a list written ready.'

'I'll be finished in five minutes.'

It was sadly apparent to the older woman that Lilian's smile was forced, and as she smiled back again she felt her own depression deepen. Who could be content when their only child was miserable, and if Lilian would not tell her why she was in such a state there was nothing she could do about it.

A while later, basket in hand, Lilian turned Chapel Corner and walked down Main Street towards the haberdashery store. From a reasonable distance she looked as perky and full of life as ever, but closer scrutiny betrayed her bleak expression and the shadows of sleeplessness beneath eyes that never quite joined her mouth in smiling greetings to the people she knew. Ever since the night when she had succumbed to Johnny Peacock she had neither heard from him nor seen him, not even at chapel, and as she walked she found herself eagerly scanning the street on both sides in case he should be there somewhere. So intent was she on finding him that when his sister stepped out of the haberdasher's doorway immediately in her path Lilian looked at her without surprise. Seeing the easy smile on her face Annabel Peacock smiled back and asked politely after her health.

'I'm well thank you. I didn't know you shopped

47

on Main Street. Don't you go to Carlisle or Newcastle?'

Somewhat taken aback by Lilian's directness Annabel clutched the brown paper parcel she was holding a little tighter as she replied. 'I needed some things in a hurry for tonight's celebration dinner at Low Shields. It's because of the engagement you see.'

Lilian frowned uncertainly. She had never heard of the Fairburns having a son.

'You're engaged?'

Annabel's laugh was light. 'No, not me. My brother John. He's just become engaged to Arabella Fairburn. That's why her parents have invited us to dinner this evening.'

Her voice trailed off as she watched Lilian move away from her to enter the nearby grocery store as though she were sleepwalking, the shock on her suddenly ashen face as eloquent as words could ever be, and she crossed over to the other side of the street amazed that someone like Lilian Rutherford had plainly expected to be more to her brother than a passing interest. A lovely singing voice she had, and an undeniable beauty, but she was still only a hill farmer's daughter.

Inside the grocery store Lilian handed over her basket and list to the proprietor, Mr Harrison, and tried without much success to return his smile. The mingling odours of soap, strong polish and sweet biscuits in their display tins that since her childhood she had found so attractive, unexpectedly nauseated her, and she swayed against the dark mahogany counter before reaching out for the wooden chair that was kept on the customers' side of the shop for just such emergencies. List in hand, the elderly Leonard Harrison let his spectacles slip down his nose as he regarded her with concern.

'Lilian? Aren't you well?'

'I'll be alright in a moment thank you. I didn't eat any breakfast this morning and it's made my head feel peculiar.'

By sheer effort of will she offered the man a watery smile and he was doubtfully surveying her when the shop door opened to admit Louisa Marshall.

'Good morning, Lilian. I've been trying to catch up with you since you passed my house before, so I'm glad to have run you to earth.'

Setting down her basket on the counter Louisa gave Len a quick greeting as he set about supplying the items on Lilian's list, then continued, giving the other girl precious time to attempt a recovery.

'I didn't have the opportunity to speak to you after chapel last Sunday as the preacher seemed to realise it was our first visit since moving here and he kept us back at the door talking, but I want you to know that I think you sing beautifully. In fact, I've never heard anyone with a better voice.'

Beaming, Louisa gazed into Lilian's face, then began to wonder whether there might be a reason other than laziness why such a young person should be sitting at the counter rather than standing.

'Is something wrong?'

Puzzled, she looked from Lilian to Len as he set

49

down the bag of sugar he had just weighed out, and he shook his head ignoring Lilian's warning look.

'She's been feeling dizzy through not eating breakfast. Doesn't do, you know. Doesn't do at all.'

He shuffled off to bring some candles from the store room at the rear of the shop and Lilian gave Louisa a rueful smile, relieved to feel her nausea receding as her friend was now expressing the opinion that she should go home with her to have some soup before attempting to continue her journey. Gratefully she accepted. Her mind, though no less steeped in shocked misery than a few minutes ago, was beginning to clear at last and her way ahead showed plainly to be Bill Robinson with his offer of marriage if she wished to avoid the disgrace of giving birth to a child out of wedlock.

Involuntarily she cast her eyes down to the wooden floorboards for a second, then determinedly straightened her back. The damage was done, and neither lamenting the fact nor wasting time feeling ashamed was of the slightest use. She would go with Louisa and drink a little of her soup then, before going home, call and see Bill while he was having lunch. Further than that she would not try to think just yet.

Louisa took the empty soup bowl away from Lilian's place as, with a murmur of thanks, the young woman's eyes slid to the living room window once more. As she had performed this action continually since taking her seat, Louisa

50

could only assume that she was scanning the terrace in order to catch sight of someone, and that someone was probably Bill Robinson. With a slight upturn of her mouth she seated herself at Lilian's side and remarked.

'There goes the grandfather clock whirring ready to strike midday, and you can take it for granted that before it's finished your admirer will be home for his lunch.'

Looking up sharply, Lilian flushed a little as she added.

'If you keep watching the road you'll see Bill coming any second.'

'Lou, I'm sorry if I seem rude today in not giving you my full attention, but I have to see him as soon as possible on a very important matter and I can't really concentrate on anything else until it's done.'

Glancing back down the Terrace again Lilian caught a glimpse of Bill's black clad figure rounding Chapel Corner and Louisa, seeing the change in her expression, took her elbow to urge her to her feet.

'You'll have to be quick, Lilian. He'll be down those steps and into his house in no time.'

'Yes ... thanks.'

Following Louisa's slight figure out of the room, through the kitchen and into the yard, Lilian gripped her hand for a moment before the girl went back inside her home, then she opened the door of the yard and went outside to wait for the man whose footsteps were getting nearer every second.

Meanwhile, keeping her head down over the

51

sink, Louisa set about the task of preparing vegetables for the evening meal. Lilian's business with Bill did not really concern her so much as the debts that were beginning to mount here in Gilfell just as they had done back in Carlisle. Terence had been away for three days now and should surely return tonight, hopefully with some money in his pocket for a change. She frowned down into the dirty water, blackened by root soil off the carrots, and wondered why her husband spent so much time in Newcastle when he was apparently paid so little for his work; and why it was always Newcastle and never Carlisle. There was no point in living in this tiny village if it was not going to be the halfway mark between the two towns as he had claimed from the start. All it meant was that Terence was with her in Gilfell for two to three days a week, while she spent the rest of the time without the comfort she had previously enjoyed of having her family close by, and whichever way one viewed that situation it was quite clearly wrong.

Small vertical frown marks had formed between her brows as she reviewed the matter and they were still there half an hour later when her task was completed and the stew placed in the oven by the side of the black-leaded grate. It was then that she heard the clatter of Lilian's feet returning and realised that she had almost forgotten about her.

Moving swiftly to the back door to let her in she tried to banish her own worries from her mind, and the first sight of Lilian's face convinced her that her friend had succeeded very well in doing just that for herself. Smiling, she stepped back to let her in, and waved to Bill who was walking onto the terrace to go back to work. He was grinning broadly, as was Lilian who had regained much of her lost colour, and as he strode away with an unmistakable spring in his step she turned to Louisa and said

'Please don't tell anyone yet, not until Bill has had the chance to speak to my parents tonight, but he and I are going to be married soon!'

'Lilian, that's wonderful! We'll be neighbours!'

Throwing her arms around her neck Louisa hugged her then added with mock severity as she looked into Lilian's suspiciously over-bright eyes. 'Now it's no use crying. You've given your word and you'll soon be a boring old married woman like me. We'll be able to get together and grumble about our husbands.'

Later, when Lilian had picked up her shopping basket and gone, Louisa still could not understand why her remarks had appeared to upset the girl, but finally put it down to the high emotion of the moment. After all, what else could have caused a newly engaged young woman to have such a strange fit of weeping?

The lights of the Assembly Rooms blazed out from the tall windows and Lilian tried hard to keep her inner tension a secret as she and Bill made their way down the path from Roughside towards its cheerfully open door. It would be dark when the celebrations ended but her father would be waiting for her with the trap, leaving Bill free to go down to the stile then on to Hillary Terrace, and she desperately wished that the

53

evening had already progressed to that point, for this was the party given for the Peacocks' employees to mark the mine's tenth year and was to be hosted by Johnny and Arabella. Next week, so Lilian had heard, there was to be another party held at White Court, this one of a more exclusive nature to which she and Bill had not been invited, and whilst the man accepted this with resignation Lilian had shown no such philosophical leanings.

'You are a senior member of staff Bill, and you should have been invited to the house,' she had stated firmly. 'You're as good as the Peacocks any day, and so am I for that matter.'

He had swept her up in his arms, kissing her soundly and loving her all the more for her championship of him, for he knew that she was right. Certain tradespeople in the area were going to White Court along with everyone of importance to do with the mine and the Fairburns' exporting business, and he and Lilian would not have been out of place. Someone had plainly seen to it that they were not invited. Someone like Johnny Peacock perhaps.

Looking down at her face as they neared the door Bill squeezed her hand gently.

'I don't suppose the engaged couple will be here long. For decency's sake they'll stay a while but when the dancing starts they'll go, so let's make sure we look as though we don't care about the other party till then. You look beautiful Lilian, and there'll be no woman in there who can hold a candle to you.'

'Thank you, Bill.'

'I mean it.'

Gratified by his vote of confidence she tried to feel good in her 'best blue' as they entered the hall, though she was painfully conscious of how many times she had worn it before, but a certain amount of consolation lay in the knowledge that the sitting room at Roughside was, at this moment, strewn with ruby coloured velvet ready to be made into the dress for her wedding in a week's time.

The first people she saw in a group standing by the top table were Johnny and Arabella Fairburn, and she felt her social smile freeze uncomfortably as the man looked up at them then put his arm around Bella's shoulders in an unmistakably proprietary manner. Bill, seeing the office Junior Clerk Kenneth Carter sitting at a nearby table with his mother, steered Lilian towards it and expertly placed her so that her back was towards the top of the room. Immediately he felt her relax, the set of her spine losing its rigidity, and the smile he gave her upon taking his own seat was warm but neutral. At all costs Bill would keep up the pretence of knowing nothing of Lilian's feelings regarding Johnny Peacock, because once she realised that he knew how she felt about him a barrier would fall between them that might never lift.

She was talking to the Carters now, and apart from adding the odd comment himself Bill was happy to sit back in his chair and watch her. Johnny Peacock had heard about his impending marriage to Lilian yet had neither congratulated him nor commented upon the matter in any way, but the antagonism between the two men which had always lurked beneath the surface of their working relationship deepened into the personal, each sensing it in the other without a word being spoken.

To his relief Bill saw that all the guests were now seated and two women, one for each row, had begun to move from table to table pouring out tea from huge teapots, rather like honey bees in reverse.

Turning her head Lilian gave him a quick smile as the fiddler from Dalton began his tuning up process with the aid of Miss Emma Hartley, schoolteacher, chapel organist and accompanist to all manner of soloists, Lilian included, and through the intermittent scrapings of bow on strings Johnny Peacock's voice was suddenly heard asking for their attention. At once all conversation ceased and Bill looked to where Johnny was standing with a sea of expectantly seated diners, his too handsome face betraying embarrassment which he was not yet mature enough to hide. Clearing his throat he commenced by thanking everyone for attending then declared himself to be extremely happy since, in addition to the mine's tenth anniversary, Miss Arabella Fairburn had agreed to become his wife in the very near future. At this Bella smiled up at him, her childlike features set in a mask of adoration, but Bill noticed cynically that Johnny never once even glanced in her direction before rounding off his brief speech with the hope that they would all enjoy their evening to the full. A dutiful smattering of applause followed his last words whereupon Johnny sat down with obvious relief.

Across the table Thomas looked above his son's head at the hall clock, silently promising himself no more than another fifteen minutes before he allowed himself to leave, and Annabel tried not to worry too much at the sight of Bella's white and over-sensitive face.

At the far end of the hall Lilian picked up a plate of sandwiches, handing them round the table whilst wearing her brightest smile. She had not turned round during Johnny's speech, but that had somehow given his words more impact, making her blink fiercely as her eyes threatened to overflow and her throat ached on and on, and Bill, searching around in his mind for something to say to fill the silence at their table felt a deep gratitude to Mrs Carter as she leaned forward to say in suitably lowered tones.

'Poor little scrap isn't she? Looks too delicate if you ask me. No good for that one at all.'

Bill looked amused. 'What do you mean exactly?'

'Well, she won't be strong enough to stick up for herself when they're married, and you know how full of himself that Johnny is! Peacock by name and peacock by nature.'

Lilian laughed a little while Kenneth muttered 'Mam,' warningly, but she had no more to say on the subject having turned her attention to the meal.

Around them the buzz of conversation grew gradually louder as the supper wore on. The fiddler flirted with a tune or two between he and Miss Hartley sorting their music into performing order ready for dancing, and bursts of laughter came from various tables as the atmosphere lightened into a more relaxed sociability.

Looking down the room Johnny Peacock found himself unwillingly watching Lilian and Bill, his stare quite fixed now that he felt sure no one was taking any notice of him. The contrast between Lilian and Bella was extreme and his regret at the way things had turned out surprisingly real, but none of that made any difference now that his course had been set, and as though sensing his scrutiny the girl abruptly turned round, her eyes staring accusingly into his for a few seconds before she presented her blue-clad back once more. He glowered at her slim shoulders, willing her to turn round again. Damn her for getting herself engaged to that dullard Robinson, and damn her even more for not having the common-sense to stop away tonight, invitation or no!

Bending towards her Bill said 'This time next week we'll be back here, remember? Tonight is just a duty but our night will be happy, Lilian, I promise.'

Her answering smile was genuine as she offered him a cake off the plate nearest to her. Today she had seen the situation between Johnny and herself as it really was, and despite being unable to discipline her inner feelings she was quietly determined to focus her energies where her real future lay. Love had done her no good and she would bother with it no more, but she would be such a good wife to Bill that he would be the envy of all who knew him. One way or another she would make this village sit up and take notice, and that would definitely include the Peacock family.

James Rutherford took out his fob watch and sighed, his ears straining for any sound that might indicate that his daughter was on her way downstairs at last. The bustling whisper of skirts descending to the hall a few moments later gave him a burst of hope, but when his wife entered the room alone he turned to the mantelshelf and reached for his pipe and tobacco.

'She's almost ready and she looks lovely.'

'Good.'

'That shade of red really suits her. It's so warm.'

'She should be in white, Emily. You know what people will think.'

Watching him tamping down the tobacco into the bowl of his pipe Emily fought to keep her gaze steady in case he should see his suspicions mirrored in her own expression.

'She's a practical girl, James, and she wanted something that would make a suitable best outfit afterwards, and as for "people" they must think what they please.'

'Fair enough.'

Through the steadily growing cloud of smoke James watched her as she picked up her handbag off the table, pushed one of her best lace-edged handkerchiefs into its interior, and snapped it shut. Her mouth was tightly closed and he noticed a faint blue tinge around it, wondering if it were really there or simply a trick of the light. He was about to ask her if she was feeling well when the welcome sound of more feet on the stairs signalled the end of his long wait.

'She's coming,' Emily said unnecessarily, smiling towards the doorway as Lilian appeared in its frame, slim, elegant and beautiful in her red velvet dress and jacket. Holding her small posy of flowers in her gloved hands she looked uncertainly from one parent to the other and James placed his pipe carefully in the grate after knocking it clear on the hearth.

'You look lovely, Lilian...' Emily began, then stopped as James walked across the room to offer his daughter his arm.

'You're the prettiest picture I've ever seen,' he said gruffly, 'and I'm proud to walk beside you today.'

Coming out of her bedroom, overnight valise packed ready for her trip to Low Shields, Annabel Peacock walked across the landing to her brother's door and knocked softly on the centre panel. At first there was no reply, but when she knocked again she heard a muffled grunt which she took to be a sign of admittance. Johnny was lying on top of the eiderdown with his hands linked behind his head, and Annabel noticed the glass and half empty bottle of port with misgivings as she went to stand at the window which, for almost two miles, gave a clear view of the Gilfell to Dalton road.

'I'm all ready now.' She remarked lightly. 'I expected to see Fairburns' trap coming for me as I'm to be there for dinner, but there's no sign of it yet. It's a pity that fancy new motor car they bought could not manage these steep roads or I might have been going in style.'

'What time is it?'

His voice was slightly slurred and the creak of bedsprings indicated that he was rising at least some of the way from his prone position: Annabel twisted round to see him sitting on the edge of the mattress with his head in his hands.

'The clock on the wall is right, John. It's six o'clock.'

'Thirty six hours left of freedom then, comparatively speaking of course. To be coerced into marriage at twenty one by one's own father is hardly the mark of a wonderful existence is it? If we'd still had our mother he probably wouldn't have found it so easy to use us as pawns in the game called "strengthening my family's finances," and I wouldn't be ... feeling like this.'

'But John, he really can't make you marry Bella if you stand your ground.'

Johnny gave her a bitter look. 'Can't he? I have no private means, no home of my own. Every part of my life is overseen by father and when he says "Jump!" I jump, just as you'll have to do sometime in the future so don't think it's only going to happen to me.'

Alarmed by the indisputable logic of his warning Annabel convulsively clasped her hands, turning back towards the window where, high on the fell slope, the lights of the Assembly Rooms were burning despite the daylight outside. Lilian Rutherford and Bill Robinson's wedding celebrations were obviously in full swing now. For a few seconds her thoughts flew back to the morning some weeks ago when she had met

Lilian outside the haberdashers on Main Street and seen her stricken look at the news of John's engagement, and she was far from being the only one her brother had charmed.

'I trust you'll settle down now, John.' She ventured, and he gave a short humourless laugh.

'Settle down? With Bella?'

'You've chosen her instead of Constance; it's only fair that you do your part to make the marriage work.'

In the distance Annabel glimpsed Fairburns' trap topping the rise on the outskirts of Gilfell and turned round to bid her brother goodbye, ashamed of the relief she was feeling. He grimaced as she picked up her valise, and before she left the room he said 'I really hope dear Bella will learn to keep herself as inconspicuous as possible and not be a nuisance in any way. If you can pass on that vital piece of advice there's a slender chance that our lives may be reasonably free of strife.'

The dinner table at Low Shields was more lively than Annabel had ever know it before, and she silently studied the fresh faces of the Fairburns' guests as she ate her dessert. The usual diners, Gerald and Elisabeth Fairburn with Arabella and Constance, were now augmented by six guests including herself, and the girl found her eyes moving continually towards the young man seated opposite. He was the sisters' cousin Raynor, son of Mary and Edward Fairburn who were also present, along with Elisabeth's brother and sister-in-law Wilfred and Ann Ruddick. All, it seemed, except Raynor and Annabel, were vying with each other to see who could speak loudest and longest, and when Raynor leaned comfortably back in his chair to smile at her she blushed furiously as she smiled back.

'Have you travelled far, Miss Peacock?'

His voice was well modulated and seemed to Annabel a perfect match for his features which she was finding increasingly pleasing.

'Gilfell lies three miles further up the valley. It was a pleasant journey by pony and trap on an evening like this.'

Raynor lifted a wine glass to his lips briefly, his eyes flirting with her over its rim as she set down her spoon, pushing her plate away a little.

'If we hadn't come by train I suppose we would have passed through your village, but Newcastle is too far for pony and trap and the route too hilly for our motor.'

'You have a motor?'

'A Dion Bouton.'

'How exciting!' Annabel gazed at him in wonder, all self consciousness forgotten. 'I suppose we would see more of them here if it were not for the terrain, but I have noticed one or two motors down the valley in Dalton. It must be marvellous to ride in one.'

He responded impractically, but as she had hoped he would, by saying that she would have to ride in their motor one day to see how 'marvellous' it felt, and she was about to make a suitable reply when a burst of raucous amusement from the end of the table cut her short. Constance was leaning back in her chair roaring with laughter at

some remark made by her uncle, Wilfred Ruddick, and unabashed by the stares of the other
dinner guests, she wiped her streaming eyes with
the back of her hand while the joker looked on
sheepishly.

'He really is a card, this man.' Constance
choked. 'Tell them what you've just told me,
Uncle Wilf.'

Elisabeth Fairburn cast her brother a withering
glance.

'I imagine we can all do without that Constance,
thank you, and we would appreciate you making
an effort to control yourself for the remainder of
the meal.'

'Oh ... right.'

Unrepentant, Constance picked up her cutlery
to continue eating, grinning down at her plate
and giving Wilfred Ruddick a quick wink at her
first mouthful. Greatly entertained by the
incident Annabel smiled down the table at
Constance before becoming aware of the icy look
her hostess was giving her, and quickly re-
targeted her smile towards Bella who appeared to
be completely mystified by it all.

Raynor had now joined the majority of the
guests in making desultory over-polite conversation which continued until the ladies withdrew
at the end of the meal, and Constance was heard
to sigh loudly as she cast her eyes despairingly at
the ceiling.

'Here we go,' she muttered to Annabel as they
moved to the door. 'A group of women together
all seeing how boring, or catty, they can be.'

Bella, walking in front of them, turned round to

remark innocently. 'Oh, it won't be for long. Mother says we are all to retire early tonight so that we are completely refreshed in the morning.'

Disappointed that she would have no further opportunity to speak with Raynor that evening, Annabel risked a quick backward glance before passing from the room and was gratified to see that he was looking after her with obvious regret. He smiled as their eyes met and she smiled back at him feeling her spirits rise. There was always the rest of tomorrow after the wedding ceremony, and she would definitely be looking her best then.

True to her promise Elisabeth Fairburn hurried Bella and Annabel off to bed at nine. Constance, who was to be a bridesmaid too, simply ignored the instruction knowing that her mother would back down rather than risk a scene, and Annabel wished she had possessed the courage to do likewise.

'I'll never sleep, you know. It's ridiculous having to go to bed at this time of night as though we are naughty children.' She grumbled as they climbed the magnificent green and cream staircase, and Bella nodded in agreement.

'I know, and I'm sorry, but at least we're out of the way of the aunts with their dull talk. Heaven knows why Constance insisted on staying.'

'Possibly because she knew the men would be joining them very shortly.'

Following the slight figure of her future sister-in-law into her bedroom Annabel wondered yet again just how she would fare as John's wife, especially as she was already dominated by her own mother who had unwittingly prepared Arabella to be the wife of a bullying man. Startled, she stopped short, watching Bella sit down at her dressing table minor to commence her toilette. Could that really be what her brother was? A bully?

'I think I'd better take off my dress before brushing my hair. I always do normally, but tonight I forgot.'

She smiled at Annabel through the glass as she stepped forward to help her, and after her dress had been discarded she sat down again to allow her bridesmaid to begin brushing her hair.

'I wonder what my John is doing now?' She murmured half closing her eyes, and Annabel smiled wryly.

'I should think he's already asleep, Bella.'

'I do love him, Annabel. I think he's a wonderful person.'

'Well ... he's just an ordinary mortal like the rest of us, and sometimes you may have to stand up to him if he gets too bossy.'

'Stand up to him! What kind of talk is that about the man who will be my husband? I love him, Annabel.'

She twisted round on the boudoir stool and Annabel looked down at her helplessly.

'He's a very strong-willed person Bella, that's all I meant, and he may need to learn how to consider someone else's feelings.'

'Then we'll learn together won't we? Please don't worry, Annabel. I know how happy I feel tonight and how happy I'm going to be as John's wife.'

Resuming her position facing the mirror Bella smiled brilliantly at her companion's reflection through the glass, and Annabel turned her mouth determinedly upwards at the corners knowing that her eyes still showed her strain. Lifting the silver-backed hairbrush she drew it slowly through the fine pale hair.

'I wish you every happiness as John's wife.' She said quietly. 'I just hope he appreciates your devotion.'

It seemed as though she had gazed at the same black star-scattered rectangle for an eternity listening to Bill's even breathing at her side, and Lilian tried to turn away from the bedroom window in the hope that the boring darkness would send her to sleep at last. In her mind she could still hear the violin and piano music they had danced to at the Assembly Rooms, and see the bright happy faces of her relatives and new in-laws as they celebrated the wedding. It had been a truly happy occasion and she realised, to her surprise, that she had never once thought about Johnny Peacock even though she had been painfully aware earlier that day that his own wedding to Arabella Fairburn was to take place the next day. Bill had been so exhilarated by it all, as though he could not believe it was actually happening, and she had felt humbled and guilty at the depth of his love for her.

Unlike Johnny, Bill had proved to be a considerate and tender lover, certainly never seeming to doubt that his bride was a virgin, for which she felt deeply relieved. She was married now and safe from scandal. In three weeks' time she would tell her new husband that she believed herself to be pregnant then visit Dr Hatton and give him the wrong dates upon which to calculate the birth. Their firstborn would obviously appear to favour the mother, with Johnny having dark colouring like herself, but she hoped all subsequent babies would look like Bill. That, in the circumstances, was the least she could do to make up for the love she wished in vain to feel for him.

Sighing, then yawning, Lilian snuggled closer to the man at her side. Perhaps in time love would come, but if it did not Lilian was determined that Bill would never suspect the truth. For a moment she allowed her imagination to replace him with Johnny, and her breath caught in her throat before she swiftly banished the thought. All that was finished now for good, and this time tomorrow Bella Fairburn would be lying beside Johnny Peacock as his wife. Surely only death could be more final than that.

Constance Fairburn looked across at her fellow bridesmaid as the carriage taking them to Dalton church set off along the tree-lined drive towards the road.

'Thank goodness the sun's shining.' Annabel remarked. 'Your sister will look lovely arriving in an open carriage.'

Constance shrugged. 'Well, at least she doesn't have to wear this insipid pale blue outfit like us. I tried to get orange, but she and mother threw one of their fits and they're a bit much doing that at the same time. I did think they could have stretched a point seeing this is the third time I've been a bridesmaid.' She grinned wickedly and mimicked her mother's prim tones. 'Three times a bridesmaid, never a bride. I simply despair of you, Constance.'

Annabel laughed. She liked Constance and found her liking deepening the more she got to know her; in fact, she had to admit that she liked Constance a good deal more than she liked Bella.

'Johnny should be marrying *me* really! You know that don't you?'

'I ... um...'

'Oh, it's alright, you don't have to answer that, but I still can't imagine what he sees in her when she's such a duffer. She's no fun at all. He would at least have had a lively marriage if he'd picked me, and I would have accepted him if he'd asked me, even though he's younger than I. Still, it's done now, and dear little Bella will soon be dragging her dreary person up the aisle all decked up like the dying swan with that sickly sweet expression in her eye when she looks at your anything-but-sainted brother.'

Against her will Annabel began to laugh again and Constance joined in heartily, her dark eyes sparkling with mischief as she contemplated the coming celebrations now that she had found such an unexpected ally.

'Don't look at me in church.' She warned. 'If we laugh in there we'll never be forgiven.'

As their carriage pulled out into the road another one, liberally trimmed with white ribbon and obviously intended for Bella and her father, passed it and turned in at the gate, while coming up on the highway behind them a trap carrying Johnny, his father and college friend Best Man Angus McLeod, was moving along at a spanking trot trying to make up for lost time. Raucous as ever, Constance waved her bouquet and shouted to the men.

'You're supposed to be in church now! Are you going to wreck everything?'

Thomas Peacock and Angus both smiled obediently, but Johnny stared straight ahead, not even sparing the bridesmaids a glance as their carriage passed the colourful duo, and Constance gave Annabel a significant look.

'See what I mean?'

'He probably has a hangover, Constance. He drank rather a lot last night.'

Constance's lip curled cynically. 'I wonder why.'

'For goodness sake John, stop looking as though you're going to a funeral.'

Thomas regarded his son balefully as the distance between the two carriages grew, and Angus turned his head away in embarrassment as his friend replied. 'I'm going to the funeral of my own freedom. How do you expect me to look?'

'If you can't manage to look happy at least try to look pleasant. You have until we reach Dalton to practise so you'd better start now.'

The curious crowd clustered round Dalton church watched proceedings with unnerving concentration as the bridegroom and party alighted from the carriage and walked quickly up the path to the porch where the bridesmaids were already waiting. Johnny, almost feeling relief as he stepped within its shade, was only half aware of his sister and the mocking Constance.

'Will those gaping idiots still be there when we come out?' he muttered, and Thomas gave him an exasperated look as he paused to remove his hat.

'They're here to see the bride. You and the rest of us are merely unnecessary additions to their viewing, so don't get too self-conscious will you?'

Passing through the door into the church Thomas left the Groom and Best Man to follow him down the aisle at a discreet distance and felt his thoughts worrying around the subject of his son seriously, but far too late, while in a nearby pew Elisabeth Fairburn was entertaining similar thoughts about her soon to be son-in-law. As he and Angus moved to sit down in their places she slid her head away to the right of them as though deeply interested in the memorial plaques on the wall. All too soon she heard her daughter's carriage arriving and the brief swell of admiring gasps from the waiting crowd of women; a rustling at the top of the church as Johnny and Angus got to their feet, then the organ music changed to the first wedding march and Bella was starting her journey towards her bridegroom.

'For better, for worse.' Elisabeth thought grimly. 'There's no help for it now.'

Standing behind her sister throughout the ceremony, Constance, though appearing attentive, was merely allowing the rituals to wash over her as her restless mind wandered away from the

71

cloying scent of freesias, roses and chrysanthemums which seemed to be stuck in every
possible nook and cranny of the building.
Tomorrow it would all be over and life could
return to normal, uninteresting though that was.

Glancing first to one side then the other she
was surprised to see a woman in the congregation as obviously as bored as she. Somewhere
in her forties, and sitting with a man who was
probably her husband, the unknown guest wore
a warm brown silk dress and hat which were the
perfect foil for her particular shade of red hair,
and her impatience with the service seemed to
hang around her like a cloak. For an instant their
eyes met and a slight smile passed between them
before the vicar announced a hymn. As she
opened her hymn book Constance wondered idly
who the woman could be, for although she and
her partner were sitting on the Fairburn side of
the church, she was unfamiliar. Maybe later she
would have the chance to find out.

Terence Marshall looked down at the supper
table then back at his wife who stood still beside
him, her expression defiant.

'Surely Louisa, when this is the first Saturday
I've been home for weeks, you could have
provided a better meal than this.'

'If it hadn't been for Lilian and Bill's wedding
yesterday I doubt whether I would have been so
honoured.'

Lifting his hand Terence touched the plate which
Louisa had put down at his place and nudged it
away contemptuously. 'What exactly is this?'

'It's exactly what it looks like. A sausage. A big one from the local store. There has been a local pig killing and the farmer supplied the shop with part of the spoils, but of course you are so rarely here that you wouldn't know about things like that would you?'

'Oh please, don't start that again.'

'Terry, it's true! You're hardly ever here, and now that Lilian has married Bill I don't suppose I'll see much of her anymore.'

'She has come to live next door to us, for heaven's sake. Any logical person would naturally expect to see more of someone in those circumstances, not less.'

With a sigh denoting long-suffering patience Terence pulled out his chair and sat down, picking up his knife and fork with studied reluctance as Louisa walked to the hearth to brew the tea.

'I see you aren't partaking of this wonderful sausage.' He remarked. 'Don't tell me I've taken your share as well as my own.'

Taking his first mouthful of the offending meal Terence found himself agreeably surprised by its flavour, and reached across the table for the bread and butter with a grunt of satisfaction.

'Hmm. Not bad at that. Sorry Louie, but it looked so poor on its own.'

Whitefaced, Louisa tilted the teapot over his cup and as he glanced up at her he burst out laughing.

'Oh don't look like that, Lou. Anybody would think you were going to be sick any second, and I've already apologised.'

Setting down the teapot with such force that a

spurt of hot liquid erupted from the spout, she turned and ran out of the room, through the kitchen and into the outside toilet where unmistakable sounds of retching now reached his ears. A gloom descended on him as he followed his wife to where she crouched over the primitive wooden seat and when at last she straightened herself, leaning weakly against the wall, he turned her gently around and led her back indoors. Like a rag doll she slumped into the fireside chair and closed her eyes.

'I'm expecting a baby.' She said dully, and he knelt beside her smiling in spite of himself.

'I rather gathered that a few moments ago. Poor little Louie.'

His voice was gentle but his words seemed strange and inappropriate. Fighting the nausea, that was beginning to rise again Louisa felt her eyes prickle with unshed tears as she wondered why he had never said he was happy about becoming a father, and she kept them tightly closed as she added. 'Do you think you could arrange to come home more often now, or at least provide some more money?'

'Yes, yes of course. You know I'll try my best.'

Patting her on the knee Terence got up and went back to the table to finish the meal he had barely started, and a chasm of silence fell between them until his wife finally rose and announced that she was going to bed.

Left alone, the man abandoned all pretence of normality as he pushed his plate away and, placing his elbows on the side of the table, cupped his head in his hands as he stared into the fire. After a while it occurred to him that there was really a very simple solution to the situation if he just failed to return from his next business trip, but he knew he would have to be totally desperate to put it into effect.

Upstairs, Louisa drifted into an uneasy sleep.

Annabel's eyes sparkled up at Raynor as the strains of the waltz died away and as he walked her back to her seat he held her elbow just a shade more tightly than necessary, slyly squeezing from time to time.

'You'll be lonely now that your brother's gone on his honeymoon. Can I come over in the motor?'

She laughed up at him as she took her seat. 'All the way from Newcastle? I know the Dion Bouton is a marvellous machine, but do you really think it can manage the distance and extreme slopes of these fells? Just think of some of the roads into Gilfell, Raynor. They're almost vertical!'

Raynor sat down at her side and gave her a rueful look.

'Well, it was a nice idea. The train will be a better one, I'll admit.'

'I'll meet you with our trap. Just let me know what time you'll be arriving.'

Unashamed of her lack of coyness Annabel enjoyed Raynor's attentions to the full as she sat back watching the rest of the people in the room while they talked. The Station Hotel was the biggest in Dalton, certainly the only one with a small ballroom, and from its polished floor to its glittering chandelier the venue had done the wedding party proud. Conscious that less than an hour remained until it was all over Annabel looked round the guests with eyes that meant to remember this night. Aunts, uncles, cousins, friends, all relaxed and happy, maybe more happy than they had been earlier in the day before the bride and groom had left on the London train, but she refused to blight her enjoyment by thinking of that now.

'Do you go home this evening?' she asked idly.

'Tomorrow ... by train. Would you like to walk round the gardens for a while to get some air?'

'But it's dark.'

He looked at her solemnly. 'Yes, I know.'

Quickly spying her father at the far end of the room deep in conversation with certain other members of the Fairburn family, Annabel got up without a word and took Raynor's arm as they walked without haste towards the French windows a few yards away.

Sitting at a table by the exit she saw Constance having a spirited discussion with a woman wearing brown silk, and a man whom she took to be her husband joining in with the occasional comment as he leaned back in his chair and smoked his pipe. For a short while she felt intrigued by the few words she overheard, including the name of the politician Keir Hardie, but once outside with Raynor she soon forgot about anything except the man at her side.

Gerald Fairburn cast his elder daughter a black look as he pushed away his breakfast plate with the food hardly touched. Trust Constance to begin annoying him when his liver was suffering so badly from his indulgences in both food and alcohol at the wedding reception the previous day.

'Of course you have my permission to stay with Eleanor and Graham; I noticed them monopolising you yesterday and wondered what on earth you were finding to talk about, and I'm still surprised that you wish to visit. You may find Manchester a little grimy after what you've been used to. It's very industrial.'

Waving that fact impatiently aside Constance tried hard not to let her parents see the full extent of her excitement in case they decided to question her more closely, and thanking providence that they had not talked long with their distant cousins, the Hemmings, she rose with studied casualness whilst announcing her intention of going upstairs to begin packing.

Elisabeth looked surprised. 'But you won't be leaving until Thursday, and that's four days away. Why start packing already?'

'I understand we will be attending quite a lot of functions so I had better make sure I take plenty of clothes with me.' She smiled, and wanted to laugh out loud at their unsuspecting faces.

Once she had sedately shut the dining room door behind her the woman ran across the hall then up the thickly carpeted stairs on feet that barely seemed to touch the floor at all. Just a few days to go, she told herself gleefully as she opened her wardrobe seconds later, and then she would have some excitement in her life at last. One by one, dresses, jackets, suits and underwear were all flung unceremoniously onto her bed ready to be folded and placed in a trunk, for with a little luck Constance felt it might be quite some time before she returned to Low Shields.

Humming softly under her breath she picked up her perfume bottle and hand mirror off the dressing table to place in the bottom of the trunk as her lips moved with relish over the words 'Womens' Social and Political Union.'

Manchester might well be a grimy northern town but it was also the home of a family called Pankhurst whom the Hemmings knew very well, and whom Constance also meant to get to know well in the near future.

CHAPTER THREE

Even the railway station excited Constance. Enormous by Dalton's standards, Manchester's bustling noisy crowds and trains hissing and growling like great prehistoric beasts brought a sparkle to her eyes. This was life indeed, far from her own dreary backwater.

'Ah, here you are, my dear! Welcome to Manchester.'

Eleanor Hemming, appearing at her side as though by magic, quickly embraced her relative before summoning a porter to retrieve her luggage and take it out to the street where Graham was waiting with the motor. Trying not to betray the fact that she had only ridden in a motor once before, and then merely travelled up and down the drive at Low Shields after they had bought their own largely useless machine for their extremely rough terrain, Constance smiled broadly at the sight of the magnificent green vehicle with its many brass fittings gleaming like glass. Standing proudly at its side Graham was sporting the unofficial uniform of the motorist; leather jacket, gauntlets, helmet and a pair of goggles to keep the dust and insects at bay, and he came forward gallantly to help her into the passenger seat while his wife prepared to take the less comfortable perch at the back.

'There's a chiffon scarf on your seat, Con-

79

stance.' Eleanor called, pulling down her own voluminous veil from the top of her hat. 'It has been raining recently as you can see, so the dust won't be a problem, but there are still the flies to consider.'

Finding the garment behind her Constance fastened it over the hat as Eleanor had done with hers, and watched Graham hiring a trap and driver a few yards away to transport her trunk to their address as there was no room for it anywhere on the motor. That done, he cranked the engine with the starting handle and quickly took his place beside his guest.

'We'll soon be home, but it's a good job you're wearing warm clothes, Constance, although the drive is no colder than a carriage would have been.' He shouted cheerfully over the engine's splutter.

'It's wonderful!' She responded as they began to move off, and Eleanor added. 'Some of the newer motors have roofs and windows, which must be better at this time of year, but the open car is still the best in summer.'

'Oh Eleanor, it's just fine. There are quite a lot of motors here aren't there?'

'It's easy motoring here, Constance; Manchester's flatter than Dalton.'

The drive to the Hemmings' rambling terrace house took around twenty minutes during which Constance eagerly took in every possible detail of the streets of the city. Trams chugged to and fro, their overhead cables clicking, and various other motors shared the route with horse driven carts and brewers' drays. Grimy it certainly was, there was no denying that, and as they drew further away from the centre of the city she stared in fascination at the many factory chimneys rising high above the rooftops, some near and some distant, but all belching the same thick black smoke into the air.

Once in the residential areas away from the pulse of industry and commerce Constance noticed that, despite the buildings and streets becoming more pleasing to the eye they were still showing the effects of the smoky air, the bricks in every house coloured varying degrees of grey by the sootfall, but it was all alive and exciting. Things were happening in this metropolis that were scarcely ever heard of at home.

By her side Eleanor was explaining certain landmarks and places of interest, but Constance was only half attentive. Later today she was going to her first gathering of the Womens' Social and Political Union with Eleanor, and her mind was beginning to centre around that event to the exclusion of even the new sights about her, and as though sensing her train of thought the older woman suddenly began to speak of it.

Tonight they were going to meet at Mrs Pankhurst's home, but tomorrow they had to go to the Free Trade Hall where a pre-election rally for the Liberal Party was to be held at which two professed supporters of womens' suffrage were to speak: Sir Edward Grey and Winston Churchill.

'Mr Churchill is the candidate for North West Manchester and we are determined to publicly question both men on their attitude to our cause, so in case anyone there should miss the point we

81

are painting our message on a piece of calico.' She explained. 'It is vital to get the open support of these figures instead of the privately mumbled encouragement they tend to give on social occasions, or no one will take us seriously.'

She gave Constance a long steady look. 'We won't be very popular with the predominantly male audience, you know. Women are not usually at these events and those who attend are expected to remain silent, so there's almost certain to be trouble of one kind or another. Are you prepared for that possibility?'

Constance's returning stare was unflinching. 'Do you mean trouble with the audience or with the police?'

'Probably both.'

The motor turned into a shady tree-lined road of three storey houses with Graham giving a squeeze on the rubber hooter to clear their path of a flock of strutting pigeons before drawing up in front of an imposing looking residence whose name, Elm Villa, was carved into one of the stone gateposts. The older woman, mistaking the reason for her hesitancy, put her hand on Constance's in a conciliatory gesture.

'It's really quite alright if you'd rather not come along, dear. I realise it must be rather alarming to contemplate a fracas of that nature.'

Turning her head Constance laughed softly. 'I wouldn't dream of not being there, Eleanor.'

The office door of Thomas Peacock and Son opened after a brief knock and Kenneth Carter, in the absence of his senior, Bill Robinson, ushered in Gerald Fairburn, who greeted his new in-law warmly as he removed his hat and hung it on the stand in the corner.

'Sit down Gerald, sit down.'

Rising to his feet Thomas shook hands genially over his cluttered desk then indicated for his visitor to take the seat opposite himself before opening the lid of the wooden cigar box invitingly.

'You've just missed young Clive I'm afraid. He arrived yesterday instead of today and I sent him off to Kenhope where I'd already booked accommodation in advance for his stay. He should be finished there in about a week or less and able to report back to us. He's a bright young lad in his profession and seems fairly confident about what we'll find there, but I've cautioned him to keep quiet until he's left the area. He found other seams of lead on his first trip, as we expected him to do, but he believes we'll find something else on the Kenhope site and I hope to have everything finalised before Robinson returns from holiday.'

Gerald applied a match to the end of his Havana and puffed busily, his mind assimilating these developments, some of which were beginning to strike him as decidedly risky.

'If Robinson's away from here he could be anywhere.' He said reasonably. 'How do you know he won't be visiting at Kenhope when Clive shows up, or even when he's working there?'

Selecting a cigar for himself Thomas removed the tip and sniffed delicately along its length with studied nonchalance.

'I can't be sure he won't do that, to be honest.

It's a calculated risk, but I'll bet you had better things to do on your honeymoon than go visiting your mother and brother on the family farm.'

'Honeymoon you say?'

'That's right. He's a careful fellow, and had apparently saved enough money to finance a short holiday for himself away from the office. Knowing what we were planning, and wanting no interested eavesdropper on any of our meetings, I made no objection to his request.'

Turning his chair away from the desk, and more towards the cheerfully burning fire in the small black-leaded grate, Gerald gave a few more contented draws on his cigar before admitting 'Hmm. As you say, it's a risk but unlikely.'

He glanced momentarily at Thomas Peacock whose slight smile echoed his own.

'Perhaps it won't make any difference in the long run whether Robinson is there at the start or not, but I would prefer him not to be.'

'A bit too bright for comfort, you think?'

'I'll easily manage the others providing he isn't on the scene, and once they've signed to accept any offer we make it will be too late for him to complicate matters.'

'It's far too big and clumsy. We'll never have time to unroll it before we're stopped, then the message will never be seen. It needs to be shortened somehow; made more to the point with only half the words at the most.'

Christabel Pankhurst held one end of a long length of white calico while mill worker Annie Kenney held the other, and although they were

84

standing at opposite sides of the room the banner still dipped in the middle as though in secret disagreement with the message painted across it in large black letters: 'Will the Liberal Party give Votes for Women?'

Someone sitting behind Constance gloomily stated her belief that they would be laughed out of the Free Trade Hall and doubtless ridiculed in the Press.

'Then there's nothing for it but to do another one.'

The speaker was Emmeline Pankhurst, Christabel's mother, and Constance watched her in fascination. From what she had been told of the fight she had expected someone almost manlike in manner and appearance, but both Pankhurst women were attractively feminine despite being so determined, and this especially applied to Emmeline with her extraordinarily high cheekbones. She had learned in the last half hour that Emmeline's late husband, Dr Richard Pankhurst, had been the one to fire his wife's crusading spirit, having been a champion of womens' rights even before they met and married, he at age forty and Emmeline twenty years his junior. Then, being widowed in the summer of 1898 and left to raise her three younger children, Sylvia fifteen, Adela twelve and Harry eight, had further strengthened her resolve to combat what she considered to be a main item on a list of social ills totally ignored by a male dominated society.

Millworkers, shop girls, women of assorted class and status, all worked here side by side in an atmosphere of mutual support, and Constance had been immediately absorbed into the sister-hood in a manner which made her feel that she had finally found her niche in life. For years she had felt out of place and unable to relate to her expected future role as some man's passive wife, but here at the home of these unusual women she was discovering others just like herself.

'So we must get our message across, but quickly, before they have time to rush at us and hustle us out of the Hall. Any suggestions, ladies?'

Startled back to the present by the appeal to the room in general, Constance looked all around her with bright eyes. Christabel had gone to retrieve the rest of the calico and ideas were being bandied around from one group to another, but it wasn't until someone suggested a neat three-word slogan that a brief silence fell as its rightness sank in. Christabel, who had returned with a roll of white calico under her arm, stopped just inside the doorway as her mother clapped her hands in triumph.

'Has anyone an objection to that wording for our banner?' She asked, smiling.

No one spoke, but all faces wore answering smiles which were eloquent enough.

'That's it, then.'

Gesturing to Christabel to retrace her steps, she advised.

'Two volunteers to go with Christabel to the scullery, please, to paint our fresh slogan on the new banner. "Votes for Women" has a real ring to it, don't you think?'

'It's not that I don't want to sing any more, Miss

Hartley, but I just feel like having a short rest from it at the moment.'

Passing a plate of recently baked cakes across the table towards her unexpected visitor, Lilian silently cursed herself for not accompanying Bill on his walk fifteen minutes ago and hoped that he would soon be back.

'Well, I had to know you were married as I played the organ at your wedding, but I was quite surprised when you simply stopped your musical activities without a word. I waited for over half an hour for you yesterday afternoon ... it was practice day, remember?'

Emma Hartley took a cake and raised her eyebrows as she placed it daintily on her plate before accepting a cup of tea.

'I'm sorry Miss Hartley, I should have let you know, but ... well, I am on my honeymoon, and I thought you might expect my usual routine to be interrupted for a while.'

'Oh, I see.' Lifting the cake to her lips the woman hesitated a moment then gave a little laugh. 'How silly of me. I thought couples actually went away on a honeymoon, but then, that is usually only those in a higher social position than yourselves isn't it?'

A tide of warm colour rose into Lilian's embarrassed face as she poured herself a cup of tea from the flowered teapot which matched her new china, but she held back the biting retort on the subject of 'old maids' that all too quickly came into her mind. Emma Hartley had already taught her all that she knew about music, and after today her opportunities to reprise her scant knowledge would be non-existent. On that she was quite determined.

'Did you make those cakes yourself, Lilian? They're delicious.'

Lilian smiled but did not look at her guest. 'I've known how to bake since I was quite young. Being brought up on a farm gives a girl a good grounding in the practicalities of life.'

Light footfalls sounded coming down the steps outside, then the yard door opened and someone knocked on the back door; guessing it was Louisa, Lilian excused herself and went to answer it, relieved at the interruption.

'I thought I'd pop over to see you for a while until Bill comes back.' Louisa began as they walked into the living room, then stopped abruptly at the sight of Emma Hartley who was starting to look distinctly put out. 'Oh I'm sorry. I had no idea you already had a visitor.'

Introducing them to each other Lilian felt a sense of savage satisfaction at the older woman's slight discomfiture, and left her to twitter to Louisa as she brought another place setting from the sideboard.

'Oh, I'm not really a proper visitor, my dear. I've been doing my practice session in the chapel and I wondered why Lilian hadn't come as she usually does, so I thought I'd better call here on my way home to ask her...'

Louisa's interrupting laugh was like music to Lilian's ears.

'Well, as she *is* on her honeymoon at the moment I don't think *either* of us have shown much tact, but at least I have the excuse that I knew she was alone when I called.'

As she later explained, it was only a joke but Miss Hartley took offence, putting on her jacket and flouncing out of the house with a face like a wet weekend, and her new neighbour put her arm round her shoulders as she grinned.

'She only came to be catty and you turned the tables on her, Lou. Sit down and have something to eat. It's good to see you.'

Louisa watched her as she poured out her tea and there was a trace of wistfulness in her voice as she remarked.

'You look so right here in Bill's house. Are you happy?'

'Yes, of course.'

Careful not to make eye contact at that particular moment Lilian sipped her tea and wondered how 'happy' might be defined: it was true that she was not miserable but she was not ecstatic either. Maybe content was the most accurate description of her state of mind since her wedding.

'I'm sure you're happy Lilian, and Bill will be a good husband. When I saw him going out on his own I thought that it would be one of the few times you'll ever be left by yourself, and that for no more than an hour or so, whereas I seem to see Terry hardly at all these days.'

Her voice trailed off and she looked across the table at her friend with a pathetic attempt at a smile. 'Sorry. That sounded awful didn't it? I'm having a baby next April and I get into some odd moods at times.'

'Oh Louisa, congratulations!' Lilian, genuinely

pleased, beamed across the table at her. 'I'm ... er ... hoping to start a family soon too. Maybe we can have our children close enough together for them to be playmates.'

A sudden loud banging at the back door made both women jump and Lilian, looking startled, hurried out of the room to answer its summons. Her father stood on the doorstep, his face grim and red with hurrying. He spoke without preamble.

'Come on lass. Your mother's been so ill I had to get Dr Hatton through the night, and he's still with her now. He says she's had a major heart attack and might have another one within the next few days.'

For a moment Lilian remained motionless, frozen with shock, then she grabbed her coat off the hook on the umbrella stand and shouted to Louisa. 'Lou, will you stay and tell Bill my mother's ill and I've gone to Roughside with Dad?'

'Yes, I'll tell him. I'm so sorry, Lilian.'

Standing in the living room doorway Louisa watched them both almost run out of the yard and up the slope to the road where James Rutherford's horse and trap were waiting, then as their journey began with a shake of the reins she turned back to sit and wait for Bill Robinson.

Breakfast at the Hemmings home next day was full of lively chatter and, as usual, the conversation centred around the struggles of the WSPU as Eleanor held sway, her slice of toast in one hand and a butter knife in the other.

'There must have been four hundred of us, at least, all filling the Lobby and adjoining passages in the House of Commons.' She said, her face bright at the memory. 'It was last year and our good friend Keir Hardie had persuaded his Independent Labour Party to present again to Parliament the franchise amendment by John Stuart Mill and Richard Pankhurst to the Electoral Reform Bill of 1866, which would have brought women the same voting rights as men but which was later killed off in debate, despite the fact that one of the largest petitions ever sent to Westminster had been received in its support. It had taken Emmeline eight days of tireless lobbying to succeed in getting the Bill placed at all, and when she was given 12th May 1904 we felt sure something was going to happen in our favour at last, and Mrs Martel felt it too.'

Constance looked askance. 'Mrs Martel? I don't believe I've met her, have I?'

'She was visiting from Australia. Mrs Nellie Alma Martel is her full name and women already have the vote back in her country, so it just shows you how far behind the times we British are doesn't it?'

'It certainly does. Go on.'

Graham rose from his seat and quietly excused himself. 'I'm going to take the dogs for their walk, my dear, then I have some work to do in my study.'

Bending down he kissed his wife lightly on her cheek on his way to the door and Eleanor turned to wave to him before continuing her story.

'We should have known better, of course. A

Roadway Lighting Bill was to be heard first, and although we waited all afternoon the discussions on this first item went on until there was a mere half hour left for our Bill. Just a farce really, as our parliamentary opponents had intended it should be. We noted the sounds of derision when our Bill was introduced and knew we'd lost again, so Emmeline told us to follow her outside where one of our oldest suffrage members began to speak, but that was when the trouble began with the police.'

Taking a bite of her toast the woman chewed slowly, her expression darkening, and Constance sat quite still watching her intently.

'They seemed to appear from nowhere, pushing us about and telling us to disperse. We helped Mrs Wolstonholme Elmy away to the statue of Richard the Lionheart so that she could start her speech again. She was a tiny little lady and one would have expected the police, or any other man for that matter, to have had more respect than come after us again, but that's exactly what they did until Keir Hardie came running over to talk to the Inspector. After that we were told it would be in order for us to hold a gathering at the gates of Westminster Abbey, and there we marched, with Emmeline and Mrs Martel in front, to loudly condemn the government while the police took our names, or as many of them as they could.'

She looked across at Constance who was still watching her, enthralled, and her lips formed a tight angry line in her face.

'That was our first militant act, but I can guarantee it won't be the last. I need you to know that our movement involves more than marching around with banners and persistently asking relevant questions of MPs.

'I understand Eleanor, thank you.'

With a long sigh Eleanor smiled at her guest and reached for the coffee pot to replenish their cups. 'Good. I'm glad we've established that before our day really starts, because we have an awful lot to do before the meeting begins at the Free Trade Hall.'

Emily Rutherford opened her eyes just long enough to see her daughter sitting by the bed with tears coursing down her cheeks, then wearily shut them again.

'Mum, are you feeling better?'

'I will be Lilian ... in a while.'

'She's very tired.' Dr Hatton advised quietly as he closed his leather bag and picked it up ready to leave. 'Best just let her rest until she gets her strength back a little.'

Distraught at the sight of her mother's ashen face and blue-tinged lips Lilian lifted up Emily's hand and pressed it to her mouth convulsively. James, standing behind her, put his hand on her shoulder.

'I'm going to show Dr Hatton out, then I'll be back.'

'Right, Dad.'

Listening to their footsteps going down the stairs she looked around the familiar bedroom with a heavy heart as she held the cold unresponsive hand in her own. Outside the day was turning to dusk as an October mist began to fall along the floor of the valley and the two mens' voices drifted up from the yard as they said goodbye. Old fashioned ways still persisted in Gilfell and Dr Hatton had arrived on horseback, which was still the best method to travel over the rough steep fell tracks.

Placing Emily's hand beneath the covers and kissing her forehead gently, Lilian wandered across to the window to watch the doctor mount his large bay and clip clop slowly over the cobbles to the farm gate, where he looked back and waved briefly before urging his horse into a trot down the more level surface of the lane. She was trying not to think of what might still happen to her mother, yet she only had to glance at her still form to realise how ill she was.

'How could we have missed the signs?' She asked as James re-entered the room, and he shook his head helplessly.

'I don't know, lass. She never said a word about it, even though Dr Hatton said she's bound to have been suffering for quite a while, but I saw her mouth go the peculiar colour it is now a time or two. I should have made her see Dr Hatton then.'

'The wedding must have stressed her. It's my fault, not yours.'

'Nay lass, it's nobody's fault.'

Taking her arm he led her back to sit by the bed where Emily was asleep again, and she watched her father cross to the dressing table to light the candles on either side of the mirror.

'Is Dr Hatton coming back tomorrow?'

'First thing in the morning he said, and I

promised you and I would take turns sitting with her so that there's always someone there if she wakes up and wants something.'

Or if she wakes up and feels ill again, Lilian thought grimly. Aloud she said.

'You go and have a sleep now Dad, and I'll stay here. Bill will sit with me when he comes.'

The man nodded wearily. It would be a relief to go next door into the spare bedroom and let his true feelings show, for his optimism was no more than a facade for Lilian's benefit. His wife was very ill indeed, and even if she survived this heart attack James Rutherford knew that a second one was inevitable and it would not be long before he was left a widower. Pausing in the doorway he looked back at his daughter anxiously.

'Are you sure you'll be alright?'

'Just go and rest Dad. You must really need it.' She managed to smile just before he shut the door behind him, then she added softly. 'I'll be fine once Bill comes.'

'Why can't we sit with Christabel and Annie Kenney?' Constance demanded. 'They've got the banner ready to unroll and we could help them.'

Eleanor looked back over the rows of men to where the other two sisters in suffrage were sitting, and shook her head.

'We'd just be in the way when the time comes, and we really should have stayed outside so as not to arouse suspicion because women don't often attend political meetings, but I want you to see first hand exactly what we're up against.'

Constance nodded and looked towards the platform where the two speakers, Sir Edward Grey and Winston Churchill, were sitting in obvious readiness for the meeting to begin, and as the buzz of conversation died in the hall it was the older man who was introduced by the chairman.

Although she tried to concentrate on the content of Sir Edward's speech Constance found her mounting excitement a decided obstacle to that end and began to feel irritated when there was first one, then another, interrupting question put by a member of the audience.

'When are they going to do something?' She whispered as a politician laboured through his reply, and Eleanor nudged her warningly.

'Soon ... you'll see.'

A further five minutes passed as the speech droned to its conclusion and Constance felt a lurching sensation in her chest, as, before he could take his seat, Annie Kenney stood up.

'Will the Liberal Government give the vote to women?' She asked clearly and sat down again.

Holding her breath, as she felt Eleanor was holding hers, Constance waited for Sir Edward Grey to reply, but he made no move to do so and after a few seconds of silence the chairman called, 'Any other questions?'

Annie stood up once more and, amidst a murmur of male disapproval, was pulled down into her seat again by two men sitting behind her. Eleanor smiled triumphantly at Constance as Annie freed herself and, with Christabel Pankhurst, defiantly unfurled the banner and held it aloft for all to see, ignoring the harsh laughter and ungentlemanly remarks that their action inspired. This time Liberal Stewards descended on the hapless Annie to make her sit down, and she called yet again to the chairman. 'Why doesn't he answer my question?'

From the platform another figure came down into the audience to have a few words with Annie, and Eleanor who was no longer smiling, told Constance that he was the Chief Constable of Manchester. They both watched, oblivious to the noise in the hall, as Annie produced a piece of paper from her pocket which the policeman took back to the platform to be passed round the speakers who read it with insulting amusement before passing it on.

'What are they doing, Eleanor?'

There was no need to lower her voice. Whistles and catcalls were still rife and no one was taking any notice of the two women sitting quietly at the side of the Hall.

'That was Annie's question written out on paper just in case this situation arose. It is signed on behalf of the WSPU which seems to be affording them some hilarity.'

As the last man on the platform glanced at the paper and set it contemptuously aside, Annie spoke again.

'For the sake of the ninety six thousand women cotton workers, of which I am one, I wish my question to be answered.'

As a Steward made to grab her again Annie rose once more to speak, with Christabel leaping up to stand between her friend and a plain clothes policeman who had just arrived, but knowing they had not much time left before male strength got the better of them she jumped up onto her seat and shouted 'Will the Liberal Government give the vote to women?'

Grasping her cousin's arm Constance gasped as the two women were forcibly dragged out into the gangway to the accompaniment of much clapping and jeering.

'Go home and wash your dishes!' was the most polite remark thrown after Annie and Christabel, and as they were pulled past the platform Annie called angrily to Sir Edward Grey 'You're a coward!' while Christabel was threatening to hold her own meeting outside the Hall.

Too late, Constance and Eleanor stood up to follow them only to find their way barred by the many men who had now left their seats to stand up, blocking every outlet.

'We'll have to push our way through, and it's going to be tough.'

Constance placed her hand on her hat to steady it. 'Right. Let's make a start.'

For the rest of her life Lilian had a dread of the month of October because, to her, it had heralded the beginning of the end of her mother's life. To be more conveniently placed she and Bill moved up to Roughside and did not return to Hillary Terrace until the first week of November, when their little house needed fires lit, not only in the living room but also the sitting room and main bedroom, to defeat the damp chill that had settled into everything. Once this was done Lilian picked up her basket to go to the store and called at Louisa's first. It was Saturday morning and Terence answered the door on his way to the barbers.

'Good Lord, Lilian, you look awful.'

She smiled faintly at his lack of tact. 'I'll be alright when I've had a rest. I've just called to tell you that we're back home and my mother has rallied, at least for the moment.'

Cursing her weakness she felt hot tears forming in her eyes and Terence took her arm to lead her inside.

'Come in for five minutes. Lou will want to see you.'

Obediently Lilian allowed herself to be led into the living room as a rustle of activity sounded upstairs.

'Was that someone at the door, Terry?'

'It's Lilian back home.'

With the slow tattoo of someone being careful not to slip, Louisa immediately abandoned her bedmaking and made her way downstairs, where she unwittingly endorsed her husband's opinion.

'Oh Lilian, you look terrible! I heard in the village yesterday that your mother is making a recovery, but you look as though you're ill yourself.'

'I'm not ill, Louisa. I'm just tired and, like yourself, pregnant!'

Louisa's reaction to her news was very gratifying and Lilian wished she could have enjoyed this time in her life without the spectre of her mother's heart condition spoiling it all, but as she sat and talked to her friend by her cosy fireside a little comfort stole over her dark mood. Nearly three weeks in a sick room were enough to depress anyone, after all, and it might just be possible that her present depression was colouring her point of view.

'I must go down to the store now.' She said after fifteen minutes had passed, and Louisa nodded.

'I need some things too so I'll come with you. I'll leave a note for Terry in case he gets back before we do.'

It was not until they were on their way home from the shops that Louisa remembered their visitor the previous week.

'We heard someone knocking quite late one afternoon and Terry went to see who it was, but he was just in time to catch sight of a man riding off along the terrace on a bicycle and he didn't stop even when Terry shouted after him.'

Lilian was intrigued. 'Are you sure he'd been knocking at *our* door?'

'Oh yes, we could tell because he hadn't shut the yard door properly on his way out.'

'What did he look like, Lou?'

'His face was never seen, naturally, as he was riding away, but Terry said he seemed quite young with black hair.'

'Hmm ... that doesn't sound like anyone I know. Maybe Bill will recognise the description.'

Pausing a moment between both their yard doors Lilian smiled at Louisa as she placed her hand on the latch. 'It's good to be back again. I haven't lived in this house very long but it already feels like my home.'

Before she could let herself in, the door was opened from the other side by Bill who took the basket off Lilian's arm and handed her an opened letter.

'Come in to the fire and rest while you read this.' Louisa heard him say as she entered her own yard, and frowned as she found herself wishing Terence was so attentive to her.

In the light of the lamp that Bill had just lit Lilian sat in her chair by the fire and read her husband's letter from his brother Gilbert, whom she had so far met only once on their wedding day.

'He must have been the caller Terry saw leaving on a bicycle last week.' She surmised, observing from the envelope that it had been delivered by hand. 'Louisa described his black hair as he was riding away, but I never thought about Gilbert. I wonder what he wanted to talk about so urgently that he couldn't put down in this letter?'

Bill glanced up at the wall clock then quickly made up his mind on a course of action.

'Len Harrison has a pony and trap that would nicely get us over the fell to Kenhope, but it will have to be tomorrow in daylight, Sabbath or not. There's no way we'll have time to go after I finish work next day when it's dark. I'll go down to the store now and ask him.'

Bending down he gave her a quick kiss then, in seconds, was out of the house and hurrying along the downward slope to Len Harrison's store. Thoughtfully Lilian re-read the letter with its brief message to get in touch as soon as they got back from honeymoon, and she grimaced slightly. Some honeymoon indeed. The moment her mind drifted back over the past weeks she became depressed again about her mother, and determinedly set the letter aside as she got up to begin preparing their evening meal. Whatever news Gilbert had for Bill she hoped it was something pleasantly distracting.

As the pony and trap turned in at the gate Gilbert Robinson walked across the cobbled path to meet his brother Bill and his new wife. Slowly they came to a halt by the open door, and Lilian viewed Gilbert from her high vantage point wondering how any brothers could be so dissimilar as these two. Unlike Bill, who was tall and fair, Gilbert was short, stocky and dark, with a temper well known within his family for being a trifle uncertain on occasions, although he was smiling now and obviously glad that they had borrowed transport to come over Kenhope Fell in answer to his letter.

'Go on into the house and I'll tether the pony for you.' He offered as Bill handed Lilian down into the yard. 'Mam's got a meal almost made and we can talk over that. I don't suppose you want to be late starting back with the days getting colder and shorter again.'

'Well, it is November.' Bill agreed, adding with quiet pride. 'I have to take great care of Lilian now, Gil. There'll be three of us next June or July.'

Gilbert took hold of the reins, smiling broadly. 'Congratulations! You're wasting no time in making me an uncle then?'

Flushing slightly, Lilian watched him lead the pony and trap away to some sheltered tethering post while Bill took her hand in his to cross the cobbles to the farmhouse door, holding her close to him against the biting wind.

'You should have told your mother first, Bill.'

'No matter, we'll tell her now.'

Inside the warm kitchen Marion Robinson was setting the table for Gilbert and herself, but at the sight of her eldest son and his bride she threw down her handful of cutlery and hurried over to embrace them. Hugging her in return, Bill first told his mother about Emily Rutherford's illness being the reason they had not been at home when Gilbert had called, and at Marion's immediate show of sympathy Lilian felt her burden of guilt quite acutely, then even more so after the woman had been told about her coming grandchild. She had taken to Marion from their first meeting, when she had been welcomed so warmly into the Robinson family, and now here she stood, brazening out the lie that another man's child was the Robinsons' flesh and blood.

'I'll begin making a layette right away.' Marion said happily, leading them to the table. 'Sit down Lilian, and you there Bill. I'll soon set two more places. Are you taking proper care of your bride ... plenty of good food and suchlike?'

'Of course.'

Taking a rabbit pie out of the oven Marion quickly followed it with dishes of vegetables and a steaming gravy boat, then began to serve the meal talking all the while about the expected baby. Cots, perambulators, all inevitably led to reminiscences about Bill and Gilbert's babyhood, but after ten minutes on this subject her younger son interrupted.

103

'I'm sorry to stop you Mam, and you know we're happy about Lilian and Bill's news, but they don't have more than a couple of hours or so before they'll have to start back to Gilfell and we have to talk about the bottom pasture.'

Marion halted her monologue abruptly.

'Yes, you're right. It certainly must be discussed today, and Lilian and I will have plenty time in the future to talk about the new baby.'

She smiled at her daughter-in-law then looked across at Gilbert. 'Go on then. Tell them what happened.'

Clearing his throat Gilbert set down his knife and fork and began to speak.

'We had a stranger come here a month ago, about three days after your wedding as I recall. Said he was a geologist, or some such, and could he look round our bottom pasture and maybe a few adjacent fields. I asked him what his reasons were and he said he was simply curious about the land in these parts and, being recently qualified, would appreciate the practice, so I didn't see the harm in letting him look round so long as he didn't disturb anything. He was there the best part of ten days with his instruments, poking about all over the place, then he thanked me and said he was finished, so I naturally asked him if he had found anything interesting, like gold or something.'

He laughed a little at his own naivety then, at a look from his mother, retrieved his knife and fork and began to eat. Bill was suddenly very still.

'What did he say, Gilbert?'

'Well, he gave me a bit of a funny look and said

104

he hadn't found any gold, so I asked him what he had been looking for and he got all sort of evasive and wanting to be gone quickly kind of thing. I asked him if he had been hired by anybody or if he had really just been doing it for his own curiosity as he'd claimed, and he said "I'm afraid I'm not at liberty to divulge that" which was answer enough, so I pretended to let the matter drop and offered him a ride back into Kenhope on the cart as I was going there myself on business. He seemed nicely taken in by this so I took him to Kenhope, keeping the conversation on anything but the land and what he'd been doing there, and he was daft enough to let me drop him off at his lodgings.'

Taking a forkful of pie Gilbert looked round at his attentive fellow diners, his black eyes alight with triumph, and Bill urged him on.

'So?'

'So, I took the cart into Pennington's yard nearby and they let me leave it there while I went back to Tenking Street just in time to see him leaving the rooming house carrying a fair sized travelling bag and heading in the direction of the railway station. I waited until he was round the corner then I went in and spoke to the landlady and she told me his room had been booked by letter for the firm of Thomas Peacock and Son!'

Lilian almost felt the shock emanating from Bill as he stared across the table at his brother, and Marion looked at his whitening face with concern.

'Did you know about it, Bill?'

'No I didn't, but I'll soon rectify that when I go

105

back to work tomorrow.'

'We've already had an offer from Thomas Peacock.' Marion told him quietly. 'That's why we sent for you before we did anything about it. He came last Tuesday and asked to buy the bottom meadow, and although he wouldn't commit himself it is most probably for the purpose of mining. I know it's a long way from the house but I don't fancy a lead mine on my doorstep thank you.'

'It isn't lead Mam, I've told you that. I made a few enquiries around Kenhope to see if our geologist had let slip any information in an unguarded moment, and I discovered that coal had been mentioned quite a few times in the local pub.'

Lilian wrinkled her nose. 'That's worse. It's dirtier.'

'It has as good a market as lead, if not better.'

Bill looked grim as he resumed his meal, eating with slow deliberation as though the food had lost its taste. He was angrier than he had been for a very long time and considered he had every justification for being so. Enquiring how much Peacocks had offered for the land, and receiving a reply, he felt angrier still.

'Don't sell.' He looked around the table, his eyes bright in his too pale face. 'If there's coal here all we have to do is ask the bank for a loan and mine it ourselves. What do you say?'

Gilbert smiled ruefully. 'No good, Bill. I've already thought of that and approached the bank here, but they won't lend us the money unless we have sufficient collateral and also somebody with practical mining experience behind us. The manager was keen enough at first until he realised that I was a hill farmer and you were an office worker, then he explained that you have to know exactly what you're doing to start mining ... and we don't.'

Silence fell again as Bill digested this discouraging news and Lilian looked thoughtfully down at her plate, staring avidly at the blue trees and birds beneath the glaze.

'It's like stalemate, isn't it? The Peacocks can't mine without your land and you can't mine without their experience.'

She spoke idly, simply giving voice to her thoughts, but a sudden intake of breath caused her to look up at the three faces all turned towards her as Bill gave a slow smile of relief.

'That's the answer!'

Mystified, she gazed from Gilbert to Bill as they grinned at each other, and her husband laughed.

'Lilian, you're a genius! The Peacocks can either make a deal over the new mine or leave well alone, but there's no way we're selling them the land! Right?'

Gilbert nodded. 'Right.'

Not understanding the direction matters had taken Marion left the table to look at the rice pudding in the oven, remarking as she did so.

'Good! That will put paid to having an ugly mine near us. Just tell them to leave well alone, as you say.'

Opening his mouth to correct her Gilbert saw Bill quickly shake his head, and put his mind on his meal again. Whatever was to be done now he

107

knew Bill would see to everything, and when he had done that it would be time enough to tell their mother that they would indeed be having 'an ugly mine' near them.

The trap turned in at the gate of Low Shields and stopped at the newly renovated Lodge where the homecoming honeymooners would now live. Johnny Peacock, who had hardly spoken at all since he and Bella had been met at the station, jumped down and reached up to assist his bride as she put her foot timorously onto the step. Dressed becomingly in a royal blue outfit which included a coat with fur collar, Bella offered their driver a wan smile then walked up the short path to the door.

'It's a poky little place isn't it?' Johnny murmured behind her, and she opened their new front door to feel pleasantly warm air coming out to meet her.

'It will do for now, John, surely.'

'For now I suppose.'

The Fairburn Jack of All Trades brought their travelling bags then went back to get the trunk, and the young man with a spurt of impatience turned on his heel and went to assist him. Something about the feel of Low Shields Lodge told him that the place would be giving him a worse than usual bout of claustrophobia, especially in the evenings when the maid and cook had gone back to the big house to sleep. There would just be himself and Bella then, staring at each other across the suffocatingly cramped rooms.

Inside the Lodge Bella found everything spick

and span, from the highly polished sideboard to the glowing fire in the grate, and she smiled timidly as a Low Shields parlourmaid appeared in the doorway.

'How nice it all looks, Laura.'

'Thank you Miss Bella ... I mean, Mrs Peacock. Cook and I have to wait and serve dinner before we go back to the master and mistress, and will do so daily until you have had the chance to employ your own staff if you wish. Will you be dining now?'

'Yes please.'

As she went back into the kitchen Johnny came in, having just finished taking Bella's trunk upstairs, and he grimaced slightly.

'We're supposed to have room for staff as well are we?'

'Are you ready to eat now, John?'

'Why not?'

Like a cloud drifting across the sun Bella found her mood shadowing into depression again at her husband's show of petulance, but she went upstairs to freshen up before the meal without retaliating. Two things she had learnt on her honeymoon were not to start an argument with her new husband if it could be avoided, and to try not to go to bed until she was fairly sure he was safely asleep; the latter being of greater importance so far.

In her absence her bedroom furniture had all been transferred from Low Shields to her new room next door to her husband's, and she sat down at her dressing table with a sigh of thankfulness knowing that, from today, she and

John would no longer have to share a bed. His rough approach to the physical side of their marriage had left Bella completely repelled, and her partner angry and frustrated. Unlike the women he had been used to, Johnny found her passivity and lack of passion at first irritating to the point of violence then too boring to bother about, and now that they were back on home ground he knew that the only times he would make demands on his wife would be when he was too drunk to care. So tonight, the idea of sleeping peacefully in a room of his own again gave as much relief to Johnny as it did to Bella, although she would have been intensely surprised had she known this.

Later, over dinner, Johnny gave his wife a smile of studied innocence as he announced. 'I'm left with over three miles to travel to the office every day now that we live here, and I bought a motorcycle one afternoon while you were having a rest, so I expect it's already arrived at Dalton Railway Station. I'll walk down tomorrow morning to collect it.'

Bella looked puzzled. 'Why not a car? A motorcycle will only travel one of us, surely.'

'Yes I know, but it's the only way to tackle these hills, as I'm sure you will know having seen your parents buy a motor only to keep it stored in part of the stables on a permanent basis. I must have transport Bella, and I don't want to buy or borrow a horse and trap. It is the twentieth century now for heaven's sake!'

Subsiding into a reproachful silence she contemplated the freedom Johnny would have once he had access to a motorcycle, and the man kept his eyes down as he sipped his coffee, anxious to keep his inner elation a secret. It was strange how he had temporarily forgotten about his visit to Harrow's Motorcycle Showrooms in London a week after the wedding and the proprietor's cheerful promise to have the machine delivered for his return from his honeymoon, but now that he had remembered he had hope for the future. A motorcycle would not only take him to Gilfell to the mine, but also to Dalton where the music hall and moving picture theatre flourished.

Replacing his cup on its saucer Johnny put a hand to his mouth pretending to smother a yawn.

'I don't know about you Bella, but I'm exhausted. Think I'll have an early night then I'll be fit to make a good start in the morning. That way perhaps I'll not be too late getting up to Gilfell after I've collected the bike.' He smiled brilliantly at nothing in particular. 'That'll put the machine through its paces alright.'

Left alone after the dining room door had closed in his wake Bella sat still for a few seconds, torn between relief that he obviously did not want to share her bed tonight and a deep sense of insult for the same reason. At last she rose, rang the bell for Laura to clear the table, and walked into the small lounge to play her piano for a while. Somewhere deep down, where she refused to acknowledge it, Bella now bitterly regretted her marriage.

Thomas Peacock stood up slowly, his face an alarming shade of red, and as he leaned over slightly to rest both palms on his desk top Bill looked back at him impassively.

'My business was with your mother and brother, not with you.'

'I speak for them with their consent, and we have decided not to sell you the land, Mr Peacock.'

'Right. You've just stated that fact quite clearly. Perhaps now your best move will be to get back to your desk while you still have a job there.'

Despite his cool outer show Bill felt a flicker of alarm at the direction the discussion was now taking, but forced himself to continue quietly.

'However, if you wish we will lease you the land on a monthly basis, all payments to be made in advance, and we would naturally expect to become partners in the new venture!'

Watching his employer sit down again Bill almost flinched at the expression on his face, although he forced himself to return his look without giving way. With his one remaining hand still on the desk Thomas beat a quick tattoo with his fingertips for a moment before speaking.

'I think getting married must had addled your brain! In case it's slipped your mind, Robinson, I have the power to cut off your only source of income right now, and I can't see your new wife being too impressed with that, can you?'

'Mr Peacock, I'm aware that you can dismiss me, but in that event I feel sure we could interest some other person, or persons, in what lies beneath our bottom pasture for, as we both know, coal is a very lucrative business.'

A heavy silence fell as the older man fought to

come to terms with this thinly veiled threat, during which Bill found the ponderous ticking of the wall clock behind his employer's shoulder a distraction which seemed to get louder by the second. Thankful that at least this time Thomas Peacock was glaring at the office door and not at him, he swallowed and tried not to clench his fists. In the outer office he could also hear the uneven rhythm of the stenographer's typewriter and wondered, when the pauses came, if she was trying to overhear their conversation.

'For no financial outlay on your part you expect a lot, don't you?'

The challenge was thrown at him suddenly, almost catching him unawares.

'Well sir, it seems to me that our expectations are rather more fair than the price which was offered us for the land.'

'You need our expertise.' Thomas guessed shrewdly. 'If it wasn't us you'd have to find another mining company to proposition. That's right isn't it? You can't raise the money to mine yourselves?'

'Yes, I'll admit that is correct, but there are plenty mining companies and I'm sure I wouldn't be too long finding one interested in our proposal.'

Thomas Peacock was equally sure, as the slow slump of his shoulders confirmed.

'Alright. I'll talk it over with my associates and let you know in good time.'

'A week, sir, if you don't mind. If we haven't heard from you in that time we'll feel free to pursue our interests elsewhere.'

113

'A week.' The older man agreed heavily and Bill bowed slightly.

'Thank you. I'll get on with my work now.'

Back at his desk he took out the clean white handkerchief that Lilian had supplied him with that morning and gently drew it across his brow where a slight film of perspiration had formed, then he opened the ledger and dipped his pen in the inkwell. Right or wrong the deed was done, and he had the feeling that big changes were coming into his life, though whether they would be good or bad it was impossible to guess.

In the distance a strange roaring sound was growing. One by one heads were raised as the office staff of Thomas Peacock and Son listened to its approach, and after a few seconds Bill rose and walked to the window just in time to see Johnny Peacock riding in at the gates on a huge black motorcycle. He caught his breath in envy, noticing Johnny's grinning face with distaste an instant before he turned to go back to his desk. Let him grin, he thought savagely. He hadn't heard his father's news about their prospective new partners yet.

Nor was Johnny to learn of it for a while. Well aware of the thin partition between his office and the rest of the workforce, all of whom had more than their fair share of curiosity, Thomas Peacock wisely decided to keep developments a secret from his son until they met Gerald Fairburn that evening. That way he could hopefully get the uproar over in just one session instead of two, for he could imagine how they would both react to Bill Robinson's demands. Unfortunately, he could also imagine that they, like himself, would be forced to accept them.

Relieved beyond measure at the end of his working day Bill left the office and made his way home to Lilian. She was standing beside the window in the firelight staring out into the darkness, and when she turned to face him he was shocked to see that she had been weeping.

'What is it, love?'

He moved towards her quickly and she almost fell into his arms.

'We have to go to Roughside again, Bill. Mam's dead!'

Clutching the handlebars of his new machine Johnny revved the engine and grinned into the strong rush of air that his speed was creating. The sensation of flight plus freedom was even headier than the wine he had drunk at dinner earlier in the evening, and he knew he should not be riding on the public highway at all for he was too often on the wrong side of the road, especially when taking a corner. Narrowing his eyes against the slight draught that was seeping through the sides of his goggles he felt an exhilaration that he had not known for weeks, just as though he had left his family, his in-laws, and the tedious Bella behind forever instead of only for a few hours.

Johnny's destination was Dalton Music Hall in time for the second house, and it was touch and go whether he would arrive there in time for 'curtain up'. He had made no excuse of any sort to Bella, simply announcing his intention of going out, and had pretended not to see her martyred expression before she turned away from him. This was to be the pattern of their marriage, and she had better become accustomed to it. Any other woman, one less useless than Bella, might have found activities of her own to occupy her instead of expecting him to be dancing attendance all the time, but her reaction to his nightly excursions into the surrounding countryside was consistently spineless. How much better it could have been had she taken a leaf out of her sister Constance's book and got herself all fired up about something, for Constance had returned briefly to Low Shields for Christmas but was obviously counting the hours until she could return to Manchester to get up to more mischief with the Suffragette Movement.

Soaring over the top of the last steep hill before Dalton he viewed the panorama of gaslit streets beneath their pall of smoke with the now familiar excitement which the thought of its possibilities always afforded him. Music Hall first and then a supper room, perhaps with the dark-haired chorus girl who had caught his attention last night.

Slowing down as he turned into the first residential road, Johnny tried to blot from his memory the events of the last two months since his marriage, but they kept flowing to the forefront of his mind like an incoming tide bringing a frown to his handsome face in place of the smile of a few moments ago. His return from honeymoon had been bad enough on its own without finding out the following night that Bill Robinson had wormed his way into the business and, naturally, brought his new wife with him. Lilian! He hoped most desperately that he need never meet her in any social capacity where they would be expected to communicate with each other, for he was not sure how he would react. She should have been relegated to oblivion in his mind long ago, just like all the others, but for some reason her image had remained with him, stubbornly fresh and vivid in every detail.

Secretly ashamed of his cavalier treatment of her that night in the barn, he now admitted to himself that while he had wanted her he had been angry with her for giving in to him and showing herself, in the end, to be no different from all the other eager females. Lilian had always been special to him then she had spoilt it, and to make matters even worse she had decided to marry Bill Robinson, a man he had never liked and whom he had always felt despised him. His lip curled at the thought. Straightfaced Bill was learning to be a big man now alright, but how big would he feel, Johnny wondered, if he ever found out that he had married another man's leavings?

Five minutes later, his cycle safely parked nearby, the young man strode from the ticket office at the front of His Majesty's Theatre into the warmly lit foyer, pausing for a moment before the photograph board showing the cast of the evening's performance, including the chorus girls, and his eyes focused intently on the tall brunette who had taken his fancy. There were other dark-haired girls in the line-up, some of them even prettier than this one, yet she had something that attracted him deeply and which, until now, he had failed to recognise, and that was the fact that she bore a marked resemblance to Lilian.

Bill looked across the railway carriage at Lilian's white face and felt a pang of remorse.

'Are you feeling ill?' he asked anxiously. 'If you don't feel like coming with me to the solicitor's I'll book you into a hotel room for the afternoon where you can rest.'

She smiled and shook her head. 'I'm alright, Bill. It's good to be doing something different ... to take my mind off things.'

To take her mind off her mother's death two months ago and the dismal Christmas that had followed it so closely, when everyone except Bill, her father and herself, had seemed to be happy. Today, with this visit to their recently acquired solicitor in Newcastle, she had the chance to distract herself, if only for a few hours, and was glad of the opportunity.

'We'll have lunch after the interview, then I'll take you round the big stores. You'll love them, Lilian. They're better than those in Carlisle, I promise you.'

'I'll look forward to that. Perhaps we can buy some things for the baby.'

'Well, yes. There's nothing like preparing early is there?'

Lilian felt the old familiar guilt come over her again at his gentle teasing. In reality she was halfway through her pregnancy, and not two and a half months as she had led others to believe, and had recently felt her baby move, fluttering gently inside her to cause such a mighty surge of love that she had been quite overwhelmed. Unable to mention this miracle to anyone she had hugged its wonder to herself, whilst occasionally aware of some of the village womens' knowing looks when they noticed the swell of her abdomen that should never have appeared at only ten weeks. Let them whisper. She wouldn't be the first girl in Gilfell to have a 'premature' baby that was really full term.

Watching the rows of houses with their back gardens and allotments passing by outside the window Lilian felt the train begin to slow down, and she stood up stiffly to adjust her hair in the small mirror beneath the luggage rack.

Bill watched her fondly. She looked beautiful but impractical in her cream coat with matching dress and hat, and he suddenly knew what he would do with their first free time that afternoon.

'I'm going to take you to the photographer's today.' He declared. 'We'll have a portrait done together, then I want one of you on your own; a big one that we can hang on the wall at home.'

Taking out her hatpin then sticking it in again at a more secure angle Lilian regarded her husband warmly from under its brim.

'Now that really is exciting.'

'Good! I'm glad you approve.'

They stood together by the compartment door as the train pulled in to Newcastle Station at a snail's pace and Lilian looked up at Bill as she remembered something.

'You recall when we were late and boarding the train in Dalton at the last moment and I said I saw Terry getting into one of the compartments

119

further down?'

'Hmm.'

'Well I still feel sure it was him, but I can't think why he ignored me when I called to him. He wasn't that far away and he was bound to hear.'

Bill was about to reply when the train stopped with a jolt and a hiss, throwing Lilian lightly against him, and he steadied her carefully before letting down the carriage window in the door to reach the outside handle. Alighting onto the platform he took her hand to help her down before they both moved along with the crowd towards the exit. They had scarcely travelled three yards when they saw Terence ahead of them, marching quickly and with purpose as though eager to escape his fellow passengers without delay. Lilian shook Bill's arm.

'Look! There he is! Shall we try to catch up with him?'

Bill halted and people surged between them and their neighbour, but not so densely that they could not see the young woman with a child in tow running towards him eagerly. She was probably a few years older than Louisa, Lilian noticed, but with hair that was a few shades darker than Louisa's very light blonde. Watching her throwing her arms around Terry's neck she tried hard to believe that this woman was his sister, or some other female relative, but the child put paid to that hope as she clung to his jacket and cried, 'Carry me Daddy.'

Stunned, both Lilian and Bill stood still just staring after the trio as they vanished quickly through the ticket barrier without a backward glance, and she looked up at Bill, disbelief showing plainly in her eyes as she whispered. 'Who was she? And who was that child who called Terence Daddy?'

'I have no idea, although it would seem fairly obvious really wouldn't it?'

Troubled, Bill patted her hand, yet in truth he was at a loss to know what to do. Desperately he tried another theory.

'Maybe he's the girl's godfather.'

Lilian sighed. 'No child calls her godfather "Daddy", although at this moment I truly wish they did. We can see Terry has a woman here and a daughter, but what are we going to tell Louisa?'

'We're not going to tell Louisa anything!'

'But we must.'

'No, Lilian.'

Holding her elbow firmly Bill began to steer his wife along the platform again, wisely deciding to buy them both a cup of tea in the Refreshment Room rather than risk seeing his neighbour again out in the street. Seating Lilian at a table beside the window he walked to the counter to order and the woman stared out at the trains, no longer entranced by their gigantic splendour. In her mind she was remembering Louisa complaining of her loneliness when her husband was away, and seeing her frowning over the price of things in the local store while she secretly totted up the amounts in her head.

When Bill returned to their table she sipped her tea but felt too nauseated to take advantage of the plate of assorted cakes and buns.

'We can't just ignore this, Bill. Terence has a

mistress, that is more than plain, and Louisa should know of it.'

'For what reason?'

'Pardon?'

'What purpose do you suppose it may serve to tell Louisa what we've seen today? What good do you think it would do with her not just loving Terence but having his baby in less than three months?'

She sighed and turned away from his compassionate gaze to stare unseeingly at the new crowd of passengers amassing on the platform outside.

'Alright. For the moment we can't say anything.' She conceded in a low voice. 'But I don't know how I'll ever speak a civil word to Terence Marshall again.'

CHAPTER FOUR

April 1912

'I can't understand you, Lilian. You've been cool towards Terence ever since that day at Newcastle Railway Station six years ago, and now that he's going to America to make a new life you want to give a farewell dinner in his honour. Is it guilty conscience or something?'

'No, it isn't anything like that, Bill. I'm doing it to cheer up Louisa for a few hours seeing she's already pining at the thought of him leaving her for a while, but you can call it a Good Riddance party if you like.'

Through her dressing table mirror, where she sat putting the finishing touches to her toilette, Lilian smiled at Bill's reflection as he pulled a wry face. He was brushing the jacket of his suit before putting it on, and as he bent his head to the task the light from the gas fixture glinted on the wisps of white now threading their way through his fair hair. Like his dead father before him Bill was going to be completely silver-haired well before he reached forty.

'Well, at least it isn't a big affair.'

'Only eight with us, Bill. Your mother and my father, Louisa and Terence, and Dr Hatton and his wife. We all know and feel comfortable with each other.'

123

'Thank heaven we don't have to bother with anyone from the mine this time.' He remarked thankfully, and Lilian's expression hardened a little.

'The less we have to bother with them the better, at least socially. It doesn't seem as though they'll ever get used to having the peasants trespassing on their territory, does it?'

Straightening up after donning his jacket Bill took a clean white handkerchief and tucked it into his breast pocket, then bent down briefly to kiss his wife's shoulder.

'I'll go and see to the fires. We must have a good blaze when they arrive and not a sullen smoking mess.'

Left alone, Lilian looked around her gold and green bedroom with an appreciation which had never faded once in the five years they had inhabited Ivy House. From as far back as she could remember she had loved the house from the outside, and the moment she had stepped inside its front door she declared to an amused Bill that the place recognised her and put its arms round her. Three storeys high, its rooms were large and square with shutters on the inside of the windows to keep out the icy gales of Pennine winters, and fireplaces in all rooms except the bedroom and boxroom at the top of the house.

Furnishing Ivy House had taken time, and been a pleasure that had helped a little to distract Lilian from her grief at losing Emily, as also had the birth of Edward on 21st May 1906, just a few months before the move.

Bill had been delighted with his son, telling

everyone how like Lilian he was, but she was guiltily aware that his dark colouring could have been inherited from either his mother or his real father, and that time would relentlessly mould his features in favour of one or the other.

There had lately been disturbing rumours of some diphtheria cases across the fell in Kenhope, and Lilian tried to put them out of her mind as she walked into the nursery on the opposite side of the landing. Looking down at the sleeping boy she smiled at his angelic appearance which so belied his mischievous and stubborn nature when awake, then moved to the cot where two year old Winifred lay, her fair hair spread out like a cloak over the pillow. Their daughter, Bill's child, did not so much look like her father as her grandmother, Marion, yet undoubtedly had a similar nature to Bill's. While Edward was energetic and noisy, Winifred was quiet and would sit contentedly playing with her toys with a concentration that was unusual in one so young. Her birthday, February 3rd 1910, had been the day when Lilian had privately considered that she had paid back at least part of the debt she owed her husband and had begun to feel a little better about Edward.

With silence born of long practice she moved out onto the landing, closing the nursery door behind her, then hurried downstairs to the kitchen where their part-time helpers, Nancy Waugh and her mother Evelyn, were busy with the final pre-parations for the meal. Evelyn smiled as Lilian entered and spoke with the familiarity of one who has known a person since their childhood.

'Everything's fine Lilian, don't worry. The table's set in the dining room and all we have to do is bring in the food when you give us the word.'

'Thanks, and I wasn't worrying, honestly. I know what wonders you work together and I just wanted to know if you have everything you need.'

Lilian's smile was still on her lips as she walked down the short passage to the sitting room where Bill and her father were sitting at opposite ends of the cheerfully burning fire. Plainly, all was under control and ready for when their guests arrived, as they should be doing at any moment.

A short way up Kenhope Fell, looking directly down onto Ivy House, White Court was also receiving dinner guests though on a slightly smaller scale. Thomas Peacock was playing host to his daughter Annabel and her husband of three years, Raynor Fairburn, but with a familiar sinking of his spirits he had just heard the sound of Johnny's latest new motorcycle entering the gates.

'There he is now.' He remarked without enthusiasm, and his daughter lifted her eyebrows.

'Surely not. You mean Bella is riding pillion?'

He smiled thinly. 'I mean Bella, as usual these days, has been left at home.'

Raynor looked away from Annabel, who was trying to catch his eye, for he secretly sympathised with his brother-in-law; Bella had always been spiritless and boring and she was worse since the two miscarriages she had suffered during her marriage.

Quick footsteps sounded across the hall then the door opened and Johnny entered, having divested himself of his motorcycle gear to the maid on his way in. He looked even more hand-some now that he was older, both in years and experience, and Annabel ran over to him, kissing him on the cheek, and taking his arm.

'You look well, John. Don't you think so Raynor?'

'You look fit yourselves.' Johnny returned warmly as he sat down on the sofa with his sister. 'And how are you today, father?'

'Enjoying some good company, which is obviously more than can be said for your wife.'

Rising to his feet Thomas pulled the bellcord to give the signal for dinner arrangements to go ahead, and his son gave an elaborate sigh.

'I'm sorry to say this, but Bella just didn't want to come. She complains continually about her health, her delicate stomach, her endless migraine...'

'Yes, yes alright! There's no need to start all that again. Let's go in to dinner now that you've finally arrived.'

Testily turning his back on his son Thomas began to usher his guests through the newly opened doors into the adjoining dining room, and Johnny rose to follow with a scowl of resignation which Annabel tried to soften with a backward smile. Secretly unperturbed by his father's disapproval he offered her a quick grin and a wink before taking his place at the table, his expression so hastily changing back to one of repentance this his sister had to cover her upturned mouth with her handkerchief.

Conversation during dinner was pleasantly general until the coffee was served, then Thomas gradually lapsed into silence. Leaning back in his chair he seemed merely to be listening to the young ones talking on their particular subjects, but in reality he was unwell. Throughout the laughter and trivial chatter he felt as though he were drifting away, yet all the while his discomfort grew; his head had begun to ache and he felt hot and sick.

Glancing down the table at her father Annabel felt a stab of alarm at his changed appearance and enquired anxiously whether he was feeling ill. Slowly he raised his eyes to her but looked as though he neither recognised her nor understood her query, and she rose, walking round the table to take his hands. Startled into silence now, Johnny and Raynor watched uncomprehendingly.

'I'll take you to bed, father,' Annabel was saying, her hand on his flushed moist forehead. 'You obviously aren't at all well.'

Looking round at her husband and brother she added urgently. 'Help me to get father upstairs, then I think we should call the doctor at once. There's something very wrong here.'

As though objecting to the proposed plan Thomas said something in a voice that was loud but too slurred to be understood, then, trying to push Annabel aside he fell heavily to the floor where he lay with closed eyes, his breathing rough and laboured.

Well pleased at the success of her dinner party

128

Lilian now sat relaxing with her guests in the sitting room as Louisa and Terence light-heartedly entertained with a succession of music hall songs and a few sentimental ballads, all rendered in Terence's rather reedy tenor, while James stood at the piano by Louisa's seat ready to turn her music pages. He was half smiling, Lilian noticed, and she wondered uncomfortably if he wasn't leaning just a little too close to her friend than was necessary. Firmly she banished her suspicion and turned to speak to Marion who was seated beside her.

'Louisa plays well doesn't she?'

'Very well. She sings prettily too, but it doesn't seem likely that she will be given a chance tonight.' Marion responded, grimacing as Terence attacked a final top note with a harshness that strained the sensibilities.

After only a few seconds polite applause Bill cast Lilian a pleading look then suggested that she give them all a song too. He had stood up to get his pipe off the mantelshelf and was filling the bowl with tobacco under the large framed photograph which they had both posed for in Newcastle five years previously. Noticing it now made Lilian remember the events of that day once again, and as Terence stepped away from the piano with a smile she shot him a look of pure venom before taking her place beside Louisa.

'What shall it be, Lilian?'

Louisa smiled up at her enquiringly as she rustled through the music on the stand and Lilian, thinking still of the faithless Terence, chose a ballad composed long ago of a woman badly treated by such a man. It was an untypical choice for one of Lilian's no-nonsense temperament, and while she sang she noticed the slightly puzzled expressions on every face except his; unable to meet her eyes Terence gazed fixedly at the carpet, his skin a dull red as his discomfiture grew, and as the brief song ended she saw him look up at her with fear and dislike. Smiling brilliantly as she refused an encore on the grounds that Louisa must surely be tired of playing the piano by now, she deliberately sat down near Terence, her bright eyes belying the savagery of her intent.

'Now, won't you tell us of your plans when you reach New York?' She requested. 'Have you any idea where you will live or who will employ you?'

He shifted uneasily in his chair as everyone in the room turned with interest to hear his reply, and only Lilian was aware of the final surfacing of their mutual hostility.

'Of course I haven't. That is why I am going alone to a new country so that I can establish myself in these respects before sending for Louisa and little Helen, and I'm sure no-one in their right senses would expect me to take my wife and daughter with me before, at least, having some control over their living conditions.'

Thinking of her fair-haired god-daughter, almost the same age as Edward, now lying peacefully asleep under a kindly neighbour's watchful eye back in Hillary Terrace, brought a slight softening to the woman's features.

'Of course not. I'm sure you would always have the welfare of your daughters at heart, Terence, as every good father should, but make sure you take your time won't you, for it will break my heart to part with Louisa and Helen.'

Although Lilian was not looking at her husband she was aware of his tension at her use of the plural 'daughters', and also of the rather bewildered looks she was receiving from other parts of the room. Putting her hand to her mouth in an over-theatrical gesture of dismay she laughed lightly.

'Oh sorry, I said "daughters" didn't I? Whatever could I have been thinking of? I must have been in a dream thinking you have more than one.'

The man gave a strained smile. 'Yes Lilian, I think you must indeed be in a dream.'

'Ah well, no matter.' Rising to her feet, feeling well satisfied with her small charade, Lilian was pleased to see everyone chatting amiably among themselves as she went to fetch some playing cards while Bill set up two card tables in the middle of the room. Plainly, the only person she had disturbed was Terence Marshall, and that suited her very well.

The game of Whist was just getting underway when a loud knocking sounded from the direction of the front door and Lilian excused herself briefly as she got up to answer it. Attired as she was in a dress of her favourite colour of cream silk, she stood in the open doorway of Ivy House looking tall, slender and beautiful in the gentle glow of the gaslight from the passageway behind her, and for a moment the man stared at her without speaking. Sighing slightly as though bored, yet feeling her heart beginning to pound with uncomfortable speed, Lilian said 'Come in

131

won't you? Do you want to see Bill?'

Johnny stepped inside the doorway and for the first time Lilian could see how ruffled he looked.

'I've been to Dr Hatton's house, but his maid told me that he and his wife are here. Is that right?'

'Yes. I'll get him for you if you'll step into the study for a second. I take it there's some emergency.'

'It's my father. He's collapsed and lost consciousness ... I'll have to get back to him now ... if you could just give Dr Hatton my message.'

'Please.' Unthinkingly she placed her hand on his arm and he drew back as though her touch had burnt him. 'Just wait. He only has to put on his coat.'

Obediently the man stayed where he was, gazing out of the open doorway at the lights of White Court, barely a quarter of a mile up the fell, where his father might already be dead for all he knew, so long had he seemed to be away. He could hear Lilian talking to Dr Hatton in the sitting room and tried to keep his thoughts off her with no success. Why, he wondered, after five years, and at a time like this with his mind in such conflict, did he still find himself thoroughly distracted by her even to the point of trying to leave the house without the doctor when they could both use his motorcycle and be at White Court in seconds?

He was running his fingers through his unruly hair when Dr Hatton emerged into the passage with Bill, who helped the older man on with his coat whilst making sympathetic comments on

132

the nature of Johnny's visit. Still aware of Lilian's close proximity while he was describing his father's symptoms to Dr Hatton, Johnny almost stumbled out of Ivy House in his relief when it was time to go, and called a stiff 'Goodnight and thank you' over his shoulder as the door closed behind them.

Left alone in the warmly lit passage Lilian and Bill looked at each other in silence for a moment before he took her hand in his, squeezing it gently.

'We'll talk about it later.' He whispered. 'Better get back to the game.'

She nodded, knowing that her husband was wondering what effect Thomas Peacock's illness, or even death, might have on their relationship with the other partners, but put it firmly aside as they rejoined their guests.

'We're one short now. We'll have to change to another game that doesn't require partners.' Marion was complaining, her hands shuffling the pack irritably.

Lilian patted her shoulder. 'It's alright. There's no need. I have something to do for a while in the kitchen so you'll have even numbers again.'

Outside the sudden roar of a motorcycle told them that Johnny and Dr Hatton were on their way to White Court, and speculation began in earnest as to the condition of the invalid.

Safely out of the room Lilian stopped at the umbrella stand in the passage to study her reflection in its tiny square mirror. She knew she should also be thinking of the welfare of Thomas Peacock, but her wayward emotions refused to

133

centre round anyone other than his son. Sombrely her hazel eyes looked back at her from the glass, accusing and apprehensive for a future where Johnny Peacock could still have such an effect on her, and she turned away quickly to walk into the kitchen.

Nancy and Evelyn had already gone leaving the place immaculate, and on the table they had left a tray which held serviettes, tea plates and knives, along with a magnificently iced cake bearing the message 'Bon Voyage'. Beside it an ivory handled carving knife waited to cut into this offering and Lilian allowed herself the doubtful luxury of imagining for a second just how much better she would feel if she could use it on her guest of honour instead, then she picked up the tray and walked back into the sitting room.

Thomas Peacock lay propped up on his bed, where his family had managed with difficulty to bring him earlier that evening, and Dr Hatton looked down at him gravely. His medical bag, which Johnny had driven him home to collect upon leaving Ivy House, lay open on the floor, but after he had examined Thomas he replaced his thermometer and stethoscope before shutting it with depressing finality.

Sitting on a chair at the other side of the bed Annabel was watching him anxiously as she twisted her handkerchief round her fingers in a compulsive action of distress.

'What do you think is the matter with him, Doctor?'

Further back in the room Annabel's husband

134

stood beside Johnny, and George Hatton was aware of a different kind of watchfulness emanating from the two men, but mainly from the dying man's own son who seemed to have calmed himself considerably during the last half hour.

'He's suffered a serious stroke I'm afraid. As you can see, he's in a coma now and unlikely to come out of it ... keep him as comfortable as you can and I'll be back in the morning to see him.'

'You mean he's not going to get better at all?'

'I think he'll probably just sleep away, my dear. Try not to upset yourself too much. It's a very peaceful way to go.'

Raynor crossed to his wife's side as Dr Hatton looked away from her tear-filled eyes, and as he picked up his bag and turned for the door he felt chilled by the speculative expression on Johnny Peacock's face. No trace of shock there any more, nor even any anxiety now that he was used to the idea of his father's illness, but a sly ticking over of all the implications for himself when he took over as head of the Peacock family business.

'I'll soon walk down to Ivy House.' He stated as Johnny followed him out onto the landing and, ignoring the young man's sounds of polite protest about taking him on the motorcycle, he hurried down the wide staircase, across the hall, and out into the refreshingly cool night air.

The news of Thomas Peacock's serious illness arrived at Ivy House with Dr Hatton just as the cake and wine were being served to the guests before their journey home, and although they voiced their concern for the old man neither

Lilian nor Bill added any kind of theory as to what changes Thomas's incapacity might bring to their lives. 'A stroke' was all George Hatton had told them, uncomfortably aware that he should not have revealed that about his patient, but in a small village the facts would be public knowledge by the following day as these things always were. At pains to steer the conversation off the subject he raised his glass to Terence, who was looking bored to the point of rudeness, and wished him good luck. Smiling his thanks, Terence hugged to himself his relief that the ghastly evening was almost over and even sent a mocking grin in Lilian's direction as the company turned their attention upon him once more. Only two more days and he would leave Gilfell for good, and for that pleasure Terence Marshall could hardly wait.

'Please Louie, try to cheer up a little. It's only for a while that we'll be apart and then we'll have the rest of our lives together in a country where we can make something of ourselves.'

'I know, and I'm sorry. I just feel peculiar about everything and I wish I didn't.'

'In what way peculiar?'

'I keep feeling that I won't ever see you again.'

Terence, his knife and fork held motionless in his hands, stared across the supper table at his wife whose eyes were filling with tears for the umpteenth time that day, and fought hard to keep up his veneer of understanding.

'My dear, you're only feeling this way because you know I'm leaving in the morning. I feel gloomy myself if truth be told, but we must keep our spirits up and plan for the future even while we're waiting or, like myself, in transit.'

'Yes, of course.'

Sitting back in her chair Louisa pushed away her food, hardly touched, and tried to smile. It was a weak effort which failed miserably.

'I think I'll go up to bed now, Terry. It's late and we have to be up early in the morning for you to catch the first train...'

She bit her lip as the man sighed and looked away, and as she climbed the stairs to their bedroom Louisa tried to stave off the dark mood of dread that had grown steadily as the time for her husband's departure drew nearer. He was losing patience with her, she could feel it. Perhaps he was even looking forward to getting away from her for a while or, how it really felt to her, for good.

Pausing on the landing she listened for any sounds of activity from the room below, but there were none and she continued quietly into the bedroom and shut the door.

Downstairs, Terence stared moodily into the dying embers of the fire as he drank the last of his tea. On first putting forward his plan to Louisa he had felt a great sense of hope but since then other emotions had crept in, especially following the dinner party at Ivy House when Lilian Robinson had made it quite clear that his secret was known to her. He had been well aware of their presence on the railway platform that day in Newcastle, and he guessed that her five year silence on the subject had only been out of consideration for her friend, for she detested him. Months after the event he had still been living on a knife-edge of suspense wondering if the Robinsons were going to tell Louisa what they had seen, but as time had passed with no developments he had gradually allowed himself to believe that they had somehow missed seeing Hilda and little Emma running up to him like that. The almost certain knowledge that they had actually witnessed enough to put two and two together and then kept quiet about it for so long, was chilling. Would they now wait until he had left and then tell Louisa, or maybe confront him in the morning before he had time to get away?

Taking a handkerchief out of his pocket he mopped his suddenly moist brow and tried to put a stop to his dark imaginings, which included the spectre of a prison sentence as his bigamy was revealed. Next day he would be leaving Hillary Terrace before six o'clock to walk down to Dalton Railway Station where he was bound first for Newcastle, a fact which he had naturally omitted to tell Louisa, and would afterwards be making his way down to Southampton after spending a few days with Hilda and Emma. Maybe the last few days he would ever spend with Hilda and Emma.

Having recklessly told both women some weeks ago of his plan to go to America, Terence now deeply regretted that he had not simply disappeared out of both their lives without a word to either of them, but once he reached Southampton he would be safely on his way to a peaceful solitary life. No more wives. No more children. Only himself to think about and work for, and with an assumed identity he would never be traced in a country so vast.

In the room above the bed creaked as Louisa lay down, and Terence wondered if he could really be so heartless as to turn his back on her forever. If only he had met her first instead of Hilda, things would have been so different. Hopelessly undecided again he tried without success to put the whole mess out of his mind, and for the last time climbed the stairs of Hillary Terrace to the bedroom he shared with Louisa.

'Why don't you let me bring the pony and trap over one day when I don't have supplies to pick up in Dalton for the shop, then I would have room to take you back over the fell to Kenhope. You could stay overnight with Jenny and I and see how the old place looks since the mining began; after all, you've never once been back to the farm since you moved to this little cottage, have you? Even when Jen and I got wed you insisted on side-tracking onto all those narrow byroads to miss seeing it.'

Marion looked away from Gilbert and out of her parlour window at Gilfell Main Street.

'I don't want to see the farm, Gilbert. It would be too much like viewing a corpse with it being deserted like that, and doubtless covered in grimy coal dust. The farm was my home as this poky little place can never be, and I'll keep it safe in my memory as it was.'

'Well, if you're sure.'

He stared at the black-leaded grate where a fire burned a comforting red in the still cold April weather and wondered whether to extol the financial virtues of the mine to make his mother feel better, but decided to simply change the subject. Before he could begin, however, Marion did it for him.

'And is the shop doing well?'

'Hardware was a good choice and we are flourishing Mam, make no mistake about it, especially since I've been leaving Jen to mind the shop while I take goods to local markets, but I suppose that can't continue much longer with the baby coming.'

'Well, make the most of it while you can,' Marion smiled. 'As long as you can make a living you'll have no need to worry.'

They were quiet for a while, but it was the companionable silence of people who know each other well, and was finally broken by Gilbert who remembered some gossip he had picked up in the village.

'Is it true that old man Peacock is dying? I've heard it's only a matter of time.'

'I've heard the same. I was at Bill's last week when his son came looking for Dr Hatton, who was also a guest, and a fine old state that Johnny was in too. Mr Peacock had apparently collapsed, and word has it that it is some kind of stroke which has put him into a coma.'

'Do you think it will make any difference when he's gone and Johnny has charge of their part of the business?'

Thinking of how her eldest son and Johnny Peacock disliked each other Marion sighed a little. 'I think it might, but we'll just have to wait and see and try not to worry.'

Gilbert nodded and stood up after glancing at the clock.

'You're right, as ever. Well, I'd better be getting back over the fell again, Mam. Are you sure you won't change your mind about coming to stay with us?'

'Not at the moment, Gilbert. Later maybe.'

He kissed her as she rose to see him to the door, then hugged her tight.

'You'll have to come after the baby's born. You'll have to see your new grandchild.'

'Oh I will Gilbert, I promise.'

He halted a moment, his hand on the door leading to the street, and added. 'Jen's so big that some of the local women are of the opinion that we could be having twins! She looks almost full term although she still has three months to go yet, but if it isn't twins they reckon she's still too big to last much longer.'

Marion shook her head, smiling slightly. 'Gilbert, it's your mother you're talking to now, don't try that tale on me. We both know that Jenny has only one month to go, not three.'

The young man looked shocked and embarrassed. 'How did you know?'

'How would I not know, you silly?' She reached up and patted him on his reddened cheek. 'I guess my new grandchild will be another like Bill's little Edward.'

Gilbert frowned, puzzled. 'How do you mean, like Edward?'

'I mean a premature baby who is really full term ... just as Edward was. But I'm not supposed to

141

know that either, am I?'

In an effort to distance herself from proceedings Lilian kept her attention firmly fixed on the dripping edge of the black umbrella that Bill was holding over both of them as they stood at the back of the crowd of mourners in Dalton churchyard. She felt damp, cold and depressed, and hoped that Thomas Peacock's funeral would soon be over.

Just in front of them stood Annabel with her husband, Raynor, and beside them Johnny and Constance, who appeared to be standing in yet again for her ever absent sister.

'...ashes to ashes, dust to dust.'

The words she had always hated about the burial service intruded into Lilian's thoughts before she determinedly closed off her mind again by covertly studying some of the other mourners. Those who were not related to the deceased, either by blood or marriage, were obviously in similar mood to herself, she decided, especially those who were representing a family whose men worked at one or other of the mines. Casting a swift glance at her husband's expression she saw that he was frowning at the back of Johnny Peacock's neck, and guessed that he was wondering how they would manage to get along now that Thomas was no longer around to act as a buffer between them.

At the graveside Johnny kept his features as devoid of expression as possible while his thoughts hurried ahead of present events. He had already told Bella that they would be moving up

142

to White Court as soon as his father was buried, and they would do that tomorrow simply by removing themselves and their clothes from Low Shields Lodge. The furniture, all of which had been provided by his in-laws, could remain exactly where it was and he, at least, would be glad to see the back of it.

Suddenly aware that the funeral was almost at an end and people were looking at him to conclude the proceedings, Johnny bent down, took a handful of earth from the pile near his feet and dropped it ceremoniously onto the coffin while Annabel moved to repeat the gesture. Shaking hands with the officiating vicar and the rest of the mourners, including Bill and Lilian, passed for the man in something of a dreamlike state and when they were left by themselves at last Constance nudged him sharply.

'Johnny. Mr Carstairs is waiting for us to leave.'

The vicar tucked his book under his arm and hastened to make noises of denial, none of which were sincere. Thomas Peacock's funeral was the second service he had held that day and he was as conscious of the icy wind as anyone else as his robes flapped damply around his legs. One more handshake and Johnny and his party turned to leave, walking slowly down the path towards the only two carriages now remaining, while the vicar made his way back to the vestry by another route, thankful to see the last of the young man with the cold emotionless eyes. It was common enough to see close relatives of a deceased person looking blank at their funeral service, for that was often due to shock if the death had been sudden or the simple wish to keep their grief private, but the son of Thomas Peacock had fit into neither category.

Left alone in their carriage after Annabel and Raynor had driven back to White Court, Johnny relaxed and studied Constance who still looked like a gypsy despite being clad entirely in black. She was holding her head slightly to one side as she looked back at him.

'What are your plans now then, Johnny?'

He stretched out his legs as far as they would go and let out a sigh of content.

'Annabel and Raynor will be returning to Newcastle tomorrow. Bella and I will be moving up to White Court.'

'That will be bound to please you. Will it please Bella?'

He shrugged. 'Who knows what may please Bella? I'd be willing to wager that nothing has pleased her since the day we wed, so why should I waste my time worrying about it now?'

'You were a fool when you married her. She has no life about her and you could see that when you proposed. Why didn't you ask me instead?'

Amused by her forthrightness Johnny grinned. 'I didn't know you loved me, Constance.'

'I don't love you Johnny, and that's why we would have made a better marriage together. I like you, and I believe you like me, but I'm under no illusions about love in any of its forms. Life's for living, not for getting oneself tangled up in a lot of self-destructive emotions.'

He smiled across at her, thoroughly enjoying their exchange.

144

'Life's for living is it? Did you still think that a few months ago when you were festering in a London jail?'

'Who told you about that?'

'Your Aunt Eleanor was silly enough to write to your mother to tell her how "the struggle" was progressing, mentioning that you were in jail at that particular time, and Bella, who began to weep yet again once your mother had told her, couldn't wait to unburden herself to me.'

'Stupid little ninny!'

'That's Bella.'

After a few moments silence they grinned at each other and Johnny took up the reins ready to begin the drive home.

'I suppose in many ways I did choose the wrong sister,' he conceded suddenly, 'but at least Bella and I won't end up murdering each other as I'm fairly sure you and I would have done.'

'You and I would definitely have ended up murdering each other Johnny, but I'm certain it wouldn't have been the only passion to mark our union! However, that's all speculation now isn't it? Let's go home.'

Constance laughed as she always did, too long and too loud, but the happy mood was like music in his ears and he was smiling as he shook the reins to urge the horse into motion.

Bella watched through the rain-spattered window of her living room as the carriage drew to a halt. Both passengers should have looked miserable, as wet as they obviously were, yet Johnny seemed disgracefully cheerful as he handed Constance

145

the reins before jumping down. Trying to imagine how she would have been feeling had she just attended *her* father's funeral, Bella felt even more outraged and glared at her husband as he waved towards the carriage then walked jauntily up the short path to their front door. As her parents' carriage had returned fully half an hour ago she wondered where they had been in that time as, moving out into the hallway, she found him handing his soaking overcoat to Laura with instructions to 'hang it up somewhere warm.' When he saw *her* his whole manner sharpened.

'Why are you not upstairs getting the trunks packed?'

Bella looked startled while Laura swept past her into the kitchen holding the coat.

'Surely we don't have to do that today. It's disrespectful to your father.'

'Disrespectful! You don't think *you* might have been disrespectful to my father by refusing to attend his funeral, do you?'

'That's not fair. I wasn't well.'

He scowled, his good humour vanishing as though it had never been.

'That's always your excuse, Bella, but you look alright to me. You can come upstairs now and we'll begin to get everything gathered together ready for tomorrow. We can hardly expect one maid to do everything.'

Mounting the stairs with brisk strides Johnny was aware of Bella trailing after him like a dispirited waif and felt his impatience turning into the inevitable angry frustration. Without turning round to look at her he entered his wife's bedroom, flung open the wardrobe doors and began to throw piles of her clothes unceremoniously onto the bed, after which he commenced to do the same with her chest of drawers. Squealing slightly, Bella stood looking helpless in the doorway, her hand fluttering nervously at her lips.

'What are you doing?'

'What does it look as though I'm doing, Bella? I'm putting your clothes and personal items on the bed for you to pack in the trunks I'm about to bring from the spare room!'

Opening the door into the adjoining bedroom that he occupied, the man began the same procedure with his own things then went to get the trunks. When he brought the first one across the landing Bella was still standing where he had left her, blocking his way into the room.

'For heaven's sake, woman, move! It's late afternoon already and we are leaving for White Court in the morning.'

Bella stepped aside sluggishly and stood with her hands stubbornly at her sides while he pushed the trunk to the bedside and opened it for her to begin.

'I don't understand why we have to leave so soon, John. Surely another few days wouldn't make any difference.'

On his way back to the spare room Johnny Peacock paused beside his wife and spoke in a tone of soft menace that she had grown to fear.

'Bella. It is now April the sixteenth, just over halfway through the month. I have lived with you in this shoebox for over five years and I promise you that this date will mark the end of that particular misery for both of us. Tomorrow morning, thanks to your parents hiring replacement staff for Low Shields, Laura and cook will make and serve our last meal here before they accompany us to White Court where, at least, we won't have to live in each other's pockets!'

Next morning Louisa made her way along Hillary Terrace and on to Main Street towards the village school. Her brow was furrowed, as it had been ever since Terence had gone with never so much as a letter afterwards to tell her how he fared, and when Helen ran off to join her friends in the schoolyard the woman made her way back to the shops where she had some purchases to make.

Len Harrison had recently taken to selling a few copies of a national newspaper, and these lay on the counter where Louisa eyed them with growing unease.

'Terrible tragedy.' Len said, nodding towards the paper as he wrapped up some bacon from the written order she had given him. 'You weren't in yesterday or you'd have seen the first report of the sinking where they said the miracle of radio communication had resulted in every passenger being saved, but today it seems that hundreds have died. Your husband didn't sail on the Titanic did he? I heard he was going to America and this ship was bound for there, so I couldn't help wondering...'

'I don't think so, but I'll take a newspaper if you please.' Louisa interrupted faintly, and reached for her purse as the bell tinkled inside the shop door to admit another customer. Wheeling round she saw that it was the mother of one of Helen's friends and smiled at her, automatically exchanging pleasantries, but a deep fear had settled like ice in the pit of her stomach.

Once outside again in the fresh air of Main Street Louisa ran to its end, round Chapel Corner and along the length of Hillary Terrace with feet that scarcely seemed to touch the ground. She had no way of knowing whether or not Terence had boarded the much publicised Titanic, yet something inside her was certain that he had, and equally certain that confirmation would come when she entered her house.

Setting down her basket she used both hands to open her back door, then stumbled through the living room towards the front of the house where a postcard lay face up on the doormat. Dropping to her knees on the rug she picked it up, took note of the sepia view of Southampton Docks, then slowly turned it over.

The message was brief. 'Dear Lou, have secured passage on new liner Titanic. Sail mid April. Will write soon. Terence.'

CHAPTER FIVE

'Go upstairs to the toy room and take Winifred with you.'

With her hands gently pushing at their shoulders Lilian encouraged Edward to take Helen and his young sister away from the adults who were facing each other beside the black-leaded fireplace of Ivy House kitchen. Hearing the door shut behind them as Edward led the girls enthusiastically in the direction of his toy soldiers, Louisa raised red-rimmed eyes towards Bill Robinson.

'I know I've no proof that Terence is dead, but inside myself I'm very sure. Will I have to travel to Southampton to find out officially, because I don't know how I'll ever afford such a journey...'

'No Louisa, of course you won't have to go to Southampton. I'll write to the shipping company tonight explaining your position and asking for verification on Terence either way. If your worst fears are confirmed the next step will be to contact a solicitor to claim compensation from the owners of Titanic on behalf of Helen and yourself.'

Lilian put her hand on Louisa's as she sat down again at her side.

'Well, at least we now have a plan of action. Meanwhile Lou, you and Helen must stay here with us. I won't have you going back to that house on your own in the state you're in.'

'Thank you, Lilian.'

Looking down sharply to hide the fact that tears were again threatening to overcome her, Louisa was aware of Bill getting to his feet in a manner which suggested that he was more than ready to leave.

'Right. I'll get down to that letter without delay and send it with the next collection. The sooner we start the better.'

Hoping that simply addressing the envelope to The White Star Line, Southampton, would suffice, as he had no immediate way of discovering their correct address, Bill entered the cool of the room he used as a study and sat down in the corner at his desk. Pulling paper and pen towards him the man hesitated with the nib poised over the inkwell stand. Writing the letter on Louisa's behalf was a straightforward matter, but he wondered uneasily just what the outcome might be. Had the woman they had seen greeting Terence that day in Newcastle been a mistress or a wife and, if the latter, would Louisa find that she herself was the legal spouse? The very age of the other child at the time seemed to suggest not, and if that should prove the case then her position would be very serious indeed. Her only hope lay in the possibility that the woman at Newcastle knew nothing of Terence's voyage to New York, but as the man's journeys east by train had not decreased even slightly over the intervening years salvation through ignorance did not seem likely.

Sighing slightly Bill shook himself out of his reverie and began the letter. Distantly, through

151

two closed doors and a length of corridor, he could still hear Lilian and Louisa talking, while overhead came the clear sounds of Edward supervising his lead soldiers' battle positions in the toy room. Peace at home would have been pleasant at the moment with Johnny Peacock limbering up for some trouble at the mining office, but there would be time to think of that later.

Fussing around Louisa like a frantic mother hen Lilian tried to push her sense of guilt firmly out of her mind. Together they set the table for the childrens' tea, Louisa's movements jerky and automatic, while Lilian kept up a constant monologue of reassurance regarding her friend's future.

'Fancy you just sitting in your own house all day after finding out a dreadful thing like that.' She muttered, taking items from the wall cupboard to place on the table. 'You should have come to us straight away Lou. Bill and I will look after you whatever happens.'

'Thank you.'

'Sit down again. You look absolutely exhausted.'

Obediently Louisa sank down onto the nearest seat keeping her mouth tightly closed as her thoughts tumbled on their troubled way, rather than risk losing control yet again. Taking in her stricken face on her way to the door to call the children for their meal, Lilian felt her secret fears intensify with the knowledge that Terence was much more likely to be dead than alive. Maybe the following day's newspapers would contain more facts about the disaster, but the article in

Louisa's paper had carried a stark headline that repeated incessantly in her mind despite all her efforts to banish it. 'Hundreds feared drowned.'

'Oh Constance ... I really don't know how you can live that way, getting into trouble all the time and going to prison, of all things! Surely you don't have to go back to London. Let the others do it.'

Bella clasped her hands in front of her beseechingly as she watched her sister carefully hanging up Johnny's suits in the empty wardrobe that had recently belonged to his father, and the woman's dark eyes surveyed her in amusement.

'That would certainly appear to be *your* motto Bella, especially at this very moment ... "let the others do it".'

'Oh.'

Half-heartedly picking up a tweed jacket Bella began to smooth it down with her fingers in an aimless way.

'But I don't want you to go back to Manchester and London, Connie. I want you to stay here with us.'

'For heaven's sake, why?'

'Because we all worry about you, and it must be horrible in jail.'

Constance took the jacket out of Bella's hands in an impatient swoop before consigning it to a hanger.

'I'd be bored to death back here, Bella, and you know as well as I do that I get into mischief when I'm bored. So how would you feel if I came back home and decided to add a little excitement to

153

your husband's extremely uninteresting life? Would you stop worrying about me then?'

A dull flush spread over Bella's normally pale features and she recommenced twisting her hands together, driving Constance into a rage of frustration which slamming the wardrobe doors shut did nothing to alleviate.

'Right. That's Johnny's clothes sorted out at last, and for all the help you were you might as well have spent the time lying down somewhere whimpering through another migraine. It seems to be about all you're good for these days!'

Ashamed of her outburst, yet unable to stop feeling aggressive towards her younger sister, Constance marched past her into the next bedroom where a variety of trunks were waiting to be unpacked and knelt down to wrestle with the leather fastenings and locks. As Bella came to stand beside her she kept her head bent down, but her voice when she finally spoke filled Constance with guilt.

'What did you mean about John's uninteresting life?'

'You know what I meant Bella, so don't pretend to be sillier than you already are!'

There was no reply, and as the silence grew heavy with accusation Constance lifted the lid of the trunk and sat back on her heels where she was able to view Bella's tear-stained face with a distinct sinking of spirits.

'Oh Bella! You really must stop weeping at absolutely everything!'

'I've lost babies... I've been ill, Connie, and I never feel well any more...'

Sitting down on the edge of the bed she added miserably. 'John doesn't love me.'

Knowing that almost anyone other than herself would have offered Bella a few meaningless words of reassurance, Constance found she could do nothing but stare back at Bella who mistook her silence for disbelief.

'It's true, Connie. I don't think he's ever cared for me at all.'

Reluctantly Constance moved to sit down by the side of her sister, who looked pathetically like a bedraggled crow in her black mourning dress, and, putting an arm round her shoulders, she shook her gently keeping her voice low.

'Johnny Peacock loves no one except himself, Bella, so you'll just have to accept that sad fact, but he chose you to be his wife so he must have some regard for you.'

'He didn't choose. He was instructed by Thomas. He told me that once when he was angry about something.'

Having guessed at the time the true state of things Constance was not surprised at this revelation, but she found herself feeling untypically vitriolic towards her brother-in-law with whom she normally sympathised.

'Just because he said that doesn't necessarily mean it's true. I know you care for him, and that he's a handsome kind of rogue, but even you have to admit that Johnny is often not a very pleasant human being. In fact, if we're going to be honest here, we should say he's a really nasty man a lot of the time.'

'If you think that, how could you threaten to ...

155

add a little excitement to his life?'

'Oh Bella, you must know I didn't mean that. I was trying to startle you into doing something other than simply lying around persuading yourself that you're ill and, therefore, helpless. You've married a man who is never going to be the sort of husband you and most other women want, but that doesn't mean you can't make some kind of life of your own. Heaven knows, *he* does. Why do you imagine he's always jumping on that motorcycle of his to go to Dalton at night? It isn't to see other men, you can be quite certain of that.'

'I don't know what to do. What do you think I should do, Connie?'

Bella's voice was little more than a whisper and Constance looked sharply away from her.

'There's little you can do except try not to let him affect you so deeply. He hasn't got it in him to love any woman, Bella, and it's no good pining over that. Try to find something to interest you outside your marriage or, better still, have another try to have a family.'

'I couldn't go through all that baby stuff again, I just couldn't.'

'Alright then. Something else. It's your choice whatever you decide to do, whether it be people or things like painting or music, but give it all you've got and let it take over enough of your life to block out some of Johnny, and you never can tell; once you've shown a bit of backbone he might begin to pay you some attention.'

Bella looked at her hopefully. 'Do you think so?'

'Anything's possible.'

In spite of her encouraging expression Constance acknowledged to herself that the situation was hopeless so long as Bella insisted upon making Johnny Peacock the motivation behind every action in her life, and she stood up briskly.

'Come on then. You can think things over while we sort out your clothes, then you can tell me whether you've decided on any particular pastime.'

Giving her usual wan smile Bella rose obediently to do her sister's bidding.

Helen and Louisa stayed at Ivy House for a week, returning to Hillary Terrace immediately after the letter was received from The White Star Line confirming that Terence Marshall was not among those who had survived the disaster. Lilian walked back with them to number fourteen where she helped her friend light the fire and was given her Marriage Certificate to take back to Bill so that he could continue with the correspondence on Louisa's behalf. The little girl was subdued and pale now, having been gently told of her father's death some four days ago, and after watching her mother and Aunt Lilian working for a while she went quietly upstairs to her bedroom window where she had so often watched for Terence coming home. She could cry there in peace, but later she and her mother would weep together.

Louisa sighed, straightening her back as she stood watching the newly lit fire catching hold.

'You never liked Terry did you, Lilian?'

'I'm sorry Lou. I have to admit that I didn't.'

'Can you tell me why?'

'No.'

Louisa smiled faintly. Just the one word in reply to be interpreted however she pleased: either 'no' Lilian did not know why she had disliked Terence, or 'no' she would not tell her why.

'Then I'm sorry too, Lilian, but you're still the best friend I've got. And Bill too, of course.'

With the Marriage Certificate tucked down the side of her handbag Lilian hurried back home an hour later conscious of a strange feeling of foreboding. Louisa and Helen's lives had been suddenly disrupted with probably worse to come, yet Lilian sensed that it was only the beginning of a chain of events which would somehow effect many lives, including her own. Abruptly she stopped walking as the certainty coursed through her, bringing with it the strong impression that the ground beneath her feet was beginning to crack and crumble as her present life started to lose its form.

'Morning, Lilian. How's the young widow?'

Startled, she turned her gaze towards Albert Stamper, a young man of about her own age who was on his way to number three where he lived.

'Louisa's stunned at the moment, but she's being very brave. Thanks for asking, Albert.'

'If there's anything me and the missus can do...'

'I'll let her know. She'll be comforted I'm sure.'

Now that the feeling of menace was fading Lilian tried hard to dismiss it, but its depressing residue lingered on in spite of all efforts to overcome it. Briskly she continued the few remaining yards to her home, shivering a little as she crossed its threshold thinking of that word Albert had used. Widow. There was something really desolate and threatening about that title, almost as though it would soon apply to herself.

She found Bill sitting at his desk with Edward and Winifred playing a noisy game around his feet. He smiled, setting down his pen.

'You look flustered, love. Is Louisa in a bad way again?'

Perching on the wooden armrest of his chair Lilian leaned her cheek against his shoulder and Bill reached up to take her hand in his, surprised at this sudden show of affection from his usually undemonstrative wife.

'She just seemed to freeze over emotionally once we were in the house. Didn't even react when I admitted that I had never liked Terence.'

'Oh, Lilian.'

She got up, taking the Marriage Certificate out of her handbag and placing it on the desk.

'Well, there wasn't any point in denying it, although I couldn't tell her the reason, and I know I should probably have lied, but Louisa isn't so easily fooled.'

'Not by us at any rate.'

Spreading the document in his hands Bill frowned over it for a moment before pushing it under a paperweight.

'If what we suspect turns out to be true it won't be all that likely that Terence will have any information about his supposedly non-existent family hidden anywhere in the house he shared with Louisa, but I hope she'll remember what I

159

told her and look anyway. However legal, or otherwise, Louisa and Helen may be they are still morally within their rights to approach any of the Marshall family for financial help.'

Bending down, Lilian took each of her children by the hand.

'Come with me now and leave your father in peace. I'll give you both an apple seeing you've been good. Lunch is in an hour, Bill.'

'Right.'

She had just chased her family up to the toy room with an apple each out of the barrel in the pantry when she heard the back door open and her father's voice calling.

'Hello! Anybody home?'

'I'm coming, Dad.'

He was standing in the middle of the kitchen floor twirling his hat round and round in his hands, and she put her arms round him impulsively, kissing him soundly on both cheeks. James Rutherford looked both startled and pleased at this unusual greeting, and she laughed as he said. 'By gum lass, you're in a good humour today!'

'I've just realised how lucky I am to have such good men in my life and I felt like showing my appreciation. Sit down and I'll make some tea. You'll stay and have lunch with us won't you? It's roast beef, your favourite.'

'I'll be glad to, especially if it tastes as good as it smells.'

He seated himself on one side of the fireplace and stretched out his legs to catch every iota of warmth.

'I've come about Louisa Marshall ... well, to ask

your advice really, Lilian. I've heard about her plight and I was wondering about her position moneywise. Is she provided for?'

Sitting down in the opposite seat Lilian grimaced a little. 'Louisa's position may be even worse than it looks at the moment I'm afraid. Bill is making all enquiries on her behalf and we realise that she should be due some compensation from the shipping line, but we think ... for the last few years, after we saw Terence meeting a woman and a child on the platform at Newcastle Station, that Louisa may not actually be his legal wife.'

James looked shocked. 'You mean she's been living in sin with the man? That she's sharing him with his proper family?'

'No Dad. She doesn't even suspect their existence and she and Terence had a Marriage Certificate which she has sent to Bill for submission to the authorities, but the child we saw that day ... she called Terence "Daddy!" Both Bill and I heard her quite clearly.'

James looked down into the fire with an expression Lilian found hard to fathom as he felt in his jacket pocket for his pipe and tobacco pouch.

'And all this time you've never breathed a word to a soul, not even me. I knew you disliked the man, of course, but I put it down to your resentment of his stand-offish attitude, as a lot of people here felt the same.'

'I resented everything about him.'

'If he does turn out to have been a bigamist, what will that mean for Louisa?'

Busying herself with making a pot of tea Lilian

161

shook her head and sighed. 'Bill says her only hope then will be to appeal to his family for support, but Terence always told her that his parents were dead. If she really isn't his legal wife there'll be no compensation of any kind from White Star and a massive local scandal to boot! Please promise me you'll not breathe a word of this to anyone, ever. In the eyes of people locally, and her own family in Carlisle, she must remain a widow with no hint of the truth to be chewed over in the village. You know what some people are like.'

'I promise I'll say nothing, Lilian. You should know me better than to ask.'

'Yes, I know. Sorry.'

Watching him apply one of Bill's tapers to the bowl of his pipe Lilian gave the freshly brewed tea another stir before prompting. 'So what kind of advice did you want about Louisa? You said you'd come here to talk to me about her.'

'Well, it's even more relevant now I should think. I came to ask you whether you could find out if she needs work, but from what you've told me I should imagine that goes without saying.'

'Yes, I agree. What did you have in mind?'

'I had the notion to offer her a sort of housekeeper's position. I know you bake for me and give the place a clean now and again, but you have enough to do Lilian, and I'd like something regular, so I thought I'd ask you what you feel about my offering Lou a job.'

Reaching carefully for a cup and saucer Lilian found herself remembering the night of the Farewell Party for Terence Marshall when a similar uneasiness had crossed her mind regarding her father's feelings for her friend, and now it had settled in her stomach once more like a lump of lead.

'I know you mean well,' she began cautiously, 'but you're bound to realise what the village busy-bodies would make of that. The minute Louisa moves in to Roughside...'

'I'm not going to suggest her moving in, Lilian. I mean a live out position for a few hours a day, probably when little Helen is at school. During the holidays she can come with her mother, of course, but I thought I could pay her to clean and bake and do my laundry; that way I'd be more comfortable and she and Helen could continue renting their present home.'

James smiled at her through his ever expanding cloud of pale blue tobacco smoke and Lilian let out a long breath of relief as she smiled back.

'In that case it sounds perfect. I'm sure it will make all the difference in the world to both their lives. Are you going to approach Louisa about it or do you want me to mention it?'

Taking the tea which Lilian was handing him, and reaching for the sugar bowl, James Rutherford stirred in a couple of spoonfuls and leaned back in his chair, well content.

'You ask her, lass. In her present circumstances it will sound better coming from you.'

The month of May was already ten days old when the reply from White Star was received by Louisa, who read it through several times before bundling it into her handbag together with a pair of James' socks which she had brought home to darn. Outside the morning was fine and mild with all the gentle hopefulness that spring seemed to bring, and she was eager to be on her way to Roughside to begin her daily duties. She had worked for James Rutherford for two weeks now and was finding that the job suited her more with each passing day, bringing satisfaction, a temporary freedom from the bereaved emptiness of her own home, and the relief of having a small regular income.

Although she had cried many times since learning of Terence's death Louisa was still in a shocked state where, at times, the whole thing appeared to be more like a nasty game than reality, and she found herself often glancing out of her own parlour window hoping to see her husband climbing up the sloping path towards the front gate. Once Helen had seen her and her eyes had filled with tears as she advised 'It's no good, Mammy. He never comes.'

And now this strange letter had arrived returning her Marriage Certificate and asking for 'proof of divorce'. Louisa did not understand a word of it, but as she pulled her back door shut behind her she felt sure that James Rutherford would. He was a kind man who had sympathised warmly with her plight, whilst remaining unobtrusive, and already she felt able to talk to him with ease on almost any matter that bothered her. After all, he was old enough to be her father.

Since hearing of her tragedy her mother and sisters had all written to her begging her to return to Carlisle, yet from the start she had felt curiously reluctant to take advantage of their offer. She had her own home now and her own friends, while Helen was too fragile emotionally to cope with being completely uprooted in addition to losing her father. In her reply to their letter she had thanked them for their concern, whilst tactfully explaining that she wished to defer her decision on whether or not to leave Gilfell until she and Helen had recovered a little from their loss, but knew in her heart that she would never do anything but exchange visits with her relatives, dear though they were.

It was a steady uphill pull through the churchyard and along the lane to Roughside, and Louisa was panting a little as she came within sight of the farm gate where James Rutherford could be seen in conversation with a richly dressed middle-aged man. Studying the swarthy stranger covertly she decided that he was a typical 'townie' trying to look properly dressed for the country in his tweed jacket and deerstalker hat, and felt relieved when she drew near enough to relax her facial muscles into a smile.

'Good morning, Louisa. This is Mr Leo Bondini, the famous opera singer. Mr Bondini, meet Mrs Louisa Marshall, my housekeeper and friend.'

Thinking how absolutely like James it was to introduce her to a person of apparent note as though she were of more importance than they, Louisa shook hands with the man and smiled again before moving quickly through the gate only to find both men accompanying her across the yard to the house.

'Will you be kind enough to prepare breakfast for Mr Bondini, Louisa? I have already eaten, but I feel sure my guest will appreciate some eggs and bacon after his long walk from Dalton.'

'Yes, of course.'

Hurrying ahead of them Louisa went straight to the kitchen and took down a ham from the hook in the ceiling, shaving off several thick slices with a sharp knife before placing them in the frying pan on top of the range where they began to sizzle gently. James and his allegedly famous guest seated themselves at one end of the large scrubbed table to continue their discussion, and Louisa quickly set a place for Leo Bondini a little to his side to avoid disturbing him, then put two eggs ready to fry on the plate she was warming for him.

It was futile to pretend not to be listening, for it was impossible not to hear their conversation, and she soon realised that the singer was negotiating to rent the cottage further down the valley that belonged to her employer.

'I must have country air, good food, and complete rest for three or four months.' He told James, smiling at Louisa when she finally set down his breakfast plate. 'Food like this, so wholesome and expertly cooked by your beautiful housewife.'

'Housekeeper, Mr Bondini.' Louisa corrected. 'It's excellent ham and I'm sure you'll enjoy your meal.'

She had just left the room and was moving up the stairs to begin tidying the bedroom when she remembered the sudden scowl on James Rutherford's face when Leo Bondini had paid her the rather clumsy compliment, and automatically made a mental note of the incident to tell Terence when he came home. Halting abruptly as the illusion shattered, she gripped the banister and fought to control the tidal wave of emotion that threatened to engulf her. Terence was dead, and there would never again be a time when she could tell him things that had happened to her during the day, nor listen to his stories by the fire after supper.

Downstairs, listening to Leo Bondini talking, James' keen ears heard the muffled sob from the staircase then the rush of Louisa's feet before a bedroom door closed and cut off all further sound. Looking down at his guest's plate he suddenly wished it empty and the man gone.

At the Kenhope mining office, which had once been the kitchen of the Robinsons' farm, Bill sealed the last wages envelope for the week and handed the tray with the employees signature book to Kenneth Carter who was now Chief Clerk.

Married now, Kenneth lived in Kenhope with his wife and two young children, and looked forward to Bill's weekly visits when he made up the pay for the workforce then enquired about any problems regarding either personnel or the running of the mine. At present all was quiet, but Kenneth knew that the most recent conflict between Bill and Johnny Peacock was still simmering beneath the surface of their working relationship. Less than a week after his father's death Johnny had begun a determined campaign to try to persuade Bill and Gilbert to sell him the land rather than go on leasing it, and had made several offers of an over-generous nature in an attempt to swing the matter in his favour. Gilbert, who took no active part in the running of the mine, agreed with Bill that they would keep the present arrangements, and left all negotiations to his brother who simply dug his heels in and waited for Johnny to tire of it all which he now appeared to have done, but in reality, as the Robinsons well knew, he was only taking a brief rest while he thought up some other tactic for getting his own way.

'Right Ken, that's it for another week,' Bill smiled getting to his feet. 'I'll go and have a look at my new niece before I start for home, and see how her Granny's coping. I brought her over to Gilbert's last week, and only just in time it seems judging by young Sara's early arrival.'

'Yes indeed. Please pass on my good wishes to your brother and his wife.'

Bill was still smiling when he left the mining office behind and started on the journey to Kenhope village on his newly acquired bicycle which he liked so much better than the pony and trap, even if it was hard work up the steepest slopes.

Coasting down into the village he was aware of a deep feeling of well being. Bill had a good life and he knew it. Sometimes he could hardly believe just how good it was, and all the things that had forged this fine existence had begun after Lilian had become his wife, which to Bill still seemed like a miracle in itself.

Gilbert and Jenny's home lay on the rim of the village nearest the mine and he was soon leaning his bicycle against their parlour wall in Kenhope's Hutchinson Street and entering the premises by the hardware shop doorway a few yards further on. Behind the counter of his cluttered little store Gilbert looked up from serving a customer and grinned happily at his brother, indicating the curtained opening to his rear.

'Go on through, Bill. The ladies are in the living room ... all three of them.'

Clutching the parcel of baby clothes that Lilian had given him to present to the new arrival Bill passed through the short corridor into the private quarters where he found his mother happily overseeing the sleeping baby, Sara, while Jenny sat on the sofa folding newly aired nappies.

'Ah Bill, come and look at our Sara. She's the spitting image of Gilbert.'

Looking down at the baby Bill smiled then winked across at Jenny.

'I reckon you're wrong there Mother. To me she looks just like Jen.'

Jenny laughed. 'And I think she gets more like herself every day, but carry on arguing. It makes for good entertainment.'

Handing over the parcel of clothes to his sister-in-law Bill fished in his pocket for a couple of half crown coins, placing them at the bottom of the pram to comply with the superstition of giving a newly born infant some silver money.

'They're too big for her to hold so I'll just leave them at her feet if that's alright. And how are you feeling Jenny? You look a bit tired if you don't mind me saying so. Shouldn't you still be in bed?'

'That's what I keep telling her.' Marion nodded. 'Sara is only four days old and there'll be plenty sleepless nights to come without getting bone weary already.'

'I'll go upstairs in a minute, I promise.'

The small knitted dresses, coats and bootees were admired profusely, and Bill felt proud of Lilian's delicate work as each garment was commented upon and replaced in its nest of tissue paper ready to be taken upstairs by the regularly yawning Jenny.

'Off you go for a sleep girl, before you swallow us all.' Marion urged, cutting Jenny's apology short. 'If he has to cross the fell on that bicycle of his Bill won't be staying long anyway. You should have bought a motorbike like that young Peacock has, then you wouldn't have to pedal.'

'I'd rather walk than copy him!'

Sitting down on the sofa that the young woman had vacated Bill listened to the regular tinkle of the shop doorbell as Gilbert's customers came and went in an apparently endless stream, and Marion nodded towards the linking corridor.

'Business is booming. It's a good job I came to look after Jen and little Sara because Gilbert would never have had the time.'

'Hmm. I can see that.' Leaning forward, elbows on his knees, Bill studied his newborn niece. 'I would hardly call Sara little. How much does she weigh?'

'She was just over seven pounds at birth.'

'Good grief! That's a pound more than Edward was! If that's what premature babies weigh it

170

seems odd to me that full term ones often don't come near that. How can it be, do you suppose?'

Marion laughed teasingly. 'Oh, you men! Gilbert tried a similar trick on me and I'll remind you both, it's your mother you're talking to so just cut out the fibs.'

Bill looked bewildered. 'What do you mean?'

Bending towards him his mother lowered her voice into a mock stage whisper. 'I mean that, as you and Gilbert both know well enough, neither your Edward nor little Sara were premature babies. They were each fine healthy full term infants, and while you may keep up the pretence with other people that your wives became pregnant on your honeymoon, please don't do it with me. I have a strong feeling about families being honest with each other whatever stories they choose to tell the outside world.'

She expected Bill to laugh, albeit a little sheepishly perhaps, but his stillness and the way he was staring began to unnerve her, and in an attempt to lighten the mood she added jocularly. 'Come on, Bill. Don't sit there looking as though I've slapped you.'

He blinked as though trying to clear his head. 'Are you trying to tell me that Lilian was pregnant when we got married?'

'Well, she wasn't the first and she won't be the last. The main thing is that you got married and Edward is a fine boy. I assume Lilian didn't tell you about it, but I knew on your wedding day, Bill. Women in that condition have a certain look.'

'A certain look ... do you think anyone else

171

noticed it?'

'Probably. You know what village gossip is like. Why trouble yourself over it now?'

He got up and stood looking down at Marion for a few moments before stating heavily. 'I have to go.'

'But you haven't had any lunch, Bill. If I've upset you by mentioning what I did, I'm sorry, but don't leave like this.'

As though she hadn't spoken he turned and left the room, and Marion sat quite still as his quick footsteps ended with a loud slamming of the shop door. A second later Gilbert appeared looking alarmed.

'What's going on with Bill, Mam? He just walked right past me and out of the store with a face like thunder. Have you said something to upset him?'

Helplessly, the woman looked towards the parlour window where Bill could now be seen pedalling his bicycle as fast as he could away from Kenhope.

'I'm very much afraid I must have done.' She admitted slowly.

James Rutherford looked across at Louisa and then quickly down again at the letter from the White Star Line. He was beginning to wish that he had not been in such a hurry to offer comfort and help in an area that had turned out to belong to his son-in-law, and hesitated to answer her query as he sought to find the kindest words of explanation.

'What do they mean about "proof of divorce",

Mr Rutherford? I don't know what makes them imagine that Terence and I had been divorced... I don't understand at all.'

Her voice was small and her pretty face pinched and ravaged with signs of the weeping she had done earlier in the day, making the man feel even more miserable at the news he had to break. He began carefully, wishing he could look away from her pitifully red-rimmed eyes.

'The situation is this, Louisa. Bill has applied for compensation on your behalf from the White Star Line and sent them your Marriage Certificate as proof that you are Terence's widow. However, it appears that they have also received a claim from a woman of an earlier marriage which Terence entered into, and they want you to send his divorce papers from his first wife to prove your entitlement to claim.'

'First wife? Terence had no first wife.'

'I'm very sorry, my dear, but it appears that he had.'

'So why did he never tell me about her? And if they were divorced, how did she know about him being on the Titanic?'

After a slight pause James replied. 'Only he could tell you that, but the fact remains that this woman *did* know. She seems to have known as much as you, Louisa.'

Across the kitchen table the man and young woman stared at each other and her face crumpled a little. 'But she couldn't have done ... unless he had told her.'

James said nothing but he saw, with dread, the realisation dawning in her eyes as the facts fit together for her, and the way her already slight figure seemed to shrink. Slowly Louisa held out her hand for the letter and he watched her as she read it through once again.

'I don't know how I could ever have misunderstood.' She said in a small voice. 'It says here quite distinctly that an earlier marriage took place in Newcastle-upon-Tyne in 1900 to a Miss Hilda Blaylock, and it is divorce papers from that marriage that I have to find and send to them. I think I'd better go home now, Mr Rutherford, if you don't mind.'

'Of course. I'm going down to the village for some groceries, so I'll give you a ride in the trap if you don't object to going by the longer route.'

'That will be very kind. Thank you.'

Unconsciously lifting her chin Louisa walked into the hall and began to put on her outdoor coat. She was pale and shaking slightly but her expression dared the man to even notice it, let alone make any comment. On his way out of the kitchen door to hitch up the pony and trap James said 'When you find the divorce papers, give them to Bill right away.'

'I will, of course.'

He walked out into the cobbled yard, his mood sombre. Louisa Marshall would not find any divorce documents relating to her husband and this Hilda Blaylock, and he had an inkling that she knew that very well.

Dusk had almost turned into darkness when a worried Lilian saw the dim light of Bill's bicycle weaving carefully down the track of Kenhope

174

Fell, and she turned from the bedroom window where she had been keeping vigil for almost an hour, calling into the lighted room next door.

'Come downstairs children. I see Daddy coming at last, so we can have tea.'

Her voice was light with the relief that was making her heart beat too quickly for comfort, and she ran swiftly down the two short flights of stairs and into the kitchen where the table was partially laid and the kettle singing on the hob. Edward and Winifred were scrambling into their seats, and Lilian was busy at the range making a pot of tea, when the back door opened and Bill came in.

'Thank heaven you're home.' Lilian said without turning round. 'I expected you back shortly after lunch and when you never arrived I began to worry in case you'd had an accident. I still think a pony and trap would be safer than that new fangled bicycle.'

With a crash the door closed behind the man and a silence fell in the room as the children stared at their father. Lilian spun round with the teapot in her hands. He was standing by the wall cupboard watching her with hostility glittering in his eyes, and she set the teapot down on its stand and hurried to his side.

'Bill, what's happened? You look awful.'

She placed her hand on his arm and he looked down at it with distaste.

'I'm not hungry. Just carry on with the meal, but when you've finished I would like a word with you.'

'But you must tell me what's wrong, Bill? Is the

175

baby alright? Jenny? Your mother?'

'They're all fine, Lilian. I've got some work to do.'

Brushing roughly past her Bill left Lilian staring after him as though turned to stone, and only when he had shut the study door behind him did the man slump down at his desk and give way to despair. He had turned off the road on the way home and spent over two lonely hours sitting on the edge of Hanson's Dam, its murky black depths mocking him as he painfully began to piece together the last seven years of his life, and he realised that the truth had always been staring him in the face had he just possessed the courage to acknowledge it.

Lilian's 'premature' labour with Edward had thrown him into a panic at the time because he could clearly remember such babies being born weak and sickly and usually dying. The fact that Edward had not been like that had seemed like a sort of miracle to Bill; a miracle which, in his thankfulness, he had not bothered to question. But perhaps the most telling sign of all had been Lilian's sudden decision to accept his proposal of marriage quite a while after he had given up hope. What made sense, with hindsight, was the fact that she had found a compelling reason to be married, and he had been the obvious choice seeing the father of her unborn child was about to marry someone else.

Bitterly he let his mind dwell on Johnny Peacock, for he hardly needed to be a genius to work out that his arch rival had been the other man. Sick at the thought of him being Edward's real father, he wondered whether he knew that Lilian's son was his too and that, together, they had taken Bill Robinson for a complete fool?

With a click the door opened and Lilian walked in carrying a cup of tea and some cakes on a plate.

'Bill, don't sit in the dark like this,' she said softly, setting the crockery down on the edge of his desk. 'I'll light you a lamp.'

At once his hand shot out and imprisoned her arm.

'I don't want a lamp, Lilian. I only want you to answer me one simple question. Were you already pregnant when we got married?'

She went quite still, as though the words had paralysed her, and he looked up at her as she stood in the shaft of light from the open doorway. Her mouth opened then closed again, and as he tightened his grip he heard her gasp.

'I want an answer, Lilian!'

'Who told you?'

'So it's true!'

'Whoever they are they're only guessing because I told no one, not even my mother.'

Letting go of her arm Bill swept the desk clear of the snack she had brought and saw his wife cringe away from his rage as the delicate china smashed on the floor.

'I loved you!' he shouted, rising to his feet to tower over her. 'You were everything in the world to me, Lilian. I would never have taken advantage of you before we were wed, and now I find that you had already laid with Johnny Peacock then passed the consequences on to me! Oh yes, much as it may surprise you, I've always known how you felt about him! You're no better than a common slut and the worst kind of liar! Get out of my sight!'

Lilian began to defend herself, her desperate speech shrill and rapid.

'Alright, I'll admit I gave in to Johnny once, only once, Bill. And I'll admit I turned to you to save me from what would have been a terrible disgrace, but I've been a good wife to you haven't I? I've done all in my power to make you happy, and I've been happy myself because I've grown to love you.'

Bill's expression showed no sign of softening and he muttered almost to himself. 'All these years I've been looking after Peacock's bastard believing him to be my own son.'

'Please don't ever call him that horrible name again. It takes more than a biological mishap to make a man a father, and you know that in every way that matters Edward *is* your son.'

Even as she backed to the door Lilian kept talking, while out in the corridor Edward and Winifred had gathered to watch the nightmare charade. It was Edward's voice that brought them both up short and cooled the situation, at least for a while.

'What is a bastard?'

Turning her back on her husband the woman ran out of the room and took both children by the hand, leading them back into the kitchen as she assured the boy in shaking tones. 'Nobody said 'bastard' darling. Now we'll finish our tea. Daddy's busy.'

Left alone in the now silent room Bill Robinson sat down again at his desk. On the floor by his feet the cup, saucer and plate that Lilian had brought lay shattered among the tea-soaked food on the carpet, while his anger transformed itself into a cold hard lump in his chest. An ache had begun there that begged the relief of tears, but Bill would not cry. Everything he had achieved over the past seven years had been for Lilian, making him happy in a way he had never experienced before in his life, yet it had been for nothing except to make of him a bigger fool than she had done. Well, all that was finished now. He had been soft and sentimental for the last time.

Behind him the door of the room slowly closed itself leaving him alone again in the chill darkness.

By the faint light from the windows along Hillary Terrace Louisa guided Helen and herself to the yard door of Ivy House and saw Lilian through the room's netted window as she looked up at the sound of the latch. When they reached the door to knock, her friend had risen from her seat by the fire and ushered them in with a face that showed no sign of pleasure or welcome.

'I'm sorry to call so late.' Louisa began, and Lilian nodded.

'Helen should be in bed, Lou.'

'Yes I know, but I wanted to see Bill about the claim.'

For a few seconds Lilian stared miserably at her friend then pulled out two hardbacked chairs from around the table, placing them nearer the fire.

'I'd better go and tell him then. Sit down and keep warm.'

Clutching her daughter's hand Louisa took advantage of the proffered seating and waited while Lilian walked the few yards across the corridor to the study where she could hear the murmur of her voice speaking to Bill. At first there seemed to be no reply from the man, and Lilian's voice sounded again. This was followed immediately by a mighty crash as something heavy was either thrown or pushed over, and both Louisa and Helen jumped with fright as Bill Robinson's voice shouted 'How many more times do I have to tell you? Get out of my sight!'

Scrambling from her chair Helen pulled at her mother's arm, trying to drag her back to the outside door, but before she could move Lilian re-entered the room with eyes that were rapidly filling with tears.

'I'm sorry.' She said in barely a whisper. 'I'm afraid Bill is not himself tonight.'

'Lilian, I'm sorry I've called when things are ... awkward. Is it anything I can help you with?'

Appalled she watched as Lilian started to weep, covering her face with her hands as she sobbed, and she crossed to her side putting an arm round her shoulders.

'Don't cry Lilian. I realise you've had a quarrel but it will be alright in a while. All married couples fight occasionally.'

'Not like this, Lou. Bill and I ... we're finished.'

Her words, though garbled, were still audible, and in an attempt to pull herself together Lilian took her hands away from her eyes and looked

180

wretchedly at Louisa.

'I'm sorry Lou, but I think you'd better go. I'll come and see you tomorrow if I may, and we'll consider what we can do about your claim then.'

Louisa, feeling troubled, shook her head. 'You come tomorrow, or whenever you like, and don't worry about the claim, Lilian. I know I can't make one, but I'll tell you about that later.'

She kissed Lilian quickly on the cheek and led Helen outside into the yard, shutting the back door carefully behind her. Before letting herself out onto Hillary Terrace she looked back through the window and saw that Lilian had not moved, and the misery on her face haunted her well into the early hours of the next day as she lay sleepless in her bed. Something bad had happened at Ivy House, and whatever it was Louisa sensed that it would have a lasting effect on her friend and her husband.

CHAPTER SIX

'I'm taking the children to Louisa's for the day.'

Lilian spoke clearly and with a strength she did not feel as she looked at her husband's uncommunicative back. For all she could see he might have been sitting at his desk all night as he appeared not to have moved at all since the previous evening, but she had heard him stealthily rising from the bed in the boxroom at five am. To realise that he had abandoned the marital bed made her so sick with dread that she could not sleep any more, yet she was resolved to show none of this, and when Bill turned his head he found her regarding him steadily from the doorway, a wicker basket in her hands.

'I've left you a cold lunch on a tray in the pantry so that you may eat when you wish.'

'Thank you.'

He looked away from her and down at the ledger he was working on as Edward broke away from Lilian's side to run over to him, leaning against his knee to look up at him with pleading eyes.

'Are you going to come as well Daddy? We'll have a picnic in Aunty Louisa's kitchen.'

Automatically Bill's hand went out to touch the boy's head, and he rumpled Edward's hair for a few moments before pulling back sharply giving the boy a little push.

'Go with your mother.'

Bewildered, Edward looked at Lilian then back to Bill, and she swooped down on the child, holding him against her side.

'It seems we have both been mistaken about each other, doesn't it? You can't forgive me for falling off my pedestal and now you're willing to punish your six year old son for my sins; and he *is* your son in every way that really matters.'

'I suppose that depends upon what you think really matters. If I brought a child to this house whom I had fathered by another woman and expected you to treat it as your own, just what would you think then?'

With the greatest effort of will Lilian did not slam the door behind her as she and the children left Bill alone, nor did she give way to the temptation of tears as his words struck home. Briskly she escorted her children out of the house and let them run ahead of her towards Louisa's home, with Edward for once lagging behind his sister, his attention seeming to be only partially with the race.

Within seconds the familiar sound of her back door opening and closing caused Lilian to pause and turn her head, and she saw Bill emerge from the yard to walk swiftly round Chapel Corner into Main Street. He never once glanced their way and seemed to have something fairly urgent on his mind. Uneasily she wondered just where he was going with such purpose, and whether it had anything to do with herself.

Bella sat at her easel, her paints untouched, as

she gazed out of the large landing window of White Court. She had decided that painting would be her new hobby but it seemed a rather useless one when she was alone in the house, while Johnny, as usual, pursued his own pastimes without her, and watching the doings of her neighbours proved much more interesting. During the last minutes she had seen Lilian Robinson set out along Hillary Terrace with her children and a few moments later her husband, Bill, also leave the house to hurry off the other way into the heart of the village with his normally mild features set in a grim expression.

Down in the hall the parlourmaid passed by on her way to put more coal on the lounge fire, glancing up at her mistress with a mixture of indifference and contempt, and Bella picked up one of her brushes defensively. She should begin her picture instead of sitting here speculating about possible events in the area in a way which made her look idle and stupid.

Having decided half-heartedly to use the Assembly Rooms as her subject she had just chosen a piece of charcoal to commence drawing when something else caught her attention. A young man in working clothes had crossed over from Main Street to begin climbing Kenhope Fell Road, and he was looking right up at White Court as though it were his destination. Realising that he could see her where she sat Bella nevertheless remained still as he drew nearer, her eyes riveted on his pleasant homely face. He was moving up the steep slope with a practised climber's long strides and within minutes had disappeared from

184

view behind the tall pines that shielded the front of the house, but Bella felt sure she would hear his knock on the side door in a short while. Holding her breath she listened, feeling strangely disappointed when the appropriate time passed and nothing happened, then he appeared below her window walking very slowly with his head bent over the flowerbeds as though studying them.

Recalling that Johnny had spoken of hiring another gardener since old Cavendish had retired, she smiled slightly and leaned forward in her chair to watch him more intently as he lowered himself onto his haunches to pick up a handful of the dark moist soil.

'Excuse me madam, but Daniel Heslop has come to see Mr John about the gardener's job, only the master's out. Will you see him yourself if I bring him in?'

Bella stared down at Laura for an instant before setting down her sable brush.

'Yes, certainly I'll see him. Show him into the small parlour ... or wait. I have a better idea.'

Descending the stairs Bella indicated the landing window, still smiling.

'That is the young man in question squatting by one of our rosebeds, isn't it?'

'Yes madam, I noticed him through the window when I was in the lounge.'

'Right. I'll go out and speak to him while I show him round the place. It's a pleasant day and I fancy some air.'

Afterwards, thinking over the events of that morning, Bella recognised that it was the young gardener's action in picking up the soil and crumbling it through his fingers that had triggered a response within her which at first she could not identify, but from the moment she stepped out into the air she lost all interest in trying to paint.

The side door opened onto the small rose garden and the young man straightened at her approach, a flush of embarrassment on his skin.

'Good morning, Mrs Peacock. Mr John told me to call about tending your garden on a regular basis, and I thought I'd have a look at it before knocking at the door.'

Bella scanned the weed engulfed plants.

'My husband is out I'm afraid, but you and I can discuss arrangements, Mr Heslop. What do you think of the garden now that you've examined it so closely?'

Daniel Heslop gave her a keen look, trying to ascertain whether she was being sarcastic, but could find no hint of it. He cleared his throat.

'It depends what you have in mind, Mrs Peacock. If you only want the present garden kept tidy it's a simple matter, but if you would like mistakes rectified and a proper garden begun then we'll have to discuss and plan together. It's up to you.'

He waited as she walked the few remaining steps to his side and saw her bite her lip in a brief moment of indecision before she turned her head to answer him.

'Let me show you over the rest of the grounds and you can tell me what is wrong as we go, then we'll decide what's to be done. I haven't lived here long, but even I can see there's scope for improvement.'

A bluster of cool air blew round the corner of the house scattering some late dead leaves onto the lawn from the beech trees across the road, and Bella and Daniel Heslop began their tour of White Court grounds, the young man explaining his point of view as they walked.

'It's the climate.' He told her earnestly. 'You can see that Mr John's other gardener didn't study that at all. It's harsh and exposed up here in the hills and things like roses, for all they are so popular, just don't do well. They're not really hardy enough. Now, what you should do is take out the plants that are fighting a losing battle and replace them with things like tough purple pansies, bright marigolds that reseed themselves each year and spread, and snow-in-summer based rockeries here and there.'

Fascinated Bella let him talk on as she mentally visualised how the garden would be after Daniel Heslop had reorganised everything to work with nature. His enthusiasm grew as their journey progressed and when he saw the greenhouse at the rear of White Court, dilapidated through lack of use for many years, he begged to be allowed to restore it. Bella opened the door with difficulty as the wood had warped along its edge.

'I don't see why not. Can you replace the broken glass panels as well?'

'First thing I'd do, then plane down the door to fit again. After that I'd need to clear out the existing soil and disinfect everything before putting in fresh earth ready for planting whatever you fancy.'

'Whatever I fancy.' Bella repeated smiling. 'I

love greenhouses. I used to beg our gardener at home to let me try and grow something in ours but he would never allow it. Could we try grapes do you think, as well as a few tomatoes?'

'Whatever you like, Mrs Peacock.'

Warming to her subject Bella began to walk down the length of the run down horticultural palace while Daniel added some suggestions of his own.

'It's a fair size alright. Big enough for quite a few things. You could grow chrysanthemums in here and even roses, then it wouldn't be such a wrench when we've cleared them away outside.'

'Could I have one side of the greenhouse to myself? You could advise me, because I know nothing about gardening yet, but I can soon learn.'

She was like a child in her eagerness and Daniel felt vaguely uncomfortable with her pleading attitude, which in his opinion was no way for the mistress of White Court to behave. Since the young Peacocks had taken over from the old man at the family home there had been rumours in the village that their marriage was far from happy, and he would have preferred Bella to have kept indoors out of his way like any normal wife.

'It's your greenhouse, Mrs Peacock. I'm here to do as *you* say.'

'Good!' She clapped her hands, oblivious to the subtle rebuke. 'When can you start?'

'Mr John told me I could start on Monday, madam, but that I could come this morning to discuss wages and hours with him. He must have forgotten about me.'

'Oh well, he's very busy. Maybe something cropped up at one of the mines. If you come on Monday, as arranged, you'll be able to see him before you start.'

'Very good madam.'

Ten minutes later Bella stood once again on the landing of White Court watching Daniel Heslop returning to Gilfell, and noticed with surprise that his gait was considerably less sprightly than when he had ascended the hill. Had she not known better she would have thought he was downcast.

Gathering up her palette and paints she called down to Laura, whose white apron she had glimpsed briefly through the banisters.

'Can you put the rest of these things in the boxroom please? I won't be needing them again.'

Louisa helped her friend on with her coat aware that while they had talked for three hours she was no nearer finding out exactly what had gone wrong at Ivy House the previous day. Lilian had quietly insisted upon discussing Louisa's immediate problems, and they had talked long and hard about Terence's 'other wife' and whether or not he had actually divorced her before marrying Louisa.

'I suppose there'll be official records of divorce cases somewhere, but I feel he didn't divorce her.' Louisa admitted, and her voice thickened with unshed tears.

'You and I could still try to find out for sure, Lou. Bill is not himself at the moment, so we'll leave him out of things for now, but we could ask Dr Hatton what to do or go down to Dalton and get a solicitor there to act for us...'

189

'No Lilian! It's kind of you to suggest it, and I do feel curious about this Hilda Blaylock; what does she look like, what kind of person is she? That sort of thing. But I don't want to risk the details leaking out and people in the village getting to know about it. I really couldn't stand that humiliation. It's hard enough being almost sure that Terence deceived me without having it proved beyond a shadow of doubt.'

Wanting to tell her what she and Bill had seen that day in Newcastle, yet feeling afraid to broach the subject, Lilian kept silent on the matter and spoke of things of a more mundane nature that bothered Louisa, while all the time her mind refused to move away from her own problem. It was only when she was coming away from Hillary Terrace that she forgot herself enough to remark 'It seems as though both our worlds have collapsed around us, doesn't it, Lou?'

It was cool and beginning to rain as Lilian walked back home, and she was about to open the yard door when she noticed a group of men standing at the bottom of Kenhope Fell road gazing with apparent fascination at the front of Ivy House. A peculiar rustling noise could be heard like someone walking through undergrowth, and she made her way round the corner to see what the idlers were staring at. An elderly man, who made his living in the village doing odd jobs, was up a long wooden ladder pulling the ivy off the walls strand by strand, and Bill was leaning on the front gate watching him. Appalled, she forgot to be discreet, and marched up to him, her face white with shock.

'What are you doing to the house? It's the ivy that gives it character.'

Bill looked down at her coolly. 'It is damaging the structure of the house, Lilian. It has to go.'

'But you know I've always loved the ivy. Without it the place will never be the same.'

'That may be said of many things.'

With tears filling her eyes Lilian looked up at the marks left on the stone by the displaced creeper, like broken veins on a body, and had no doubt that this was part of Bill's revenge.

As she turned away to take the children inside through the back yard rather than push past her husband, the men gathered by the wall watched her curiously while muttering to each other about the Robinsons, both of whom they considered to have inflated ideas of their own importance. Well aware of their attention, Bill kept his head averted and chatted nonchalantly to Eli Dobbs as more and more ivy was ripped away to fall onto the piles of recently dug up roots that proved his act of petty spite could not be undone, even had he wished it. Ivy House that Lilian loved so much now had a name that was a mockery, and he hoped that each time she heard it she would be reminded of everything else that had been lost. That was the least she deserved.

'What the dickens are you doing in here? I've been looking all over the house for you.'

Johnny frowned into the interior of the toolshed at the back of White Court where his wife was apparently sorting through a variety of garden tools. A smudge of grey lay across her

191

cheek and wisps of cobweb stuck in her hair as she faced him, a spade in each hand.

'I came out right after breakfast, John. You weren't up, so I couldn't tell you where I was going. What do you want?'

He grimaced, looking her up and down. 'To get you cleaned up for a start. We're due at Low Shields today for lunch, remember?'

'Oh.'

In an untypical show of petulance Bella threw down the spades on the floor, slapped her palms together to dislodge any grime and stamped past him onto the path, her mouth set in a mutinous line. Johnny laughed.

'What's the matter, Bella? Don't you want to go home to see Mummy and Daddy?'

'I was busy.' She began to stride ahead of him, her skirts brushing against the weeds growing in the walkway. 'I'd forgotten about it and I had other plans for today.'

'Had you indeed? Well, that certainly makes an all time first for you doesn't it? Am I to assume that your "plans for today" included doing the garden?'

Bella halted so abruptly that he almost bumped into her, and when she turned to face him her expression had lost all traces of aggression.

'In a way, yes it does. A young man called Daniel Heslop called yesterday and said he had come to see you about becoming our gardener, but seeing you had gone out *I* interviewed him!'

'You!'

Her husband was openly grinning now and Bella felt her burst of energy beginning to seep away leaving her with the old familiar feeling of weariness again. With sinking spirits she pressed on.

'The garden is not as good as it might be, and he offered either to simply keep it tidy or refashion it to take into account our less then mellow climate. I thought a change would be good. Wouldn't you agree, John?'

'What kind of change?'

'Plants and flowers that grow well in a cold wet area like this.'

As she waited for Johnny to answer Bella pushed back a strand of hair that had fallen untidily onto her forehead, leaving yet another dirty mark on her face, and a speculative gleam appeared in the young man's eyes. Bella with an interest was a novelty indeed, and definitely one which could operate to his advantage.

'And you want to take part in this transformation do you?'

Bella clenched her fists at her sides, took a deep breath and said 'Yes. I want to help reshape the gardens.'

'Then by all means do so.'

She blinked and he smiled faintly. 'Just make sure you're not in this state when we're either expecting guests or due to go out somewhere.'

'Oh I won't, John. I promise.'

Bella turned and ran up the path rubbing her hands down her skirt as she went, and the man let out a long breath of satisfaction. If his wife had suggested doing a daily shift at the lead mine he would have encouraged her, but gardening would do well enough. He called after her before she vanished round the corner.

'I assume Heslop will be starting work here on Monday.'

'Yes.'

Back in the house she bathed and changed her clothes, already impatient for her forthcoming visit to her parents' home to be over, and Johnny took a cigar out of the box in the lounge, his thoughts now firmly on other matters.

The Fairburns had recently bought another motor, one able to cope fairly well with the local terrain, and he was looking forward to Gerald arriving in the vehicle to drive them down to Low Shields. Had it not been for the fact that owning a car himself would necessitate transporting Bella everywhere, he too would have invested in a similar motor.

Thinking of his father-in-law made his thoughts drift to the mines which led on to the subject of Bill Robinson, who seemed destined to remain a major thorn in his side along with the stubbornly unforgettable Lilian. Without him realising it the memory of her brought a frown of vexation to his brow, and a few seconds later when he turned to face Bella it was still there. She paused, looking at him uncertainly.

'You haven't changed your mind about the garden have you?'

'Of course I haven't. Why do you ask?'

'You looked so cross just then. I thought you'd decided against it after all.'

The distinctive sound of the Fairburns' motor labouring up the short incline towards their gate cut short any further reassurances, and Bella walked quickly to the hall table where she had left her veiled hat.

'There'll be no dust. It only rained a few hours ago, Bella, so I'm sure you don't have to travel looking like a bee keeper today.'

Johnny's voice was mocking as they walked out onto the front porch, but his wife ignored him. Her mind was on the fascinating subjects of flowerbeds, garden tools and greenhouses, and she was not to be easily distracted.

Reaching across the pew past Winifred Lilian tapped Edward sharply on the knee and he stopped fidgeting, but sighed and looked pleadingly at his mother as the preacher's boring sermon droned on, apparently forever. Disregarding it she gave him a stern look before sitting back, hands folded over her personal hymn book. In truth, she was as weary of the morning service as they were but hid it better, her thoughts still on her husband's intractable attitude towards her and their dying marriage. She had hardly been surprised when he had made no move to accompany them that morning as he usually did. In her heart she had wanted to plead with him, not just to attend chapel but to put the past behind him and go back to being the Bill she had grown to know well over the past six years, but she knew better than to try and felt that every member of the congregation was secretly watching her, well aware of how things now were between them. It was nonsense of course. Louisa would not tell anyone else that they had quarrelled and neither would Bill.

She began leafing through her hymn book as the sermon ended and wished that they had sat down in the body of the chapel instead of being the only people in the gallery, but the children more easily endured proceedings when they could sit upstairs. As always she felt better the moment she began to sing, and Edward looked up at his mother then down at the people below who kept glancing up at her because her voice could be heard too clearly above theirs. Lost in the balm of the hymn Lilian was quite unaware of the attention she was attracting until the end of the piece when a sea of upturned faces reminded her that, this time, she had forgotten to sing quietly so that she blended in with everyone else. Flushed and self-conscious she sat down for the final prayer, holding back after that until she felt fairly sure everyone else had left the chapel, but upon coming down the stairs to the porch she found the recently appointed resident preacher, Victor Dallow, waiting patiently by the door.

'Ah, Mrs Robinson! I've been waiting to see you about the concert tomorrow night in the Assembly Rooms, and to ask why you haven't already volunteered your services.'

He was smiling, setting her teeth on edge with his irritating affability, and she replied shortly. 'I had no idea there was to be a concert, Mr Dallow.'

'Oh yes indeed, and we would certainly appreciate a song or two from your good self. The small admittance charge is to go towards the upkeep of the Assembly Rooms, especially its long overdue redecoration, so can I count on your support?'

'Yes, I suppose so, but I have no accompanist and it isn't giving me much time to practice.'

'I'll accompany you, Lilian. It's been quite a while since we worked together but I'm sure we haven't lost the touch.'

She turned to find Emma Hartley emerging from the body of the chapel and was surprised at the friendly smile on her face.

'Can you call at my house later today, or would you rather I come to you? We can soon run through some suitable songs for you to choose for tomorrow night.'

Across the road Lilian saw the yard door of Ivy House open and Bill step outside; at once Edward and Winifred rushed from her side to greet him. Holding her breath she watched their meeting, unaware that the preacher and the organist were puzzled by her intentness, and when Bill scarcely gave the children more than a few seconds of his time before hurrying away down Main Street her lips twitched with anger even as Miss Hartley's enquiring voice brought her back to the present with a jolt.

'You will help us out, Lilian, won't you?'

'Yes, of course.' She gave the woman a strained smile before adding. 'If I may bring Edward and Winifred I'll come to your house to rehearse. You have more music than I.'

'I'll expect you after lunch then.'

Victor Dallow and his organist exchanged glances as Lilian walked out to her children and Winifred piped 'Daddy wouldn't take us with him, Mummy. Why wouldn't he take us with him?'

Hustling them into the yard Lilian desperately hoped that they had not been overheard, but feared that the lack of communication between Bill and herself could hardly have passed unnoticed.

Making the children their midday meal, she put her mind on the concert and decided to ask Louisa to look after her young family for her rather than risk a refusal from Bill. Trying to make it sound like a rare treat she told them that they were going out again soon to Miss Hartley's, after which they would call on Louisa and Helen, which latter part of the plan was pleasing enough to pacify them as they fell avidly to their food.

Lilian sat beside them feeling the emptiness of the rest of the house pressing in on her while her throat began to ache. There was no life for her any more with Bill, that was very clear, and she knew she would now take any excuse to get out of this once warm house, if only for short intervals.

Bill leaned against the low stone wall looking at the rare patch of flat land behind it. The man at his side, still mystified by his request, wondered whatever he could want with such a useless acre and hoped he wouldn't change his mind about buying it. The smallest of fields, it could not even be rented as grazing to a sheep farmer, but he was careful not to mention that in case it put paid to the sale.

'My children have been playing in it lately.' He remarked, indicating the row of cottages on the opposite side of the road where he lived. 'The missus doesn't care for them running about in the garden. What was it you wanted it for?'

Bill made a non-committal comment about still needing to make more enquiries but to think over his offer and let him know as soon as possible, and with that Fred Walton had to be content.

The Assembly Rooms were almost full and the concert minutes from starting when the stranger walked in. Too smartly dressed for a village like Gilfell, and obviously foreign with his swarthy good looks, he caused a momentary hush as he took a seat near the back, but Leo Bondini was used to attention and paid it no heed. He had been out walking, and feeling the need to rest his legs a while, had decided to attend the concert on seeing the notice posted outside the door. Prepared to adopt a polite facade Leo settled down to rest his body and endure the concert, no matter how bad the performers were, as the gaslights along the front of the stage were lit one by one by a young man on his hands and knees.

Lilian had agreed to go on in second and fifth places, and stood in the wings watching a troupe of five year old girls thumping round the stage to Miss Hartley's rendering of 'The Dance of the Sugar Plum Fairy'. Louisa had insisted upon attending the concert with their children in tow, and Lilian felt glad that she would not have long to wait before she could go home and put Edward and Winifred to bed. In different circumstances Bill would have been at home minding their young family, but it was useless thinking of those days now.

Walking out onto the stage a few moments later, she smiled automatically at the audience en masse as her first introductory notes tinkled out on the piano, then she began to sing.

At the back of the hall Leo Bondini opened his eyes slowly before closing them again, the better to appreciate the tone of the young woman's voice. Her appearance was too distracting, in any case, and he wanted to be sure that what he was hearing was the truth and not a myth suggested by the beauty of the soloist. In his opinion, women with inferior talent had all too often made their career on the operatic and concert stage simply because their looks ensured their popularity, but by the end of the song he knew without doubt that this singer was not like that and the old familiar excitement of discovery began to stir within him. Uncertain of whether she would be performing again, and seeing no printed programmes available to inform him, he sat in hopeful anticipation through the next two acts, pleased to find that Lilian Robinson was being introduced once more for her 'final song'. Ignorant of how intently she was being studied by the stranger, Lilian sang her way through another popular ballad while Leo Bondini found he had no difficulty in picturing her as Bizet's Carmen or Saint-Sean's Delilah, although whether or not she could act either part was something he had yet to find out.

A short while later, between a comic monologue and an amateur magician, Lilian emerged from the door at the side of the stage dressed in her outdoor clothes, and was joined in the aisle by

Louisa with the children before they quietly left the hall. Leo Bondini rose from his place in the shadows and followed them outside where he quickly caught up with the group, lifting his hat courteously to Louisa.

'Good evening, Signora Marshall.'

'Oh ... Mr Bondini. How nice to see you again. This lady who has just been singing is my friend, Mrs Robinson. Lilian, Mr Bondini is an opera singer who has recently come to stay in the area, and he knows your father.'

'Really?'

Leo took her hand, raising it briefly to his lips.

'Your father is Mr Rutherford, who lives on the farm?'

'That's right. How did you meet him?'

They began to walk on slowly as the Italian explained that he had taken leave of a musical comedy touring company back in Newcastle and had rented Moss Cottage to take an extended rest. Lilian expressed interest in his stage career and, as he was obviously taken with her to the exclusion of anyone else, Louisa drew back with the children leaving them to talk. Once over the stile and into Hillary Terrace Louisa and Helen bid them goodnight. Lilian turned to her, smiling, and made hasty arrangements to see her on the following day, then she, the children, and Leo Bondini walked the rest of the way to Ivy House. On the way there he told her quite sincerely that her voice was exceptional and asked about her training, shaking his head regretfully when she admitted that her only teacher had been Miss Hartley.

'Not good enough for you, Signora. Would you allow me to teach you properly? A voice like yours should be treated with care. Would you not like to sing in better places than your village hall?'

Standing beside the yard door with her fingers on the latch Lilian knew that in the past she would not have hesitated to ask this stranger inside to meet her husband, but now as she looked into his admiring eyes she felt that the decision to go further was her own and that she had very little left to lose.

'I would be glad of your help,' she said quietly, 'and I would love to sing in other places if I should ever be considered good enough.'

'Have no doubt of that, Signora. You and I will work on the voice together until it is perfect. It will be hard work for you, but rewards will come.'

His parting smile was brilliant, and long after she had gone into the house Lilian kept remembering it *and* his promise to give her proper training. Tomorrow morning she would take her music to Moss Cottage to commence her lessons and, for the first time in days, she found she was giving no special thought to Bill's absence.

Johnny rose from his solitary place at the dining table and pulled the bellcord by the side of the fireplace. Within seconds Laura entered.

'You may clear away now. I take it my wife has got one of her migraine headaches today seeing I haven't set eyes on her since breakfast.'

'No sir, I believe she's just tired. She went to bed over an hour ago.'

'Hmm.'

He poured himself a brandy from the decanter on the sideboard and wondered whether he might go to the music hall. Second House would be starting in half an hour, but it would be too much of a scramble to get there in time. Tomorrow night maybe or, better still, when he had finally solved the problem of Bill Robinson. Behind him crockery clinked as Laura loaded the dishes onto her tray and he wandered into the adjoining lounge to sit by the fire, thankful that Bella was not there to aggravate him. He smirked for a moment thinking of her wish to garden, of all things, and how quickly she had fallen back into her old ways again as the maid, guessing his thoughts, hid her amusement behind a deadpan expression, for at four thirty that afternoon Bella Peacock, dressed in her oldest clothes and canvas apron, had come in from the garden as dirty as a scarecrow and as happy as a child. She had requested a light meal on a tray, bathed and gone to bed with the avowed intention of getting up as early as possible in the morning to begin again.

Daniel Heslop looked round Robinson's hardware store with a handyman's appreciative eye while Gilbert began to work his way down the list he had given him, muttering softly to himself from time to time.

'White exterior paint and undercoat ... yes, I have that. Nails, putty ... three panes of glass cut to...' He looked up at Daniel apologetically. 'I don't do glass at the moment I'm afraid. You'd have to go to Dalton for that. Do you want me to cut some wood to these measurements so that you can nail them in place temporarily?'

'That will be fine. Thanks.'

Gilbert nodded towards the far end of the shop. 'If you'd care to help yourself I think you'll find all that you require in gardening equipment up against the wall, but if you get stuck let me know.'

Turning eagerly the young man advanced on the interesting collection of gardening and agricultural tools and accessories and began to pick out what he wanted, setting the items in a pile by the counter, his many journeys making a pounding noise on the floorboards as he trod backwards and forwards. He had just finished when a small elderly woman emerged through the curtained alcove behind the counter and smiled at him encouragingly.

'Excuse me young man, but did I hear you mention before that you had travelled by pony and trap from Gilfell and, if so, might I travel back there with you?'

'Mam, there's no need.' Gilbert looked embarrassed but Daniel took the request in his stride.

'I'm sure you're welcome to a lift as far as White Court. I work in their gardens and that's where I'll be going.'

'Then I'm much obliged. I'll get my bags. I have two but they're not heavy.'

Disappearing behind the curtain again Marion went upstairs to collect her luggage, packed already for a journey she had planned to make to Gilfell with her son the next day, then she slipped into the parlour to say goodbye to Jenny and Sara.

Kissing her daughter-in-law and her little

granddaughter, Marion tried to hide her relief at finding herself going back to her home a day earlier than expected. She loved them all, and had enjoyed her stay, but she had begun to feel homesick for her own tiny cottage again and felt happy to be on her way.

'It will save Gilbert having to take me tomorrow on his afternoon off. You can have a restful time together for a change.'

As she took her seat outside in the trap Marion waved to Jenny who was standing at the window with Sara in her arms, then bent down to kiss Gilbert who had finished stacking her luggage and had come round to her side to tuck the travelling rug more securely round her legs.

'Thanks Mam.' He said simply. 'We couldn't have managed without you, as you know. Give our love to Lilian and Bill when you see them.'

Daniel climbed up beside Marion and shook the reins then the trap began to move off slowly, and as the outskirts of Kenhope gradually gave way to open country the woman wondered again just what had upset Bill when he had last called at the shop, then, ruffled by such thoughts, she turned her attention to Daniel.

'Have you worked for Mr Peacock long?'

'I only started a few days ago, and it's more Mrs Peacock I'm taking orders from.'

'Really?'

Daniel nodded and smiled. 'She's very keen on the garden, young Mrs Peacock. Got a lot of ideas for improving it.'

He stopped talking, afraid of saying too much that might later be interpreted as gossip, and

Marion obligingly changed the subject onto something more general.

Two hours later the loaded trap stopped at the gates of White Court, and Daniel jumped down from his seat to assist Marion who was feeling stiff and chilled from the long open ride.

'I'm sorry I can't take you all the way to your home, but I'll bring your bags on for you later if you like.'

'That's nice of you, Daniel, but they're not heavy. Thank you for bringing me this far.'

He stood for a moment watching her slowly descending the hill, a bag in each hand, and after satisfying himself that she really didn't seem to be finding them too great a burden he opened the gates and led the horse inside with its load of gardening equipment.

Round the back of the house he found himself confronted by an excited Bella who had been taking barrowloads of soil out of the greenhouse, and he grinned at her now familiar gesture of rubbing her dirty hands down her apron skirt. Seeing his amusement she smiled back and shrugged.

'I know I'm a sight, Daniel, but I'll soon get cleaned up once I'm indoors. Now, let's see what you've brought.'

'Mam! What are you doing?'

Marion set down her bags and beamed at Bill as he crossed Main Street towards her, his expression incredulous, and she hurried to reassure him that she had not walked over the entire fell from Kenhope.

'I begged a ride from a young man who works at White Court, Bill. He was buying some goods at Gilbert's store, and I thought how nice it would be to come home a day sooner than I'd planned.'

'Well, I'll carry you these bags now and I'll light your fire for you. Do you want to stop at the grocery store on the way?'

'Yes, I'd better just get a few staple items until tomorrow when I can take in an order for Len to deliver. I'll give you my door key if you want to go ahead.'

Less than fifteen minutes later Marion walked through her open front door and found Bill kneeling before her hearth where a coal fire was encouragingly gaining strength. He looked up, the flames casting a warm glow on his face as he smiled.

'I've put your bags upstairs in your room and the kettle will go on the hob in a moment for your bottles.'

He nodded towards the kitchen table where two heavy pottery bed warming bottles lay ready to be filled and she set her shopping down beside them with a sigh of pleasure. 'I've enjoyed being away for a while but it's lovely to be back home, especially when you're doing so much of the donkey work for me. I see you've brought me some more coal in too.'

'What else are men for?'

'To have a happy life I hope.'

Turning his head away from her Bill thrust the poker through the bars causing sparks to fly up the chimney like small red fireflies, and Marion advanced on him, aware that there would probably not be another such perfect opportunity to question her son for a long time to come.

'Bill, what upset you so much that day when you came to Gilbert's? You went rushing off as though all the demons in hell were at your heels and I've wondered about it ever since. Won't you tell me about it now?'

He took a deep breath to steady himself but it came out sounding like a sigh, and he replied gruffly. 'I'm sorry I was rude. It's all sorted out now. Don't worry about anything.'

'Well, if you say so.'

She could see by the set of his shoulders that he would tell her nothing more, and before she could utter another word he began to speak on a subject which pushed the mystery firmly to the back of her mind.

'I've just bought that piece of land belonging to your neighbour, Fred Walton. I'm going to use it for a business of my own, quite independent of Peacock and Fairburn, and I expect to launch the new venture before the end of this year, or next spring at the latest.'

Marion sat down on her fireside chair, her hands folded demurely but her eyes bright with curiosity.

'What kind of business will that be in a small empty field?'

'It won't be a small empty field forever, and you'll have to wait a while until I've finalised arrangements before I tell you all about it, but I can promise you there's nothing like it in the area, so I'll be the first.'

'How exciting. What does Lilian think of this plan?'

'Nobody knows about it yet except myself. I promise I'll let you all in on the secret as soon as I can.'

'Good.'

Later, after he had gone, his mother stood looking out at the piece of land in question as she tried to ignore the implications of his admission that his wife had been told no more than anyone else, and knowing that if her son had closed in on himself to the extent of excluding Lilian from his plans then something had to be very wrong indeed.

The first person Bill saw upon entering his home was Edward. Playing with his toys at the bottom of the stairs he froze his habitual smile of welcome at the sight of his father and gazed up at him with wide apprehensive eyes. Bill stood still for a moment, ashamed to realise how the boy now reacted to him, then dropped on his haunches beside him picking up a toy to join in Edward's game. Wary at first, his son remained distant for a while then slowly began to relax as Bill made no move to go away, and it was there that Lilian found them both some ten minutes later as she and Winifred came down the stairs.

'Lilian.'

He straightened after placing the train he had been holding in Edward's hands and ruffling his hair affectionately, and the woman held her breath at this sudden ray of hope between herself and her husband. Winifred broke free of her hand

and sat down beside her brother to play as Bill spoke again.

'Can I speak to you in private for a moment?'

'Yes, of course.'

She began to smile at him but he turned and walked towards the lounge holding the door open for her to precede him into the room, and she felt her hopes for a reconciliation dwindling sharply. There was an uncomfortable silence for a few seconds as they sat at either side of the empty fireplace looking everywhere but in each other's eyes, and as Bill cleared his throat to begin Lilian felt her despair returning. By no gesture or word had the man hinted at a change of heart and she braced herself for what he was about to say, her hands clenched tightly in her lap in an effort to stop her aching throat finally bringing her to tears.

'I have thought about matters regarding Edward,' he began heavily, 'and I have to admit that my feelings towards the child cannot be denied. You were right when you said that in all the ways that really matter he is my son.'

He looked down as a spasm of pain crossed his face, then continued, 'But towards you, Lilian ... it's just no use. What I felt for you has changed and I know now it will never be as it was. I have, as I said, given the matter much thought and suggest you follow either one of the two possibilities I shall put to you for your consideration. Firstly, while we shall present a united front to the outside world, inside our home we shall live quite separately. The house is big enough to allow for that, as I'm sure you'll agree, but if you do not then you must go and I'll make arrangements for the children to be looked after by some suitable person during my working hours.'

She rose to her feet, staring down at him in disbelief.

'You wouldn't do that to me, Bill! How could you ever contemplate Winifred and Edward living without me? I'm their mother.'

'Then you must stay and live as I have suggested. It's entirely up to you.'

Wanting to scream at him and beat him with her fists, she stayed helplessly silent as he stood up and walked to the door. He turned before leaving her alone, his pale blue eyes like twin points of ice in a face that no longer held even the faintest shadow of the love he had once professed to feel for her.

'You may consider your future over the next few days and let me know what you decide, but don't take too long.'

The door shut behind him with a quiet click and she sat down again putting her hands over her burning face, yet she was too shocked to weep.

Hours later, when the sounds of Bill playing with the children then putting them to bed had ebbed into silence, Lilian moved swiftly through the dark room and let herself out into the passage. For all the signs of life she could detect the house might have been empty apart from herself, but she crossed the few yards to the study assuming that Bill would be at his desk.

At first he made no move to lift his eyes from the book he was reading and she realised that she

211

had entered so quietly he had not heard her. Coughing slightly she watched him raise his head and turn to face her, his features shadowed now that the soft glow of the oil lamp no longer shone on them directly.

'I can't leave the children.' She said simply. 'I will stay on your terms.'

Bill nodded. 'That will be our agreement then.'

A fire burned in the grate making the room pleasantly warm, but Lilian began to shiver as he returned to his book as though she had done little more than remark on a matter of the most minor importance. She hesitated, wanting to try one last time to break through the implacable barrier of his indifference, but after a few fruitless moments she backed out into the passage and closed the door.

Making her way to the back of the house she entered the kitchen and sat down by the side of the hearth, picking up pieces of coal from the scuttle with her fingers and throwing them onto the day's dying embers. Her concentration was total, each coal being tossed where it would stand the best chance of flaring into life, and when the first flames appeared she relaxed a little, leaning back in her chair. Her old life with Bill was as good as dead; but she would resurrect something new for herself out of its ashes just as she had done with the fire. Twenty six was far too young to endure the emotional prison Bill had in mind.

The faint sound of the study door closing, followed a short while later by the familiar creak of the first landing floorboards, told Lilian that her husband had now gone to his bed alone and without bidding her goodnight. She sat still for a while longer, ignoring the tears that kept running down her cheeks.

James stamped into Roughside's kitchen, smiling at the sight of Louisa baking, whilst Helen, wearing an apron that reached her ankles and an intense expression, furiously stirred a substance in a small white basin.

'Ah, I see you're determined to earn the florin I promised to give you at the end of your school holidays. Are you making a cake?'

Helen nodded. 'For today's tea, Mr Rutherford. It's going to be chocolate.'

'Good. That's my favourite.'

Sitting down in the hardbacked chair by the door James bent to remove his boots while he studied Louisa's pale face.

'And how are things with you, lass? Any improvement in the village?'

She grimaced and shook her head, cutting out the scones she was making with unnecessary violence. 'The men speak but their wives are still not prepared to forgive me for going to the concert that night while "in mourning". The silly thing is that if I hadn't been looking after Edward and Winifred I wouldn't have been there at all, and the concert made no difference to how I was feeling inside.'

James grunted agreement as he pushed the mud caked boots under his chair. He was about to take the trap down to the village for various supplies, and he secretly hoped to encounter as many as possible of these women before returning to the

213

farm. On his way through the room he patted Louisa's shoulder lightly.

'Try to ignore them if you can. Every village has its share of uncharitable old crones and you're happy enough up here aren't you?'

'Oh yes. We both are.'

'Good.'

On his way up the stairs to his room to wash and change James hummed tunelessly to himself, his thoughts pleasing. Things were beginning to go his way at last.

The first frost of the autumn was just beginning to melt away as Bill arrived at White Court and he was unsurprised to see Gerald Fairburn's motor parked by the front door. He himself had firmly intended to be last, as sitting around waiting for other people was no longer his style.

Stepping inside the hall he could almost feel the maid's disapproval as she took his hat and coat, and her prim 'The others are waiting for you, sir,' fell onto the air as the man strode across to the heavy oak door, knocking briefly before entering the room.

'Good morning gentlemen. I hope I haven't kept you waiting.'

Despite his conciliatory words Bill's tone implied very clearly that he hoped exactly the opposite, and while Gerald treated him to a scowl of irritation Johnny Peacock leaned back in his chair behind the desk with a slightly mocking turn of lip.

'It's of no importance. We've had plenty family business to discuss.'

Bill seated himself in the spare chair facing Johnny wondering how good it would feel to smash his fist into that too handsome face as he played the old isolating game again; we are kin, but you are odd man out.

'I hear your prospecting in the Gilbury area has been successful. You've found more coal.' He said bluntly, and Gerald nodded.

'If you want a share in this mine you'll have to come up with your portion of the costs, and that will include geologist's fees and all that goes with securing the mine for ourselves, then there will be new equipment to purchase.'

'Thank you, Gerald, but I have no wish to buy into the new mine.'

'You haven't?'

Gerald's surprise was echoed in Johnny's raised eyebrows and slightly open mouth and Bill, enjoying the moment to the full, pressed on.

'I have my own plans for the future and shall be opening a new business within the next two months. I won't bore you with the details at the moment, especially as I still have a number of small matters to clear up before it commences, but I'm sure you'll appreciate that any spare energies I have must be directed towards my new venture.'

A heavy silence fell, and the two men regarded him with distrust. Eventually Johnny spoke.

'You mean you've bothered to come here just to say that? You could have sent us both a note, or even told us that you were not interested in expanding your mining investments with the rest of us.'

'Now there's a point of view.' Bill smiled thinly

and crossed his knees. 'It seems strange that you both consider I should have kept you informed of my every move when I have no recollection of either of you telling me about the prospecting. I had to learn of that through local gossip.'

Gerald shifted uncomfortably. 'Well, we're telling you now. We didn't think you would have the spare capital to invest in the search.'

'You could still have informed me and given me the option.'

Johnny cut in sharply. 'It hardly matters now does it? You aren't interested. It beats me why you came here this morning at all.'

'Oh, I had a reason, you may be sure.'

Taking two long envelopes out of his inside jacket pocket Bill handed one to each of the men and sat back to watch as they opened them, not bothering to hide his satisfaction. Gerald Fairburn read in silence for a few moments then looked up, first at Bill and then across the desk at the furious Johnny who had risen threateningly, the document still in his hand.

'Exactly what do you call this?' He snarled, waving it in Bill's face. 'Is it some kind of financial blackmail?'

Gerald gave him a warning look. 'Sit down John, and keep calm.'

'Sound advice. Maybe you'd better take it.'

Deflating like a pricked balloon Johnny reseated himself with reluctance as the older man asked. 'Will you be good enough to explain what this means? You must know that we can't possibly agree to this new leasing price for the Kenhope land.'

Bill looked unperturbed. 'As I recall, it was yourselves and Thomas Peacock who insisted upon the clause for a review to take place after seven years, and that time is now only months away. I always imagined that you had thought that up as a way to dislodge me at that stage if you possibly could, but maybe I'm wrong. Anyway, that will be the new price if you still wish to continue leasing the Kenhope land from my family, so I'll leave you to discuss the matter and let me know your intentions within a month.'

He stood up to leave and Johnny stood up again with him, his mood ugly.

'If we pull out you'll have no steady income, any of you, and you'll also have put over forty men out of work. Don't think for one moment that we'll be taking the blame for that, Robinson! We'll make quite sure that every man and woman in the area knows exactly who's responsible for their predicament.'

Having moved across the room during the tirade Bill now turned to face Johnny as he opened the door a fraction ready to leave.

'You seem to forget that I have had experience of the difficulties of mining for almost seven years and am no longer the novice I was before. If you both leave, the mine will carry on. You can pay the increased rate or allow me to buy you out. Either way, I can't lose.'

'You can lose if we take the equipment out, and that is all ours remember?'

'Hmm. A risky if not impossible business, don't you think? Might lead to a nasty accident or two during the actual operation, for which you would

217

both definitely be responsible. However, in view of that threat, I'll make enquiries about buying my own equipment so that the mine would only be closed for as long as it took to reinstate. Of course that would result in a drastic reduction of the buying out price to yourselves, but it's up to you.'

Leaving them staring after him Bill walked into the hall, retrieved his hat and coat once more and strolled back into the sunshine with a spring in his step that had not been there for some time. He had almost reached the gates when a light female voice called. 'How are you, Mr Robinson? Well I hope, on this lovely morning.'

He halted, looking in the direction of the sound, and saw a woman whom he could not quite place yet who seemed to be vaguely familiar. Her blonde hair was tied back with a blue ribbon giving her a childlike appearance which was heightened by the grubbiness covering her skirt, hessian apron and well worn jacket. In her hands she was holding a seed tray full of uprooted bedding plants, and she was smiling broadly through a pair of steel-rimmed spectacles.

'You don't recognise me, do you?'

'I'm sorry. I feel I should know you but I can't quite...'

'Bella. Bella Peacock.'

'Bella?'

She laughed. 'It's my gardening clothes. That's why you didn't know me. I get rather dirty sometimes but it's worth it. Haven't you noticed the difference in our gardens this summer?'

Wishing he had been light-hearted enough to

concern himself with such things, Bill smiled. 'They've been beautiful. Congratulations.'

As he touched his hat and walked out onto the road he heard her cheerfully promise. 'Wait until next year. They'll be even better.'

From the study window where he had witnessed the encounter Johnny tightened his lips in anger, cursing his wife for adding her particular brand of insult to Bill Robinson's injury.

'Will you look at Bella?' He unguardedly complained to Gerald. 'I think it was better when she laid about the house all day, or played her piano, instead of roaming the grounds like a scarecrow for all to see.'

Gerald rose and looked over his son-in-law's shoulder at his daughter briskly going about her business without seeming to have a care in the world.

'Well, one thing's for sure, John. It's the first time I've seen her looking happy since she left home, even her mother agrees to that, and she soon tidies herself up when she comes indoors.'

'Oh quite, quite.'

Realising his faux pas Johnny waved to Elisabeth who was walking across the lawn towards Bella, then crossed to the sideboard to pour a drink for Gerald and himself.

'Help yourself to a cigar. The box is on the desk.' He invited gloomily. 'We have plenty to think about now.'

Outside Bella hurried in the direction of the potting shed with her mother at her heels. Elisabeth had a letter in her hands, and as it was probably a further chapter from Constance she guessed that she would have to listen to yet another mournful monologue from her parent on the activities of the Suffragettes.

'I'll just put these plants on the shelf for Daniel to see to later, then we'll go inside and I'll clean myself up before lunch.' She promised. 'I take it you're worrying about Constance again.'

Elisabeth waved the letter towards Bella. 'It's all getting too much. I just fret all the time. She tells me that a friend of hers has died in prison from being forcibly fed, and that she has recently been through the ordeal herself but has learnt to vomit it all back later! Can you credit it? She actually writes about it in a letter!'

Bella laid down her burden with a short sigh of relief and a feeling of growing depression.

'It seems much worse to think of her doing those things than merely writing about them. She's so brave, mother. Why aren't you proud of her?'

'Brave? Proud? Have you gone mad, Bella? All I want is for her to come home instead of worrying me all the time!'

Coming across the lawn with his spade Daniel Heslop heard the twitter of disagreeing females before actually sighting his employer and Mrs Fairburn, and he doubled back towards the shrubbery with long swift strides. Mrs Bella would be all quiet and moody again now, just as she always was after her parents had visited, but at least he would have the garden to himself for the rest of the day and that was a rare treat in itself.

Down the slope, hidden by the bushes, he sat

down on a large rock and viewed the panorama around and below him. The chapel, the Assembly Rooms looking down onto Gilfell, and immediately in his line of vision, Ivy House, where he could see Lilian Robinson sewing at the sitting room window as Bill walked in at the front door. Idly he watched, expecting her to get up and go to meet him or to see him come to the window to speak to her, but nothing happened. Bill disappeared into the house and Lilian remained exactly where she was without so much as lifting her head.

CHAPTER SEVEN

Spring 1914

'I think you'd better go home now, Louisa, before the snow gets worse. The wind's rising and the lanes and roads will be blocked with drifts in no time, so it's doubtful that you'll be able to come back tomorrow.'

James, looking into the kitchen through the door he was holding open, glanced back at the yard where snowflakes the size of half crown pieces were turning the air into a moving curtain of white. Louisa nodded and began to put away the dishes she had been washing.

'That's good of you, James. The school will be shutting soon if the last blizzard is anything to go by, and Helen will need me to be at home to let her in. I'll just finish clearing the crockery then I'll get my coat.'

'I'll take you home on the trap and then go down to the store, so if you want anything from there I'll drop it off for you on my way home. Don't be long.'

He disappeared abruptly as the door closed again while the occasional howl of the approaching gale threatened Louisa's peace of mind as she hurried to get ready, and she cast her eye quickly over Roughside kitchen before stepping out after her employer. Her coat was warm, but it would shortly be wet, and as she tucked her scarf round her head and into her collar she shivered, taking James' hand to help her up onto the seat of the trap.

They spoke only when they had to on the journey to the village, but their silence was companionable. Louisa had worked for James Rutherford for two years now and they had become accustomed to each other's ways to the point where they used first names when alone, only now and again letting them slip out when in company. Louisa had found it hard to understand James' insistence on observing the convention of giving each other their full title before any third party, for to her it seemed natural after all this time, but since he had once gruffly explained that he was guarding her reputation from the more deadly of the village gossips she had thanked him and protested no more. The idea of anyone gossiping about herself and James Rutherford had affected her strangely, and sometimes still did. Until then she had never thought of James as anything except a kindly employer, yet she realised that he must have privately entertained the possibility of being more otherwise he would not have acted as he had, and the notion had made her feel awkward in his company for a while until his continuing failure to advance matters finally reassured her.

By the time he dropped her off at Hillary Terrace the snow was at a depth of almost five inches and its unbroken line to her yard showed that Helen had not yet arrived from school, but she had not been in the house many minutes when the sound of childish voices preceded the opening of the back door and Helen, Edward, and Winifred came bursting in, their clothing liberally marked by the force of recent snowballs and their eyes sparkling with excitement.

'Aunty Lilian isn't in, so Winnie and Ted have come here.' Helen panted, throwing off her coat as she turned back to her friends. 'Come on. Take your wet things off.'

Louisa smiled. 'Sit down at the table and I'll make a meal, then we'll see if we can find your mother.'

She spread their coats along the arms and seats of the fireside chairs then stirred up the smoking coals into a cheery blaze, trying not to look as worried as she felt at the sight of the storm. Lilian would be at Leo Bondini's cottage, a mile below Gilfell, and although it was situated near the Back Road the blinding ferocity of the blizzard would blank out all landmarks. It had happened before when people got lost and were not found until it was too late.

Working to prepare the meal as quickly as possible she wondered how Bill Robinson might feel should his wife die in the storm, for it had been obvious to her for a long time that their marriage was a sham and that Lilian's underlying unhappiness was in direct consequence of this: not that she did not make every effort to hide her real feelings, and probably succeeded in fooling everyone except those closest to her. Marion Robinson always struck Louisa as being quietly aware of the barrier between her son and daughter-in-law, but whether she knew the reason for it, or was as ignorant as she was herself, Louisa did not know. Lilian had never mentioned their quarrel since the night she had gone down to see Bill then heard him shouting at Lilian in his study, but she could still recall the words she had uttered afterwards.

'Bill and I ... we're finished.'

James was coming out of the store when he saw a tall figure moving through the storm, bracing with difficulty against the strengthening gale, and he loaded his supplies in the back of the trap and called to her.

'Lilian! Is that you?'

She was wet, exhausted and anxious, and almost fell into the trap in her relief.

'I need to get home, Dad. School's closed and there's no one at home yet. I met Mrs Wallace with her family ten minutes ago and she told me.'

James' mouth tightened with disapproval and he turned the pony to face the journey home, thankful that the wind would now be at their backs.

'I'll tell you this much, my lass. I'm considering giving Bondini notice to quit the cottage and, hopefully, the area. Three or four months' stay, he said, and it's now two years and he's still here. Doing what, I ask myself, and why? If he really was with a theatrical company why isn't he still with them? He isn't an old man.'

'I'm sure I don't know. He gives music lessons all over the neighbourhood and has been giving me mine this morning.'

'Then he lets you walk home in this storm by yourself?'

Lilian fell silent, shivering as a gust of east wind chilled her. It would be useless trying to invent a plausible excuse when the real one was simply that Bill had threatened her should there ever be any gossip about herself and the Italian, causing her to vehemently refuse the man's offer to escort her.

Although they often sang together locally, Leo Bondini was now himself a leading figure in the musical life of Gilfell Moor and neighbouring Dalton, and also sang with various other performers too. A concert party had been formed, often travelling far afield during the summer months, but as Bill's new business had become involved from the start no harm was done to her reputation.

The bus, now expanded into two buses with a third one planned for the future, had arrived with its hired driver/mechanic just over a year ago after the garage and adjacent living quarters were completed. The first vehicle was a draughty affair in bad weather with a large glassless area by the door and a windscreen that opened out in heavy rain or snow, supposedly to enable the driver to see the way ahead more clearly, but the miners living in outlying places who were transported to and from their shifts were fascinated by the vehicle which displayed the name Lacre and had only come on the market the previous year. The second bus, which Bill often drove himself, was used for more sociable reasons like the concert party dates, local market days, and twice weekly excursions to Dalton's moving picture palace where longer films had recently become part of

226

the programme.

Outwardly relaxed and genial, Bill appeared just the same as ever to everyone except his wife who felt the strain of daily play acting more acutely than she would admit.

Dropping her off at Ivy House a short while later James refused her invitation to have lunch before going home, and Lilian had expected nothing less knowing how quickly the roads could be blocked in such a storm.

'I think the children will be at Louisa's.' He shouted above the wind. 'She tells me they often go to her house and Helen would come with them from school.'

Believing him to be right Lilian hurried inside to change into some dry clothes, hesitating only a moment beside the new telephone that Bill had installed in the passage at the same time as the one in the garage. Would he be there now if she rang? She knew that he would come to her assistance at once, but he would also be angry that she had not been at home when the children came from school. Reluctantly abandoning the idea she ran up the stairs to her bedroom to change.

This particular blizzard was late in the season. It would bring all travelling to an abrupt halt for its duration and Lilian felt helplessly frustrated, as though the elements had brought about the fourth paralysis of the winter just to annoy her. A concert party date was due in Kenhope Village Hall on the evening of Saturday 2nd May, but as that was a mere four days away she did not doubt that the affair would be cancelled due to impassable roads and her small beacon of excitement extinguished yet again.

Since the secret breakdown of her marriage Lilian had relied heavily upon her singing activities to bring some personal meaning to her life, and the music together with her children brought her a solace she could not have done without. Left alone by her husband most of the time, as he was either driving or working in the study, she found the house she had once loved feeling more and more like a prison and became eager to escape its walls as often as possible. Winters were bad, with the few concerts being confined to the local Assembly Rooms, and during her long days and nights spent indoors Lilian sometimes pondered bleakly upon her future once Edward and Winifred were grown up. With searing honesty she admitted to herself that her voice would be past its best by then and her family living their own lives, where her part would probably be small. What then?

Reaching into her wardrobe for her thickest coat she heard a loud thumping noise from the direction of the back door while, at the same time, the telephone began to ring. Hurrying downstairs she found the children and Louisa in the yard and kissed them all in her relief as they crowded round the fire to get warm, then hastened out to the passage lifting the receiver from its hook.

'Hello?'

'Are you alright? Are the children home yet?'

'Yes Bill. We're all here.'

Polite words spoken in politely distant voices.

'Albert and I are taking the buses over to

228

Kenhope while it's still reasonably penetrable, and when we've brought the local lads back to the village we'll be moving down the moor towards Dalton once the snow stops. The Kenhope village men will tackle the fell road as usual.'

'Thank you for letting me know.'

Abruptly the line went dead as Bill replaced his receiver and Lilian sighed as she did the same. By now she should be used to their communications, bereft as they were of such things as goodbyes, but the coldness of them still depressed her.

Walking back into the kitchen she smiled at Louisa who was urging Helen not to remove her coat as they would have to go back up the Terrace in a very short while before the track was completely buried.

'That was Bill. He and his driver are going to bring back the miners then they'll be taking a bus with as many volunteers as they can muster to clear the road between here and Dalton as soon as the snowfall stops. What a job! All those men with spades clearing the road yard by yard, and if it starts again later their hard work will be cancelled out.'

Louisa grimaced sympathetically and Lilian gave a small hollow laugh as she added 'It's exactly like life really, isn't it?'

Bill took out his fob watch and tried to ignore the weariness that weighed more heavily upon him with every passing minute.

'One o'clock. We'd better get started. Everything's in the bus I think, but we'd better check before starting off.'

Two miners recently brought home from Kenhope were rolling a drum of petrol back into position in the corner of the yard after the vehicle's fuel tank had been topped up, and six others stood ready to board, their spades in their gloved hands. Albert came out of the garage carrying a pair of lanterns which he set on the ground before locking the doors.

'Everything else is loaded?'

'Yes.'

Bill looked grimly at the uneven blanket of snow now lying under a clear starry sky. Gusts of wind blew clouds of stinging white powder from its miniature slopes, smarting on the faces of the men as they walked to the road to begin their task. They would be lucky to advance two miles before morning with the bus following behind ready to provide shelter when necessary and bring them back home when they could go no further. If they were fortunate they would meet up with a similar team of snow clearers working their way up the valley from Dalton, but they all knew that was unlikely and that the long night would, in all probability, be followed by a long day tomorrow when another voluntary shift would take the place of the present one to forge a passage through snow almost three feet deep in the worst drifts, the lifespan of which could either be mercifully short or long enough to have a stranglehold on the villages in its grip.

Already beginning to grow drowsy in the icy air the men set to work with a determination they did not really feel but which would help them to build up some more body heat.

No one spoke much as shovel after shovel of snow was thrown to each side of the road to make a single track with an occasional passing bay, and from her bedroom window a few yards away Marion Robinson tightly clutched the blanket she had wrapped around her night clothes as she watched them making their slow progress. Even in the bedroom her breath vaporised in the extreme temperature and her heart went out to the men, all volunteers, who served their village so well each winter. Bill, typically, never missed going out 'clearing' and worked with everyone else instead of taking refuge in driving the bus as many in his position would have done, yet it had seemed to her for some time that he seized any opportunity to be somewhere other than his home.

Shivering, she returned to her bed. Her joints ached continuously these days and she had forgotten how it felt not to be tired, especially in a winter like this one that didn't seem to know when to stop. Through half closed eyes she lay watching the dim glow of the lanterns, and occasionally the brighter light of the bus headlights as it moved a few yards further on, but as darkness slowly replaced them she drifted uneasily back into sleep.

Over three hours later the team had advanced a mile and a half towards Dalton and decided to call a halt for the night. The wind had dropped and the still cloudless sky suggested that the blizzard might be over, hopefully for good. Straightening their aching backs the men banged their spades briskly on the ground to knock off excess snow and made for the door of the bus as

Bill got into the driver's seat. It was then that the irregular mound just ahead of where they had finished digging showed signs of being something other than mere snow, and the man left the motor running as he hurried off the vehicle with the rest of the team at his heels.

Nobody spoke as they drew level with the body but all bent down to clear away the snow with their hands, revealing more and more of the man's dark coat that had become visible in the lights of the bus. Breathing through their mouths in their haste they scrabbled frantically to push away the snow from the storm's victim, and Bill smoothed the man's face clear as he took off his gloves to feel for the neck pulse beneath the sodden clothes.

'There's a faint beat.' He said tersely. 'Let's get him on the bus.'

'Poor bugger's had it.' Someone muttered as they laid the man down along the back seat a few minutes later, but no one replied. After the last few hours this unfortunate half-dead stranger was a dismal end to their efforts and they all knew well enough that his survival would be unlikely after such savage exposure. Covering him with the blankets they had brought they made their way back to Gilfell as fast as conditions would allow, stopping en route at the home of Dr Hatton where, to combat the intense cold, a fire still burned in the surgery waiting room.

Most of the clearing team walked off to their homes as soon as they had helped the doctor to remove the man's wet clothes and wrap him in warm dry blankets in front of the hearth. Bill looked miserably across at the doctor over the man's body.

'It looks as though he may be going to recover after all … do you want me to stay?'

The older man shook his head. 'I'll do what I can to help him, Bill, and I know what it will entail. Just get along to your bed.'

'None of us know who he is. Do you recognise him?'

'He arrived in the area recently to work on a farm down Gilbury way. You know how Len will always serve people at any time in weather like this, and with the stuff we found shop wrapped in his coat pockets he must have been on his way home from there and become disorientated. He was probably wandering about in circles for hours before he finally fell … wish him luck.'

Trying not to see the grim look in Dr Hatton's eyes Bill thankfully left him with his new patient and let himself out again into the night. He badly wanted to be out of earshot if the man came round for he had experienced such a near fatality before and knew what unspeakable agony recovery was for an almost frozen man, but he had just successfully turned the starting handle and was climbing into the vehicle when the screams began. Hastily he shut the door of the cab and took his seat behind the wheel, urging the engine into greater and noisier life whilst trying not to notice how his hands were shaking.

Lilian heard about the stranger's brush with death a few days later, but the news came via one of the snow clearing team's wives whom she met on her way to Roughside on the following Saturday morning. Afterwards she tried to ignore the sinking of her spirits at yet another incident where communication between Bill and herself had been nil and concentrated her attention on the fact that the snow had finally gone and spring was in the air at last. It was the birdsong that made everything seem more cheerful, and the clear sky, although she was carrying her umbrella as a safeguard.

Bill had taken the children down to Dalton on the bus half an hour earlier and, feeling more hurt than usual to be excluded on such a morning, she had decided to pay a surprise visit to her father, purposely taking the Back Road to avoid passing Louisa's home. It was not that she did not want to see her friend but that she did not wish to be sidetracked if she were seen passing by; on her way home she would travel via Hillary Terrace and call upon Louisa then.

Half an hour later, as she passed through the gate into Roughside yard, the first sight to meet her eyes was Helen Marshall sitting on the kitchen step playing with two kittens. Surprised, she halted a moment before walking towards the girl who stood up smiling at her approach.

'Hello, Aunty Lilian. Mam and Uncle James are in the kitchen. Do you like Tiger and Marmalade?'

'They're lovely, Helen.'

Stroking the tabby kitten and then the yellow one as Helen held them out, one in each hand, Lilian tried hard not to give in to the uncharitable irritation that this intrusion was causing and knocked briefly on the door before walking into her old home.

For a moment no one spoke. James and Louisa were sitting at the table pressed close together holding hands, and they both stared at Lilian as though struck dumb. She stared back at them for a few seconds then turned blindly to leave.

'Wait! Lilian!'

James' chair fell back with a crash as he jumped to his feet, crossing the floor to take her arm, and when he steered her towards the seat at the table opposite Louisa she sank into it thankfully as her knees buckled. Louisa watched Lilian with frightened eyes but could think of nothing to say.

'We need to talk to you.' James announced with a firmness he was far from feeling, and when Lilian looked up at him he flinched slightly.

'Well, I hardly have to ask what you wish to discuss, do I? It's very obvious what has been going on between you!'

His hand was on her shoulder as though its desperate pressure could alter her attitude, and she turned abruptly to shake it off as he spoke again.

'There's been nothing going on between us, Lilian, but I have asked Louisa to marry me and she has said "Yes".'

He walked slowly back to his seat and Lilian looked incredulously from one to the other.

'Marriage? You're old enough to be her father! How can either of you even contemplate such a thing?'

Louisa ventured a reply. 'We're lonely.'

'Lonely!' The word was halfway between a laugh and a sob and Lilian repeated it with venom as she stood up, her knuckles whitening as she gripped her umbrella. 'Let me tell you both something; neither of you know the meaning of the word! Try living with someone who will hardly speak to you. Someone who tells you that you have no longer got a place in his life, but if you leave he is keeping your children!'

'Lilian, what is all this...?'

James began to stand up, his expression both pleading and uncertain, and Lilian, on the verge of hysteria, raised her arm and brought her umbrella down on his head with a sickening thump. He recoiled and fell back against Louisa's chair, holding his hands to his face where a thin trickle of blood was now oozing out of his hair-line, and Louisa screamed as she held out both arms in front of him in a protective movement.

'You're disgusting! I never want to see either of you again! Sneaking around behind my back ... behind everybody's back...'

Stalking to the door Lilian paused for one last look behind her, although her tears distorted the image of both her father and her once best friend, and the last words she heard were from James as he begged. 'Look lass, please wait and we'll talk...'

Wide-eyed Helen Marshall sat hunched up on the side of the doorstep and looked fearfully at Lilian as she swept out of the house, skirts flying as she ran across the yard leaving the big gate wide open before rushing down the lane out of sight. The child had heard every word of the quarrel and knew now that her mother was going to marry Uncle James. Helen did not really know whether she was pleased about this or not, but if Aunty Lilian did not like the idea then she felt sure she would not like it either.

The excited shrieks of Edward and Winifred echoed round the long wide room at the side of Dalton's Market Hall, but Bill was oblivious to their noise and unruly behaviour as they chased each other between the double line of tables. Marion sighed and put her hands over her ears in protest.

'Make less racket, children, please. I can't even hear myself think, let alone listen to what your father is trying to tell me.'

Glancing at his offspring in quick irritation Bill roared 'Be quiet!' only once before peace was restored, Edward and Winifred reluctantly seating themselves on one of the long benches lying against the wall.

'The machines arrive next week, and I'm having extra gas brackets put in the walls so that the women will still be able to see no matter what time of day it is.' He enthused. 'They will be seated down the middle of the room looking out towards the windows or gaslights, as the case may be, so there will be no eyestrain to cause headaches. I already have two expert seamstresses ready to take charge of a line each so I'm leaving the hiring of their team to them; after all, they know more of what is required than I do.'

His mother nodded, although she still looked slightly bemused.

'How on earth did you get into the military uniforms business with no experience, Bill?'

'It's a sub-contract from a firm in the north-east, but when I've had a few months to find my feet I'll tender on my own behalf because there'll be plenty of money in it soon, believe me.'

'Oh Bill, you don't believe all this war talk as well, do you? Gilbert seems to be incapable of discussing anything else these days.'

Walking across to the nearest window Marion stared through its dirty panes at the back stretch of wasteland leading down to the river. She was chilled by this continuous speculation about a possible war in Europe, and wondered whether it had ever occurred to her sons that if Britain became involved they might both be fighting in it instead of running their respective businesses.

'Maybe it would have been wiser to have stayed with what you are familiar with and not sold the mine to that Reddings company who had plenty pits of their own. We were doing well enough with it, weren't we? And after the effort it took to keep the place going after the others pulled out, I would have thought you'd want to hang on to the Kenhope mine just to show them how wrong they were.'

Raising a warning finger at his son and daughter who were beginning to slap each other playfully, Bill walked to Marion's side and said quietly. 'We all got a tidy sum from that sale, Mam. Are you complaining?'

'Of course I'm not. I just can't understand your motive for letting the mine go when you could easily have borrowed the money to start this place. You know what you told me once about needing collateral to secure a bank loan, and the

238

mine was surely that.'

'The sale of the mine left me with enough to invest without the need to borrow from a bank, and I had a personal reason for letting Redding and Company have Kenhope. Mining's a dirty business in more ways than one. Even when I was only Peacock's Chief Clerk I never felt comfortable knowing that children were employed to sort both coal and lead before going on to a miner's life cut short by the 'black spit'. Haven't you noticed how many young widows live in Gilfell? Women married to miners who died before reaching forty, leaving their children and wives to follow in their footsteps in order to keep body and soul together? A vicious circle of mine owners' greed and mine workers' need, and although I tried to make better conditions for the men at Kenhope I could only do so up to a point, but there'll come a day of reckoning there, mark my words.'

'At Kenhope?'

'At every mine! Especially with a war coming when coal will be more important than ever, yet the men will still be expected to work for a pittance and their women and children the same. Men like Fairburn and Peacock need a lesson.'

She nodded, seeing his jaw tighten as what she had privately come to call Bill's Grey Devil settled on his shoulders. Whatever it was that had caused it Marion knew that it had begun at the same time as his marriage had foundered, and the cause of that was also a mystery. Sure that had there been any gossip regarding either Bill or Lilian she would have heard it, Marion was completely bewildered by whatever had come between them replacing their once warm relationship with such unrelenting coldness. They spoke to each other only when circumstances dictated, and sometimes with a forced cordiality that was painful to see, yet she could sense no lover in the background for either of them.

Anxious to smooth over his ruffled feelings she placed a conciliatory hand on his arm.

'I'm sure you know exactly what you're doing, Bill. Now, shall we take these two young people for lemonade and cakes as we promised? We should just have enough time before your passengers gather at the bus for the journey home.'

Ten minutes later they were seated in The Primrose Cafe eating cakes with the now silently absorbed children when the door opened and a cheerful female voice exclaimed 'Ah! The Robinson family! I'm waiting to ride home on your bus. May I sit with you?'

Bill stood up, trying to make his sociability seem stronger than his surprise, and Marion moved over as he slid a chair from a neighbouring table into place for Constance Fairburn.

'Thanks Bill.' She grinned up at him without affectation. 'Are you driving this wonderful vehicle I've heard so much about?'

He smiled. 'I am indeed, but surely you've seen plenty buses in Manchester and London.'

'One or two.'

Edward nudged his grandmother and enquired in a clear voice. 'Who is this lady?'

'This, children, is Miss Constance Fairburn, daughter of a previous business associate of your father's.'

Constance raised her eyebrows. 'Previous? Have you parted company?'

'Fairly recently, yes.' Turning quickly as he resumed his seat Bill beckoned the waitress to order more tea and cakes for Constance, who added a request of her own.

'And an ashtray, if you please, or an old saucer if you don't have such a thing.'

The woman stiffened. 'An ashtray?'

'Certainly.' Opening her handbag Constance took out a cigarette holder, silver cigarette case and a box of matches, proceeding to place a cigarette in the tortoiseshell holder and light it, blowing a cloud of smoke towards the waitress as she explained further in a tone of cheerful patience. 'You see, when this cigarette has burned for a while ash forms on the end of it and if I don't have an ashtray it will fall over the table, probably onto the food.'

Embarrassed, Bill and Marion tried to ignore the way the entire room was intent upon watching the exchange, the only sound being Winifred's giggle as she saw the funny lady doing such strange things, and the waitress vanished into the kitchen returning a few seconds later with a chipped blue saucer which she placed rather forcefully beside Constance.

Marion, looking offended, said to Bill. 'Maybe it would be better if I took the children out now.'

'I don't think so...' He began, but his mother was already on her feet commanding her grandchildren to follow her out of the cafe, which they did amid much grumbling that they had not finished. Constance watched them go with unconcealed amusement.

'I'm sorry, Bill. I seem to have offended your mother.'

He smiled, feeling somewhat more relaxed without Marion. 'Never mind. Are you home for good now or only for a while? How are things with the Suffragettes?'

Her eyes clouded slightly, and she looked down at the tablecloth for a second before answering.

'I've decided to do something more constructive in future. It was fun at first, you know, I won't deny that, but people have been getting themselves killed and lately some of the movement have taken to setting churches on fire because the clergy won't speak out on our behalf. It isn't that I'm religious, but it's all a bit extreme even for me. Then there's all this talk about war, so I've decided I would be better employed as a nurse of some kind.' Her black eyes stared into his and she added quickly 'Please don't laugh.'

'I wasn't going to.'

That at least was the truth, as amazement was what he was feeling, not mirth. Hesitantly he said. 'Nurses perform a great many rather basic tasks, Constance. Do you feel you could be happy in such a job?'

'Basic?' She gave him a swift mocking glance, tapping the first of her cigarette ash into the saucer. 'I've been in prison, Bill, twice as a matter of fact, and nothing is much more basic than that.'

The return of the waitress with Constance's tea and cakes saved Bill the need to reply and, later, when he stopped the bus at the end of Low Shields drive, he wondered just what kind of reaction she would get at home to her latest scheme. The children smiled at her and bid her goodbye, fascinated by this colourful friendly woman, but Marion merely nodded icily and turned her head away as the bus drove off, feeling angry with her son for waving as he had. Constance Fairburn had always been a law unto herself, but to smoke cigarettes in public was outrageous!

Something was wrong. Lilian lay still in her bed trying to work out what it was as the green and gold colours of her bedroom filtered through her half closed eyes. Yesterday had been terrible, of course, and she had spent most of the night weeping over her father's intended marriage to Louisa, but it was more than that. Her body felt strange somehow, and she was hot and sickly.

Thinking that it might be better just to keep on the go she pushed back the covers to get up, then found she could not move her legs! Again and again she tried to shift her limbs but they lay useless on the mattress, and in panic she began to shout for her husband. It seemed an age to her, although it was in fact only two minutes, before the bedroom door was flung open and Bill stood looking down at her in angry disbelief.

'What on earth has got into you, Lilian? The entire village must be listening to you shrieking like a fishwife and the children think you're dying!'

Once more she tried to rise, lifting herself up on one elbow while her face contorted in an effort rendered almost superhuman by her fear, but in vain nevertheless. Defeated, she sank back on her pillows and began to plead indistinctly through a bout of weeping.

'For heaven's sake get Dr Hatton! I can't get up!'

Emma Hartley, for the past twelve months Emma Dallow, kept quite still as she listened at her husband's study door, determined to hear why James Rutherford and Louisa Marshall had called upon him together and in such a manner of harassed intimacy. They seemed to be both happy and bothered about something, and if her suspicions were correct she could guess why. Scarcely breathing she leaned forward to get her ear as near to the thick oak door as possible, and her eyes widened as the words 'banns' and 'wedding' floated into her hearing. She had been busy preparing the Sunday lunch, which they always ate late due to the first service of the Sabbath taking up so much of the morning, and still held her oven cloth in her hands, twisting it convulsively as the voices rose and fell.

Suddenly there came the sound of papers rustling on her husband's desk, almost always a sign to a frequently eavesdropping Emma that an interview was ending, and she scurried soundlessly back along the narrow passage to her kitchen, pushing the door to behind her. Within seconds she heard the trio emerging and was careful to chink some dishes together as though she had been working all the while, then ran the tap into the sink for good measure. Emma's actions were as unnecessary as they were sly because Victor would naturally tell her all about their visit over lunch, but since becoming his wife the woman had derived great pleasure out of beating him to it whilst keeping him in ignorance of her new pastime.

Humming softly to herself, she was standing at the stove testing her pans of vegetables with a fork when the front door closed behind James and Louisa, but instead of coming straight on into the kitchen Victor's footsteps returned only as far as his study. Annoyed, Emma dropped all pretence of having been engrossed in her work since their arrival and tripped lightly back up the passage to make enquiries. Victor offered his wife an odd little half-smile from behind his desk, where he appeared to be doing absolutely nothing, and she raised her eyebrows.

'What did they want?'

'To raise Cain I think.'

'What?'

Victor sighed. 'They want to get married as soon as possible, and I'm trying not to think of the trouble it may cause with James' family.'

'With Lilian you mean.' Emma corrected as a gleam of satisfaction showed in her eyes. 'Oh, I think there'll be trouble alright. Knowing James' daughter, you can quite safely rely on that!'

'Now, my dear, don't let's cross our bridges before we come to them. Lilian may well be delighted. Louisa is her best friend after all.'

Emma looked down at him in silence, wondering if he really didn't realise that Louisa being Lilian's friend would be the main cause of any turbulence that might lie ahead, then she turned and walked to the door saying lightly over her shoulder. 'Lunch is in five minutes, Victor.'

'Good.' He shifted things on his desk ready to return to them after the meal, then stood up and followed his wife. 'I'm ready for it, I'll admit.'

Outside in the trap Helen watched her mother and Uncle James being shown out of the Dallows' home by the smiling preacher, and bent her attention determinedly upon the doll she had been allowed to bring with her. Surely her mother could have waited after chapel to see Mr Dallow instead of going home first and waiting for Uncle James to come. Of course it was true that they had travelled in the pony and trap which she always enjoyed, but life was becoming rather peculiar all the same. Her mother had not noticed her in the same way since yesterday when Aunty Lilian had been so upset, nor had she actually told her that she was going to marry Uncle James. Looking at the man from under her fringe, as the couple advanced on her across the fine gravel, Helen felt the first stirrings of resentment knowing that her life was due to change, yet no one had actually told her so to her face. It was as if she no longer mattered.

Climbing into the trap Louisa gave her daughter a quick smile from the front seat she was sharing with James, then resumed the discussion they had been having as he got up beside her and they started on the journey to Hillary Terrace.

As they approached Chapel Corner Helen made up her mind exactly what she would do upon reaching home, and within ten minutes of going into her house she escaped unnoticed then ran helter skelter back towards Ivy House to see Edward and Winifred.

CHAPTER EIGHT

Johnny lifted his head from the Gilbury Mine Ledger and stared in angry disbelief at the horse drawn dray pulling into the depot entrance with its outgoing load still intact. This was the second order to return in such a way, and if it continued the situation could very easily panic him. On his way outside he tapped a brief tattoo on the door next to his own where Gerald Fairburn was busy making up wages for their workforce, and as he heard the door open he called over his shoulder 'Harry Benson's brought back his load now. I'm going to get to the bottom of it if I have to go down to The Station Hotel myself this very second!'

The older man followed his son-in-law at a slower pace, grimacing at the rain as they emerged into the muddy yard. Beneath his mild exterior Gerald was as worried as Johnny but refused to show the workers how agitated he felt, either by rushing about like a madman or bullying them for things which were not their fault. Now, as he watched Johnny marching towards the dismounting Harry, he indulged in one last gulp of tobacco smoke before removing his pipe and calling across to the two men.

'Wait a moment. Don't start to unload until we've talked.'

Johnny spun round. 'Talked? About what, pray?

It hardly takes a genius to work out that Reddings have undercut our prices again and we have lost two more customers in a week.'

Harry nodded at Gerald, his expression apologetic. 'Sorry Mr Fairburn. Reddings' man called on them a few days ago, as seems to be happening everywhere, and his quotation for a ton was so much lower than ours that they went over to him.'

Johnny's scowl deepened. 'How kind of them to let us know.'

'They gave me this letter.'

Taking a grubby envelope from his jacket pocket the man handed it past Johnny to Gerald, who thanked him as he slit it open and read the short message inside. As he refolded the page to return it to its envelope he suggested. 'The best plan now will be for you to get back down to Dalton with that load and offer it to householders round the streets. They'll take it at our regular price so we won't lose out on it.'

Harry Benson's face mirrored his dismay very clearly as Gerald finished speaking, and the man added quickly. 'Put the team undercover with their nosebags and have your own meal first.'

In the office Johnny stood with his back to the pot bellied stove and frowned heavily in spite of its warmth; they could lay the blame for this growing catastrophe firmly at Bill Robinson's door, and he still had a tenuous hold on their affairs by transporting many of the local miners over to the Kenhope pit where pay had remained marginally better than what they could offer. Fortunately, the sometimes ferocious winter weather that occasionally prevented the bus from making its journey was enough to make the more cautious men decide to stay in Gilbury, but this price cutting of Reddings would be hard to survive. He glared at Gerald, irritated by his calm.

'How wonderful to be so lacking in imagination that you can't see how this could end for us.' He snapped, and Gerald retorted sharply.

'Save your sarcasm for those who may be impressed with it, John. Reddings have us by the throat now, which is probably just what Robinson intended to happen when he sold them the Kenhope mine.'

'We should have paid the higher rent when he demanded it and kept the place under our control.'

'Certainly. With the wisdom of hindsight we can clearly see exactly what would have been the wiser course to pursue, but we opted to start this place instead so we'll have to carefully think over how to keep it afloat.'

A sharp gust of wind blew the rain against the grimy office window, and Johnny's eyes followed the meandering trickles gloomily.

'They'll gradually take over all our customers and then, just before we sink without trace, make us an offer we'll be forced to accept. Maybe we'd be better trying to sell out now to a rival company of Reddings. At least we might stand a chance of avoiding too heavy a financial loss.'

'Maybe ... maybe.' Gerald, unconvinced that immediate surrender was desirable, reinstated his pipe feeling extremely depressed to discover that it had gone out. Reaching into his pocket for a box of matches he added. 'There's no point in being too hasty, John. If all these rumours of a European war turn out to be fact there'll be plenty custom for every mine in the land as the factories increase their demand and trains need more for extra journeys ... let's just hang on for now and try to compete until Reddings' threat is cancelled out by circumstances. War is a terrible thing, but there's many a fortune been made through it.'

'Hmm.'

Slightly mollified Johnny suggested. 'Well then, how about me going round our remaining customers in person offering whatever discount we can afford? Reddings don't do domestic deliveries so we don't need to concern ourselves with them, but the local big boys ... the schools, village halls, the other two Dalton Hotels and the theatres, we need to keep. I've got the motorcycle. I could start to visit them within the next half hour if we can agree to a new figure.'

His pipe lit now, Gerald seated himself behind his desk and pulled a notebook and pencil towards him.

'Good idea. Let's get it worked out, then you can be on your way.'

Bill stood just inside the bedroom door carefully avoiding his wife's eyes as Dr Hatton tried to solve the mystery of her paralysed legs. Reflexes had been tested and found to be intact while various other possibilities had also proved to be no answer to Lilian's affliction, and the older man lifted his patient's useless limbs back into bed and covered them up.

'I must admit that you have me puzzled.' He said honestly. 'I think we are going to need an expert opinion here and will gladly send for a Specialist to visit and give us the benefit of his superior knowledge, if you will agree to that.'

George Hatton raised an enquiring eyebrow towards Bill, who nodded.

'Of course. Whatever it takes.'

Lilian noticed that the doctor was the only one of the two men to actually bid her goodbye, and listened to hear what else they said to each other on their way downstairs as the bedroom door had been left ajar. George Hatton was again expressing his bewilderment that her illness could not be called a stroke, admitting that he was at a loss to know exactly what it was, and Bill was making non-committal muttering sounds that could have meant anything.

Elisabeth Fairburn looked out through the lounge windows at the long stretch of rain-freshened lawn leading to the shrubbery, and tried not to let her growing disquiet get too firm a hold on her.

'I hope you realise just what a nurse's job entails, Constance. It's not at all suitable for a young lady who has been well brought up.'

'Oh mother! Who cares about that sort of thing now? If a war starts do you really imagine a wounded man is going to wonder about his nurse's upbringing?'

The older woman protested, 'I thought you were happy being a Suffragette.'

'Happy? How could you possibly think that I,

or any other woman, would be happy whilst being brutally treated by the authorities in public, and even more brutally in prison? The Pankhursts are split into two groups now: Emmeline and Christabel are carrying on the struggle as they have been doing for a long time, but Sylvia has branched off on her own. She claims that the violence is out of control and that we should be trying to help the country's poorest people in more practical and peaceful ways. I agree with her, surprising though you may find that, but I have experienced and seen things that you probably could not imagine in your darkest nightmares, and I know what I want to do with my life in future.'

Elisabeth stood up, her expression angry. 'Oh yes Constance, you have certainly received brutal treatment, but is it any wonder? Despite your very low opinion of my intelligence I have actually kept reading the newspapers these past twelve months. Your group have smashed windows, gone into museums and art galleries and destroyed valuable works of art, set fire to buildings, including churches, and even managed to plant a bomb in Lloyd George's house!'

Now also on her feet Constance confronted her mother, red-faced with fury.

'I notice that you have left out one notable incident that injured no one except a woman who felt strongly enough about our rights to sacrifice herself!'

'Indeed? And which sainted martyr might that be?'

'A Suffragette called Emily Davidson who, you

252

may recall, threw herself to her death under the King's horse on last year's Derby Day.'

'Yes, I do recall, although what good she considered she was doing is quite beyond me. The government has not exactly rushed to grant women the vote because of her death, have they?'

'If women like you would only speak out in our support they might think again, but if you continue to behave as though you don't have a brain we'll all be tarred with the same ignorant brush, won't we?'

'How dare you?'

The opening of the lounge door saved Constance from making a reply, and she gave her father and Johnny Peacock a rather strained smile as Elisabeth immediately assumed her sociable persona.

'Ah, here you are at last. Constance and I have been having a little chat to catch up on each other's news while we've been waiting.'

Johnny grinned quite openly as he stepped into the room and Gerald patted his wife on the shoulder on his way to the sideboard.

'Yes, dear. We heard you both chatting the minute we entered the house. Now, shall we have sherry or port before we leave for White Court? Constance?'

She reseated herself with reluctance. 'Dry sherry please. I can't bear that horrible sweet stuff mother drinks.'

Perching on the arm of her chair Johnny looked down at his sister-in-law noticing the very fine lines that had formed round her eyes since the last time he had seen her. Some of her previous

253

exhibitionism had been replaced by a maturity that he found attractive, and he would have been surprised had he realised that Constance was covertly studying him while entertaining very similar thoughts.

'How is Bella these days? Still up to her eyebrows in soil?'

'Obsessed by it, actually, but I have to admit that it's put some life into her which wasn't there before, and she's hardly ever bothered with migraine these days. She's even gained some weight lately, and it suits her.'

Smiling as she accepted a glass of sherry from her father Constance hid her surprise at Johnny's flood of words on the subject of his wife. In the past he would have responded to such queries with a curt word or two, usually dismissive, and to hear him speaking of Bella with any degree of enthusiasm was amazing.

'I'll look forward to seeing her and her gardens.' She murmured, adding a little sarcastically. 'I suppose she'll have grown the vegetables we'll be eating at dinner too.'

'I wouldn't be at all surprised.'

Gerald took a quick gulp of the whisky he had poured for himself and Elisabeth frowned at his glass as she delicately sipped her own drink. He was tense about something, she could feel it, and she wished she could ask him about it at once instead of having to endure dinner at White Court first.

The grandfather clock in the corner was ticking its ponderous way towards ten o'clock as Bella gave yet another yawn. She had been up since seven that morning and was more than ready for her bed.

'Coffee, madam?' Laura enquired at her elbow, and she nodded, watching the dark liquid steaming into the small cup. The smell, usually so delicious, mingled with the assorted cheese on the wooden board at the centre of the table and nauseated her. She had been ravenous at the start of dinner, so much so that she had previously doubted her ability to wait for the others, but now that she had eaten voraciously of three courses Bella had begun to have serious regrets. Taking up her cup as Laura moved along the table with the coffee pot, she sniffed the aroma once more but there was no mistake. It was horrible.

Constance was, as usual, furiously debating some issue with Johnny while her father joined in from time to time, and only Elisabeth noticed the sudden whitening of Bella's face as she sat back in her chair.

'Bella, are you feeling ill?'

Silence fell at once as all eyes turned in her direction, and she smiled weakly. 'It's the coffee. I think there's something wrong with it. It smells awful.'

'It smells how it tastes, Bella, absolutely delicious.'

Johnny's tone was lightly amused but his eyes held a warning to his wife not to spoil the social occasion, and she made an effort to pull herself together.

'Oh ... it must be me then. Maybe I smelt the gorgonzola or something.'

'There is no gorgonzola is there?' Constance queried, frowning suspiciously. 'You're not getting a migraine are you?'

'No, I don't think so. I'll go into the drawing room now though if you don't mind.'

Elisabeth agreed. 'I'll come with you.'

Relaxing with her mother before the huge stone fireplace Bella felt her nausea begin to recede, and smiled up at Constance a few minutes later as she joined them.

'Are the men being boring?'

'The men as good as chased me out of the room. It seems they have business to discuss.'

Constance's smile was without rancour as she sank down into a comfortable armchair. She had brought a valise with her, intending to stay for a few days, and was more than content to drift with the flow for the moment.

'Bill Robinson is taking a coach to Newcastle tomorrow morning.' She remarked. 'Shall we go on it and do some shopping?'

Elisabeth looked shocked. 'Certainly not! You don't have to be so vulgar, Constance. If you wish to visit Newcastle we'll run you down to Dalton to catch the train.'

'With Bill's bus we get virtually from door to door, so I'll put up with the so-called vulgarity if you don't mind, and so will Bella if she has any sense.'

'Oh, I'm not going to Newcastle. I have far too much to do in the garden at the moment. It *is* spring you know.'

Constance scowled. 'Yes, I do know, and it will be summer next, then winter, and you'll have nothing to wear once your weeding and pruning activities are finished. Take a look at yourself Bella! You've worn that dress for so many years it isn't just out of fashion, it's coming to pieces on you. Your waistband is gaping round the back.'

'John thinks I've put on weight, and maybe he's right because all my clothes seem to be getting tight in places, but I really can't be bothered to go shopping at the moment, Connie. Once I've been outside to my greenhouse I'm completely tired out these days, honestly.'

Elisabeth exchanged an exasperated look with her eldest daughter.

'But if you're growing out of your clothes it's all the more reason to buy some more, surely. I think Constance and I had better have a look through your wardrobe with you right now.'

'Quite right.'

Grinning in triumph Constance rose to her feet holding out a hand to Bella who sighed deeply but protested no more. On the way upstairs she helped herself along by gripping the banister and, behind her, Elisabeth wondered at her obvious weariness when her health had improved so much after her interest in gardening had first manifested itself.

'You must see Dr Hatton, Bella. I simply don't understand this at all. If you were overworking in the garden you would be losing weight, not gaining it.'

'Alright mother. I promise.'

Once in the bedroom Constance flung open the wardrobe doors and began fingering through the hangers while making the occasional comment to

Elisabeth, and Bella, sitting on a chair by her bedside, watched them indifferently. Let them do as they wished. She felt too tired to care.

Within minutes the clothes had been sorted into a large pile on the floor with a smaller one on top of the bed, the latter being the only ones Constance and Elisabeth considered worth keeping.

'You can throw those out or give them to the church to distribute among the poor, but please don't ever wear them again.' Constance said sternly, and Elisabeth held up the first dress off the pile on the bed.

'Come on. We'll see how the remainder fit before you go to Newcastle. It's a pity you can't find a dignified way to travel, but one can't have everything and the situation really does call for desperate measures. Walking behind you on the stairs I could see that your waistband wasn't even fastened, and it looked as though it wouldn't have been any good trying.'

'It isn't. None of my clothes fit now.'

Obediently, just wishing they would leave her alone, Bella allowed them to subject her to a critical trying-on session with first one dress then another, and it wasn't until her petticoat tapes became undone and the garment fell round her ankles that a sudden silence fell. Standing in her chemise Bella looked from her mother to her sister, puzzled by the change in their expressions, then bent uncomfortably to retrieve it.

'Oh ... it feels so peculiar when I have to stoop; I've got so fat round my front lately it's no wonder none of my clothes fit any more.'

Constance grinned as she looked from Bella to Elisabeth, whose face had taken on a decidedly pink tinge.

'Honestly Bella, you *are* the limit! Having seen you in your chemise I'd say it's little wonder your clothes don't fit you any more, and the reason is that bump on your front which looks like something more substantial than mere fat.'

'Hmm?'

'You look as though you're having a baby, you ninny! I'm surprised Johnny hasn't drawn your attention to it, even if you have been too busy to keep track of things.'

'A baby!'

'That's what I said.'

Shocked, Bella began a series of proddings upon her abdomen which amused Constance and embarrassed her mother, before bursting into tears and flinging herself sideways onto the bed.

'Now Bella, let's have no hysterics please. You should be glad after all.'

'Of course you should. It's a good job mother and I came tonight or heaven knows when you would have realised. Whatever are you carrying on about?'

'I can't go through it all again.' Bella sobbed indistinctly, her face pushed into a pillow. 'You know I never get further than three months before it all goes wrong.'

Elisabeth leaned over her, gripping her shoulders. 'By the look of you, you're quite a way further on than three months already, so maybe this time is going to be different. Sit up and dry your eyes.'

Watching her slowly pulling herself together Constance felt surprise taking over from her initial reaction of humour. Bella had followed her advice and developed an interest in something, which seemed to have sparked off a certain kind of attention from Johnny, and she wondered whether or not he would be pleased at the prospect of becoming a father.

Lilian closed her eyes and gritted her teeth as the voice of Dame Adelina Patti escaped shrilly into the room from the phonograph Bill had bought for her a few days ago whilst driving a coachload of villagers to and from Newcastle. Turning round from the machine, which fascinated him enough to cause him to spend a much longer time than usual in her bedroom, he frowned slightly at her expression.

'You look as though you're in pain, Lilian. Don't you like Adelina Patti?'

'And so I am in pain! I'm amazed and outraged to think that she is considered to be one of our top opera singers when that is the noise she makes...'

'Well, let's wait until *you* are sixty and see how good *you* sound then, shall we? I'll agree that she is very obviously past her best, but she has had an illustrious career and I thought you would like a memento of such a woman.'

Lilian opened her eyes. 'Sixty! Was she really that old when she made this recording?'

'Yes. She was born too soon for this machine, but it's a wonderful invention just the same. I'll play you The Merry Widow Waltz if you like.'

'Thank you.'

Conversation between them ceased and Bill seated himself by the window to wait for the aria to finish, and Lilian studied his remote expression through lowered lashes. She knew she was being peevishly unpleasant, even though he had brought her something to relieve her boredom, and she felt guilty as well as worried about that afternoon when the Specialist was due to visit. Would he know what was wrong with her or, like Dr Hatton, profess himself completely baffled? And if he did, what would happen then?

Down the Back Road, which curved round the front of Ivy House, came one of James' neighbouring farmers leading two small ponies towards the Kenhope Fell road, and Bill watched them sombrely knowing that they would never again see the light of day once they entered the pit. Behind him Lilian stirred restlessly.

'What's that noise? Is somebody riding past?'

'It's Ben Mulholland taking two ponies to the mine, poor beasts.'

'Oh yes, poor beasts indeed! Maybe you could strain your sympathy to extend to this poor beast who cannot walk and may never do so!'

Abruptly Bill got up, walked to the phonograph and turned it off. His face was set in hard angry lines but, as though a devil were driving her, Lilian rushed on.

'I'm sure it must be extremely tedious for you to spend time with me just because Marion is here and you want to appear in a good light, but it makes me feel uncomfortable. I'm no longer used

261

to being treated like a human being by you, and knowing it's all false just makes everything worse.'

'You are plainly in need of a rest. I'll leave you to it.'

Without glancing at Lilian her husband left the room and closed the door behind him as tears of helpless frustration spilled from her eyes. She had lain in bed for almost a week since Dr Hatton had visited and was in a state of dread over the Specialist's possible diagnosis, for if he offered no hope for their future then that would truly be the end of everything. If only she had felt able to confide her fears to Bill instead of repelling him with her ill humour the situation might have eased somewhat, but the distance between them was too great to be bridged in a matter of days. Perhaps it was now too great ever to be bridged at all.

The familiar rustle of skirts coming up the stairs heralded the arrival of Marion a few moments later, wiping her hands on the corner of her large apron. Anxiously she surveyed her daughter-in-law, having deduced by Bill's manner that all had not gone well between them.

'It's almost lunchtime, dear. Once you've eaten I'll bring you some water so that you can wash and put on a clean nightdress. I don't suppose you'll be able to relax until the Specialist's visit is over, but it won't be too long now.'

Opening her mouth to offer a polite 'Thank you' Lilian found herself saying instead 'I'm scared Marion.'

Listening from the bottom of the stairs Bill felt a stab of shame, and wished he could go out for a long walk before his mother returned to lecture him yet again on his lack of patience in the sick room. Dismally he let himself into the study, where he could no longer hear the womens' voices, and tried to get to grips with some correspondence that was long overdue. If Lilian was scared he was equally so, yet no one would allow for that, even though the fact remained that while their life together had been a minor hell for two years it could very easily turn into a major one if the prognosis was bad.

Looking down at the blank page beneath his hand Bill blinked as a drop of ink fell from his pen onto its pristine surface, then he pushed it all away and sat in silence gazing out onto the road where Winifred and Edward were playing with a ball. Three long hours remained before the Newcastle Specialist was expected but they would feel more like three years.

'I am the person most concerned in this difficulty, and I would be most obliged if you would address your remarks to myself instead of going downstairs to mumble to my husband!'

Lilian glared towards the black-clad figure of Sir Hubert Bannister, who had concluded his examination of her and now stood with his back towards her putting various instruments into his medical bag. Unperturbed, he gave the contents a final shuffle before closing the bag with a snap. Bill was waiting with Dr Hatton downstairs, but Marion had remained in the room during the investigation and stood clasping her hands in agitation.

'Lilian ... please...'

Ignoring her, Lilian fixed the Specialist with an aggressive eye as he finally faced her.

'I want you to tell *me*, Sir Hubert. Whatever my illness is, I must know.'

He sighed slightly. 'Very well, Mrs Robinson, though I doubt whether you will appreciate my diagnosis.'

'Go on.'

'As far as physical causes are concerned I can find nothing wrong with you. As Dr Hatton has already pointed out, your condition in no way resembles a stroke, and I am very much inclined to favour the view of hysterical paralysis.'

Aware that Marion had sat down with a thump on the wide windowsill, Lilian continued to stare at the man as she persisted.

'Hysterical? What exactly does that mean? That I am some kind of lunatic I suppose!'

'Not at all. Hysterical paralysis refers to the trigger for the complaint arising in the mind of the patient and not in their body. Your legs refuse to move, even though there is no physical reason for this, and modern medicine now believes that in those circumstances the mind has caused this condition to manifest for emotional reasons.'

For the first time since he had entered the room a hint of compassion showed in his eyes as Lilian turned her face towards the wall. Setting down his bag Sir Hubert moved to the bedside to sit in the chair beside her, then looked quickly and significantly at Marion who stood up at once.

'I must go downstairs and see to the children,' she muttered. 'I'll be up again later, dear.'

Lilian made no reply, but when the bedroom door had closed behind her she relaxed a little and turned back to Sir Hubert.

'Are you saying that I'm making this up and only pretending that my legs won't move?'

'Very far from it, Mrs Robinson. What I am saying is that your legs won't move because something buried deep in your mind doesn't want them to move. Have you had anything happen recently that has deeply upset you? Maybe something that might have felt like the last straw in some way?'

She nodded, feeling her throat begin to ache, and he said gently.

'Is there anything you can do about this circumstance?'

'Nothing at all.'

'Then you must give some thought to coming to terms with it, if possible, and when you feel you can, I am sure you will find that you begin to walk again. Meanwhile, I will instruct your mother-in-law in how to exercise your limbs to keep up the muscle tone, and maybe your husband...'

'Not him!'

Rising to his feet Hubert Bannister felt a flicker of surprise at her vehemence but made no comment. Instead he promised to return in a month's time if no progress had been made by then, and wished her a courteous goodbye before going downstairs to join the others.

Left alone, she tried not to give in to despair. Like a nightmare come true the prognosis of the expert was far from the clearcut answer she had wanted, and something so nebulous was difficult

265

to understand, let alone fight. Determined not to weep, as she had done so often lately in private, Lilian turned her head on her pillow and gazed longingly through the window at the pleasantly sunny day outside. The leaves were out now on the chestnut tree in the front garden and, as she watched, a small bird came to land on its branches giving full throat to a song that seemed to mock her lack of freedom.

The opening of her bedroom door interrupted her gloomy reverie and she looked across at her visitor with lacklustre eyes. Marion smiled a little awkwardly.

'Bill is seeing Sir Hubert to the door, dear, so I thought I'd come and see how you are before we go down to my home with the bus.'

Lilian blinked. 'Bill's taking you home in the bus?'

'Oh, it's only to pick up some of my things. I thought he would have told you about it.'

Something about the woman's manner gave Lilian a feeling of unease which deepened considerably as she noticed that her mother-in-law seemed unable to meet her eyes for longer than a second. Raising herself onto one elbow she stared hard into Marion's face as she asked slowly. 'What did you think Bill had told me?'

'I thought you had discussed it...' she broke off to clear her throat, turning to leave the room at the same time. 'Bill wants me to move in here in case ... until you are well again, and we're going to bring my things up today. Not everything, of course, just those things that I want beside me.'

For a moment they looked at each other,

Marion with guilt and Lilian with an odd kind of hopelessness, then the older woman moved out onto the landing leaving the younger one alone once more.

CHAPTER NINE

August 1914

Bella glared at Daniel from her place at the greenhouse door and he noticed the two high spots of colour forming in her cheeks with faint alarm.

'Don't upset yourself, Mrs Bella.'

'What will your mother do, Daniel Heslop? What, for that matter, will *I* do?'

Plucking the last ripe fruit from a tomato plant the young man stood looking at Bella, his homely face a picture of discomfort.

'Please understand. There's a Mobilisation Notice in the Post Office window, but they say the war will be over by Christmas and if I wait for the gardening season to be past its peak before volunteering I'll miss everything.'

'Oh, of course, the war is more important than anything else, isn't it? Heavens knows, it's all people talk about these days from morning till night, and I could scream! Just when are you going to join the army, Daniel? Today? Tomorrow?'

'Tim Huntley and I are going to enlist tomorrow, and we're stopping at his Aunt's in Carlisle until we get our orders.'

Speechless she stared at him suddenly aware of how close she was to tears, not all of which were because of her garden. Her clothes fell inelegantly over her burgeoning shape and she put both hands over her abdomen as her baby kicked, feeling embarrassed as Daniel looked quickly away from her.

'So, why don't you get a miner's job and do your bit for your country that way, Daniel? My husband says that miners won't be expected to volunteer as their work is too important, but many of the younger ones are talking about it so there are bound to be vacancies if they leave. Couldn't you settle for that, and do some gardening here when you can?'

'If I'd wanted to go down a mine I'd have done it years ago, but my father died of the "black spit" and I don't want that to happen to me.'

'This is your last day here?'

He nodded, relieved to hear the resignation in her voice, and she turned to go knowing that she would miss Daniel's companionship much more than his work in the garden, excellent though it had always been.

'I'm very sorry you feel it necessary to do this, Daniel, but if you like I'll take your wages to your mother later in the week when they've been made up. See me before you leave today and I'll have a small bonus for you.'

'Thank you, Mrs Bella. That's very kind of you.'

Beaten, she walked swiftly back towards the house. The prospect of life without Daniel and her garden was unbelievably bleak and she desperately wanted to reach the sanctuary of her bedroom before beginning to cry.

'I can walk a few steps now and I'm getting better

every day. Dr Hatton is very pleased with me, and so was the Specialist when he made his second visit last month. He doesn't have to come back again, so Marion tells me.'

Leo Bondini tried hard not to let Lilian see his dismay as he perched uneasily on the chair by the wardrobe, his hat on his knees.

'It is many weeks since I last saw you, but you were bedridden then so it is a pleasure to find you up and dressed so prettily.'

Her summer dress was swamping her once womanly figure, and the life seemed to have drained out of her since her illness, but not for the world would he have hurt her by betraying his feelings. The whole house seemed oddly isolated from this over neat bedroom, and he remembered that shortly after his arrival Marion Robinson had gone out with Edward and Winifred, apparently not bothering to say goodbye to Lilian. Where Bill was he could not say.

'It is bad news about the war.' He ventured. 'I'm afraid I cannot share the views of those who find it exciting.'

'People say it won't last long.'

Leo grimaced. 'Over by Christmas. I've heard that very optimistic declaration too. Let's hope it's true.'

'Bill's new factory in Dalton is already working very hard making military uniforms and Marion tells me that he's thinking of introducing a night shift to keep up with the orders, even if it is only temporary. Everybody's busy, and I feel so useless, Leo.'

Her hands, that had been compulsively pleating

the material of her skirt, clasped together in her lap and he leaned forward, eager to divert her onto more positive matters.

'Listen, Lilian. I need you to get better as quickly as you can ready for the victory show we are going to put on in Dalton's theatre next spring. Edward German's "Merrie England" will be ideal and has wonderful solos for a mezzo soprano, as I'm sure you know.'

For the first time she looked at him with real interest while a smile slowly transformed her features.

'I know one of them well: "Oh Peaceful England". It's a beautiful song, though rather ironic in the circumstances I suppose, but will it not be expensive to secure the Performing Rights of a show just over ten years old, let alone hire scenery and costumes?'

'We have a few months, Lilian. As you say, the Performing Rights will not be cheap, but I don't see why we should not make both our scenery and our costumes. We will need to expand the Concert Party to allow for a chorus for both male and female voices, and also some people who are generally willing to work in the background in all sorts of ways. Think of it, Lilian! If the war is over it will be a marvellous victory show, but if heaven forbid, it is not finished, it will still boost morale.'

'Yes. It's a wonderful idea, Leo.'

The man smiled as he looked into her face. Her cheeks were flushed with excitement and her eyes sparkled with life just as they had done when he had first watched her singing.

'So all you have to do now is get well. Once you

can walk properly again we can begin rehearsals. I'll be back to see you in a week or so, if I may, and I'll let you know then what progress has been made.'

Standing up he put on his hat, then reached into his inside jacket pocket producing a soft bound book which he handed to Lilian with a flourish.

'Here is the libretto for you to study during the times when you are not walking round the room further and further each day. Try Queen Elizabeth's part. You can shine in "Merrie England" as never before, my dear, so start today to work very, very hard.'

For a while after Leo had gone Lilian sat still in her seat in the window with the warmth of the August sun on her back and felt hope beginning to take the place of despair in her heart. Since Marion had moved into Ivy House she had felt as though Bill had deliberately frozen her out of every part of their marriage, leaving her with no role of any kind except that of useless invalid. Her father and Louisa had called once before their wedding but had never come back after being politely, though firmly, turned away by Bill. Learning of this from the children some hours later she had been both puzzled and frustrated by her husband's action, and when he had refused to discuss the matter with her she had fretted over the incident. Letters had followed, one from her father and the rest from Louisa, all requesting her understanding, but she had failed miserably in her attempts to compose a reply and, in time, they had ceased altogether leaving her to feel bitter and abandoned all over again. For weeks since their last letter she had mentally shrunk away into the self-imposed backwater that was her life and, until today when Leo had offered her some kind of future, had felt no need to do otherwise.

Through the half open bedroom door she heard Bill entering the house by the front gate, yet for once gave the matter little attention. Standing up with the aid of her two walking sticks she fixed her determination on the phonograph four yards away and began to move towards it jerkily like a puppet, but with strength summoned up by her newborn will to succeed.

Five minutes later Bill paused over a ledger on his desk as the sound of The Merry Widow Waltz drifted through the ceiling from the room above, and with it his wife's voice, singing softly at first and then with growing confidence. Listening with an intentness he wished he could banish he felt his throat begin to ache as her mezzo soprano gained in richness and volume, soaring effortlessly to the higher notes just as it had done years ago in chapel when he had watched and listened to her with love; and if that love was really dead why did he want to weep with longing for her now?

Entranced, he sat still until the song finished, then jumped to his feet as something crashed down heavily onto the floor above and Lilian could be heard crying out. Rushing up the stairs into her bedroom he found her lying beside the phonograph where she had fallen, but before he could reach her she levered herself onto one elbow and reached across to the bottom of the brass bedstead with her other hand.

'Don't help me!' She commanded breathlessly as he came forward. 'If it takes the rest of the day I'll get up myself, Bill.'

'Lilian, don't be so stubborn. Let me lift you.'

'I'll do it myself.' She repeated, then laughed as though at some private joke of her own. 'I *will* walk properly again. Just wait and see!'

Daniel was half a mile from the remote cottage he shared with his mother when Leo Bondini stepped out from behind the large gorse bush where he had been waiting. He stopped and looked at the older man with a mixture of nervousness and aggression.

'Well Daniel, I hear you are leaving the village in the morning to go and find glory in this accursed war.'

'That I am.'

'You will never make a soldier, you silly boy. You are too sensitive, too gentle...'

'Stop that! I'm going with a friend to volunteer because I need to get away from this place. I need to get away from you!'

Daniel's voice suggested panic more than rage and Leo shook his head as though saddened.

'That will solve nothing. You will leave me behind, it is true, but the army is full of men, Daniel, and you cannot deny your nature forever.'

'Leave me alone! I'm not like you!'

Roughly pushing past the Italian, Daniel began to run along the lane breathing deeply in his distress, and Leo Bondini called recklessly after

274

him. 'But you *are* like me, Daniel, as you have proved several times. Running away will not work.'

He did not slacken his pace until he was safely inside the cottage where he immediately looked out of the window to see whether Leo had followed him.

'What is the matter, Daniel?'

Coming into the room from the kitchen Mrs Heslop regarded him with concern and he grinned sheepishly.

'Nothing really. There was a stray dog and it growled as I passed it, but it must have wandered off instead of coming after me.'

The woman placed a pie on the centre of the table. 'You're a country boy and should have known better than to run from it. Now, sit down and get your meal. Are you going out again tonight?'

He looked at her sharply on his way to wash his hands in the scullery. 'Why should I be going out?'

'I thought you might be meeting up with the lad who is going with you tomorrow, that's all.'

'I'll see him in the morning, Mam. I'm staying with you tonight.'

She nodded, averting her head sharply. Nan Heslop had spent many futile days trying to dissuade her only son from becoming a volunteer and now that they had only a limited time left together she did not want to spoil it by showing her distress. Perhaps this war would not last long, as so many people claimed. Or maybe it would take Daniel from her and never give him back.

It was after midnight when the familiar soft knocking came from the front door and Leo, sitting on his rocking chair, smiled down into the fire's dying embers for a few seconds before getting up. He was wearing a maroon silk dressing gown over his pyjamas with a grey cravat at the neck, a pretension that would have looked ridiculous on any other man, and he glanced at his reflection in the small mirror in the hall before opening the door. At first he could see no one, but finally discerned the dim shape of the person he had been waiting for so patiently.

'Come in, my dear. Why stand back like a stranger?'

Daniel moved forward into the hall as though drawn there against his will, and as Leo closed the door and bolted it he protested quickly.

'Don't do that, Leo. I can't stay long tonight. I had to wait for Mam to fall asleep and I've only come to say ... goodbye.'

The older man's smile was regretful. 'I'm glad you have, but let's hope it's only au revoir shall we?'

10th September 1914

Someone was keening; a long shrill primitive sound that came again and again, breaking through her barrier of pain, and Bella twisted helplessly as the noise began to repeat itself after only a slight pause. Dr Hatton's voice made her open her eyes and she stared into his face,

276

realising that the cries had been her own.

'Just be brave a little longer, Bella. Your baby is almost here now.'

'I can't ... I can't.'

Closing her eyes as the agony gripped her once more she heard the sharp command to 'Push! Push as hard as you can!' and tried her best to obey, but it was a weak effort even though the moisture broke out on her brow with the strain. Eighteen hours had passed since her labour had really got into its stride and she was weary almost to the point of collapse; her fair hair dark with sweat clung flatly to her head, while her eyes stared in panic out of shadowed sockets.

'You must try harder then it will soon be over. I can see your baby's head. Just a few more, Bella, that's all.'

Dimly aware that all the time he had been speaking Dr Hatton had been looking under the sheet that covered her, Bella, summoning every last vestige of her strength, gave a long drawn out push to the discomfort within her, this time roaring out with the effort before falling back onto her pillow again.

'Good. Now, no more pushing.'

Suddenly, there came a sensation of sliding and turning, a grunt of satisfaction from the man then, as she opened her eyes, the first cry of her baby who was being attended to by a smiling Dr Hatton.

'You have a son, Bella. Congratulations!'

The young nurse the Peacocks had hired to assist at the birth and stay on afterwards as nanny for the baby, moved forward to deal with the afterbirth while the umbilical cord was cut and the child sponged and wrapped warmly in a shawl to sleep off his ordeal. Hardly conscious that her pains had returned, Bella kept her eyes on her son as nature dispelled the afterbirth, then at last held her prize in her arms while tears of joy coursed down her cheeks.

'He's like John, isn't he?' she said, half laughing. 'He looks just like him, especially with that cross little face.'

Privately hoping that the baby's 'cross little face' would be the only way he resembled his father, Dr Hatton announced that he would go downstairs for half an hour while nurse made her more comfortable and that he would give the good news to Johnny.

He was in the lounge staring out of the window at the garden and wheeled round sharply as he heard the older man's approach, his face wearing a scowl that underlined his wife's statement that the baby resembled him, and George Hatton suddenly found it easier to smile at this man whom he disliked.

'You have a fine son. Nurse will let you know when you can go up.'

'A son!'

Like magic the frown melted into an answering smile and Johnny walked to the sideboard to pour drinks for them both, shaking his head a little as though unable to quite believe it.

'Sit down doctor ... stay to dinner won't you?'

George Hatton accepted the port and nodded. 'That would be welcome. Thank you John!'

'Is Bella ... is she...?'

'Bella's fine. Nurse is helping her wash and change then she'll have a sleep; a very happy sleep I should imagine.'

'Yes.'

Having listened for hours to the noises from his wife's bedroom, Johnny shuddered a little, yet half an hour later as he mounted the stairs to see his new son his steps were hurried, the more unpleasant aspects of the day forgotten.

Bella watched him intently as he looked down into the bassinet. He had neither kissed her not paid her any direct attention since entering the room, but she was used to that and expected no more, although the nurse who had noticed both discrepancies thought little of him for it.

With her freshly bathed body and clean clothes Bella felt good despite her exhaustion, and nodded happily as Johnny said 'He's a fine boy, Bella.'

'Yes, he is.'

'We'll call him Antony John.'

Putting down his hand to touch the small dark head Johnny saw neither Bella's wry smile of resignation at not being consulted nor the nurse's slightly tightened lips as she busied herself in the corner of the room.

Later, on his way downstairs, he paused on the landing to look down on the village. From that vantage point Ivy House lay in his direct line of vision, and in the sitting room window alcove he could see Lilian Robinson seated whilst attending to some needlework. Not realising that word of the baby's impending arrival had spread round Gilfell that morning like a forest fire, he felt a little shocked when she continued to stare at him then raised her arm to wave. After a few seconds he waved back to her then turned and walked the rest of the way downstairs. He wished he had not stopped there and seen Lilian, and he wished she had not waved to him so that in an unguarded moment he had responded, for even now, after all this time, she still had the power to ruffle him.

CHAPTER TEN

Friday 7th May 1915

Behind the front door Marion watched Lilian putting on her hat with the aid of the mirror on the umbrella stand, and noticed the savagery with which she plunged in her hat pin. Her clothes were fashionably short at mid-calf and she had been restored to good health for some months now, her old vigour more than evident in her personal affairs despite her making no effort to take back her rightful place from her mother-in-law.

'Are you going out to another practice, dear?'

Marion's voice was uncertain and Lilian deliberately did not look at her but turned away to pick up her music case.

'It's the final one before tomorrow night when we are at the Assembly Rooms singing "Merrie England" in concert form. Will you be there with your children?'

Marion looked flustered at the obvious jibe regarding her role with her grandchildren, and twisted her hands as she tried to find something soothing to say. She had wanted to go back to her home months ago after Lilian had really got her strength back, but neither she nor Bill would hear of it, and when it had become obvious that her daughter-in-law was making a different life for

281

herself whilst leaving her other duties to Marion on a seemingly permanent basis she had become increasingly depressed. Her son refused to listen on the rare occasions when he was at Ivy House for any length of time, and Lilian, who seemed like a totally different person these days, simply dismissed her protests with ill-concealed mockery.

'But Marion, Bill brought you here to look after Edward and Winifred and I wouldn't dream of going against his wishes, or yours either.'

As the young woman opened her front door to leave, Marion tried again.

'It's early for a practice isn't it? Will you be back any sooner?'

Lilian sighed impatiently. 'I hope so, but it's difficult to say. This is our last rehearsal and we may need to go over some songs several times, that is why we are starting at two o'clock instead of seven. I really must go or I'll be late.'

Stepping out into the bright May afternoon she felt almost light-headed with relief as she heard the door shut quietly behind her, and walked quickly round Chapel Corner into Hillary Terrace. In the field at the back of Ivy House she could hear Edward and Winifred playing with some friends from school and was pleased that they sounded so happy and normal, for their home could certainly not be described as either. Marion's misery made her feel rather guilty, yet in fairness she had only her son to blame for that, and had he not made such an effort to push Lilian out of her rightful place in his life she would not be pursuing her own interests so strongly now. It was an act of self defence rather than revenge, for she had decided as she began to recover from her paralysis that the more she kept her distance from her husband the less opportunity he would have to hurt her again. So far her plan had worked quite well, although Bill stayed down in Dalton a lot to oversee matters at the factory.

Leo had told her recently that there was talk about Bill and one of his leading machinists, a young widow, and she had tried hard not to care, but the truth was that she cared much more than she would have thought possible.

Just behind her a woman's voice said 'Hello' and she turned to find Annie Castle, one of the lead miner's wives, drawing level with her.

She smiled. 'Hello Annie. How are you?'

'I'm fine thanks, and I'm glad to see you looking likewise. Are you on your way to rehearsals again?'

'That's right. It'll make a change from knitting socks and scarves for the troops.'

Annie smiled in agreement. 'It was more fun buying Bella Peacock's flowers on Primrose Day last month. They say she made quite a reasonable amount for The Red Cross.'

'Her sister's a VAD Nurse now, isn't she? She has been sent abroad recently I believe.'

They began walking along the terrace together at a more leisurely pace and Annie lowered her voice as she confided.

'Robert Elliot's parents had a telegram from the army this morning, and so did Douglas Armstrong's people.'

Halting again, Lilian gazed at her in dismay. 'Oh Annie, how awful. Those poor boys...'

Annie blinked as her eyes filled with tears. 'And my sister's son, Ronald, went to volunteer yesterday. They don't know how they'll manage on the farm without him, but he wouldn't be reasoned with and it will break their hearts if he doesn't come back. He has been taunted several times by some of the local girls, and some kind soul slipped an envelope containing a white feather into his pocket last market day.'

Looking down at the music case in her hand Lilian suddenly felt guilty for the triviality that had become her life in the midst of a worsening war that had been widely predicted to be over five months previously, but which showed no signs whatever of coming to an end. Young men, and some not so young, had left Gilfell and Dalton in a steady stream since the previous August, while the women in their families took over their duties as best they could. Many who had not volunteered were often subjected to the cruel message of the white feather, and the straight choice of remaining at home or leaving as a heroic patriot could hardly be deemed a choice at all in an insular area like Gilfell. Loyal speech was on everyone's lips, while depression closed in on the valley as news of the deaths of its sons grew more grim each day. The terrible battles of the winter just gone had resulted in the first batch of dreaded telegrams to the volunteers' Next of Kin, followed later by parcels containing their dead hero's personal effects. Lilian shivered, trying to imagine how she would feel if one day she received something like that belonging to Edward. Miserably she looked into Annie's troubled eyes as they began to walk again with slow tread.

'Everything's changing isn't it? There's always somebody crying over a loved one who's never coming back, and it doesn't make sense to me. I don't even know why we're at war really, even though the men say The Kaiser wants to rule the world and must be stopped.'

A short while later she said goodbye to her companion at the back door of her house, so like the one both she and Louisa had once lived in, and climbed over the stile at the end of the terrace feeling none of her usual happy anticipation at the thought of the coming rehearsal.

Arriving at the Assembly Rooms Lilian realised that she was late, for she could hear Leo singing 'The English Rose' as she pushed open the door. Emma Dallow glanced over at her from her place at the piano, raising her eyebrows briefly to indicate her disapproval whilst never losing a note of her accompaniment, and she sat down on one of the chairs near the back of the hall.

In an attempt to take her mind off the recent war casualties from the village she wondered how it would have been if Leo had been able to go ahead with his ambitious plan to stage 'Merrie England' in the theatre at Dalton with its red plush seats and opera boxes. At first there had been a rush of enthusiasm as people of all ages flocked to join the Concert Party, and a start had actually been made with preparations for the big production. Some scenery had been painted, chorus members and principals selected, with practice sessions of the music held for two hours each week, then as the younger men drifted away to become volunteers and Christmas drew nearer with the expected victory nowhere in sight, membership began to drop until the project had to be abandoned in its original form. Living and working conditions were daily becoming more spartan and Bill, who had privately considered the idea of a Victory Show ridiculously optimistic from the start, kept secret his relief at no longer having to ferry the Gilfell half of the Concert Party down to Dalton each week to meet the new faction. By this time he had less frivolous matters to concern him, mostly to do with the need for ever speedier production at the factory, and began staying overnight at a lodging house near his work when circumstances demanded it.

When her strength had finally returned to her Lilian sought every opportunity to leave the house until practice sessions and fund raising activities took up all but a fraction of her waking hours, and she knew that once the concert was over she would once again be in limbo unless she found some new direction in her life. Unconsciously scowling at her own thoughts the woman reflected that now she was back on her feet Marion was clearly anxious to return to her own home, a fact which had only rendered her pig-headedly determined to make her stay until Bill himself suggested it, and if he did not then she considered that it served her mother-in-law right for stepping too eagerly into her territory in the first place.

With a start she suddenly realised that she was being called to the front to rehearse and was moving down the aisle towards the piano when the door of the hall opened to admit James Rutherford, who stood uncertainly holding his hat whilst watching his daughter. The abrupt silence as Emma Dallow arranged her music for 'Oh Peaceful England' alerted Lilian to the changed atmosphere in the room, and she turned round to look directly into her father's eyes. For a moment the entire company froze into immobility; even Emma Dallow paused halfway through the act of turning a page of her score, then James began to walk forward again and the spell was broken.

Excusing herself, Lilian hurried to meet him as her face took on an ever deepening shade of pink. News of their estrangement had swept through Gilfell before the wedding and Louisa had rarely been seen in the village since becoming James' wife, general opinion being mostly against her, although Helen still made the occasional clandestine visits to play with Edward and Winifred.

Once level with her father she touched his elbow and they walked out of the hall to where Louisa was sitting in the pony and trap. Behind them the door swung shut cutting off all the distracting whisperings and mutterings, and James took Lilian's hand, holding it firmly.

'Look lass, we had to come here to speak to you because we've been banned from the house by Bill and you never answered any of our letters, but it seems we've mistimed our visit. When everything was quiet we thought the rehearsal must have finished, or that we had got the timing wrong ... that's why I just walked in. If you were still around I was going to ask you to come back to Roughside with us for a while.'

Looking from one to the other Lilian noticed that Louisa was not quite as slender as she had once been and that her father had more frown lines across his forehead and greyer hair, and her throat began to ache as the woman who had been her closest friend smiled down at her.

'It's good to see you again, Lilian. Please come back with us. We have something important to tell you.'

'I'd love to come but I can't miss this practice as it's the last before the concert, so I'll walk up when it's over if that's alright.'

James beamed. 'You do that, Lilian. I'll come back for you if you can give me an idea of when you'll be through.'

'I really can't say, but I'll soon walk to the farm from here. It isn't far.'

James patted her hand with enthusiastic vigour, and she rubbed her throbbing fingers ruefully along her side after he had climbed back onto the trap.

'I'm glad you came.' She said, smiling broadly as a surge of happiness swept over her, and Louisa, leaning backwards so that she could still see her as the trap moved forward, laughed aloud.

'Oh, so am I, Lilian. So am I.'

Watching them until they turned out onto the narrow road leading back to the farm Lilian heard her father's voice urging her to be as quick as possible, and waved before going back into the hall.

'Oh dear, how dreadful. Have you seen this, Lilian?'

Breakfast at Ivy House had finished ten minutes ago, over an hour after Bill had left to take the bus down to Dalton, and Marion and Lilian were alone at the table after the children had gone to play in the back field. Looking over the rim of her almost cold tea cup Lilian raised enquiring eyebrows towards her mother-in-law who was holding The Times as though afraid it would explode.

'The Germans have sunk a ship called The Lusitania and 1500 passengers, including women and children, are lost out of just over 2000.'

'Oh no; surely not another like the Titanic with insufficient lifeboats. How horrible.'

'It says here that there were adequate lifeboats for all the passengers and that the ship must have sunk very quickly to have suffered so many dead. How could the Germans torpedo a passenger ship like that? It's barbaric!'

Setting down her cup Lilian rose and began to stack the dishes rather savagely onto the trolley at her side, her happier mood born from the reconciliation with her father and friend the previous day dying slowly in the face of the morning's stark facts.

'With all this mindless killing going on and on it seems ludicrous to think that we ever planned a Victory Concert for last spring.'

'But it was never held, dear.'

'No. Tonight will see the remnants of it performed in aid of The Red Cross, but I can't see us carrying on with anything else once it's through. None of us have the heart for it any more, nor the time ... nor the male voices.'

Turning a page of The Times, Marion's eyes fell on the depressingly long Obituary Column giving the latest details of the men most recently fallen in France, and she folded the newspaper quickly before setting it aside.

Lilian's next remark distracted her a little from her ever deepening gloom.

'I'm sorry I was so late coming back from practice yesterday, Marion, but I was at Roughside. Dad came down to the Assembly Rooms with Louisa to see me, and after rehearsals were finished I walked home to have supper with them.'

'Oh Lilian, that *is* good. I'm very pleased for you.'

Through her pleasure at the news Marion felt a twinge of sadness at her daughter-in-law's use of the term 'home' for Roughside Farm.

'How are they both these days? We never seem to see them much in the village any more.'

Lilian smiled, ruefully reflecting on the retort she would once have made about Bill barring them from the house, and said 'I'm to have a little half-sister or brother towards the end of the year. That is what they wanted to tell me, and although it's quite a shock I feel happy for them. Helen is a lonely child, and although a baby wasn't planned, both Dad and Louisa are pleased about it. In fact, I think Dad would like a son. Most men want that don't they?'

'Oh my dear, that's quite ... wonderful!'

She had been going to say 'shocking' but changed it swiftly, and Lilian propped open the dining room door before wheeling the laden trolley into the passage.

'What's wonderful really is that we're all friends once more. I've felt so lonely without them, and now that everything's alright again I'll rejoice in anything they do. It's as simple as that.'

Left alone in the room Marion turned listlessly and walked to the window which overlooked the sloping vegetable garden at the side of the house. 'Simple' Lilian had said, but was anything simple these days? Guiltily her mind echoed the words 'I've been so lonely without them' and she wondered again just what could have caused such a serious rift between her son and his wife, for it had lasted three years now with the couple even further apart since Lilian's illness.

Part of the strain of living in Ivy House was the atmosphere of separation which lay behind the couple's stiffly polite dealings with each other, and she knew suddenly that she would have to leave as soon as possible if she wished to avoid any worse depression than the one plaguing her at present. The war itself was enough to darken the spirits without living in a house filled with silent hostility.

'Marion.'

Lilian's voice from the doorway made her start.

'I thought we might go for a little walk this morning and take the children; just as far as Hanson's Dam maybe. Will you come?'

'That would be pleasant, Lilian.'

Smiling at this unexpected overture of friendliness Marion made a heroic effort to hide her dismay at the prospect of dragging her aching joints up the steep Kenhope Fell Road and went upstairs to put on her coat and hat while Lilian called to Edward and Winifred. Later today, she decided, she would really have to announce her departure and go back to her cottage.

'Ah, there you are, Nanny! And how is master Antony this morning?'

Entering the nursery Johnny looked down at his son who was lying kicking on a rug in the middle of the floor, and felt again the familiar surge of pride that the sight of the boy always gave him.

'He's very well, sir.' The girl responded. 'I'm taking him for a short walk before lunch, or maybe to sit and watch his Mama in her garden. He likes that.'

'Hmm. The fresh air will do him good whatever you decide, I'm sure.'

Bending down he touched the child's chubby cheek and smiled into his eyes as the infant raised his head showing features so like his own.

He grinned. 'Good boy! You're a chip off the old block already.'

'He's the image of you, sir. No doubt of that at all.'

In the last few months Nanny Sarah Brewster had recovered from her initial disapproval of the master of the house and now harboured a secret passion for Johnny, of which he was not entirely unaware, but as Sarah was too short and plump for his taste he left her disappointingly unsullied. Now, as she gazed up into his handsome face she felt her heart begin to race again, and was both thankful and sad when he gave Antony a final pat before striding out of the room. Not for the first time she wondered just how he had ever come to marry someone like Bella who never seemed to care how she looked any more and was always pottering in the garden in old clothes with her spectacles constantly falling to the end of her nose. The maid, Laura, had told her a few weeks ago that the Peacocks slept apart and that the master had 'interests' outside the marriage. No doubt that was where he was always going on his motorcycle, Sarah thought, and who could blame him?

Picking up Antony she kissed him soundly and smiled as he wriggled to be down again.

'We're going out now, little love. You'll see your Mama and I may see your Daddy again before he leaves.'

Her voice was soft so as not to carry out of the room, and she walked to the window with Antony just in time to see Johnny emerge from the side door in his biking clothes and walk quickly towards the old stables where he kept his machine. He looked so dashing on the motorcycle, she thought dreamily, just like a modern day knight on a shiny black steed, and she stayed where she was until her hero had ridden by the house on his way to the gates.

Before coming out into the road Johnny halted beside Bella who was working on new rockeries on either side of the gate posts, and informed her in a tone of resigned patience that her son would soon be brought to visit her. She beamed briefly in his direction, and as he revved the engine he saw her mouth form the word 'Good.'

Once on the road he turned his thoughts to the business of the day and wondered how much longer he would be left in peace to attend to it. So many of his peers had volunteered long ago, including his brother-in-law Raynor, and criticism of his cowardice was growing daily both in quantity and boldness. At a recent dinner party some chit of a girl had sarcastically praised his courage in refusing to join the patriotic fray when even his wife's sister was serving as a VAD in France. He had defended himself by pointing out that the mining of coal was vital to the war effort and that someone had to run both the coal and lead mines, but his tormentor had retorted that Gerald Fairburn was more than capable of that task, leaving Johnny red-faced and uncomfortable.

As he rode out of Gilfell his thoughts turned once again to his little son, and the probability that when conscription came it would exclude men with young children for as long as possible. Older men were firmly of that opinion whenever the subject came up, and he took comfort in it. Not only did he truly love Antony and hate the idea of leaving him for any length of time, but he had never been taken in by romanticised notions of the glories of war, and the tales that were now filtering back from The Front more than confirmed how right he was to be so cynical. Annabel had confided in Bella that when Raynor had come home on leave last autumn he had woken screaming every single night with terrible nightmares.

Johnny grimaced into the wind as he accelerated. He would try not to think of things like that any more. After all, it did no good.

'Oh look, there's Bella Peacock with her baby in the pram beside her. Let's hurry and see how he's coming along. It's months since I saw him when his nurse had him in the village, but he was asleep and all wrapped up so I couldn't really get a close look at him.'

Lilian's voice was carefree as she turned round to wait for Marion. The children were ahead of both of them, anxious to have their lunch after walking up Kenhope Fell road and around Hanson's Dam, and were already nearing the foot of the slope that was mere yards from their home.

'I hope there's a seat.' Marion tried to smile, but her joints were painful and she was weary.

Lilian looked at her with concern. 'I'm sorry, Marion. I didn't realise how tired you are. We'll just keep going and get you home as fast as we can.'

'It's alright, dear. A few minutes won't make any difference. I'd like to see the babe as well.'

Bella looked up as they drew nearer, then smiled and wiped grimy hands down her hessian apron.

'Good morning, or is it afternoon now? I've lost track of time, I'm afraid, but Antony seems to be getting hungry so it's bound to be a mealtime of some sort.'

Bella's son was propped up in his pram throwing an endless stream of small toys onto the ground then chortling with glee as his mother picked them up, and Lilian smiled down at him then turned to Marion.

'Isn't he a fine boy? You must be proud of him, Bella.'

'Oh yes, and so is John, but that's because he can see how Antony looks just like him.' Bella laughed, adding honestly. 'If he'd resembled me I doubt whether he would have doted quite so much.'

'Men do like their children to look like themselves, don't they?'

Glancing once more at her mother-in-law Lilian saw her face freeze into an expression of shock as she stared at the baby, and Bella frowned slightly.

'Mrs Robinson ... is something wrong?'

Marion gave a little start, then shook her head. 'I must get home ... please don't think me rude, but I really am so tired.'

With stiff jerky movements the older woman moved away and Lilian muttered a few embarrassed words of apology before following her. Holding Marion's elbow as she reached her side she enquired anxiously after her health, but the woman shook her off angrily.

'Marion, whatever is the matter?'

'I know it all, Lilian!' She looked straight ahead as she spoke, keeping her voice low. 'These past few years I've often wondered just what had gone wrong between you and Bill, for he would never talk about it, but it's all fitting together now.'

She was panting with the exertion of walking faster than was wise and talking at the same time, but when Lilian tried to slow her down she managed a few more sentences before falling silent, and still she did not look at her companion.

'Edward looked exactly like Bella's son at the same age, and even now they could be brothers, but that's because they are half brothers, isn't it Lilian? When you married Bill you were expecting Johnny Peacock's child and soon the entire village will see the obvious, for they both look so much like their father and each other I wonder how I could ever have missed what was staring me in the face.'

She halted for a moment, panting fiercely in her distress, and Lilian looked back at her helplessly. There was nothing she could say in defence of this accusation, and she knew that the pain in Marion's eyes was echoed in her own.

Finally, as though the life was slowly draining out of her, the older woman's shoulders hunched and her lower lip quivered as she began to walk again. With only a few yards between herself and the back yard door Lilian accompanied her in silent resignation, making no comment as Marion said heavily. 'I shall go for a lie down when we get indoors, then I'll begin my packing. Bill can take me home either tonight or tomorrow.'

CHAPTER ELEVEN

Beginning of December 1915

Constance knelt on the floor beside the first casualty trying to close her ears to the groans, cries and sometimes screams of pain from the wounded men who had been brought in from the ambulances. The entire ward was in chaos with stretchers lying between the occupied beds and down the centre aisle, dirty khaki blankets covering body wounds, and smashed limbs that were bound to splints by bandages, many of which were soaked through with blood.

Unlike the hospital in Camberwell that she had just left, the wounded arrived here not in twos and threes but in twenties and thirties, and as she bent to the bandage on the young man's leg the smell of infection rose in a sickening cloud making her fear in case she should vomit. For that 'insult' she could never forgive herself. Reaching for her scissors she began to cut away the binding as quickly and gently as she could, muttering 'Sorry' as her patient moaned in protest.

Constance, one of eight VADs, had arrived only hours before and knew now that she had simply left hell to come to a worse one, as had many of the injured and dying men in her care. The women had begun their shift at 7.30 am and were due to end it at 8.00 pm, with three hours off in early afternoon, but the rest period had immediately been cancelled when the Red Cross convoy arrived with its cargo of broken heroes; heroes just like her Ralph, but she must not think of him in this awful ward or every man's face would become his, and every man's torturous condition his too. Ralph had to be alive and well, because if he were not she could not bear it.

'Try to hurry, nurse. We have lots of men to treat and more may arrive at any time.'

'Yes, Sister.'

She felt no resentment at the Ward Sister's words, although her job, which was to clean then apply a sterile dressing to the mens' wounds until a doctor could examine them, could not be done any quicker.

During the brief period of normality before the convoy had come Constance had worked with the rest of the staff to get the ward in order for nine o'clock. As in the hospital she had just left, beds were meticulously lined up by their rear castors with the same pernickety attention to detail applied in many other areas, all of which struck her as unnecessarily time wasting in the circumstances.

Her first real shock came upon approaching a patient who wanted more water, and upon looking down at his exposed leg she saw an open wound which appeared to possess a life of its own. As she replaced the water jug she stared down at the maggots, writhing obscenely in the odorous mess on his thigh, and turned sharply away from him without speaking. She had heard of this method of dealing with gangrene, and knew that it was saving his life, but her first sight of the treatment had come when she was overworked, stressed and exhausted, and her immediate reaction made her ashamed. Since becoming a VAD many terrible sights had upset her, and the maggot cure was yet another part of her working life that she would have to get used to, but it was too late for the young man who had doubtless seen the disgust in her expression.

Hours later, lying in her bed at last, she listened to the muffled irregular boom of the big guns miles away at The Front and prayed to a God, in whom she found it increasingly hard to believe, to end this terrible war. Sleep was elusive despite her urgent need of it, and her thoughts centred as ever nowadays on her fiancé, Major Ralph Miller, whom she had met less than a year ago during his convalescence. He was a childless widower of forty one, his wife having died in 1910 from tuberculosis, and had resigned from his post as headmaster of a rural school in her home county of Cumberland in order to return to the military life of his youth. Constance had been drawn to him from the start, and her delight on discovering that the attraction was mutual had been tempered with an untypical shyness. Clean shaven, with light brown hair and grey eyes, Ralph was pleasant looking rather than handsome, and Constance, now thirty three, had been shocked to find herself in love for the first time.

Both Ralph's parents were dead, but he had a married sister living in London and had taken Constance to meet Sybil and her husband on her first day off, then they had gone to stay there on his final few days convalescence before returning to The Front. On the afternoon of her visit there had been a Zeppelin raid a few miles away and he had taken her hand in his and said 'You asked me last week why I volunteered when I am basically a pacifist, and those exploding bombs are my reason. Battlefields are bad enough without the enemy attacking civilians ... old people, mothers and children ... they have nothing to do with this war.'

'Neither have we, Ralph.' She pointed out quietly. 'Nor probably any of the men who are being killed and injured in France. Maybe there'd be fewer wars if the politicians and heads of state had to fight things out themselves.'

He had looked grim for an instant. 'If we could only bring about that change, my dear, I'm sure we could eradicate war in one fell swoop.'

They had become engaged the day before Ralph's return to active service three months previously and she now lived precariously from letter to letter, writing back to him whenever time and energy would allow. Before leaving Camberwell the expected letter from Ralph had been almost a week late, and she had written to him on her last night in England giving him her new address. Delays in postal matters were extremely common and nothing to get too alarmed about at this point, as Constance knew, yet her whole being yearned for the reassurance of a message from him, however brief. To have lived all these years, comparatively unscathed emotionally, only to enter a war and love a man

301

so deeply who might be killed at any moment was an irony as cruel as it was unexpected, and probably explained why she had not yet mentioned him in her letters to her family. The engagement ring he had given her, a modest single diamond set in gold, she wore beneath her uniform on a chain around her neck, as jewellery was inappropriate on a hospital ward.

Looking back on her activities as a Suffragette it seemed like a life lived by a completely different person, and her prior existence on Dalton Moor even more so. Her mother wrote often, and Bella slightly less often, but their letters did more to irritate her than to comfort. Her mother grumbled about the food shortages and the growing number of able-bodied men leaving the valley to enlist so that they had been forced to employ two men in their sixties to tend the gardens at Low Shields, and even had to do without half of their domestic servants as they took jobs that had once belonged to men, or better paid positions at the military clothing factory belonging to William Robinson.

No mention of stress at the mines, she noticed; just silly things that did not really matter. And Bella was no better. After telling her every fascinating detail of Antony John's progress she inevitably fell to worrying in case Johnny should be involved in conscription, as she had heard several people opine that this step must soon be taken by the government. Thinking of it, Constance curled her lip. Whatever else happened, the war must not upset Bella's precious family round whom the entire universe must surely revolve!

Closing her eyes as a wave of soothing weariness swept over her she pleaded silently before falling asleep 'Just one letter, please God, and let it be tomorrow.'

Marguerite Rutherford, just two days old, kept her blue eyes firmly closed as Edward and Winifred leaned over her cradle to examine her intently. Sitting on Louisa's bed Lilian smiled as she looked into the new mother's flushed face.

'Just think, Lou, Marguerite is my half sister and Edward and Winifred are the baby's nephew and niece.'

'That's right. I hadn't thought of the various relationships before. Isn't it odd?'

Winifred looked up at them both, her small features a mask of disappointment.

'She won't say anything. She won't even wake up. Can we go out to play in the yard now?'

Helen, standing uncertainly in the doorway, scowled fiercely at Edward as he said 'I think she's nice,' and Lilian held out her hand to the lonely little girl who had stayed with them at Ivy House from the moment Louisa felt the first twinges of labour. Her pretty face betrayed her vulnerability all too clearly, making the woman's heart ache for her.

'Off you go and play then, and leave us three together with the new baby. Come here, Helen, and sit on the bed beside your mother. You and I are related now, you know, and so are Edward and Winifred. We're all one big family since your mother married Uncle James and made him your step father.'

Helen came forward and stepped into Louisa's

arms burying her head in her shoulder as tears ran down her cheeks into the abundant fair hair. Clattering noisily down the stairs the other children called up to her not to be long coming to play 'Tig', and Lilian gave her a quick kiss then excused herself to go and see James who was outside in the byre.

Pausing in his task of stacking the mangers with hay, James smiled as she walked towards him.

'How do you like your little sister? Fair little cracker isn't she?'

'She's beautiful Dad, no doubt of that at all. You must be very proud.'

'No more than I was when you were born, lass, believe me. You had all that dark curly hair and you squawked most of the day, but maybe you were just trying to sing for the first time.'

He grinned down at her, leaning on his fork, and she put her hand on his arm.

'Dad, could you perhaps make more fuss of Helen for a while now that Marguerite's here? She's a sad little girl really and obviously needs some reassurance if she isn't to feel displaced. After all, a new baby doesn't know that someone else is getting the lion's share of attention, and by the time she is old enough to know you'll have Helen quite willing to share her parents with her new sister.'

James sighed, watching Edward and Winifred chasing each other noisily across the cobbles outside, and Lilian held her breath as she saw his expression darken.

'I've tried with her, Lilian, heaven knows. We used to get on well together once, yet she just won't have me now no matter what I do. Louisa's told her to call me "Dad" but she refuses, and I don't know what to say to her any more.'

'Louisa should have had more sense than try to force things like that. Helen's father was killed, and she still loves and misses him ... perhaps she could call you Uncle James as she used to do. Shall I suggest that to her?'

'If you think it will help. This whole thing with Helen has me beat, I'll admit that, although Lou said that someone in the village had told her she was to have a new brother or sister before she'd got around to saying so herself, so that may have upset her a bit.'

Considering this to be something of an understatement Lilian contented herself with a slight smile of agreement before changing the subject.

'Would you like to come down to Ivy House for Christmas Day? It's less than two weeks away and it would probably be easier for Louisa and more fun for Helen to have Edward and Winifred to play with.'

'If Louie wants to come it's alright by me, lass, and providing we don't have a lot of snow.'

'Good!'

Coming out into the air Lilian saw Bella Peacock walking past the yard gate and called across to her in surprise, realising as she did so that the woman was probably on her way to visit Daniel Heslop's mother whose cottage lay a little further on from Roughside. At once Bella stopped, and when she drew nearer Lilian saw that she had been crying. Her shoulders were hunched in her fur-collared coat, but it seemed to be something more than the temperature that was causing such a stance.

'Bella? Are you alright?'

'Not really ... I heard about Daniel today, although they say his mother got the telegram days ago.'

'Oh no.'

Tears welled up in Bella's eyes and she put up a gloved hand to wipe them away.

'John says I shouldn't go bothering her in person when a note of sympathy would do, but I was very fond of Daniel and I can't believe he won't ever be coming back to work with me in the garden. I *hate* this horrible war.'

'I'm so sorry. There are so many telegrams like that these days and I'm afraid I hadn't heard about Daniel either. Do you want me to come with you to visit Mrs Heslop? I could leave the children here until we get back.'

'No thanks. I'll be alright. I apologise for losing control, but you're the first person I've spoken to since leaving the house and it just overwhelmed me.'

Taking out a handkerchief from her pocket she wiped her face rather fiercely then gave Lilian a determinedly bright smile before turning on her heel and hurrying away along the lane. Slowly Lilian looked round to where James was watching from the byre door.

'Daniel Heslop's dead.' She told him bleakly. 'It's practically impossible to keep count of all these poor young men any more, isn't it?'

Seated at his desk in the corner of the study Bill

glanced first out of the window at the fading daylight then at the grandfather clock which showed the time to be almost three thirty. Lilian and the children should have been home at least half an hour ago, he decided, then relaxed as he heard the noise of Edward and Winifred's familiar bickering approaching the front door.

A fire was burning in the grate casting faint moving shadows over the walls, and as he rose to put on the light Bill wondered how much longer he would be free to enjoy the comforts of his family and home. Since Marion had returned to her cottage, leaving him in no doubt as to her reason for going, he and Lilian had begun to experience a more peaceful co-existence both still going their own way but in an atmosphere of acceptance rather than hostility. He quite often marvelled to himself that she had never taken a lover since his desertion of the marriage bed, and the knowledge that she had invariably conducted herself with dignity and restraint for all that time had gradually given him a new respect for her. It did not look as though Marion would ever forgive Lilian, but Gilbert and Jenny had refused to join her in her condemnation. He could still hear Gilbert pointing out quietly that 'It's a matter for you and Lilian, and nothing to do with the rest of us.' Lilian's indiscretion had probably been as she had claimed, a single mistake, and the guilt he felt at knowing his own mistake to have been quite deliberate haunted him like a bad dream.

Maura Harker, a young widow of twenty nine, had worked in his factory and rented him a room in her house during the harsh months of the last Pennine winter, and for a while they had bonded together in a relationship that soon had tongues wagging in both Dalton and Gilfell. Did Lilian know? It would be strange indeed if no one in this small village had told her about it, and pondering on this possibility held him back from approaching his wife at a time when he genuinely wished for a reconciliation. Bill, who had moved on quite a distance from his first violent reaction to the truth about Edward, was now neatly trapped in a snare of his own making.

'Dad! Dad!'

He smiled at the sound of Edward's voice and opened the door into the corridor just as Lilian and the children entered the house, and both Edward and Winifred hurled themselves towards him vying with each other to gain his attention. Lilian halted beside them, her expression pleasantly distant.

'One at a time, children. How can your father understand what you say when you both talk at once?'

Lilian inwardly warmed to Bill as he took Edward's story about baby Marguerite first, then Winifred's excited chatter about their game of Tig, and after they took off their coats promising to race each other up the stairs to the toy room she hung their outdoor clothes in the cupboard under the stairs. Bill smiled, watching her.

'I was beginning to worry about you. It's almost dark.'

'I should have started for home sooner, I know, but I saw Bella Peacock on her way to Mrs

Heslop's cottage. Bill ... Daniel's dead! Isn't it awful? How many more have to die?'

Above their heads the childrens' feet scampered across the first landing before the toy room door slammed shut behind them, and Bill shook his head, at a loss to say anything although he wanted to tell her so much.

'I'll make the tea.' Her voice was low and she paused in the act of turning away.

'Is it true that conscription will be introduced soon?'

'I think that will happen ... maybe in the next few weeks.'

'They won't want *you* to go will they?'

She was tense waiting for his answer, and he wanted to sweep her up in his arms and ask her if it really would upset her if he had to enlist, but he just answered honestly.

'I don't know Lilian.'

'But you're not a young man and you have a factory, a garage and young children to think about.'

Bill grimaced a little. 'As you so rightly point out Lilian, I'm not a young man, but there are now severe shortages in that department and I hardly think the government will take either my family or my businesses into account when considering whether I should enlist.'

'Oh, I'm sorry Bill. I didn't mean to sound insensitive, but if the worst comes to the worst you won't have much time and there would not be many men left who could learn to stand in for you. Old men wouldn't know how to service the buses, let alone drive them, and the factory is probably even more complicated than that. Shouldn't you be thinking of a possible replacement now, just in case?'

The sudden coldness in his eyes warned her that she had gone too far and she walked briskly into the kitchen to begin preparing the meal, pretending not to hear the familiar creak of the door opening again to admit her husband. His voice, heavily sarcastic, came from behind her.

'How touching. How practical. No worries about whether or not I might be injured, or even killed, I notice.'

'Why should that matter to you? I've learned the hard way to live my life along strictly practical lines these past few years, and I think my point about planning ahead is a valid one.'

Picking up a tablecloth she shook it free of its folds in an unmistakably aggressive gesture in Bill's direction before smoothing it over the table and delivering her bombshell question.

'How about training *me* to run the factory? Women all over the country are stepping into absent mens' shoes, doing horrible jobs like making munitions and just whatever they can to keep things going, and I want to be useful, Bill! God knows, I've got to be of value to somebody!'

Two patches of high colour burned in her cheeks as she finished her impassioned plea, and behind the man's icy stare a gamut of emotions struggled in vain to break out into speech. Instead, he looked down at her as though she were some half-witted stranger then shrugged and walked back into the study, closing the door firmly behind him just as something heavy crashed to the floor in the kitchen.

There was sense in what she said, and he knew that Lilian was more than capable of running the factory and maybe even the garage as well. What had upset him so deeply was her indifference towards him on a personal level, yet he acknowledged that he had treated her in a similar manner since learning about Edward and that she could claim with justification to have been taught by an expert in the art.

Long after he had gone to bed that night Bill could still hear her voice echoing in his mind. 'God knows, I've got to be of value to somebody!'

'It's almost dark now, Mrs Heslop, and I will have to go while I can still see a little. Shall I light you a lamp?'

Bella looked across the room at Leo Bondini who had arrived fifteen minutes ago, then at Daniel's mother rocking slowly back and forth in her chair before the fire. All her efforts to communicate with the old lady had so far proved to be futile, and although she had wondered just what the Italian was doing visiting Nan Heslop she felt grateful for his silent support. He looked haggard, she could almost have thought grief stricken despite the fact that he was obviously just extending neighbourly courtesy, and he reached forward to the oil lamp on the table at his side, saying quietly. 'Allow me Signoras. A taper?'

Taking one from the container on the mantel-shelf Bella waited until he had the lamp ready then lit the end in the fire before handing it to him. The comforting glow filled the small room and Nan said suddenly. 'That parcel on the chair by the table ... will you open it for me please?'

With sinking heart Bella watched Leo lift the large parcel onto the table, looking hard at the marking on it then back at Mrs Heslop.

'I think maybe you might like to be alone now?' Bella looked enquiringly at Daniel's mother. 'Would you like us to leave, Mrs Heslop?'

The old woman rose slowly and walked over to the table, where she re-seated herself on a hard-backed chair.

'You were both Daniel's friends. Please stay.' She pushed the package slightly towards Bella. 'There are some scissors in the dresser drawer.'

Daniel's personal effects were sparse: a comb, tobacco pouch, half a dozen letters, a pencil and a penknife. Small objects that spread over the chenille tablecloth in a pathetic display, including a round gold coin-shaped article which Nan picked up and held out to Leo. He took it from her, and Bella was appalled to see tears falling down his cheeks.

'It is a St Christopher medallion ... the patron saint of travellers. I thought it might help keep Daniel safe. I offer again my sincere condolences Signora.'

He placed the gift in his waistcoat pocket, bending his head as the old woman patted his hand as though to comfort a child, and Bella lifted out a heap of mud-caked underclothes all stinking with the odour of filth and stagnant water. They gazed at them in silence for a few moments before she quickly replaced them in the package, for underneath she had glimpsed the

312

tunic of Daniel's khaki battledress and her eyes as they met Leo's were filled with horror. Folded neatly, it too was a mess of dried dirt, but worse than that was the dark stiff stain down the front of it surrounding two holes that had obviously been made by bullets.

She cleared her throat fiercely. 'Mrs Heslop, the rest of the parcel contains Daniel's uniform and I understand that it is the custom for the man of the house to bury such things, especially when ... when the soldier is to be interred abroad. Would you allow me to take these to White Court and bury them for you?' She faltered a little, then went on. 'I would really appreciate you letting me do this in his memory.'

Nan, whose sense of smell was telling her enough of what her eyes could not see, understood the purpose of Bella's request and leaned over, pushing the paper down over the offending garments.

'Yes, do that Mrs Peacock. Maybe Mr Bondini will help you back to White Court now. I see it is almost dark.'

'I will certainly do so, Signora.'

Leo rose, gathering up the cut away string to tie around the middle of the parcel, and Bella gave Daniel's mother a kiss on the cheek as the old woman re-seated herself wearily by the fire.

'Do you have a favourite tree, Mrs Heslop? I want to plant a new one for Daniel.'

For a few moments silence fell, with Leo standing awkwardly by the door as Nan gripped one of Bella's hands, then she spoke quietly.

'A silver birch. It's a beautiful tree ... not as

313

strong as an oak or a beech ... but more beautiful, like my Daniel.'

'A silver birch shall be Daniel's tree. I'll come back when it's done, then maybe you would like to visit White Court and see it.'

Giving Bella's hand a final pat Nan turned away from her visitors, and they left her cottage with their burden.

It was eight thirty next morning when the first thin column of smoke rose into the frosty air at the back of White Court. Bella watched the paraffin-soaked sticks crackling in the flames for a few seconds then took the bundle of white underclothes and dropped it in their midst. At once a cloud of acrid grey spread towards her before it too began to rise, and she jumped as an irritated voice at her side exclaimed 'What on earth are you doing?'

She turned her head, surveying Johnny with an unusually cool eye.

'I'm burning some clothes John, as I'm sure you can see.'

'Of course I can see, but we do have a few servants left Bella; people who would have put them in the kitchen furnace for you.'

He kicked his foot against the brown package on the ground, unfolding the wrapping at the top, and the tunic with its grisly message lay visible now to both their eyes.

Bella said quietly. 'I told Daniel's mother I would bring his clothes here to bury them, but it somehow seemed more appropriate to burn them.'

'Yes… I see.'

He looked faintly shocked, as indeed he was, for the sight had reawakened in him the dread of his own possible involvement in the war very shortly.

'I should have gone with you to Daniel's home. How did you carry this heavy parcel yourself?'

'It wasn't heavy, just clumsy, and Leo Bondini was there to see Mrs Heslop so he carried it back for me.' She looked thoughtful. 'He and Daniel must have been very good friends because I could see the man was as upset as I.'

'Oh Bella, will you always be so naive? Rumours were rife about Bondini and Daniel for months before he volunteered. Why do you think Daniel never had a girlfriend nor Leo Bondini take up with some woman in the valley?'

Glaring up at him, Bella clenched her fists at her sides.

'You're a nasty wicked person, John, and I don't believe you!'

'As you please, my dear, but they were probably only a short time away from being arrested. Little wonder he left his alleged touring company to "rest" up here, then stayed for years. If this place wasn't such a backwater Bondini would have been in trouble long before now, so he can count himself lucky on that score!'

He turned and began to walk down to the house and she bent down and added Daniel's tunic to the funeral pyre, repeating softly, 'I don't believe you,' as she watched the flames slowly consume Daniel Heslop's uniform through the flickering curtain of her own tears.

Her heart began to beat out a suffocating tattoo the moment she knocked on the cottage door, and as she heard the shuffling footsteps approaching on the other side she wanted only to turn and run away, then Marion Robinson opened the door and stared at her uninvited visitor.

'Marion ... it's Christmas Eve.' Lilian pleaded. 'We would like you to spend the day with us tomorrow as you always have, and I've come to see if we can talk over our present ... difficulty.'

'I have no difficulty, present or otherwise, but you'd better come in I suppose.'

Grudgingly the woman stood back to let Lilian step inside, and she sighed as she took a chair by the fire. Every sign so far pointed to a negative outcome from this meeting, but she would not give up just yet. Marion hovered by the kitchen door and asked. 'Would you like some tea?'

'Yes please.'

'Then push the kettle over the fire and I'll bring a tray.'

With the black kettle hanging on its hook over the flames Lilian felt a faint relief as the 'singing' noise began at once. She had left the children with Bill, but he had a meeting at the garage in less than an hour so saving time was vital. Within minutes Marion returned with a tray and set the teapot down on the fender to warm.

'Marion ... I hope you won't object to my bringing this subject up, but we have known each other many years now and I don't feel I can let this situation between us continue without at least trying to make amends. I know I did wrong

316

marrying Bill when I'd had an accident with another man, but I've tried so hard to make up for it and be a good wife.'

Her mother-in-law looked away from her, but not before Lilian glimpsed the pure distaste in her expression, and she went on desperately.

'Bill and I were happy, and I'm sure we could have stayed that way had he not found out about Edward ... and I don't know how he did, for I never told anyone, not even my mother. It just ended every good thing we ever had together. I'd grown to love him Marion, and I really believed I was making him happy...'

Her voice trailed off as the older woman guiltily busied herself lifting the kettle from the hob to make the tea. Lilian finished lamely.

'I wanted you to know that I truly regret hurting Bill, that's all.'

A heavy silence fell. With the tea brewing in the pot Marion Robinson seated herself in the chair opposite her daughter-in-law, staring thoughtfully into the fire while Lilian studied her impassive features with lowering spirits, then she leaned forward to arrange the crockery on the tray and remarked.

'This war is very depressing isn't it? I shall be so glad when it is over.'

Her tone was quite normal, and Lilian realised that this was her strange way of accepting the apology she had been offered. Relieved, she responded in kind.

'Yes indeed. I suppose we're luckier up here than in the south where they have those terrible Zeppelins coming over with bombs ... it said in

317

the paper the other morning that over fifty people were killed in London through one of those raids. How can they do that, I wonder?'

Marion poured out a cup of tea, passing it across the table as Lilian added 'Bill and I have been talking about the future in case things get any worse, and we have decided that I shall take over the management of the factory and garage if he has to enlist. God forbid that it should come to that, but it's best to be prepared. He's already explained to me quite a lot about the running of both places, and last week he took me down to Dalton to meet the women who work in the factory.'

A spasm of pain crossed her companion's face as she digested this unwelcome information, and she shook her head suddenly as though to deny everything she had just been told.

'But Bill is too old to go into the army, isn't he? And Gilbert too.'

'It's only a precaution against some of the wild rumours that are circulating these days. Please don't worry about it, Marion. I only mentioned it out of interest.'

Wishing now that she had done no such thing Lilian offered her an encouraging smile before sipping her tea and hurrying on to a less disturbing subject.

'I'll need something to do, in any case, seeing Leo Bondini left the village last week. No more Concert Party do's, although no one is in the mood for them now.'

'Yes, I heard he'd gone quite abruptly. I met your father in the village one morning and he

318

told me that Mr Bondini had left the cottage keys on the doorstep at Roughside, and that was the first they knew of his intention to leave. No "goodbyes" to anyone. He must have walked down to Dalton for an early train, and that would have been far from easy in the dark.'

Outside the window a light flurry of snow swept giddily past and the women gazed at each other in dismay.

'I must hurry. Bill has a meeting at three o'clock and I've left him with the children.'

The front door rattled in a gust of wind as Lilian set down her teacup and Marion nodded, knowing well how quickly a snow shower could turn into a blizzard. As she walked to the door Lilian said 'If this keeps up Dad and Louisa will probably have to stay at home tomorrow. There's no point in them risking coming away if the weather's bad to find they're not able to get back again, but I did so want us to be together this Christmas Day. Bill will come for you Marion. If he walks down you can both come to Ivy House in one of the buses seeing the garage is only over the road.'

Marion smiled. 'And providing the road is still visible, dear.'

As she walked briskly along Gilfell Main Street Lilian held onto the memory of that unguarded endearment from her mother-in-law, for it proved that despite Marion's shocking discovery about her grandson she still harboured some affection for the relationship they had built up over the years, and on that slender foundation she could hope to rebuild.

Constance straightened her back, her face red with the heat from the stove she had been stoking, then hurried to wash her hands before rushing on to her next job. Her shift was almost over and she was thankful for it. The horrors of everyday life on the ward had frozen part of her sensibilities out of emotional self-defence, but she knew she could never get used to the harrowing way so many men called out for their mother in their last minutes of life, and three soldiers had died already that day.

Dysentery, the curse of the wounded, regularly swept through the wards to sap the meagre strength of the patients, who sometimes wept in protest while they were washed clean, and the only quiet men seemed to be those who were unconscious or simply too ill to speak. Yet still the casualties kept coming in a constant stream, filling her heart with despair as she searched each new face in case Ralph should be there. Ten days ago, in desperation, she had written to his sister, Sybil, asking if she had any news of Ralph that she could pass on, hopefully to set her mind at ease, and every day she looked for a reply. So far none had come, but maybe today would be different.

Pushed to the back of her mind as she carried bedpans, took temperatures and attended to various wounds, a message from Ralph or his sister was still uppermost in her thoughts when she left the ward half an hour later to find a letter in Sybil's handwriting waiting for her. Torn between joy and terror she took it back to the nurses' quarters before tearing the envelope open, and as she read the single page Constance sank down on the side of the bed, her eyes staring blankly into a future which had once promised everything but now held nothing.

Across the room her fellow VAD, Christine, paused in the act of putting on her shoes and asked gently, 'Is anything wrong, Connie?'

'Wrong?'

'Your letter. Have you had bad news?'

She nodded, unable to speak for the pain in her throat, but held out the page towards her and the girl silently read the sympathetic, though brief, message that a telegram had been received by Sybil and her family some weeks previously stating that Major Ralph Miller was 'Missing in action, believed killed.'

CHAPTER TWELVE

1915/1916

Christmas and New Year were subdued affairs in
the valley. The reality of so many bereaved
families, some mourning more than a single
loved one, had long ago brought the war's harsh
facts to replace patriotic wishful thinking, and as
Lilian retreated to her kitchen to baste her goose
on Christmas morning she let slip the smile she
had worn since breakfast for the childrens'
benefit. What would next Christmas bring, she
wondered, then cast it out of her mind to
concentrate determinedly upon the present. The
snow had stopped after covering the ground with
a one inch blanket of white, and both Marion
and the family from Roughside would be arriving
within two hours: it might be a pity not to make
the most of it this year.

At White Court, Annabel, a constant reminder
of the threat world events posed to relationships,
seemed to have a permanent smile fixed on her
pale face while her eyes glittered as she put on a
desperate show of enjoying herself which fooled
no one. She cringed when Bella told her about
Daniel Heslop, and thanked providence that his
mother had refused her sister-in-law's invitation
to come to the house for the day. Was Christmas
not hard enough to endure without having a

grieving parent added to the company? Bella and little Antony were the only ones with any real life about them, she thought, for she herself was tense and Johnny silent and moody. He had several times questioned her when they were alone, asking about Raynor's experiences and whether there was any truth in the terrible conditions some of the local men had spoken of after being invalided out of the army. Annabel had replied in a manner which she hoped would deter him, but Johnny's anxiety spurred him on so that she had finally shared with him the substance of her husband's nightmares. At the time Bella had been upstairs bathing Antony, for which Annabel was grateful, and when she came down again Johnny was locked in his study with a bottle of brandy.

Conscription began on January 5th when Prime Minister Asquith introduced The Military Service Bill calling up all single men and childless widowers between the ages of eighteen and forty. At first a secret relief was felt by certain of those not covered by this criteria, but by March the Bill was extended to include married men, and by 25th May a further Bill was passed calling up every man of conscription age.

At Roughside, Louisa's thoughts flew to her dead Terence and she secretly wondered just how happy their extra four years might have been had he not boarded the ill-fated Titanic, whilst at Ivy House a curious calm fell.

The night before Bill left for Carlisle he and Lilian spent a long time in the study after their children were asleep. Earlier in the day he had said goodbye to Marion as cheerfully as he could, but she had been deeply upset by the imminent departure of both her sons, and knowing how the memory of his mother's tears gave him pain Lilian tried to be as matter of fact as possible, unaware that her apparent lack of emotion was causing Bill even more distress.

He looked at her profile as she bent over the factory ledger, lips moving silently as she added up yet another column of figures under his supervision, and wished he knew whether she was at all sorry to see him leave. Their marriage had turned into a travesty long ago but now that he was going away, maybe forever, the issue of Edward's parentage no longer seemed important. Twice Bill opened his mouth to tell her this, and twice closed it again without uttering a word. It was true that on what was possibly their last few hours together there was no longer any hostility between them, but equally, there was no warmth either, and when he left Ivy House next morning they remained imprisoned in their emotional stalemate. Wounded by his seeming indifference towards her as he said goodbye to Edward and Winifred on the front steps of their home, Lilian felt her resolve beginning to crumble and turned abruptly as tears overwhelmed her, walking swiftly along the passage and up the stairs where she shut herself quickly in her room with her head buried in a pillow to stifle her sobs. Perceiving this as a callous gesture on Lilian's part Bill stood still for a few seconds listening for a clue as to what might be going on up the stairs, but heard nothing, and quickly kissed Edward and Winifred before reaching into his trouser pocket for a coin which he held out towards both children.

'Do you know what this is called?'

Winifred shook her head but Edward nodded. 'It's a shilling.'

'Yes, but it's a special shilling. It's called The King's Shilling which soldiers are given before going to fight for their country, and I'm giving this special shilling to you.' He took Edward's hand and placed the coin in his palm. 'I want both of you to keep this safe until I come back. Can you do that?'

'Yes Daddy.'

Feeling both sadness and pride Edward turned to show the precious keepsake to his sister and Bill walked away, his footsteps sounding resolute and strong to Lilian who was trying to pull herself together in the bedroom above the front door. In a way it had been a relief to weep as she had, if only for a few minutes, then Winifred's voice came from outside her door telling her that Daddy had gone and she answered in a falsely light tone.

'Alright darlings. I'm coming.'

As she rose from the bed she could still hear her husband's footsteps fading into the distance and wondered if she would ever hear them coming back, for he had made it clear that he intended spending his Embarkation Leave elsewhere than in Gilfell as one goodbye would more than suffice.

Of the many men who left the valley that day

only a handful returned. Three in the higher age group with lung trouble and acute arthritis, Robinson's garage mechanic-driver with varicose veins, and Johnny Peacock of White Court who had been found to have a heart defect.

Relieved at being legitimately able to stay at home, yet alarmed at his previously unsuspected ailment, Johnny huddled in the corner of the railway carriage and stared out at the darkening landscape. The procedure had taken most of the day with men passed like cattle from one point to another, often stark naked, and by the time he returned to Carlisle Railway Station he was unable to feel anything other than total weariness. The platform on the opposite side of the station had that morning been packed to capacity with men who had previously had their medical and were now en route to their basic training barracks, and for an instant he had glimpsed Bill Robinson standing talking among a crowd of other men. He had seemed quite at ease with his pipe clenched between his teeth as he talked, removing it once for a few seconds as a wave of laughter swept the crowd, and Johnny wondered how they could joke about anything when they were going to The Front in a matter of weeks. Had they not heard of the conditions there that sounded worse than hell, and the way the war was going it was more than likely that most of them would never see their families again.

Now, on his way back to Gilfell, he smiled as he thought about Antony. His son was the only person he had ever truly loved and he could even

326

feel pleasure at the thought of the long walk he would have from Dalton to Gilfell because it would be so good to see little Antony at the end of it.

He closed his eyes, sighing slightly with a deep relief that he knew he would have to hide very carefully from others in the future. This day, a black one for so many men in the area, had undoubtedly been a very lucky one for him, heart condition or not.

Almost an hour later the train stopped in Dalton Station disgorging its few passengers in seconds before moving on, and the Gilfell men walked out onto the street to find Robinson's bus waiting at the exit as usual. Unable to believe his luck Johnny surged forward with the others, feeling in his pockets for change to put in the fare box, then looked up to find Lilian sitting in the driver's cab viewing him with disdain. The mechanic was grinning at her, and after putting his suitcase on the luggage rack he pushed past Johnny to go outside again where he walked round to the front of the bus to speak to Lilian.

Sitting down on the front seat Johnny listened. 'Well, missus, I see you're not to be beat. Are you going to let me drive us home?'

'I'll do that with pleasure, Albert. I took my time bringing the bus down in the daylight, but I wasn't feeling very brave about taking it back up in the dark.' Opening the cab door she jumped lightly down to the ground and Johnny heard her ask in low urgent tones. 'Did you see Bill at all before he left?'

'No missus ... sorry.'

'Oh well, it was just a thought. I take it they wouldn't accept you.'

'It was my legs. Varicose veins they said. No use for marching.'

'Well, it's good to have you back, believe me. We'll talk about reorganising everything again tomorrow.'

'Righto.'

Tensing himself as Lilian mounted the steps into the bus Johnny watched her lip curve slightly downwards at the sight of him, and as Albert turned the starting handle and the engine spluttered into life she sat down facing him in a seat across the aisle.

'Of all the poor fellows who left here today I might have known you would be one of those to come back again. Has there ever been anyone with such a charmed life, I wonder?'

He scowled, shifting uncomfortably. 'They wouldn't have me... I have heart trouble.'

Her burst of laughter was the last response he had expected and he glared at her defensively.

'The army must have some really clever doctors, Johnny, for I don't think the rest of us ever suspected that you had a heart to have trouble with.'

'I'm glad you find it so amusing.'

The bus moved forward, beginning to gather speed as Lilian settled more easily into her seat, and as though they were puppets worked by the same hands both turned away from each other to stare out at the black square of their window.

One by one the other passengers left the bus as the journey progressed, and Johnny and Lilian were alone for the remaining half mile to the garage where Albert drove the vehicle straight inside before switching off the engine.

At once Johnny rose, pulled open the door of the bus and stood at the bottom of the steps ready to help Lilian down. Surprised at this unexpected courtesy she took his hand while descending, thanking him rather awkwardly for his assistance as Albert vacated the cab intent upon securing the premises for the night. Touching the handle of the big sliding door he frowned for a moment at the two figures, still standing by the bus staring at each other like statues, until his voice made them both jump.

'Shall I walk you to your home, missus? It's late.'

Johnny answered for her without looking up. 'It's alright. I'll see Mrs Robinson to her door on my way to White Court.'

Looking towards Albert, Lilian nodded. 'I'll be fine with Mr Peacock, thank you Albert.'

Following them both out into the night Albert ran the door along its track then walked round the corner to enter the building again, this time by his private accommodation entrance which he had never dreamed he would be lucky enough to see again so soon. His curiosity about Lilian and Johnny was already dead, and seconds later as he drew the curtains across the window of his small living room he gave no more thought to the couple making their way through the deserted centre of the village.

Outside, the man and woman walked from the outskirts of Gilfell towards Main Street as fast as their limited vision would allow, and when she felt him put his hand under her elbow her heart began to beat rather too quickly for comfort. It had been so long since she had felt a man's protective touch, but she wished it could have been Bill's instead of Johnny's.

'I'm sorry about Bill having to go.' He was saying. 'You must be very disappointed.'

'I am, but it isn't your fault, and I shouldn't have said what I did about you having a charmed life. I don't think any of us have that now.'

'No.'

They were silent for a while until they reached Chapel Corner when Johnny suddenly remarked 'Everything's changed. I remember the year I came to your farm to help with the haymaking, and it seemed like a totally different world then. A nicer world. Maybe a world we'll never see again.'

Lilian stopped walking abruptly as she realised with horrified certainty that she was going to cry. Johnny was right. None of them would ever see those days return, even families lucky enough to have their menfolk survive, and the person she missed most from that time was Bill. Dear kind Bill, who had once wanted more than anything else to have her as his wife.

'It hurts thinking of it all.' She whispered, then covered her face with her hands and wept, leaning against Johnny as he put his arms around her. She heard him murmuring in her ear as she sobbed and smelt the faint tobacco-leather odour of his clothes that had once helped to separate her from her commonsense for a few fateful minutes, yet did nothing to her now.

Waiting until her storm of weeping had died Johnny tilted her face up to his and kissed her full on the lips, a long warm kiss that should have thrilled her but did not, and her voice as she disengaged herself was distant though a little unsteady.

'I'm sorry I've cried all over you, Johnny, but it's been awful lately for every one of us, and you were just here at the wrong time.'

'Is that all it was, Lilian?'

In the starlight she could see the faint gleam of his teeth as he smiled, and an emptiness came over her as she acknowledged that what she had told him was the exact truth. Johnny's kiss had meant nothing to her other than the fact that he had taken advantage of her temporary vulnerability, while the one person she really needed was speeding further and further away from her every moment.

'That's truly all it was.' She said quietly. 'Thank you for seeing me home.'

Inside the yard she waved briefly in his direction, unsure of whether he could actually see her or not, then shut the door and hurried into the house.

Everything lay under a blanket of silence. Upstairs, the children and Marion, who had agreed to stay overnight, were plainly fast asleep, and Lilian sat down at her kitchen table staring into the glowing embers of the fire. Was Bill on a train at this moment or already lying in some comfortless barracks? Wherever he was he would surely be thinking of home.

Her tears came quietly this time, for the floodgates had already been opened, and after laying her head on her outstretched arms she slowly fell into an exhausted sleep troubled by jumbled snatches of dreams where she was being kissed again, only this time it was Bill who was holding her in his arms, not Johnny.

Midsummer was fine and warm with July and August the same. In the valley, so depleted of men, the haymaking workforce was made up of elderly men and as many women as could be spared from other jobs. At Roughside, Helen worked alongside her mother stacking sheaves into stooks, and tried not to grumble about her aching bones as the sweat ran down her forehead and into her eyes. Red faced and weary they toiled from light to dusk making each second count while the dry weather held. Once it was all safely inside the barn they would be able to relax, and the widows and grieving mothers go back to their homes to rest and feel a little better off.

Baby Marguerite kept her mother out of the meadow a lot of the time for she was eighteen months old now and, unless asleep in her pram, was far too difficult to watch as her tendency to toddle towards the shire horse's massive feet seemed irresistible.

In Dalton, Lilian helped the women pack the completed uniforms when she was not busy with ledgers and invoices. The work was piling up daily, and she knew it was more than time to introduce a permanent nightshift, but for that she must have a supervisor whom she could trust to

332

run it for her. A name had been suggested to her by two of her machinists quite independently of each other, and she was waiting for the woman to arrive for an interview having sent one of the younger girls to her address with a note. She had apparently worked at the factory until around six months ago but had left suddenly for reasons of her own. The only cause Lilian could think of for a childless widow to leave such steady and lucrative employment was bad eyesight, but she hoped it was not true for if she could not see properly she would be no use as Night Supervisor.

Above the intermittent whirr of the sewing machines in the next room Lilian heard a gentle cough and glanced up to find a young woman standing in the doorway holding in her hand the note Lilian had written. She was around thirty, slim and pretty with blue eyes and reddish-gold hair that fell unfashionably to her shoulders. Afterwards Lilian remembered the abrupt cessation of noise on the factory floor and the nervousness of the woman's manner as she looked at her with wary eyes, but for the duration of the interview these telling points escaped her.

Smiling, she pushed back her chair to stand up while beckoning her visitor into the office, then shut the door behind them.

'Mrs Harker, isn't it? Please have a seat. I'm Lilian Robinson.'

'Yes, I know.'

Maura Harker's eye contact with Lilian was brief, and she stared down at the desk as Lilian talked to her about the Supervisor's post.

'It seems that you are the only person with a

333

working knowledge of all stages of production, and I would be very glad if you would accept the job of Night Supervisor and help me find some more workers for that shift too if you can.'

'I think I could find some finishers, Mrs Robinson. Is that what you'll want for the nightshift?'

'Well yes, I suppose it is.'

Surprised that this simple fact had not previously occurred to her, she gave Maura Harker a grateful smile.

'You see? You're proving your worth already. My husband tried to teach me as much as he could before he left, but you can't beat experience.'

They were together for fifteen minutes while Lilian asked her advice on various issues and promised her a wage commensurate with her responsibility, but while she talked she wondered why her new employee had so little to say and why she still seemed to be so ill at ease. When the time came to show her out, she asked her 'Would you mind telling me why you left the factory before, Mrs Harker? Was it the money, or was your eyesight bothering you?'

The woman shot her a startled look. 'No, it wasn't anything like that. I had ... personal reasons at that time.'

'Sorry. I didn't mean to pry.'

It was the few seconds after Maura Harker left the office and was walking down the factory floor towards the outer door that finally alerted Lilian to the cause of the woman's discomfiture. All machines ceased working as every head turned first in the direction of the widow, and then towards herself, and as she looked into their faces the secret amusement there told her clearly just who Maura Harker was and why she had left the factory. Sickened, she returned to her desk and pretended to resume work on a ledger while her feelings towards the women who had caused her such humiliation hardened, for there was no way out of it now without making matters worse, both practically and emotionally. Bill might find it funny if he learned that his wife and recent mistress were running the factory together, and no doubt the inhabitants of Dalton would appreciate the joke too.

Aware of a sly spate of whispering and giggling from the adjoining room Lilian rose to her feet and opened the door.

'So far as I am aware none of you are being paid to gossip, and in future anyone talking too much will be sacked!' She said coldly. 'Good workers I can gladly employ, leaving personal feelings aside, but malingerers won't be tolerated. I hope I've made myself clear.'

Deriving some satisfaction from the now startled faces of her machinists Lilian returned to her desk, but this time left the office door open. If they found anything else to be amused about she wanted to know.

The heat was stifling, but the three young men in the column in front of Bill still had a little breath and energy left to sing. 'Tipperary' and 'Take me Back to Dear Old Blighty' had long ago been rendered with gusto, the mens' feet marching easily to its rhythm, but weariness was setting in now and only the trio were left giving voice. Bill, who had never been able to sing two consecutive notes in key, smiled grimly as he listened to the words and wished he could join in. Sung to a hymn tune, and sounding equally fervent, the young soldiers carolled:

'When this bloody war is over,
 Oh, how happy I shall be.
When I get my civvy clothes on,
 no more soldiering for me.'

Someone near the back shouted a loud 'Amen' at the end, and a few subdued guffaws responded before all sound ceased except for that of heavy boots hitting the road in a grim concerted beat.

Half an hour ago a soldier had fallen in his tracks, unconscious from dehydration and exhaustion. The line had soon resumed its tempo, and after a spell in the medical van he had returned to his place, obviously unwell, but once more capable of putting one foot after another despite his ghastly pallor.

This was the second day on their journey to The Front, and Bill wondered why it had never occurred to any of them that they would have to march there in suffocating heat carrying heavy packs and rifles. The flies plagued them mercilessly, even before they began to sweat, and as the nightmare trek went on men with glazed eyes took inner refuge from the torture of their own thoughts. Thinking once of the home he had shunned during Embarkation Leave, Bill found it so incredibly painful that he concentrated instead on events of the last few weeks' basic training and his first sight of war upon landing on French soil in the dark of night. The horizon had been lit up by a moving fringe of light from the big guns, like a gigantic necklace reflecting a candelabra's brilliance, while above it coloured lights rose into the sky before falling to earth in a slow graceful curve. Objects that appeared like bright stars hovered in the air for a few seconds then faded into oblivion, and all the time the ominous muffled rumblings reminded him that its strange beauty was only an illusion. Wandering a short distance away on his own Bill viewed the raging line of war in silence, for whatever he had imagined a battle-ground to be like he quickly forgot in the face of this awesome reality.

Since enlisting he had made many friends, but within an hour of landing the platoon split up into different factions to replace the many casualties in other companies, and with the last remnants of familiarity gone a dark depression came down on him which he fought valiantly to hide from his new companions, although he suspected that most of them felt the same.

Beside him a dark-haired young man of heavy build cursed frequently under his breath. Malcolm Dawson was an ex factory worker from Sunderland who had left his wife and two children in straitened circumstances and constantly worried in case the army failed to send on to them his meagre wages. Trying his best to give reassurance that all would be well, Bill would find himself wondering about Lilian, his mother and the children, and then his brother Gilbert, of whom he had so far heard nothing.

A sudden scuffle up ahead drew everyone's attention to yet another victim of the march, an older man this time who had stumbled out of the line and fallen awkwardly on his rifle, but a harsh cry of 'Walk on!' set the column in motion again after its initial hesitation. At Bill's side his companion muttered 'That's Horace Babcock who lives two streets away from me and the wife. He's over forty-five but they never asked for birth certificates and I think he fancied himself as some kind of hero, poor bugger!'

Towards the end of the day's march word filtered down the line that Babcock would not be returning. He was dead.

The factory took up most of Lilian's time while Albert ran the garage to the best of his ability. As there was no way that one driver could hope to do the work of two, chaos prevailed more often than not, and at home she was paying various women to look after Edward and Winifred as well as having Marion reinstalled in Ivy House.

She tried hard not to mind that her mother-in-law had received three letters from Bill whilst she had not had any, but it seemed yet again to widen the gulf between her husband and herself. Of Maura Harker she had seen very little other than the few minutes when their shifts overlapped in the mornings, or when something needed to be discussed, then Maura's voice would drop as Lilian's sharpened into hostility, yet in spite of it all the factory was running with maximum efficiency and making a fine profit. Sometimes

Lilian felt guilty about this, even though it was a fact that most home manufacturers were reaping huge benefits from the war which was severely restricting all imports, and she took comfort from the knowledge that her workforce was one of the most generously paid in the area.

She was sitting in her office on the morning of 6th July unable to concentrate on the ledgers for the anger she was feeling at an article in her daily newspaper. According to this particular war correspondent the ongoing battle near a river called The Somme, which had begun on the first of the month, had been 'on balance, a good day for England and France' yet a blizzard of telegrams had started in the valley forty eight hours ago and showed no signs of slowing down. Lifting her head above the wooden partition Lilian watched the women, heads bent over their machines, and wondered how many of the dreaded forms had already arrived within their families, or were at this moment on their way; might there also be one destined for Ivy House or the little hardware store in Kenhope? Shivering she began to fold the offending newspaper, then twisted it savagely into the smallest shape she could before ramming it into the wastepaper bin at her feet.

'Excuse me missus, but I've brought a man to see you who is looking for a job driving our buses.'

Albert was standing in the office doorway with a stranger by his side, and Lilian felt grateful for their timely intrusion as she smilingly motioned both men inside.

'If you can drive a bus, and are free to do so, then you have a job. It's as simple as that.'

The stranger, swarthy as a gypsy, held out his hand to her.

'Sean Curtis, Mrs Robinson, late of the King's Own Scottish Borderers. Invalided out two months ago.'

Shaking his hand Lilian looked into deep brown eyes, unaware of how intensely her own were responding, then drew back sharply as though his touch had burned her. Albert spoke again, saving her the trouble of trying to think of something to say to break the sudden tension.

'We've already discussed shifts and I've told him what the wage is, so if it's alright with yourself I'll be doing the miners' run and Sean here can do Gilfell to Dalton.'

'Yes, that's fine. If it suits both of you please carry on. Have you got anywhere suitable to stay, Mr Curtis? You don't strike me as being a local man.'

Amazed at how steady her voice sounded despite the sudden turmoil of her senses, Lilian offered her new driver a cool smile which he returned in kind.

'I originally hail from Annan across the Border, as my accent probably tells you, but as I left home a few years prior to 1914 I decided to convalesce with some relatives who have a farm on Dalton Moor. I heard that you were looking for a driver, and I told them that if I got the job I'd be seeking new lodgings in Gilfell to be near the buses.'

'Try the row of cottages opposite the garage, or

failing that, let me know tomorrow and I may have a better prospect for you to consider.'

'Thanks.'

He turned and walked away after Albert, and she noticed that he limped quite badly. She also noticed how tall he was and how broad his shoulders, and as though aware of her scrutiny Sean Curtis glanced back towards her quickly. Startled, she looked away, but their mutual show of interest seemed to hang in the air like a promise for the future.

'Another day's marching'll do it, or so I've heard from the NCO., and even if he was lying just to make us all feel better it shows he's a decent sort I suppose.'

Bill nodded and leaned forward to take off his boots. The village square was picturesque, and might have seemed peaceful had it not been for the depressingly familiar sound of gunfire which was now much louder than it had been before.

Malcolm Dawson looked over his shoulder at the window of the house on whose cobbled frontage he and Bill were sitting, then followed his companion's example by taking off his boots and beginning to scrape them clean with a clasp knife.

'Some bloody rest period,' He grumbled, and grinned as Bill looked at him. 'Go on professor, have a good laugh.'

Smiling good naturedly at the nickname he had acquired since the start of the march Bill looked over the square to where a crowd of their fellow soldiers were filing into a building that looked

341

like a tavern.

'Some of us will sleep well tonight, even if it is here on the street.'

'And I'll make sure I'm one of them.' Malcolm promised. 'All this polishing leather and brass, plus blancoing and rifle cleaning, is a job that deserves the reward of alcohol in some form, even if it's only wine. What do you reckon, Prof?'

'I can't say, never having tasted any.'

Dawson stared at him in silence for a few seconds then slowly shook his head. 'I might have known it. You're teetotal.'

'Guilty.'

'Well, I promise you this, Prof. After tonight you won't be, and what's more you'll sleep like a baby for the first time since we set foot on these shores.'

Half an hour later they crossed the cobbled street to enter the tavern and Bill looked back at the village in sunset, its atmosphere so evocative of serene summer nights in Gilfell. He paused for a moment, almost against his will thinking of Ivy House, then, as Malcolm beckoned him on, he turned his back on the scene and walked into the crowded noisy room. Within minutes he was sitting at a table with a group of his fellow soldiers, drinking the same as they were and admitting, to their raucous delight, that he had obviously spent many dull years missing out on this wonderful substance.

'It's good.' He acknowledged as the relaxing warmth began to spread through his body. 'I haven't felt like this in weeks.'

A few tables away Private Jimmy Jones grinned

342

ruefully across at the convert. 'Enjoy it while you can, boyo. Its effect doesn't last forever, more's the pity.'

In the far corner of the dimly lit room a mellow baritone began to sing 'If You Were the Only Girl in the World', to be joined bar by bar by other voices, and Bill closed his eyes as he leaned back against the wall. Dawson had been right. He would sleep well tonight wherever they were billeted, and that would be as well seeing they were so near The Front.

As the song ended someone called out 'Where's Stan Harris? C'mon Stan. Give us a rendering.'

A tense silence filled the room for a few uncomfortable seconds, then the man was heard to mutter, 'Sorry. I forgot.'

Thirty five year old Stanley Harris had often sung on the marches, and the battalion had enjoyed his cheerful tenor, but this morning he too had been taken to the Medical Van never to return.

Constance pushed her grisly burden into the depths of the furnace, slammed the door shut and began at once to gag into the tray that had carried it. Yet another amputation with the hapless VAD left to dispose of the limb, this time an arm, and the horror of it was often overwhelming, even for a woman whose emotions had largely frozen over through personal bereavement.

Eyes stinging partly with tears and partly through the effort of vomiting, she walked over to the door once she had sluiced the tray and leaned on the jamb for a few minutes in an effort to regain her equilibrium. She was both feeling and showing weakness, and with the seemingly endless deluge of badly injured men that they had dealt with since July 1st Constance knew she must pull herself together somehow.

The ward was a daily nightmare with men enduring unimaginable pain through wounds going septic, bones shattered by shrapnel, and the added misery of pneumonia and all manner of fevers. Five men had died since she had come on duty two hours ago, four of them through the terrible effects of mustard gas, and each time a sheet was pulled over a face the memory of her lost love, whom she acknowledged was almost certainly dead, added itself to the anguish she felt for the victim and his family.

This morning she had received one of many rather peevish letters from her mother asking her why she so seldom wrote back, but there was no polite way to answer that question. The world of her parents and Low Shields, and even that of the Suffragettes, were many universes removed from the one she now inhabited, and as she could not write about her reality neither could she pretend to relate to the old one. Every six weeks or so she managed to compose a note of around four lines hoping all was well with them and citing the heavy workload as an excuse for her brevity, but she had grown to dread the arrival of her mother's pale blue envelopes with their familiar spidery handwriting.

A sudden rustle of skirts in the corridor alerted Constance to the approach of another member of staff, and she straightened herself quickly just as her Ward Sister came into view.

'Come along nurse, don't loiter! We have more patients coming in again and need every pair of hands on the ward.'

'Yes Sister.'

Passing her superior, Constance was careful to keep her eyes away from whatever it was that she was carrying beneath a white cloth, but the smell that touched her nostrils as she walked out into the passage told her clearly enough what gangrenous obscenity lay there.

CHAPTER THIRTEEN

1916/1917

The Battle of The Somme, like a ravenous man-devouring monster, raged on for over four months. Following the first major defeat of the German army with its terrible cost in British lives, the process of wearing down the enemy began in earnest and a French contingent under General Foch added their military shoulder to the wheel on the right flank of the British. At first the enemy stumbled slightly, surprised that the French were still in action after the Battle of Verdun, but soon recovered their resistance to launch fierce counterattacks after each allied onslaught, the first often closely followed by a second of equal ferocity, whilst casualty lists on both sides swelled to monumental proportions. Two more days of marching through now sparsely populated country and Bill's battalion were drawn into this hell, the survivors to live with its terrible images for the rest of their lives; Ulstermen, Highlanders, Newfoundlanders, South Africans and Australians were among those who were to remember The Somme and the thousands of their compatriots who fell on foreign soil.

Becoming accustomed to life in the trenches put a stop to most of the nostalgic mind-wandering that Bill and certain of his companions had occasionally indulged in, as personal survival hour by hour became their prime motivation.

'For Gawd's sake, keep your bloody 'eads down!' had at first struck Bill as Corporal Tanner's most overworked phrase until one morning during a lull in shooting when a young soldier, no more than eighteen, had risked a peep at the enemy. At once there was a burst of gunfire and Private Anderson fell back as his face disintegrated, blood and brains spattering the uniforms of his comrades as he slumped to the bottom of the trench. Stunned, the men stared down at the mutilated corpse that mere seconds earlier had been a living human being, and a harsh voice from further down the line called 'Don't just stand there! Move 'im to the end for the Medical Corps to take away, and if you don't want to be next keep yer bloody 'eads down!'

Hunger and thirst were constant companions, as were the incessant flies and body lice, the latter being the harder to bear for the more fastidious spoiling what little sleep could be snatched during the night. Water, which had to be collected every day, was rationed to very small amounts for each man and the half mugful put aside for cleanliness was used first for teeth cleaning, then washing and shaving. On occasions when there was a surplus of the slightly petrol-tainted liquid other parts of the body could be washed, but those times were rare and more urgent worries than fretting over personal hygiene occupied the men.

Like many others Bill slept standing up, having carved himself an appropriate niche in the trench wall where he could lean back and feel a little support until waking at dawn, when for a few minutes he would watch the strands of mist lying across No-Man's-Land. Fingering their gasmasks and listening for the sound of the warning gong kept the men in a state of nervous anxiety many times, for the stories about the effects of mustard gas were now known not to have been exaggerated. Shot from the enemy lines in shells, the gas escaped to form earthbound clouds of a sickly-greenish yellow which would melt into one another to move forward on the prevailing wind, changing colour to a bluey-white. Its resemblance at this stage to harmless mist frequently gave rise to alarm if a breeze happened to be blowing towards newly awakened soldiers, but just when they were sure of their safety from this threat the enemy would begin to send 'The Breakfast Ration' of shells called 'plum puddings' or 'flying pigs'. These could be shot from a distance of over a mile and would fall suddenly on a steep curve, the sound of their flight giving a few seconds warning of their approach, and were the usual overture to the rest of the day's horrors.

Between bouts of hostility Private Dawson kept up a stream of almost constant comments which Bill found oddly comforting, and they became friends as far as was possible in their circumstances. He spoke of Lilian and his children as though they were just like any normal family, forgetting their true situation in the telling, and Malcolm responded to this confidence wryly.

'Trust you to have a beautiful wife and clever kids, Prof. Bet you can't wait to get back to them.'

348

They were eating the last meal of the day, which was welcome to stomachs never full despite its unappetising taste, and Bill paused for a moment wishing he had never spoken of his private life. Dawson continued to talk in a hoarse whisper.

'Take my old girl ... a bit of a lass, as we say in the north. A right rum 'un! Had a fling with the Rent Collector a couple of years ago and ended up in the family way when I was on nightshift and too tired to do anything but kip during the day. If it hadn't been for our first daughter, Nancy, I'd have put her out, but as things were I just had to lump it and we're okay now.'

Both men chewed thoughtfully for a few minutes then Bill asked 'So, what about the baby? Are you absolutely certain it can't be yours?'

'Well, there was the odd time we got together, I'll admit, but I don't know for sure one way or the other. Young Ethel looks like her mother and the fancy man and me have similar colouring anyway. It hardly matters any more. I wanted to kill the wife at the time, but she's behaved herself since and there won't be many likely men left at home now for her to cavort with, will there?'

'I suppose not.'

'Well, I reckon we're all entitled to one mistake, and so long as there are no more...'

Dawson indicated his indifference to the subject with a shrug and finished the rest of his meal in silence.

An hour later, under cover of darkness, both Bill and Malcolm Dawson were sent with fixed bayonets as part of a raiding party, and had no time to think of anything other than the moment at hand and how to get back alive. The tension felt on such raids, relatively short though they were, was mind numbing. The two 'bayonets' were the party's guards, and Bill had often wondered whether he actually possessed the murderous instinct necessary to plunge the razor sharp steel into any unsuspecting enemy who might blunder into their expedition. As they crawled across No-Man's-Land the occasional star shell rose into the sky from the German lines, and they flattened themselves against the earth with pounding hearts as it began its graceful descent, lighting up the area as bright as day. These were some of the same lights he had witnessed when they had disembarked, and he had marvelled at their beauty then from what had been a safe distance. How ironic it all seemed now as he lay pressed to the ground and in fear for his life. Knowing that neither he nor Dawson should have been picked for such a mission, both being married men with families, meant nothing to him either during the raid nor when he, Dawson, and the grenade thrower returned safely leaving two men dead, one of them hanging horrifically from the Germans' barbed wire defences. Such deaths were a part of everyday life and grief for one's fellows settled within like a cold hard rock. Morale must never be allowed to sink any lower in this foretaste of hell.

'We must be careful, Sean. I don't want anyone to see us, and I don't want to end up in a scandalous condition.'

Hardly able to believe that she was speaking so boldly about their clandestine affair Lilian gazed up into her lover's face. Inside the garage where they had just parked the bus for the final time that day the smell of oil and petrol, that had once made her grimace with distaste, now went unnoticed as Sean put his arms around her drawing her close.

'Don't worry. I won't let that happen, Lilian. You're going along the Back Road so I'll go down through the cemetery and cut across the fields to meet you, as usual, but it does seem a pity that you can't just come to my house.'

She shook her head. 'How can I come to your house when it belongs to my mother-in-law? Anyway, we'd be sure to be seen.'

The mid September sun warmed Lilian only slightly as she took a short cut between two houses at the far end of Hillary Terrace, then up past the Assembly Rooms and on to what had once been Leo Bondini's cottage.

On occasions when she was planning to meet Sean she told Marion that she was going to Roughside at the end of her working day, feeling amazed at her lack of guilt. The older woman never seemed to wonder why she suddenly needed to visit her father two or three times a week and accepted her explanation without question, even having a meal waiting for her when she finally returned to Ivy House. The children too were content with their grandmother installed and various other women, all glad of the chance to earn a little extra, attended to most of their needs and did the housework so that domestic

351

matters were not a worry either. Fate itself was abetting their liaison, and after years of celibacy Lilian was in no mood to resist.

Now, as she shortened the distance between herself and Sean, she scanned the entrance to Roughside carefully. Louisa generally made the evening meal at this time of night and she relied upon this habit remaining unchanged as she sped past the cobbled yard and the front of the house where she could easily have been seen from the windows. The same caution did not apply to the small dwelling further on between Roughside and the cottage, for Daniel Heslop's mother lived there and was in no state to be curious about anyone's comings and goings. Once Lilian had seen her standing still in her open doorway, but although she had spoken to the woman there was no response, and the grey eyes had seemed to stare right through her as though she were not there. It was almost as though Nan Heslop had somehow died along with her son.

As Lilian had hoped, Sean was already waiting for her in the bedroom of the cottage, and he gathered her up in his arms, kissing her with the unrestrained passion he always held in check any place but here. Moments later, lying with him in a magic circle of their scattered clothing, she gave way to the sheer physical hunger that she felt for this vigorous man; the smell of his body, the sweetness of his breath on her face, and the sheer maleness of him was like a deluge of water to a soul dying of thirst and, unselfconscious in her nakedness as she had never been with Bill, the woman imbibed without restraint.

When they finally lay peacefully in each other's arms she wallowed in the satisfaction of it: this was what she had wanted, yet never had until now, and she savoured the moment to the full with no trace of either shame or regret.

Leaning up on one elbow Sean looked down into her hazel eyes, lazy now that passion was spent, and took a handful of her thick hair as it spread untidily over the pillow.

'You look like a beautiful witch.' He teased, and she touched his cheek softly.

'I wish we could stay here all night, but I must go home soon.'

'Too soon, Lilian.'

'I know.'

Wondering bleakly just how much longer they would be able to visit the cottage together Lilian turned her body towards his for one final embrace, then left him lying alone as she picked up her clothes and began to dress while he linked his hands behind his head to watch her, smiling at her through the fly blown dressing table mirror as she adjusted it to do her hair.

'I've lost a lot of pins, and I must have them or I'll look like a wild woman and probably give the game away.'

Walking quickly back to the bed Lilian bent over him, kissing him lightly as she groped around the pillows to retrieve her hairpins, and he took her hand firmly in his as she tried to pull away.

'What are we going to do, love?'

'What do you mean?'

'What's going to happen to us? If your husband comes back from the war will you leave him for me, Lilian?'

'Sean … let's just enjoy what we have now and not complicate things. Isn't it good the way it is?'

He sighed, releasing her, and she stood beside him to finish putting up her hair, her smile brightly encouraging as though he were a small child. He smiled back, although it did not quite reach his eyes.

'Yes, it's good, Lilian.'

Frowning a little after a glance towards the window showed that the sun had almost set, Lilian gave her hair a final pat and picked up her bag to leave. She decided not to kiss Sean again in case he held her back even further, for she was late enough now to cause comment at home.

'Give me half an hour before you leave.' She warned. 'You have your pocket watch with you, haven't you?'

He sighed again, lapsing into Scottish dialect in an effort to make her laugh.

'Aye, dinna fret, lassie.'

With a quick smile she was gone and he was suddenly aware of a chill in the room as he started to dress. In just over two weeks it would be October, and winter could begin as early as that in the Pennines. Certainly further visits to this secret place would be out of the question when the days were even shorter than at present, not to mention frost hardened fields that would add to the difficulty his damaged leg already had with the severe incline. All in all he decided that the outlook was not hopeful, yet hope he would, for Lilian Robinson had got well and truly under his skin.

The letter was waiting at her place and, as Marion began to serve the dinner which had been held back for the mistress of the house, Edward and Winifred watched their mother pick up the envelope as though it would burn her fingers.

'That's from Daddy.' Winifred announced. 'Grandma said.'

'It's his writing, that's how I know.' Marion confirmed, adding sharply. 'I wasn't snooping, Lilian.'

'I never thought you were.'

Opening the envelope Lilian scanned the single page in Bill's tidy hand. No censor's black marks here, for there was nothing in the few sentences to warrant it; it was a letter that could have been sent to any of the writer's friends, having no particular intimacy, yet she knew its tone was meant to be conciliatory. He apologised for not writing sooner, explaining that it was often very difficult to find the necessary time, but that he was well and hoped his family were too. There was no farewell message of love for her, only the wish that she might reply to his letter very soon. He signed himself simply 'Regards, Bill.' and against her will Lilian felt a small knot of hurt form in her throat at his formality. Edward's voice cut through her reverie.

'What does Daddy say?'

'He just says he's alright and hopes we are well.'

'Yes, but what else?'

'That's it really, except that he wants me to write back soon, and I'll do that tonight.' Handing the letter across the table to her mother-in-law,

Lilian added. 'Perhaps he's put all the important news in his other letters.'

Feeling guilty already, Marion began to look even more uncomfortable as Edward replied. 'Oh yes, he always sends really long letters to Grandma.'

As though the matter no longer interested her Lilian picked up her knife and fork and began to comment lightly upon the day's goings on at the factory, but later that evening she sat alone in Bill's study with her fountain pen poised over a sheet of paper that seemed destined to remain unmarked. Three previous attempts had already ended in the waste paper bin and she wondered why she should bother to answer his dismal note at all. It was not guilt about Sean, for she felt none even now, nor was it from any sense of duty to Bill as her husband because he had long ago stopped fulfilling that role.

Restlessly she leaned back and looked round the familiar room, remembering how many times she had opened the door to speak to him while he sat at this very desk, and knew that part of her still wanted the old loving Bill back again. Passion aside, she still cared for him, and if this letter was the first step in bridging the gulf between them then she would take it somehow. Picking up her pen again she hesitated a moment then began to write slowly 'Dear Bill, thank you for your welcome letter. It was nice to hear from you and know that you are well...'

Once started to her satisfaction the rest of the letter was easy. She kept it short, with no more emotion than Bill's had contained, but signed it boldly 'Your loving wife, Lilian.'

'Hell's teeth! What unearthly contraption is that?'

Bill did not look around to see who had made the comment for he silently echoed the sentiments himself as he stared at the peculiar cross between a monster car and a windowless bus with a great gun pointing forward from the high turret at the front. It moved slowly, like a lumbering old elephant, yet its appearance of impregnability made its threat seem very real.

The battalion had been on the move again, and although it was a welcome change from the trenches most of the men had suspected that worse was to come at the end of it. A few hours ago they had seen a demonstration of a new type of British machine gun pit shield of battleship armour plate. These were erected alongside the latest German models and some of the men had been given rifles and automatic weapons to do their utmost to destroy them both, but after the experiment when the German plates were riddled with bullet holes, the new British shields were merely indented at various points. These were the new weapons that would hopefully turn the tide of the war: the shield and the tank.

October 1916 was well underway when a letter arrived at Ivy House addressed to both Marion and Lilian. It was from Jenny in Kenhope telling them that she had, that morning, received a telegram telling her that Gilbert had been killed in action, and that she had tried to find someone to bring her over the fell to break the news in person but had been unable to do so.

Marion went up to her room clutching the letter in her hand, and from then on it seemed to Lilian that the vitality had gone out of her too, just as it had for Nan Heslop. At the first opportunity she took Albert's Miners' bus over to Kenhope to see Jenny and Sara, finding her sister-in-law running the store as though her life depended on it, not just her livelihood, and only when they sat down later in the day did her tears come for the husband she would never see again. Holding her comfortingly Lilian promised to visit every week, or as long as the bus could get over the fell during the winter, and cursed her own uselessness when the time came to leave. She would see Jenny regularly, as she had promised, yet knew there was nothing she could really do to ease the pain of her loss.

Meetings with Sean were not as frequent now, but as the winter progressed and they arrived back in Gilfell under cover of darkness she sometimes risked entering his home by making her stay as short as possible. Lighting the lamp downstairs, keeping the curtains drawn, and going upstairs to the dark bedroom where for safety's sake they had to feel their way towards each other was far from satisfactory, but they consoled themselves that when summer came round again they would go back to the cottage.

With still no sign of a cessation of the war yet another joyless Christmas passed in the valley with the New Year of 1917 following on. The snows began in mid January making the roads treacherous, and with most of the male population of the area either at war, or unfit for heavy work, the clearing process was abandoned more often than not. Sean advised Lilian to approach other business people with a view to buying a snowplough for future years, as all firms would be bound to benefit, and she spent a whole day at the factory writing to every hotel, shop and mining proprietor within a fifteen mile radius, including Johnny Peacock and Gerald Fairburn of the Gilfell and Gilbury pits. Response was slow at the beginning but by the end of April, when the last thaw was underway, she had received enough in donations to order a snowplough, and at a meeting of contributors in Dalton's Three Bells Hotel it was agreed that the plough be stationed in Gilfell upon arrival, as it was much easier to travel first downhill in a snowstorm than fight one's way upward, and a site beside the Main Street shops was decided upon.

At the conclusion of the meeting, when Lilian was gathering up her papers and feeling a heady sense of triumph, Johnny Peacock appeared in front of her table smiling in a way that made her feel a shade uneasy.

'I trust you have seen to it that we all get a good return of interest on our money until the war is over.' He said pleasantly. 'With a bit of luck we should still be able to purchase a plough by then with the amount growing every year, so to speak.'

She stared at him blankly. 'I don't know what you're talking about. We're sending for the plough at once.'

'Yes, Lilian. You're ordering it from a firm in Canada are you not?'

'Yes, of course. No one seems to make them here.'

'So, don't you think you'd better find out the position regarding unnecessary cargo during this war? I've heard it's quite strict.'

It was only afterwards that Lilian realised that Johnny had waited on purpose to speak to her alone and that he could have humiliated her had he made his point in the middle of the meeting, for investigation proved him to be correct in that they would have to wait until the end of the conflict before ordering the snowplough. Once again she sent out letters to all concerned, this time of explanation, while The Snowplough Fund lay in Dalton Bank waiting for the arrival of peacetime, and the year dragged drearily on.

On June 17th 1917, the Third Battle of Ypres began, to be known ever after as Passchendaele.

With the force of a minor earthquake nineteen mines exploded simultaneously just after three a.m. under the Messines Ridge, and as tall pink mushroom clouds rose into the air their awesome roar made a sound that could be heard quite distinctly as far away as London. Over two thousand guns and howitzers added their power to the din while eighty thousand British, New Zealand and Australian Infantry went into the attack with tanks bringing up the rear.

The Ridge was taken immediately, and by mid-afternoon every objective of the battle had been secured, although outpost fighting continued for a further week with all enemy counterattacks failing. At its conclusion German casualties stood at twenty five thousand, including seven thousand five hundred prisoners, and the British lost seventeen thousand men, one of whom was Private Malcolm Dawson who fell at Bill's side during a charge.

Thinking that his friend had just tripped up on the uneven ground Bill stopped and bent down to help him, only to hear the harsh command, 'Don't break the line! Keep going!' It was the last memory he would have of his companion of many months, and the image remained burned in his mind for the rest of his life. All around him men were falling, wounded or killed, and he stumbled on amid fumes of cordite and phosphorous as the ground trembled beneath the relentless assault of enemy artillery. His vision, already distorted, was further hampered by sudden tears that would not be controlled, yet his legs still propelled him forward with the rest of his comrades while whistling bullets, missing their intended targets, threw up deadly showers of wet earth around their feet as they ran. Half blinded by grief for his lost friend, and his erupting rage against the endless slaughter that claimed life after life, Bill kept going forward screaming his hatred at the enemy for his intent was, for the first time, truly murderous.

Directly ahead of him there came yet another sharp rattle of machine gun fire, then the ground reared up hitting him in the face as total darkness engulfed him.

Maura Harker stood in Lilian's office doorway holding a man of around fifty by the hand. They

361

looked faintly ridiculous, like an over-age courting couple, and Lilian stared at them both in silence for a few seconds before turning on her stool and motioning them to enter.

'I'm sorry not to have any other seats in here, but the office is too small. What can I do for you, Maura?'

'This is Raymond Bennett, Mrs Robinson. He travels for a textile company and passes through Dalton each week.'

'Yes?'

Maura was beaming like an excited child.

'Well, the fact is that Raymond and I are engaged now, and I wondered if you might give him a job here? He's done all sorts of work in clothing, including this one, and I thought maybe he could relieve both of us ... make two jobs into three, if you see what I mean.'

Again Lilian looked at them without speaking, unable to decide whether Maura was actually possessed of a brilliant idea or simply an abundance of insolence. Maura and Raymond looked back at her, then at each other. That they were lovers Lilian could not doubt, and the knowledge mellowed her towards the woman whom she had so recently regarded with hostility.

'Congratulations to both of your on your engagement.' She smiled. 'This idea needs thinking over and very careful planning if it is to be workable. Shall we adjourn to The Three Bells and discuss it over lunch?'

The meal, plain though it was with wartime fare, lasted well into the afternoon while Lilian and Maura considered various ideas for Raymond

Bennett's shifts, finally deciding to give the man two each of their own. This allowed both women regular time off while Bennett worked a strange week composed of two days and two nights.

'I'll have to rely on both of you to keep the factory going on any days when I can't get down to Dalton, if the children or my mother-in-law are ill or if there's a blizzard in winter causing a blocked road, for instance.' Lilian said. 'Will that be alright with you?'

They agreed at once, surprising her not at all, and as she paid the bill at the end of their conference she watched through the glass door in the foyer as Maura and the new man in her life walked away up Dalton's steep High Street, still hand in hand. On the surface the plan seemed to be a good one, yet something about the man with his thin black moustache and slicked back hair made her feel uneasy. He had rarely spoken for himself, and when she had questioned him about his previous jobs he had talked a lot yet divulged very little except the names of the towns where he claimed to have been employed. Even the title of his present firm was totally unknown to her, although that might be explained by the fact that it was, according to Raymond Bennett, very new. In any case, she reasoned, he was bound to have a job of some kind to visit Dalton every week, and she had just committed herself to giving him a chance. Whether that had been wise or not remained to be seen.

Opening his eyes Bill found himself lying at the bottom of a shell hole with a corporal ripping open his left trouser leg, and noticed with odd detachment that the man's hands and the material of his uniform were liberally stained with blood.

'Keep still. You'll be found by the medics later, but I'll have to fix you up a bit before I go. Sorry mate.'

There was no pain in his leg at that point, from which Bill deduced that he had not been unconscious for more than one to two minutes, and he raised his head slightly to look down at it as the corporal took an ampoule of iodine out of his medical bag and broke it over a rifle butt.

'Grit your teeth.' He advised, and Bill obeyed, lying back again to stare upwards through the dust and smoke into a sky that was surprisingly sunny, and tried not to remember the way the flesh of his calf lay torn away from the visibly shattered bone. Mercifully, the leg was still numb and all he initially felt of the searing antiseptic was its coolness.

'Don't stay here with me, Corporal.' He whispered. 'Go with the others or you'll be left behind as well.'

There was no reply but a grunt from his amateur doctor, who placed a pad and dressing on top of the wound, then with the needless advice to 'Stay where you are and they'll find you later.' he grabbed his rifle and disappeared over the rim of the shallow crater.

The onset of shock brought a sense of utter weariness and indifference in its wake that helped Bill deal with the pain when it began. Alone in his open grave he could hear distant cries and groans of other fallen men as his mind drifted away from his plight, sometimes into thoughts of the past and sometimes into troubled half-dreams, as the day wore on and gradually gave way to darkness. Still no one came. Maybe, he thought with a sudden burst of clarity, nobody would ever find him except the rats that fed constantly on neglected corpses. Trying to move in his horrified panic he cried out as the agony from his limb filled his whole body, making him fall back again weeping tears of frustration and weakness before his consciousness began to blur again.

He had no idea how much time had passed when the ominously familiar sound of an approaching shell pulled him back into full awareness and he realised with dread that the weapon, obviously off course, was about to fall in his area.

The earth shattering thud of its impact, the terrible noise and the blinding flash as it exploded perilously near to his makeshift refuge sent Bill once more down into the darkness, and the night wore steadily on.

CHAPTER FOURTEEN

'Oh Lilian, what have you done?'

Jenny Robinson gazed in consternation as her sister-in-law walked in at the shop doorway, and little Sara blinked in surprise as Lilian pushed Edward and Winifred forward into the shop. Jenny was busy up a ladder restocking shelves and drawers during the quieter end of the day, and Sara, almost five now, came forward eagerly to meet her cousins.

'I've had my hair chopped off, Jen.' Lilian smiled, and put up a hand to feel the edge of her new bob. 'It's so good. I just wash it and leave it and I've no more bother pinning it up. That was always such a nuisance.'

'I expect I'll get used to it in time then.'

As the children walked through the curtained passageway into the living quarters to play Jenny descended to floor level then crossed to the shop door and locked it, turning the sign in the window to read 'Closed'.

'It isn't quite finishing time but it will have to do for today. Come and have some tea and a chat.'

Gilbert's widow was painfully thin, and although she made a great effort to hide her true state of mind her inner wretchedness hung around her like an almost visible aura. Watching her as they both cut bread in the kitchen to make sandwiches, Lilian interrupted her flow of determinedly cheerful chatter to ask how she was.

'It's nearly October again, Jenny, and coming up for a year since Gilbert died. I wondered if you wanted to do anything in his memory that might make you feel just a shade comforted. Marion refuses to discuss anything like that, but she refuses to discuss most things these days. I tried to persuade her to come with us today on the miners' bus, but she wouldn't, despite knowing that the ordinary passengers' seats are reserved at the back of the vehicle and never used by the men in their dirty working clothes. I seem to be utterly useless to both of you.'

'You're not useless, Lilian. Never think that. I don't know how I'd have managed without your weekly visits, especially at the start, and I could never begin to tell you how much it's meant to me.'

'So, *is* there anything you'd like to do?'

'I think I'd rather wait until the war is over and do something then: maybe not only for Gilbert either. There's talk of putting a memorial of some kind in the village square when peace comes, and it could have all the names of the men from Kenhope and surrounding areas who...' She paused as her eyes filled up, then shook her head as though to throw off her sadness before changing the subject. 'But what about Bill? Have you heard from him yet?'

'No, but I believe things are pretty chaotic with correspondence to and from France. The most important fact to keep in mind is that we haven't heard anything awful about him. As I tell Marion all the time, no news is good news really.'

Jenny looked over to where Sara and Winifred were playing with some wooden bricks, then at Edward who was holding a book up to his face and plainly listening to their conversation.

'We have some baby rabbits in two hutches in the yard if you want to see them, Edward.'

'Oh yes! Thanks Aunt Jen.'

Springing to his feet the boy rushed from the room, all curiosity in grown up talk forgotten, and Jenny smiled slightly at an understanding Lilian.

'I'm glad you and Bill started writing to each other last year. Maybe the war has mellowed him a little. Gilbert always said Bill could be too stubborn for his own good, and I remember you telling me how stiff his first letter was, just as though he were writing to an acquaintance. Did he improve at all?'

'Yes ... a touch, but I wish you wouldn't speak of him in the past tense, Jen.' She stopped, embarrassed at having spoken sharply, then admitted 'Three months *is* a long time not to hear from him, isn't it?'

'Perhaps he can't write, or maybe he's written letters and they're still in France.'

'Maybe.'

While they drank their tea and the children ate sandwiches and cakes, Lilian found her attention continually drawn to the calendar on the wall where she noticed Jenny had been crossing off the days. It seemed to her a fairly pointless thing for Jenny to do when her husband would not be

368

among those coming home, yet something else about the counted off squares struck a chord within her that was vaguely unpleasant, and her eyes returned again and again to the month of September where only four days remained to be pencilled out. Something of significance was hovering on the edge of her mind, yet no matter how she tried to pin it down it stayed tantalisingly out of reach for the duration of her visit, but after the day's farewells had been said and the bus was moving out of Kenhope the answer came to her. Jenny's calendar had bothered her because the month of September had not brought nature's usual reassurances, and after some frantic mental calculations Lilian assessed her situation with a sinking heart. Despite all the care that had been taken between Sean Curtis and herself, her period was now three weeks overdue!

As Lilian and the children entered Ivy House the first thing she heard was a persistent peal from the telephone in the front passage, and she hurried to answer it wondering crossly why Marion could not have braved the instrument for once. A month ago she had managed to get a telephone installed at the factory which could have proved invaluable had her mother-in-law ever answered her calls, but she always insisted that she was 'frightened of it', and that was that.

Irritably her mind still worrying around her own personal problem, she spoke into the mouthpiece and heard Sean's voice over the line.

'Lilian, I'm at the garage and Maura Harker's just telephoned from the factory. That Bennett fellow has vanished, and she didn't even know he'd gone until she went to collect his laundry and found none of his clothes there. The women back at the factory told her that when he came in he was carrying a suitcase, which he hid behind the bales of cloth in the corner, then after she left for home he waited a few minutes and simply walked out with it, probably to the railway station. Maura tried phoning you at home but there was no reply so she rang here instead. I see Albert's coming in now from the Kenhope run, so I could stay with him until you've phoned Maura or run you down to Dalton to see if anything's missing.'

'I'll phone her first, Sean, then I'll ring you if you can wait a while.'

'Right. I'll be here.'

The rest of the day's events were distracting enough to call a halt to all private worries, and Lilian, after trying to inject some logic into Maura's hysterical ramblings, advised her to calm down until she arrived in half an hour to do the nightshift herself.

A search of the office upon arrival showed that all was as it should be, even to the money in the petty cash box, and Lilian realised that she had probably not been the target if Raymond Bennett *had* stolen anything, for all that lay in the safe were contracts and cheques received but not yet banked, and they would be of no use to him.

Sean looked at her enquiringly as she relocked the safe, and she nodded towards Maura who was talking to a machinist on the factory floor.

'Would you mind going home with her and staying until she's checked her house thoroughly?

I have a feeling that she may be one or two items short.'

Ashamed of her relief that the slippery Bennett had gone without harming her business, Lilian sat down at her desk and tried to concentrate until she knew whether Bennett had left Dalton empty handed. Over an hour passed before Sean returned to report that Maura had done a complete search of her valuables and found a few items of jewellery missing, including the engagement ring Bennett himself had given her that she never wore whilst working, a solid silver teapot with matching sugar bowl and cream jug which had been a family heirloom, plus her personal savings of £16. 10s found to be no longer in the large china biscuit barrel on her kitchen shelf.

With scant hope that they were in time to catch Bennett, Lilian first phoned the railway station to find the destination of all departing trains from five o'clock to the present, then put calls through to both Carlisle and Newcastle-upon-Tyne Police Stations, passing on a description given to her by the women of what he had been wearing, together with his physical appearance, but it became obvious as the night wore on that Bennett had either left his train before it reached a main station or had never boarded one at all. Neither train was an express, and the platforms in question had been watched carefully as passengers disembarked, but there had been no sign of anyone answering the description of Raymond Bennett.

The following day two detectives arrived in Dalton from Manchester and interviewed Maura,

Lilian and anyone else whom they felt could be helpful to their enquiries, as it was believed that he was a confidence trickster operating under a number of aliases whom they had been trying to track down for almost a year. Usually preying on women of much more generous means than Maura, Bennett had been well away from his usual hunting grounds, and the police believed that he would now be on his way back to a city having successfully hidden himself away for several months.

Ignoring Maura's stricken look at this information the Detective Inspector remarked that Dalton, being a bit of a backwater, had not been a bad little hideaway really and closed his notebook with a slam. At her side Lilian gave her a sympathetic look and they both rose to their feet as the policeman opened the door of the Station Sergeant's Office and thanked them for their time. The young woman had a bewildered expression on her face as though she could not quite grasp what had happened, and outside on the pavement she looked all round High Street as though she had never seen it before.

Lilian touched her arm. 'Come on, Maura. You can go home now and have a sleep. You look as though you haven't had a proper rest for weeks.'

It was true that the woman looked unwell with her skin drained of colour and dark circles under her eyes, but she shook her head as they began to walk up the steep hill towards the factory and her own home.

'I've got to find him, Mrs Robinson.'

'There's no point in finding him, Maura. The

man is a thief. In any case he won't come back to Dalton even if you do find him, but the police will probably run him to earth and arrest him, which is what he deserves.'

Her tone was brisk, denying empathy with her companion's predicament, and she went on purposely in the same vein in an effort to arouse in Maura some fighting spirit instead of her present hangdog attitude.

'Look on the positive side. I know you feel hurt, but you've still got your job and your boarding house. At least he couldn't steal those as well.'

Maura's mouth twisted into a bitter smile. 'Oh no, but he could steal my ability to do those jobs.'

'What do you mean?'

They stopped walking again as Maura turned towards Lilian.

'I mean that I shan't be able to work at the factory more than a few months, nor shall I be able to see to the boarding house as I have done up to now. You see, unlike yourself, I'm not a virtuous woman, and Raymond Bennett has left me pregnant!'

By mid October Lilian finally received news of Bill and was astonished at the depth of her relief. At the same time as the letter arrived from the army another far more detailed explanation came from Constance Fairburn telling her that Bill had been moved to her present hospital from a medical post near The Front, where he had remained a mystery for several weeks owing to confusion brought on by shock, and the fact that he had lost his identification disk somewhere on

373

the battlefield. His badly fractured leg was slowly healing and his memory was beginning to return in small snatches, but Constance knew from experience that his days in the war were over and that he would be transferred to Blighty as soon as possible to recover in a military convalescent unit before coming home. She closed her letter by expressing sympathy for Bill's plight, but added her conviction that he would return to reasonably good health in time.

Glad that Constance had fleshed out the stark outline of events passed on to her from the military, Lilian penned a grateful reply to the woman whom she hardly knew then began a long letter to her husband. She was just beginning the second page when reality stayed her hand and she stared down at the paper, amazed at what she had managed to forget since finding out that Bill was still alive. Touching her abdomen in a gesture of protection she felt a shiver of dread at the thought of Bill coming back to Gilfell to find his wife having yet another baby that was not his. Until today she had determinedly pushed the matter of her pregnancy to the back of her mind, hoping that some satisfactory answer might suggest itself soon, but her dilemma was now quite beyond any solution based in a nebulous future and her particular Nemesis was almost upon her.

Rather in the manner of someone closing the stable door after the horse has bolted she had not been with Sean since discovering her predicament, refusing to meet him at the cottage with the days swiftly shortening again. Since Bennett's disappearance Sean had initially put down to overwork her terse manner and habit of snapping at him, but after the first week Lilian had promoted Alice Coulthard from the factory floor to be a supervisor in his place, which should have relieved the situation. Having tried cajoling then confrontation, to no avail, the man finally retreated to a safe emotional distance, but she was often aware of the bewildered looks he gave her when she stepped off the bus at Gilfell, and bid him a cool 'Goodnight' instead of finding a discreet corner of the garage for a more affectionate farewell.

Putting down her pen Lilian suddenly knew that she had to tell somebody trustworthy about her trouble, and there was only one person that could be. Thankful that it was only nine thirty in the morning and that her own children and Louisa's would be at school, she left the study to put on her outdoor clothes. Marion was sitting by the kitchen fire moving slightly back and forth in her rocking chair with the letters about Bill in her lap, and when Lilian announced that she was going to Roughside to tell them the good news the woman merely nodded. Studying her intently for a few seconds she saw that the corners of Marion's mouth were slightly turned up and her eyes content, then she opened the door and walked briskly along Hillary Terrace.

Upon arriving at Roughside Lilian was happy to find Louisa on her own with Marguerite, and she blushed a little at her friend's obvious surprise.

'I know I haven't been to see you for a while,

Lou,' she apologised, 'but I'm here now.'

'Good. James has gone down to Dalton on the bus so we have until teatime to talk.'

Her smile was teasing as Lilian sat down taking her half-sister onto her knee, and she looked at the big wooden table with its selection of baking ingredients.

'You're busy. Can I do anything while I'm here?'

'You can help me with the pastry cutting when I've made it, but I'll brew some tea for us first. Now ... tell me what you've been up to. I haven't seen you hurrying along the lane to the cottage lately.'

'Lou ... what do you mean?'

'I mean I haven't seen you scurrying along to meet that driver of yours in the cottage that Leo Bondini used to rent!'

Watching her putting on a large white apron to weigh flour onto the scales Lilian stared dumbly back at her as a fresh wave of unwelcome heat spread up her face, and Louisa added gently.

'I don't think anyone else noticed it; certainly James never did or he would have said something, but I was usually at the sink washing dishes at that time of day and I saw you so often that I began to wonder where you were going all the time, then one day last year Marion remarked on how many times you were visiting us when you weren't, and I started to put two and two together. Also, your driver was observed at the other end of the village making his way over the fields two or three times a week, and people wondered why he didn't just take his walks on

376

the road when he had such a bad leg.'

Wriggling down from her knee Marguerite ran to the far corner to play with her doll's house, and Lilian cleared her throat uncomfortably.

'Do you think people in the village have guessed? Have you heard any ... gossip?'

Louisa grimaced as the scales tipped down too violently and began to juggle with the white powder, her brow creasing into a little frown of concentration.

'No. I haven't heard anything Lilian, but I hardly think they would say anything in front of me.'

'Well, it's over now.'

'Is he going away?'

'Not that I know of, although I suppose he may do. It doesn't matter whether he does or not; I was terribly attracted to him when he first came, and Bill and I hadn't been truly man and wife for four years then. Can you imagine what that's like? I'll admit I just fell into his arms, and we've been having what I believed was a very secret affair for over a year now.'

Louisa turned away from the table as the kettle began to sing on the hob and busied herself preparing the crockery as she answered.

'I remember the night I called to see Bill about Terence and the Titanic. You were in a terrible state but you never explained anything to me later, and I felt I shouldn't ask about it.'

'He'd just found out about Edward. You see, Edward isn't his.'

'Oh Lilian!'

Visibly shaken, Louisa carried the tray to the

table and sat down beside it gazing at Lilian in troubled disbelief, and seeing her expression Lilian offered her a thin smile.

'Edward is Johnny Peacock's son, Lou. I can see you're shocked and I'm sorry, because there's worse to come. You see, I had word of Bill today and it was such a relief after months of not knowing what had happened to him, until I remembered that I'm pregnant! There; now you know what a low woman I am.'

With a sizzle some boiling water shot from the spout of the kettle onto the fire and Lilian watched her young step-mother hurry over to the hearth with the teapot in her hands. She did not speak again until they were seated opposite each other with cups of freshly poured tea, then she said in a level voice.

'I'm not judging you, Lilian, so please don't ever think I am.'

'Thank you, but you'll be the only person who won't when the truth comes out, and if I hadn't been weak falling for Sean as I did, I could have been so happy now that I know Bill is coming home. He's been injured, as you can probably guess, and I expect he could be here in a matter of weeks, but that will be the end of me, Lou. He'll never forgive me for this, and I can't blame him can I?'

She began to cry, trying to choke back her sobs for the sake of Marguerite who was looking at her in alarm, and Louisa came quickly to her side with a clean handkerchief which she took from the pocket of her apron.

'Don't despair, Lilian. We'll think of something,

and whatever the gossips of Gilfell may suspect about you and Sean they don't know about the baby, do they?'

'Nobody does except you.'

'So we still have time to think of a plan. Could you leave the factory for a few months? Make some excuse to go away? Perhaps I could go with you, and when we come back I'd say the baby was mine.'

'Could we do that? Would it work? You're so good, Louisa, offering to take another woman's baby as your own...'

'Your baby, not just another woman's. Now, dry your eyes and cheer up while we explore the possibilities.'

The quick rise in spirits that Lilian felt at Louisa's support slowly began to crumble as they tried to find ways around the various difficulties in their plan. To go away together presented them with the biggest problem of all; what to do with their respective children, let alone find a convincing reason to absent themselves for so long. If they took the children along they would know that the baby was not Louisa's, and to leave them behind for months was simply unthinkable.

An hour later they finally agreed to try and think of something else and Lilian got up to help with the baking, defeat giving her a cold sick feeling in her stomach. They had not thought of an answer because there was no answer. With her passion for Sean she had wrecked her life for good and all, for once Bill came back her future would be bleak indeed. She looked across at Louisa as the enormity of it numbed her mind, and asked.

'Are you happy with Dad, Lou? Has he been good to you?'

'He's very good to me, Lilian, and I hope he's as happy with me as I am with him. He looks after me so well, and my Helen. She was very withdrawn with James at the start, you know, but she was badly missing her father and it was a difficult time for her. He was patient though, and it all came right eventually.'

'Do you still think of him... Terence I mean?'

She noticed Louisa's soft sigh which, of itself, told her all she needed to know, and her hands paused in their rolling out as she replied honestly.

'I do love James, Lilian, yet I have not managed to love him as I loved Terence. I'm sorry. I don't want to hurt you, but Terence has been like a question that was never answered, and this has kept my mind returning to him. Did he really love me or not? What was his real wife like?'

'I can tell you that, Lou!'

'What?'

Lilian took a deep breath but continued to cut out the shapes for Louisa's jam tarts as she spoke.

'You guessed once that I had not liked Terence, and the reason was that when Bill and I went to Newcastle to see our solicitor ... this would be a few months after we were married ... we saw him get off the train ahead of us and a woman and a little girl met him. The girl ran to him calling him "Daddy", and although we tried hard to think of some other explanation for it we had to agree that she would not have called him that had he

380

not been her father. They were quite a way in front of us and quickly disappeared, otherwise I would have probably confronted them, but Bill said I had not to say anything about it when we got home because you were pregnant by then and Terence might not be actually married to this other woman for all we knew. Either way, he pointed out to me that it could not do any good to reveal what we had seen, but I never liked him after that.'

'You knew ... both of you knew all that time!'

Looking up she found Louisa staring at her accusingly.

'Lilian, how could you? You didn't even breathe a word of this when the Titanic had gone down and the truth of his bigamy came out.'

'I might have done, Lou, but my own life took a nasty turn then too. I'm truly sorry. Please believe that.'

'Well, I suppose you're right, and it probably wouldn't have done any good to tell me about it then. So ... what did she look like, this woman?'

'Similar colouring to yourself, but older and nowhere like as pretty.' Lilian smiled. 'Heaven knows why he did what he did, but he really must have loved you to commit bigamy and risk a prison sentence to get you.'

'It would surely have been simpler to get a divorce.'

'Perhaps she wouldn't give him one and to sue for one himself Terence would have needed grounds, which probably didn't exist, making bigamy the only way.'

'Well, we'll never know now, that's for sure.'

Bending her head over her work Louisa cast aside the image of Terry's face as it loomed so clearly in her mind, handsome and smiling as she always remembered him. She was intensely grateful for James' kindness, but gratitude was not enough to fill the gaping hole that Terence had left in her heart when he had sailed away on the Titanic, perhaps never intending to get in touch with her again.

Making great play of attending to things in the oven she changed the subject back to Bill and Lilian's apparently insurmountable problem, but still no conclusion had been reached when Lilian left to go home.

'Tell Dad I'll come again in a few days to see him, but I can't wait until he comes off the bus today as it will be almost dark.'

Secretly rather relieved not to have to face her father just yet, Lilian made her way back to Ivy House where she still had an hour to spare before the children came home. Marion was asleep upstairs and the house was peacefully silent. The fire, which her mother-in-law usually forgot all about when left alone, had been carefully banked up with coal this time as though the news of Bill had given her a fresh lease of life.

Going out into the corridor to hang up her coat she caught sight of her reflection in the hall stand mirror. Her face was white, and her eyes stared back at her out of the glass filled with despair and fear.

Driving through the gates of Low Shields, Johnny looked over at the house and surrounding grounds with an appreciative eye whilst almost absent-mindedly ordering Antony to 'Sit down like a good boy, or you won't get a ride on the pony.' Bella smiled encouragingly at her son and pointed to the small black Shetland as it grazed in the meadow nearest to the stables.

'There's Freddy, darling. He's just waiting for us to saddle him and lead you round the field on his back.'

'Bella, don't fill the boy's head with such rubbish. The animal is feeding at the moment and isn't capable, at any time, of speculating about the future.'

Bella shot her husband a cool look. 'Oh well, you would know I suppose.'

Intensely proud of his newly acquired Rolls Royce, Johnny grasped every opportunity to take it out in his spare time and had himself suggested visiting the Fairburns yet again. His motorcycle was still quicker and more efficient for travelling between his home and the mines, but on Sundays he devoted most of his time to the car, accompanied by Bella if necessary but more often just by Antony. On the occasions when he took only his son with him he would sneak him away to the car, then, either wave to Bella in the garden on his way to the gates or sound the horn in derisive farewell should she be indoors. At first she had been petulant for days after he had left her behind, but as he clearly did not care whether she was civil to him or not she had suddenly become as sly as himself, arriving at the garage doors all dressed for a jaunt just as he was bundling Antony into the seat beside him. Today that had not been necessary, however, as Johnny had asked her to accompany them to Low Shields. He could hardly arrive at her parents' home without her and she might as well be present when he pointed out to Gerald, yet again, how very superior the Rolls was compared to the Fairburn motor.

Sounding the horn now as they turned the corner at the bottom of the drive he had the satisfaction of seeing both Gerald and Elisabeth framed in their dining room window as he cruised past them to brake beside the front door. Jumping down he strode round to the passenger seat to assist Bella, then lifted little Antony in his arms.

'Go and find Grandma and Grandpa,' he urged the sturdy three year old, and watched as Bella paused to take his hand at the bottom of the three shallow steps leading into the house. 'Don't pamper him, Bella! He'll do it himself if you'll only let him try.'

'Of course he will, John. He'll break his neck himself too if I let him do everything you suggest.'

He scowled at her as she ignored his instructions, leading Antony carefully up to the doorway where his grandparents had appeared smiling a welcome, and got back into the car to drive it round the side of the house. He would make sure they did not stay any longer than he wanted to, then if it was still reasonably light when they got back to White Court he could go out again on his own.

The afternoon was late October at its best and

Freddy was saddled up at once for Antony to ride. Delighting in the fact that his small son showed no fear of the animal, nor any other new experiences as far as he could tell, Johnny spoke sharply to Bella when she called over to them both to 'Be careful.'

'For heaven's sake will you stop being such an old woman and let the boy enjoy himself?' he snapped. 'I'm using a leading rein, and you'll just turn him into a complete sissy if you keep on this way.'

Elisabeth and Gerald exchanged significant glances behind their daughter's back and the woman's lips narrowed with an anger that she knew she should never express, but watching her son-in-law leading Antony's mount round the pasture she cursed the heart defect that had proved no great obstacle in his life, yet had kept him out of the war. Other men had gone to fight and better men than John Peacock had been killed, yet here he was, as arrogant as he had always been, still treating Bella like a half-witted servant. Alarmed at the viciousness of her thoughts she turned sharply away from the scene and urged her daughter to accompany her back to the house.

'We can have a chat until tea.' She coaxed. 'Don't worry about Antony. The men have the situation well in hand, dear.'

The cool green walls of the lounge soothed Bella as she took a seat facing her mother with her back firmly turned towards the window through which her son could now be seen sitting on the trotting Freddy whilst emitting shrieks of delight as his father ran beside the animal, still holding the leading rein. Determinedly she stiffened her shoulders and enquired.

'Have you heard from Constance lately, mother?'

'No. Have you?'

'No. I haven't had a letter either, but I know Lilian Robinson has.'

Elisabeth's eyebrows rose sharply. 'Lilian Robinson? Why on earth would Constance write to her?'

'I saw Lilian last week in the Assembly Rooms. There was a bazaar in aid of the Red Cross ... remember, I told you about it but you said you couldn't come.'

'I attend the Dalton Red Cross activities. I can't be everywhere.'

'Anyway, she told me that Constance had written to her about Bill being brought to her hospital, and the letter arrived at the same time as the official one from the army, only it contained many more details about Bill's condition. Lilian was grateful to her and wrote back to say so. It seems that he should be home in a while, although no one knows when exactly as he's been quite badly injured.'

'How thoughtful of Constance to write to Lilian Robinson, and at such length, when she scarcely ever puts pen to paper to her own family.'

Bella was exasperated. 'But that isn't the point mother. It shows that she's alright ... only busy as she has said.'

'Yes, I see.'

The woman's gaze suddenly became riveted on some point over her daughter's left shoulder and

Bella twisted around to see what she was looking at so intently, afraid that all was not well with Antony, but the sight of another car rumbling along the drive put her mind at ease.

'You're about to receive some more visitors. Would you like us to go soon?'

'Of course not. It's only the Bancrofts from Dalton to talk about the coming Red Cross sale of home produce to be held in Dalton Market Square next week. Odd isn't it, after we've just been discussing such things?'

Immediately donning her social manner like a well worn cloak Elisabeth moved out of the room to greet her unexpected guests, and Bella sighed. For her the visit was spoilt now with the intrusion of these strangers, and she would have preferred to go home instead of making polite conversation over sandwiches and cakes, but the rules of elementary politeness put paid to any such escape. For the next half hour she struggled to exchange suitable pleasantries with Gregory and Marjorie Bancroft, falling silent when the topic returned yet again to various activities of the local Red Cross, and the Fairburns' single elderly housemaid had just brought in the tea trolley and cake stand when the men returned with Antony.

Introducing the visitors to Johnny and her son, Bella wondered why Marjorie Bancroft looked so hard at the little boy and kept on glancing towards him all through the meal until he began to show signs of becoming restive. Suddenly Johnny snapped at him to keep still as he wriggled on his seat, causing Bella to speak up at once in his defence.

'I think he's wondering why Mrs Bancroft keeps looking at him all the time, John, and it's making him nervous.'

Marjorie Bancroft gave a start at her words, and hastened to explain.

'My dear, I'm so sorry to have frightened your little son, but your mother has already told me that he is your only child and, believe it or not, I have recently seen his double! I mean his exact double!'

Johnny, looking bored, cast her a withering glance but Elisabeth, polite as always, enquired where this had been.

'It was at Gilfell last weekend at our Bazaar, and there was a woman there helping ... a tall, nice looking rather stately person, and she had brought her son and daughter with her. Her son was older than Antony, I believe she said he was eleven, and when I saw your Antony today I was amazed at the resemblance between them. They really do look so alike it's uncanny. Do you have any relatives in the area with a son of that age?'

Bella, who had listened in fascination, shook her head.

'No, there's no one. Actually I was at the Bazaar myself, but I left after a short while and I can't say I saw anyone who looked like my Antony. Who was this lady? Do you know?'

'Her name was Mrs Robinson ... Lilian Robinson.'

The heavy silence that followed froze the scene forever in memory for Elisabeth Fairburn as she took in her daughter's whitening face. Bella had often seen Edward Robinson and wondered what

388

it was about him that puzzled her, but it had taken this sharp nudge from fate to show her exactly what she had been looking at. Her mind took her back to the gates of White Court on the afternoon when Lilian and Marion Robinson had stopped beside Antony's pram, and the expression of shock on the older woman's face before she had left them so abruptly with Lilian running after her in some kind of panic. Well, now she could guess why.

Lifting her eyes towards Johnny she found him sitting quite still gazing into the far distance through the large windows, yet she could almost feel his mind racing to and fro after this unwitting revelation.

Annabel Peacock had once told a story of meeting Lilian on the morning of the engagement dinner and fearing that she had been going to faint right there on Gilfell Main Street. Could that have been because she was then pregnant with Johnny's child?

'Do have some more tea Marjorie, and you too Gregory.'

Elisabeth's voice, strident in her attempt to sound normal, cut across her thoughts and, for a moment Johnny raised his head in Bella's direction, yet his eyes looked straight through her into the past where he was already beginning to suspect that he had fathered two sons, not just one.

CHAPTER FIFTEEN

November 1917

Bill lay looking up at the ceiling in a ward that was never either still nor completely quiet, and tried to isolate himself from the pain in his leg. Tonight he was lucid, but there were still times when he was unsure of where he was or what his purpose was meant to be in this depressing building. Earlier that day a brusque elderly doctor had advised him to be thankful that he still had his injured limb as other men had lost a leg or an arm, and sometimes more than one, then within an hour an amputee had been wheeled out of the ward with the sheet over his face leaving Bill feeling the familiar sickness of despair wash over him at all the futile slaughter of a war that still showed no sign of abating.

Now that he was no longer constantly primed for survival his thoughts were free to wander over all the events that he had managed not to dwell on before, presenting a replay in his mind of the deaths he had seen: the body of a soldier, who had been part of a group attempting to repair the defences, trapped on the barbed wire, his sightless eyes fixed on former comrades as his flesh rotted and bloated. The vermin that invaded the trenches, especially in torrential rain that turned the ground beneath their feet to thick mud, and the horror of an advancing charge when he had jumped into an abandoned enemy dugout to find his boot touching a German helmet that still contained its owner's decapitated head. He had screamed, but only the abrasive sensation in his throat confirmed his reaction for no other sound could be heard above the earth shaking blast of continually exploding shells, and since leaving France it was the absence of that terrible unremitting noise that had been so hard to get used to.

He could scarcely recall the journey back to England except in a few disjointed memories, each lasting no more than a few seconds, but he had vivid recall of lying with his fellow wounded on a railway station platform and seeing a young woman with dark hair bending over him. Her lips moved as she spoke to him, but none of her words made sense, and he tried to reach for her hand whilst whispering 'Lilian.' The girl smiled, tucking two Woodbine cigarettes and a box of matches under his pillow, and as she moved on to the next man a nearby engine let out a great hiss of steam causing another crescendo of pain in his leg as his body jolted in panic.

Dreams, when they came, were violent. Lilian and his mother, Edward and Winifred, Gilbert and Johnny Peacock, all played out bizarre roles in places that were a strange amalgamation of France and his own Pennine valley, and he would awake panting and disorientated, sometimes calling out until a nurse came to soothe him. It was on one of these occasions that he had first encountered Constance, and he clung to her hand like a small boy as she leaned over him speaking his name. After that she spent a little of her precious free time with him each day before going off duty to catch up on her rest, and Bill's moments of clarity grew a little longer as she talked to him about his home, the mines, the snows in winter that he and the other men battled through with spades, and how he had to relax and let the passage of time effect some healing to his war battered psyche. This process took no more than three to four minutes each time yet its cumulative benefit was invaluable.

Amid the haziness at the back of his mind lay the impression that Lilian had been writing to him but there had been no letters on his person when he had been found, so that seemed unlikely, yet he also felt that something had been wrong with his marriage. Tussling with this uneasy suspicion from time to time Bill began to remember his home, but it was back in his early life with Lilian and not in the recent years of cold truce. On two of his rather stronger days he had tried composing a letter to her, only to find on reading it through that his script had veered off into nonsense, and today he had unsuccessfully tried again, finding also that he could not recall his address. It seemed that physical weakness was now his greatest enemy and one that he felt quite unable to overcome.

There was an ominous sensation beginning down the right side of Bella's face, and she stared up at the first landing where her husband was standing once more at the large window looking

392

down towards Ivy House.

'There you are again!' she observed bitterly. 'If it's Edward Robinson you're looking for, I'm afraid he'll be in school at this time of day.'

Johnny turned his head towards her for a second before resuming his vigil.

'Don't be so silly, Bella. How many more times do we have to go through this rigmarole? Don't you have any gardening to do?'

'It's November!'

He made no reply and she went up the stairs to stand beside him, causing him to give vent to an elaborate sigh.

'Maybe you're looking for Lilian Robinson as well?'

'Maybe I am. Now, why don't you leave me alone and find yourself another fascinating hobby?'

'You may as well tell me the truth, John. Edward Robinson is your son isn't he?'

He shrugged, but did not look at Bella. 'He may be. How would *I* know?'

'Simply by looking at him I should imagine! That Bancroft woman was right about them being doubles of each other, and by now I'd be surprised if the entire neighbourhood wasn't aware of the identity of their mutual father.'

'So what?'

'So, you'd better remember that Bill Robinson will be back in Gilfell in a matter of weeks and leave his family alone. You already have Antony. Why should you want Bill's son too?'

The expression on his face as he turned to leave was almost pitying, and she flinched as he answered 'Because, my dear, as you have already pointed out, Edward is *not* Bill's son. He's mine!'

Already Bella's churning stomach was adding its warning of the approaching migraine, and she put her hand to her temple to stave off the pain that would soon begin there as Johnny ran lightly down the stairs and across the hall without so much as a backward glance.

'Maura is leaving in two weeks' time but she will work with you until then, showing you the ropes and giving you time to get used to the job. Do you feel confident about taking it on?'

'Yes I do. Thank you, Mrs Robinson.'

Ena Elliott smiled broadly at her employer, her mind already focusing on her future higher wage, and Lilian nodded her dismissal pleasantly.

'Fine. You can start your new post tomorrow then, Ena. You've always been a good worker, and I'm sure I can rely on you.'

Once the second newly recruited supervisor had returned to her machine Lilian thankfully left her office and made her way across the factory yard to the old fashioned dry toilet, where she vomited dismally for some minutes before returning to her desk. Nausea was present most of the time now that her pregnancy was around the three months mark, and already showed a little when she was wearing only her underclothes. Louisa's suggestion of hot baths she had taken aplenty, despite her guilt at her intention, but to no avail, while remedies of her own were equally unsuccessful. Running up and downstairs for an extended period of time did nothing but make her feel even more sick than she normally did, as well as cause Marion and the children to doubt her sanity, and her excuse about taking more exercise whilst remaining indoors convinced no one. Soon, for safety's sake, she knew she must see Dr Hatton. In despair at the thought of what his reaction would be she cringed even more from imagining the local womens' response to her predicament when it became too obvious to hide: and then there was Sean. She had not told him yet, and did not see how she could now that there was a barrier of non-communication between them which she herself had erected. In the face of her unrelenting coolness he had slowly but surely retreated to his original position of employee, treating her with an exaggerated show of respect that only she knew was meant to be sarcastic.

Shivering as the late afternoon temperature began to drop quite sharply, she looked outside the window where previous rainclouds had drifted away leaving the sky a pale and frosty blue. The roads would be icy soon, for it had been showery all day, and on evenings like this Lilian felt pleased that she no longer drove the buses as she had sometimes done before.

The old fashioned fireplace in the machinists' workroom was cheerfully ablaze when she went to sit by the fireguard for a few moments to warm herself until it was time to go home. Almost ten minutes had passed when the telephone bell shrilled out and she reluctantly went back to the office to answer it. Louisa's voice sounded down the line, faintly apologetic, explaining that she had mistaken today for one of Lilian's free days and had called to see her with the children after school to find Marion in a rather confused state, so James had continued home in the trap and she and the children had stayed.

'Oh Lou, thank you. She isn't ill is she? Do you think we should get the doctor?'

'No, she isn't ill, just mixed up and thinking Bill is coming home for his tea shortly. Has she been like this before?'

'Quite a few times since the news came about Gilbert, I'm afraid. Please can you wait until I get home? Sean will be bringing me to Gilfell on the bus in about half an hour, and I can get him to run you to Roughside on it by way of the Back Road if you like.'

'Helen and Marguerite will love that. I'll set your table for you and see you then.'

Replacing the earpiece with sinking heart Lilian reflected gloomily on Marion's failing mental health. Most of the time she was simply withdrawn, but when this phase passed off she appeared to have slipped back within herself to happier years and was plainly no longer able to watch the children, nor even look after herself properly, on increasingly frequent occasions.

At the end of the shift Lilian and two machinists who lived at Gilbury climbed aboard the bus and Lilian, wishing herself at home in front of a cosy fire, listened to her two companions exchanging banter with Sean through the glass partition of the driver's cab. Agonisingly slow and cold, each mile seemed to crawl by, and when the vehicle stopped to let the other women alight Lilian noticed the frost glittering in the headlights on the road ahead.

'Conditions look bad, Sean.' She ventured as they moved forward again. He answered with a terse 'Aye. That they are,' and Lilian fell silent so that he could concentrate fully on his driving. She had already spoken to him about taking the bus right to her home instead of turning in at the garage, and now she wondered whether it would be entirely wise to send Sean along the primitive Back Road to Roughside afterwards when her father would be bound to guess that Louisa and the children had stayed all night with her and come for them in the trap next morning. Rather than distract the man by speaking through his cab window again, she decided to tell him just to return the bus to the garage after he had let her off at Ivy House.

Happier with her new decision, she relaxed a little and began to breathe more easily as they passed through the outskirts of Gilfell and proceeded into the heart of the village. Exactly what caused the skid at that particular point she was never to know, but as they drew level with the shops in Main Street the back wheels of the bus suddenly slipped towards them, propelling the front of the cab straight across the road towards the low stone wall that bordered the River Gill.

In what seemed to be slow motion Lilian rose to her feet, clutching the metal bar of the seat in front of her, and heard her own voice screaming 'Sean!' as they crashed through the rocky barrier, tipping over and down in a sickening lurching dance. At once the headlights went out and

Lilian felt as though some enraged giant was hitting her as she tumbled down towards the front of the bus, then, as a swift hot pain gripped her abdomen, she fainted.

Voices were the first thing to pierce her consciousness. Lots of people shouting, then the sound of running water. Gingerly she moved her arms around and tried to sit up, aware as she did so of a warm uncomfortable clamminess between her thighs, then the door of the bus opened above her head and someone shone a torch down on her.

'Lilian! Thank God!'

It was Len Harrison's voice, and others were joining it saying that they would have to lift her up through the doorway if she couldn't climb and someone, for heaven's sake, get the driver out of the water. Dimly she was beginning to realise that the bus was lying on its side in the river, with Sean apparently having been thrown out at the moment of the crash.

Outside someone else was calling that he would go for the doctor as they needed him to look at the driver, and Lilian Robinson was probably injured too, then she slumped against the cab sinking dizzily into a twilight world where she was only half aware of strong rough hands pulling and pushing her this way and that as the pain came again more severely than before. Muted speech, the sound of the river, and occasionally lights shining into her face, then horses hooves thumping along the grassy verge mere seconds before she caught a brief glimpse of Dr Hatton as he bent over her.

'Don't worry, Lilian. We're going to take you home. It's only a few yards.'

He looked anxious despite his reassuring words, and moved off into the darkness after a man's voice asked 'Can you give us a hand here with Mr Curtis, doctor?'

She closed her eyes as another wave of pain made her cry out.

It was a week before Lilian was allowed out of bed, and Louisa and her daughters stayed at Ivy House while James visited daily. Marion, bemused by these events and unable to take in the facts of the accident although they had been explained to her repeatedly, did what was now the norm for her, and spent most of her time in her bedroom where the fire was lit to keep her warm.

Dr Hatton attended Lilian each day following the accident, and she noticed miserably that he never made eye contact with her for more than a second or so and spoke only of medical matters. Luckily no bones had been broken during her buffeting on the bus, and although she was badly bruised the crash had left her relatively un-scathed, but her miscarriage was another matter, and when it was finally over she was weak from shock and loss of blood. On his last visit to Lilian during the first week in December she looked at him as he snapped shut his black bag, and asked 'This won't be talked about in the village ... my personal mishap?'

He regarded her coldly. 'I'm a doctor, Mrs Robinson. I don't divulge any of my patients' secrets.'

'Mrs Robinson? It used to be "Lilian". I thought we were friends.'

'I am also the friend of your absent husband, and find certain circumstances deeply disturbing. Now, if you will excuse me.'

Waiting outside on the landing Louisa listened to the exchange with a mixture of pity and fury, whilst silently lamenting the fact that travelling all the way to Dalton in future to consult a different doctor was too impractical to work. Coming outside he shut the bedroom door behind him, but not before she had seen Lilian's stricken expression, and Louisa stepped aside to let him pass.

'You can see yourself out can't you, Dr Hatton?'

Her tone was hostile, and the smile he had begun faded from his face as he bowed slightly then hurried down the stairs. Inside the bedroom both women heard the front door slam as he left, but deliberately ignored the subject of his visit, and Marion, startled by the noise, wandered out of the room and into that of her daughter-in-law.

'Oh Lilian, aren't you up yet? It's almost lunch-time, dear.'

Louisa tried hard not to show her exasperation and her voice was soft as she pointed out that it was almost six o'clock, but this served only to further confuse the old lady.

'I see. Have you retired early or aren't you feeling well?'

'I haven't been well, Marion, but I'll be getting up a little tomorrow and I'm sure we'll soon be back to normal. Louisa has looked after us all for

400

over a week. I don't know what we'd have done without her.'

Marion smiled vaguely. 'Yes, it was good of her, but I expect Bill would have found someone anyway.'

Wandering back across the landing she seemed to have forgotten all about them, and was humming as she shut herself back in her room again. Louisa groaned and sat down in the chair by the bedside.

'Lilian … she's getting worse, isn't she?'

'I'm afraid so. When I get on my feet I'll have to find someone to stay with her all the time I'm at work, because she's no longer capable of looking after the children or herself.'

There was silence for a while then she spoke again, hesitantly.

'I keep forgetting about Sean, you know. I wonder how his broken arm is healing and his concussion? Dr Hatton must think me a horrible person not to have been more concerned for his welfare.'

Louisa took her hand as it lay on the counterpane, patting it comfortingly. 'Don't worry about Dr Hatton. Whatever he thinks about anything is not worth agonising over, and Sean has gone back to the relatives he was originally staying with on Dalton Moor before he worked for you.'

'Oh.'

She closed her eyes for a moment as the full implications of the month's events began to sink in.

'I know I tried quite a few times to start a miscarriage, Lou, but I truly wish I hadn't had to lose a baby to get my life back on track. However, I have to admit that if the pregnancy had continued I wouldn't have been living here much longer once Bill got to know.'

'It's over now.' Louisa soothed. 'Think of the future, not the past.'

Making no reply Lilian turned her head away towards the window as she wondered just what might now lie ahead, and when Louisa spoke again she gave a slight start at her words.

'A few nights ago Johnny Peacock came to the door to see how you were and to offer his services to you and your Gilbury girls until you find another vehicle to replace the bus. He told me that he was fairly sure you wouldn't be able to buy a replacement until peacetime, and he would be very glad to help out if you wished.'

Frowning a little Lilian plucked at the corner of her eiderdown, dismayed at this aspect of losing a bus which had not previously occurred to her.

'What did you tell him?'

'I told him that you were not well enough to see anyone yet and to come back. He said he would telephone to make sure it was convenient before calling again.'

'Well, I suppose it's good of him to think of these things. I'll see to it that I'm up when he wants to call. By the way, what happened to the bus? Did they have difficulty getting it out of the river?'

'They needed the assistance of every horse and rope in the area, and it took a long time. It's parked in a corner of the garage now with Albert making hopeful inspections every few days to see if the damage may prove repairable after all, but it seems fairly hopeless. The engine was smashed up so badly with hitting the wall and then the flagged bed of the river, that nothing can be done.'

'So there's only the miners' bus on the road and only one driver?'

'Yes.'

Pushing back the bedclothes Lilian eased her legs over the side of the bed and reached for her dressing gown.

'Something must be done then, and as soon as possible.' She told Louisa. 'I'm coming downstairs now to phone Johnny and ask him if he can call here tomorrow afternoon to talk things over. Heaven knows, in this situation, even *his* help is better than none.'

The study had always been a gloomy room and Lilian had just finished lighting the gas brackets when she heard Johnny's knock. Having assured Louisa that she could manage alone she made her way to the front door on slightly shaky legs, and as they both seated themselves on opposite sides of the fireplace she thanked him for his offer of assistance. He looked handsome, as he always did, yet his smile which had once melted her resistance completely now left her unmoved.

'You know I'll always do what I can. These accidents are such a shock.'

'Yes; it was awful ... all of it.'

'Is it true that Bill is coming home?'

She smiled then for the first time, and he felt the old useless regret starting up again as she answered.

'Yes, he's coming home, but I don't know exactly when. He was wounded at a place called Passchendaele, and after three months of silence I heard from both the army and your sister-in-law Constance, but she'll have told you all about it in her letters I expect. It would be wonderful to have him home for Christmas, but I think that may be too soon.'

Realising that there were unspoken details which he was supposed to know about, and probably would have done had Constance deigned to correspond with her own family, Johnny merely nodded and smiled again before passing on to the problem he had come to discuss.

Lilian was gratified when he told her that he had been transporting her two Gilbury workers back and forth in his car ever since the accident, and that all she had to do was agree to come along too, at least as long as the weather conditions would allow.

'That's marvellous! I must pay you...'

Her voice trailed off at the look on his face, and she added weakly. 'Well, let me reimburse you for the petrol you use. After all, a horse and trap would be too slow and no one else has offered to take us anywhere in their motor.'

'There's no question of any payment, so please don't bring the matter up again.'

Suddenly the study door opened and Winifred stood looking in, apparently nonplussed at the sight of a stranger, while beyond her Edward could be heard addressing his mother.

'I told her not to come in, but she wouldn't listen. Come on, Winnie!'

Johnny stared beyond the little girl towards her brother, and before Lilian could reply he urged both children into the room.

'Come in then. Let's have a look at you both now you're here.'

His tone was lightly teasing, attracting them inside the room where he engaged them both in conversation as Lilian looked on, surprised at his easy way with the young, but there was an almost tangible tension about him that she could not understand and after her son and daughter had taken their leave his eyes were bright with something that looked strangely like triumph.

'You have a fine family, Lilian.' He said as the door closed behind them, then smiled to himself at her puzzled expression. 'Now, you tell me which days you will be going to the factory and I'll make a note of them.'

Writing down the details in a black leather notebook with an expensive fountain pen, Johnny had difficulty getting his thoughts away from Edward Robinson. The Bancroft woman had been right. Edward and Antony, in spite of their age difference, were like doubles of each other and were both obviously his sons, although what he might do about that he did not know.

After a further ten minutes discussing various aspects of their respective business problems Lilian and Johnny parted company, and after showing him out she stood for a few seconds with her back against the closed front door. At the top of the corridor Louisa came round the corner from the kitchen and raised her eyebrows enquiringly.

'Is something wrong, Lilian?'

She gave a rather uncertain smile. 'I don't really know, Lou. He's going to run the Gilbury girls and I backwards and forwards for no charge, which is a very generous offer, yet ... I keep getting the feeling that he's really up to something else, and that if I knew what it was I wouldn't like it.'

CHAPTER SIXTEEN

1918

By Christmas 1917 a handful of war wounded had returned to the valley, changed forever from the men they had once been, but Bill was not among them and no letter had yet been received from him although Lilian had written again to the hospital where he was a patient. On New Year's Eve she sent off a desperate plea to the hospital's Almoner asking for information on her husband's whereabouts as soon as possible, and decided to go down to London to find Bill the moment she knew for certain where he was. On January fourth a reply came stating that Bill had been transferred on November tenth and giving her the address of a convalescent home in Berkshire. With the ever increasing demand for such places Lilian doubted that he could still be convalescing after two months, but sent off another letter to the Matron explaining her problem, and this time the answer came within three days. As she had begun to fear, Bill had been discharged from the Berkshire Home as far back as December the first. It had been assumed that along with other war wounded men he would be intent upon making his way back home, and it was with regret that the writer could not say what had happened to Private Robinson after that date.

Mercifully alone at the breakfast table when this last letter brought its disquieting news, Lilian moved to the calendar on the wall and counted off five weeks since Bill had apparently vanished into thin air. Knowing that many women who could afford the time and money to make a journey had travelled to see their men in these places, she wondered whether Bill had realised that her hesitation had simply been caused by the possibility that their paths might cross en route. Her letters must have reached Bill yet he had never answered them, leaving her unsure of any action she could take, and now she had no idea where he was while more than a month had passed since there had been any trace of him at all. For an entire day Lilian seriously contemplated travelling down to the Berkshire Home in an attempt to pick up his trail somehow, but James and Louisa persuaded her to drop the plan.

'You have those who need you here, lass, so it's no use going off on a wild goose chase. Bill will come home when he's ready, and all the rest of us can do is wait.' James advised, and Louisa echoed him.

'People probably wouldn't be able to recall seeing Bill, not with all the wounded men wearing those red ties and bright blue suits. They say the big towns and cities are full of them at the moment, poor things, and for all we know Bill could be heading for Gilfell at this very minute.'

'Yes ... I expect you're right.'

Retreating slowly from her determination to

hunt for her husband, Lilian listened to the sounds of her children playing happily with their cousins upstairs in the toy room and tried to quell the awful thought that maybe some accident had befallen Bill since leaving the convalescent home, and that they might never see him again.

'When is this dreadful war going to end anyway?' She demanded suddenly, then added the unthinkable. 'And when it does, do you think we will be the victors or the vanquished?'

That the tide of the war was finally turning in favour of the Allies was undeniable fact by late spring 1918, but the death toll, continuing to exact its crushing price for all nations involved, still held the country in a sombre grip. By April Lilian had still received no word of Bill and went about her duties both at home and at the factory like an automaton, trying to hide the depression growing in her heart. She had visited Maura Harker regularly since the birth of her baby boy back in January, and was pleased to see that the woman was managing to run her boarding house well enough to make a living. At first Maura had been suspicious of her motives for visiting, thinking that there must be an element of gloating behind Lilian's apparent concern, but gradually she came to realise that all the woman really wanted was someone to talk to about Bill's disappearance, which was now common knowledge in the area. Admitting that she wondered whether Maura might have an idea of where Bill might be, or what he might be doing, Lilian tried to form a theory of her own as Maura slowly lost her embarrassment in talking about her past relationship with Bill Robinson and pooled her ideas with those of his wife, who so desperately needed to track him down in spite of the gulf that had existed between them for so long.

'He still loved you.' Maura ventured one afternoon after another of their fruitless speculations. 'He wouldn't talk about you directly, so I can't tell you that he actually said it, but I always knew. Women can sense these things can't they?'

Lilian's smile was a little tremulous. 'I certainly hope so, Maura.'

Since the turn of the year the winter had been so mild that there had been no snowfall to speak of beyond the flimsiest covering from time to time, and Johnny Peacock had continued to ferry Lilian and her workers to and from Dalton, but she had been dismayed at a recent Red Cross fund raising sale in the Assembly Rooms when Bella had cut her dead. Not only that, but she had given the children, and Edward in particular, a hard and bitter look that revealed all too clearly the cause of her sudden antagonism. For a while now Bella had stopped bringing Antony along to these events, although like all mothers she had enjoyed the complimentary comments her son received, but the possibility that she had somehow found out about Edward's paternity was strong in Lilian's mind; so put together with Johnny's offer of help back in the autumn, plus his great interest in Edward at every opportunity since then, and the conclusion was more than obvious.

To Bella Peacock, Johnny's other son was a

direct and insulting blow to the only triumph she had ever felt in her life; the birth of Antony John. It was true that Johnny had been even more attentive to Antony lately, but Bella still deeply resented both Edward and Lilian and the atmosphere inside White Court had deteriorated into open hostility during the past few months.

Gerald and Elisabeth Fairburn had made it quite plain where their loyalties lay, yet Johnny remained apparently indifferent to it all. The highlight of his days were the moments in his motor after he and Lilian were left alone, when he would insist upon talking of 'old times' and once daringly suggested that he should have married her instead of Bella. To this idea Lilian wisely made no answer, but her discomfiture was becoming increasingly hard to bear. To offset his advances she would talk of Bill's absence in tones that made it quite clear that she had no feelings for any other man, but Johnny was not easy to discourage and was eventually bold enough to confront her directly.

'Edward is *my* boy isn't he?' He challenged one night after stopping the motor at Ivy House, and the panic-stricken look she gave him told him all he needed to know. Gripping her wrist to prevent her leaving he drew a long breath of satisfaction.

'I knew it! Let me get to know him, Lilian! He can come out with Antony and I on Sundays ... you can come too.'

'And what kind of scandal would that cause, do you imagine, affecting both our families and, above all, your legitimate son? You can't do that for another reason too, Johnny, and that has to do

411

with what is good for Edward, because *Bill* is Edward's real father in all the ways that matter. You were a biological mishap and can never be anything more!'

Quite unimpressed by her outburst he smiled and murmured 'I don't give up on things I really want without a fight, Lilian. So ... we'll see, shall we? Time may tell a different story.'

In despair Lilian considered renting a room at Maura's and hiring someone to stay at Ivy House during her days away, but she could not do that for the Gilbury girls who had dependent families to support, so Johnny's services would still be required, no matter how much she wished otherwise, and his constant badgering about Edward simply had to be endured. Only once did his cajoling turn into the grim threat to cease helping her, but when she calmly agreed to make other arrangements he retreated swiftly to his original position assuring her that he had only been joking. Knowing perfectly well that he had not, she again put her mind to the problem of finding another source of transport for herself and the Gilbury girls, yet was all too aware, as he was, that none existed.

Albert ran the miners' bus on a tight schedule seven days a week, stoically and without complaint, but the money made from these routes was minimal, and the factory now financially propped up the garage business until the future cessation of the war might give it a chance to prosper. In gratitude to her one remaining driver, Lilian had given him a sizeable rise in wages knowing that the garage would simply cease to

412

exist without him, and his total loyalty proved it to have been a good move as well as one she could easily afford, as the factory's credit balance rose week by week to a figure Lilian would never have imagined in her wildest dreams. Whatever things the war had taken away, it had certainly filled the Robinsons' coffers along with those of many other manufacturers in these times of severe importing restrictions.

The summer was well underway, with still no word of Bill, when another kind of casualty returned to the valley. Lilian was on her way back to the factory from the bank when she saw a woman climbing slowly up the High Street, and something about her struck a familiar note in her memory. Standing still, she covertly studied the person whilst pretending to look for something in her bag. The woman's head was bent and it was impossible to tell from her black hair, so liberally streaked with grey, just how old she was, then she looked up and with a sense of shock Lilian recognised Constance Fairburn.

'Constance! How are you?'

The tiredness of her answering smile was not lost on Lilian, nor were the fine lines around her eyes and mouth. From a young woman who had once been a monument to vitality Constance had visibly aged, and now seemed drained of life.

'Hello, Lilian. I've been sent home ... I'm afraid I am disgraced ... I couldn't seem to function any more. I may be able to go back in a few months, but I don't really know.'

The dark eyes, once so full of laughter and mischief, now had a haunted look, and Lilian

413

stepped forward and took her by the arm, steering her towards The Three Bells Hotel.

'Let us have lunch together, Constance, and give me a chance to thank you properly for sending that letter about Bill. You'll never know how much it meant to me.'

Walking through the glass doors with Lilian, Constance smiled a little, and as they took their seats at a table in the corner, she asked.

'How is Bill? He must have been home for quite a while now. Maybe I could call and see him some afternoon.'

'Of course you could. You'd be welcome any time, but Bill never came home and I still don't know where he is, or even if he's still alive.'

Their talk and their meal took so long that the manager had to approach them at four thirty pointing out that the dining room would normally have closed over half an hour ago and, while he very much appreciated their custom, the staff now had to prepare the tables for dinner. Guiltily Lilian paid the bill and escorted Constance back to the factory to await Johnny's car, greatly amused by a glimpse of the old Constance as she exclaimed with only a trace of her former weariness. 'Oh, thank God! I'll stay at White Court for a while. I couldn't stand to have mother twittering at me at the moment.'

'You look absolutely terrible! No wonder you want to hide at White Court, although you know as well as I do that your mother will arrive on our doorstep within minutes of hearing that you're home.'

414

'Yes, I know, but that's just a visit. It isn't as bad as living with her and being lectured all the time.'

'Surely, even Elisabeth couldn't find anything to disapprove of. You've served your country like a true patriot, and given your skills as a VAD nurse without even the dignity of a wage in return. I call that heroism; what do *you* say Lilian?'

'I couldn't agree more.'

Having dropped off the Gilbury girls some minutes previously Johnny and Constance had immediately launched into their blunt discussion on recent events, and Lilian had silently agreed with both points of view to a certain degree. They were still heatedly thrashing things out when Lilian left the car at Chapel Corner and she smiled to herself as their voices could still be heard over the labouring engine as the vehicle started up Kenhope Fell road towards White Court.

Busy in her garden as usual, Bella stared owlishly through her spectacles as Johnny parked the car round the back of the house near to where she was working and helped Constance alight, then, as she realised who the unexpected passenger was, she ran forward to meet her.

'Connie! Oh Connie, how wonderful that you're back!'

Flinging herself on her sister she hugged her fiercely, feeling slightly surprised when Constance responded in kind, and Johnny frowned as he threw his driving gloves onto the car seat.

'What a pity you couldn't have looked clean and tidy for once, Bella, instead of being encrusted in grime from head to foot!'

'I'm sure I'll soon amend that, John, and if Constance doesn't object I don't see that it's any of your business.'

Turning her back on her husband Bella began to lead her sister into the house, and Constance cast an interested backward glance towards Johnny to see what his reaction was to this untypical show of spirit from Bella, but he appeared to be quite unsurprised by it as he removed his goggles and leather helmet. It seemed that there had been some changes on the home front as well during these past few years.

'Where's my nephew?' she asked as they walked along the back corridor into the hall. 'I've never seen him yet, remember?'

Upstairs, in the nursery, where Constance met Antony John, his young nanny studied her slyly wondering just how much older than her mistress this ageing sister could be. Surely in her late forties judging by her hair and the lines around her eyes and mouth. Then, of course, she just had to utter the thing that always made Mrs Peacock cross when anyone else said it, even though it was true.

'He's just the image of John, isn't he? How clever of you to manage that. I'll bet his Daddy thinks there's no-one like him.'

'Not quite. Actually, his Daddy knows there's another who's exactly like him, but I'll tell you about that, later.'

Dinner had just finished when the shaking began. Appalled, Constance saw her coffee cup begin to vibrate with the sudden tremor of her hands, and as carefully as she tried to replace it in its saucer the savage crash of crockery turned all heads in her direction. Bella frowned uncertainly.

'Are you alright?'

'No ... not really.'

Her voice was barely a whisper as she stood up and stumbled from the table towards the door, and Johnny rose to go to her aid feeling humiliated for her as Laura gaped from the sideboard.

'You may clear away now.' He said sharply, and took Constance's elbow leading her out into the hall and up the stairs, where every step seemed to make matters worse. Tears spilled from her eyes and ran down her cheeks, her sobs made all the more terrible because they were silent, and in her room she fell upon the bed curling herself into a ball like a child.

Standing aside to allow Bella access, Johnny closed the door softly on the sisters and went down to the lounge. Not for the first time he was aware of the hell he had sidestepped in being rejected for military service, and as he sat down by the fire he took a steadying gulp of the brandy he had poured himself, leaning back with half closed eyes as its warmth spread through him. There were many of the opinion that the war had now only weeks to go, and if it had affected many as it had obviously affected Constance then there truly was a generation lost.

The Fairburns' reaction to their eldest daughter's breakdown was largely one of bewilderment born of ignorance. Elisabeth was loud in her condemnation of the military hospitals for not giving their nurses sufficient off duty time to properly recuperate before their next shift, and Constance soon gave up trying to explain that rest periods had not been the issue. Her mother still lived in her own cosy little world, and had not the slightest concept of the unending horrors to which she and her fellow nurses had been subjected day after day; in fact, no one understood who had not been there to share the experience.

After a fortnight at White Court she went back to Low Shields, but it seemed merely to exacerbate the situation. As though it had been trapped in time the place had the weird effect of causing Constance to feel that she was living in two distinctly separate ages, the pre-war, and the present, with the two walking uneasily out of step with each other.

More and more she took to wandering over the moor on her own, and when the chill of October brought its orange and flame leaves to blend with the heather on the upper reaches of the fells she seldom got back to the house before dark. Gerald would stand in his darkened study straining his eyes to catch a glimpse of the bright yellow scarf she always wore around her neck, sinking down into his chair in relief when he eventually realised that she had made another safe return.

Silent and withdrawn, she was a shadow of herself, and scarcely ate anything despite her skeletal figure. Gerald and the family had been delighted to have her back from France, but he found himself worrying about her increasingly each day whilst not having the faintest idea what he could do about it. Meanwhile, not even Bella had an inkling of the desolation she was feeling from having lost Ralph. On the rainy days when walking was out of the question she hid in the attic among the trunks, unwanted pieces of furniture, and piles of old books which she thumbed through by the hour, smiling to herself at various passages that she considered he would have appreciated, and at night she dreamt of him. It was always the same dream. She would see him walking towards her down the long driveway, smiling and holding out his arms, but the moment she began to run to him her dream ended and she awoke, grief stricken and more desolately lonely than she could ever have believed possible.

With November came the first snow of the winter and the much hoped for peace with the Armistice finally signed by Germany on the eleventh, following Turkey on the thirtieth October and Austria/Hungary on November third. There were no triumphant celebrations in either Gilfell or Dalton, but rather a weary relief that the nightmare had at last ceased, yet still there was no sign of Bill Robinson.

Lilian faced the approach of Christmas with deepening depression as surviving men began to trickle home. She was delighted for their families, and for them, but felt her own situation to be as hopeless as that of her sister-in-law, Jenny, for if Bill had still been alive he would surely have returned by now.

December was just beginning when Spanish Flu crept into the valley like an enemy overlooked, and the first person of Lilian's acquaintance to succumb to it was Johnny Peacock, as the car was on the road again in a bout of mild weather. He looked hot and feverish upon picking up the factory workers to take them home at five o'clock, and Lilian, alarmed at his demeanour as he slumped breathlessly into his seat after turning the vehicle's starting handle, was firmly of the opinion that they would all be staying at home the following day.

'Maybe you're right,' he gasped, and began to cough into a large white handkerchief whilst leaning forward onto the steering wheel until the spasm passed.

Later, when the girls from Gilbury alighted at their home, they assured Lilian that they would walk the two miles into Dalton the next day and try to find someone to give them a lift on their return journey after work. Failing that, they were quite prepared to walk that way too. Grateful for their resourcefulness, Lilian offered to drive herself and Johnny for the remainder of their journey, and was astounded when he agreed.

It was a strange feeling driving the Rolls Royce under instruction from its owner, who was so ill he plainly cared for nothing except getting back to White Court, and did not even react on the occasions when she crunched the gears. Parking the car outside the front door she rang the bell for help, then assisted Bella and Laura to walk the now delirious Johnny into the house. Bella, her eyes reflecting her dread at this turn of events, thanked Lilian in an abstracted way as she bent over her husband, who lay where he had fallen on the lounge sofa breathing roughly through his mouth, then sent Laura to get blankets from upstairs, and tell Nanny not to allow Antony anywhere near his father. Leaving quietly, Lilian shut the front door behind her and walked down to Ivy House, suddenly anxious to check on the health of her own loved ones.

In the space of only a few days the entire area lay in the grip of the epidemic, with scarcely a home free from it. The elderly stood little chance against its savagery, nor did small children or anyone in delicate health, and within one week the local undertakers were distressingly overworked while Dalton Hospital was filled to overflowing with staff members going down like ninepins.

It was this last crisis that brought Constance Fairburn out of her reclusive state as a call went out for all with medical experience, who were not infected, to report to the wards to help the meagre number of staff left trying to do their own work and that of their stricken colleagues. Having packed a few essentials into a valise at first light one morning just before Christmas, she was striding purposefully down the drive at Low Shields when Gerald came behind her in the car.

'Get in and I'll drive you down there.' He ordered grimly, and for the first time in weeks the woman smiled.

Stranded at home now that Johnny and his transport were no longer available, Lilian became fretful about the factory and nervous in case the dreaded infection struck down any of her loved ones. From mostly selfish reasons she told her usual helpers to stay away whilst she was able to take over her own domestic tasks and they obeyed

421

with alacrity, also hoping to isolate themselves from any needless exposure to the flu germ.

Marion, who still lived continually in her bedroom, showed no signs of incubating the illness, but on Christmas Eve both Edward and Winifred became increasingly hot, headachy and listless, as Lilian wondered miserably what would happen if she too fell victim to the illness and could not look after them.

Christmas Day passed virtually unnoticed with the children too ill to be interested in anything, and Marion ate the makeshift snacks that Lilian prepared for her alone in her room, seemingly unaware of the date.

By nightfall a harassed, and apparently immune, Dr Hatton arrived to examine the flu's latest victims and gave Lilian simple advice on how to treat the invalids, adding the only comforting words he could think of. 'They're strong, Lilian. They stand every chance of pulling through.'

That his manner had reverted to the warmth of their former friendship Lilian neither noticed nor cared. She thanked him for calling and promised to follow his advice on the care of her children, then closed the door behind him with a sigh of weariness, wondering whether she dared sleep at all that night.

With the turn of the year the epidemic slowly came to an end in the valley, which although badly hit had fared better than town areas where the population was densely packed, and George Hatton, exhausted after weeks of gruelling overwork, felt that only a miracle had prevented him from contracting the dreaded disease himself. The death toll in Gilfell by mid January included Nan Heslop, found by James and Louisa who had noticed her smokeless chimney from their bedroom windows, Emma Dallow, several people from the poorest families who had not been strong to begin with, and Gerald and Elisabeth Fairburn of Low Shields.

When the news of this catastrophe reached White Court, Bella found it impossible to grasp at first, while Constance, still busy in Dalton Hospital, found yet another burden of grief to add to the one she already had. The agent from the Gilbury mine had discovered them both mere hours before their death, too ill to be moved due to the onset of pneumonia, and also their two servants lying ill upstairs in their quarters.

Constance immediately left the wards to return to Low Shields where arrangements had to be made for her parents' funeral, and upon her arrival set to work at once to make the cook and housemaid as comfortable as possible. In the master bedroom, awaiting the undertaker's carriage, her mother and father's lifeless forms were part of a nightmare from which, like so many others, she would not be waking up.

She was relieved when Bella phoned just after the funeral directors had left, taking Gerald and Elisabeth. She seriously doubted that anyone would be able to get very far during the next few days, for the late afternoon sky promised snow and a biting wind from the east told quite clearly that the worst of the winter weather was about to start. Voicing her view on the approaching blizzard Constance was startled to hear Bella cry 'It's awful enough with mother and father gone, but the doctor says this terrible flu has caused more damage to John's heart! He has been so very long getting over it and doesn't seem able to get his strength back at all, then he has become so breathless when the pains come in his chest...'

'Bella, what are you talking about?'

'John's condition. He was rejected by the army because of an enlarged heart.'

'I didn't know that. So the flu has made matters worse then?'

'Dr Hatton says so, yes.'

Hesitating a few seconds Constance asked gently. 'Is little Antony still in good health?'

'Yes, thank God!'

'Exactly.'

'What do you mean?'

'I mean be thankful that, unlike some poor mothers, you haven't lost your child, Bella. I'm sure John will be alright in a while, and even if his heart condition has deteriorated it will mean living life at a quieter pace, that's all. But it's still a life. There are plenty who would give anything to be able to say that about someone they've lost during these past few years.'

'Yes ... of course. I'm sorry, Connie.'

'Good girl. Now, about the funeral arrangements...'

The blizzard began that night and continued for a further two days, by which time all roads were completely impassable, and the funeral of the Fairburns and all others due at the same time had to be postponed until it cleared away.

At Ivy House Lilian gave all her attention to her childrens' convalescence, relieved beyond measure when they began to recover a little of their past energy and appetite. Marion mercifully escaped the illness, continually questioning Lilian as to why Edward and Winifred were not at school, and when was Bill coming home from work as it was surely getting late. Answering as patiently as she could, Lilian often wanted to weep with frustration and longed for the thaw to come so that their lives, and those of everyone else in the valley, could return to what would be regarded as normal in the future. The days before the war, so dearly familiar in memory, were gone forever, and she tried never to dwell on them too long.

By the end of January a few days of milder temperature melted the blankets and drifts of white, and life in the valley began at last to move on.

From her landing window Lilian often glimpsed a gaunt-faced Victor Dallow, himself newly bereaved, taking funeral after funeral in the chapel while the grave diggers worked overtime in the cemetery just outside the village. Most of the population of Gilfell resembled black crows in their mourning garb, and she counted herself lucky not to be among them, especially when she heard about the Fairburns and watched a thinner pale-faced Johnny driving his family down towards Dalton Church on the day of their burial.

With the return of her domestic helpers to look after her home and mother-in-law, Lilian instructed Albert to drive her down to the factory between the miners' runs and booked a large room at Maura's for herself and the children, from whom she now refused to be separated. Seating them in front of the factory fireplace with their new Christmas books she found the last order for military uniforms almost completed and began preparations to finally shut down the unit. Without Bill to advise her she could see no other course of action open to her, and hoped to sell the workshop machines in the near future to anyone willing to try their luck in the clothing industry. Meanwhile, she thanked the women for carrying on the work during her absence, paid them up to date with an additional bonus, and promised that a list of their names and skills would be given to any prospective new employer.

Five days later she locked up the premises for the last time then posted some important letters at the nearby post office. One was to a national newspaper and another to one covering the northern counties, both publicising the availability of the small factory implements, and the third was to a firm in Canada following up on her original enquiry regarding a snowplough. Much as she regretted closing the clothing factory Lilian was convinced that the garage at Gilfell, so long a minor concern, would soon be able to flourish aided by the profits from the other business, and the plough would be a godsend in keeping the roads clear during the many snowfalls in winter.

Out on the street again Winifred tugged at Lilian's sleeve.

'Can we go home now, Mammy? Have we finished?'

Taking both her children firmly by their hands Lilian tried to make her smile convincing. 'Yes, we're finished. We'll go for some tea at the cafe for a treat until Albert comes with the bus to take us home.'

They were sitting at the window table of The Primrose Cafe ten minutes later when Johnny Peacock drove up High Street towards the Gilfell road with Bella and Constance sitting in the passenger seats. As the car laboured up the slope Lilian looked at the group with interest. It was a week since the Fairburns' funeral and the women were still in black, even though Johnny was not, but what held her attention was the fact that although he was scowling ferociously, Bella was almost grinning, and her sister looked as though she had sustained a blow to the head which had left her semi-conscious. After a few seconds' quiet musing she wondered whether they had just visited the solicitors for the reading of Gerald's Will, because if that should be the case its contents had plainly not pleased his son-in-law.

Looking down the street towards the heart of Dalton, Edward suddenly stopped eating and stared at the man with the mop of snow white hair who was almost at the door of the cafe, then he stood up and ran forward to meet him.

'Edward! Where are you going?'

Lilian was on her feet and Winifred gazing towards them in wonder as the boy re-entered the room leading the newcomer by the hand, and the man smiled a shade uncertainly.

'Hello, Lilian.'

Shocked, she sat down again with a slight thud

as her knees gave way, then, as Winifred scrambled from her chair and flung herself at her father the woman covered her mouth with her hand while tears flooded her eyes. Coming forward Bill Robinson seated himself on the chair next to his wife and pulled his son and daughter onto his lap, but he reached past them to take Lilian's hands in his own.

'Don't cry, love,' he said softly. 'It's so very good to see you. Please say you're just a little glad to see me too.'

CHAPTER SEVENTEEN

The cafe was filling to capacity as more people came in off the street, but Lilian was aware of nothing and no one except the husband she had given up for lost. The children chattered as they clung to him, asking questions which he answered automatically whilst never taking his eyes from her face, but when she managed to speak it was to utter something completely trivial.

'What happened to your hair, Bill?'

He smiled. 'I suppose the war happened to it, Lilian. Sometimes it worried me quite a lot.'

She began to laugh but it turned into a sob, and she stopped abruptly.

'So where have you been all this time?'

'I decided to work my way up the country ... I needed time. I kept forgetting things after I was hit, and I felt I must have some weeks to myself to get used to ordinary life again. I'm sorry if I caused you anxiety. I was in a convalescent place in Berkshire after the hospital, and I often tried to write to you but it would never come out right somehow. I'll try to explain things better when we're on our own.'

'That will be best I'm sure. Albert's coming down with the bus to take us home after the last miners' run. There's a lot to tell you: a great deal to catch up on.'

'I've still got the King's Shilling you gave me,

Dad. I keep it safe in my bedroom and I've kept polishing it so it's nice and shiny now.'

Cutting through their exchange Edward beamed up at Bill who smiled back at him as Winifred nudged her brother sharply.

'I polished it as well sometimes.'

Watching Bill speak to the children as though he had never been away, Lilian felt as if the world had stopped to hold its breath while she tried to grasp the wonderful truth that he was home at last. Not just home, but more like the Bill she had wanted returned to her for so long. His clothes were shabby, and at his feet lay a small cheap suitcase that obviously contained no more than the bare essentials of his life; a life that he still had to tell her about in the fullness of time. Unwillingly she wondered whether there had been another Maura involved, and knew that her own relationship with Sean Curtis had cancelled out any right she may have had to be angry. Guiltily she looked away from him, jumping slightly .as she saw the bus passing the cafe window.

'There's Albert.' She said quietly. 'We can go home now.'

At the gate of Low Shields Johnny drew the Rolls to a halt, his expression sulky as he got out to help Constance alight. Bella raised her eyebrows.

'Surely we can take Connie right to the door, John. It's a long walk to the house on such a cold afternoon.'

'It's fine here, really.' Constance gave them both a smile then turned on her heel walking briskly towards the drive, adding cheerily. 'I'll telephone you tomorrow sometime, Bella.'

She heard the car starting up again and Bella shouting 'Goodbye' but kept her eyes straight ahead, fixed on the house that her parents had left exclusively to her, together with their share of the Gilfell and Gilbury mines: a share that had always been marginally greater than that of the Peacocks and, she guessed, had probably been the real reason why Thomas Peacock had engineered the marriage between their two families which now proved to have been completely futile.

As a single woman Constance was unencumbered by a husband's rights to any of her property, and she quickened her pace as her appreciation of the situation grew. Not only would she have the final say in any decisions regarding the mines but she would also make sure that Johnny treated Bella very differently in the future, and that last resolution gave her the greater pleasure.

The rest of the journey to White Court took place in silence between Johnny and Bella, and she cast him regular looks of wary bewilderment for she could not understand why he was so angry. His face, pale when they had left the solicitor's office, now had dull red blotches on each cheek and the muscle movement along his jawline very clearly showed that he was gritting his teeth together in temper.

Waiting until they were back inside their home she turned towards him as he flung off his driving gear, most of which landed at the attendant maid's feet.

431

'What on earth is the matter, John? Surely you can't resent Constance being left everything. Heaven knows, she has nothing else in her life and we already have our proportion of the mines and this house.'

He glared at her, his eyes glittering dangerously.

'Oh, so we have my sweet, but didn't you forget to add something else to our list of blessings?'

'Something else?'

She followed him into the lounge, shutting the door on the listening servant whom she knew would be hovering in the hall for as long as she could find ways of looking busy there. Johnny took a cigar out of a box on the mantelpiece and clipped off the end with savage precision before mocking her in a falsetto voice.

'We have each other, Bella! Fancy forgetting that!'

With her back still to the door the woman studied him for a few seconds as her mood hardened. She had endured his bullying for years with very little retaliation, and even that was fairly recent, but with the death of her parents Bella felt his attitude of jealousy and greed to be a direct insult to both of them, and reacted accordingly.

'Oh, I didn't forget that we had each other, John. I simply never thought of it as a blessing, and I think you would be the first to agree that, apart from our son, we both very much regret the day we married so unwisely. However, as we did, I suggest we continue to make the best we can of a very bad job! Connie has inherited Low Shields instead of yourself, and no matter how long you have coveted my family's home there is nothing

432

at all you can do to get it, so the sooner you stop sulking the better!'

It was by far the longest speech Bella had ever made in her husband's presence and he paused in the act of selecting a taper for his cigar, staring at her as though he could not believe his ears. Defiantly she stared back as anger stiffened her resolve.

'Who the hell do you think you are?' He asked softly. 'Mummy and Daddy aren't here to protect you now, remember. There's only you and I.'

'And Constance. And Low Shields, my original and much loved home.'

'Go back there whenever you like, but if you try to take Antony I'll kill you!'

Putting down his cigar and taper Johnny took a threatening step towards her, his face contorted with rage, and Bella felt sudden fear as she realised he was right. Her mouth opened to speak, although she did not know what she could say to ward off what was obviously about to become a physical attack, but before she could think further Johnny halted, his hand on his chest and panic in his eyes. Fascinated she watched him slowly fall to his knees as his breath began to come in short irregular gasps, then she turned, opened the door, and walked back into the hall where Laura was making an elaborate show of hanging up their outdoor clothing in the large wardrobe under the stairs.

'Leave that for the moment and ring Dr Hatton to come here as soon as he can.' She said clearly. 'Tell him John Peacock appears to be having a heart attack!'

Laura hurried across the hall to use the telephone and Bella returned to the lounge where Johnny now lay prostrate, his eyes closed with the effort of fighting for every breath. For a while she stood quite still, watching him with a completely dispassionate curiosity, then she bent down to speak to him.

'We've sent for Dr Hatton to come.'

His eyes opened a fraction at her words and she touched his forehead and cheek gently with her fingers, although her smile belied their softness as she added. 'I don't think you're going to be very well in future, John, but don't worry. Constance and I will look after you.'

The windows of Ivy House were ablaze with light well into the early hours of the following day as its inhabitants fussed around Bill. Marion cried with joy, and kept on bursting into tears at regular intervals until she was too weary to do anything except go to her bed, and the children the same. It was past eleven o'clock when Bill, with Edward at his heels, carried Winifred upstairs, and Lilian noticed the lines of weariness and pain on his face as his limp became more pronounced. For a few seconds as he turned the corner on the first landing he looked like an old man, then he smiled down at her, shattering the disturbing image.

Alone at last they sat before the fire in the study, silent for a few moments until Bill asked 'Why did you want us to sit in here, Lilian? We always used to relax in the sitting room.'

'Because while you were away I always

visualised you in this room, working at your desk as you always did.'

'You did think of me then?'

'Bill, of course...' She stopped, suddenly remembering Sean, and he noticed her guilty look with dismay. Carefully he went on.

'We've been apart for a long time, love.'

She nodded, but did not raise her head.

'We've been apart much longer than my time in the war, and things can happen during long absences ... as I know myself. I'm sorry, but I befriended a woman in Dalton...'

'I know about Maura.' She cut in swiftly. 'I had a friend too for a while, but it was over long ago. I'm not proud of myself either, but at the time it began you weren't writing to me and we were still like strangers to one another.'

Bill's intense surprise at Lilian's knowledge of his previous affair was uncomfortably blended with a large portion of jealousy while he absorbed this unwelcome news, and she watched him with pounding heart, knowing that to go back to their old hostility a second time would be unbearable.

'I've been honest with you,' she offered into the silence. 'He was the second driver I told you about before, but he's gone back home to Scotland now. After the accident, which was some while after we had stopped seeing each other, I sent Albert up to Sean's relatives on Dalton Moor where I'd heard he was staying, because I owed him some pay. He sent back a polite little note thanking me for settling the money matter and informing me that he was leaving for Annan the next day.'

435

She had stood up in the middle of her explanation and Bill reached forward, gripping her hand.

'Lilian, I know both your affair and my own will always be painful for us to recall, but can't we put the past behind us and start again? I love you. I always have, even though there have been times when I've tried hard not to. We had so much once and, while I realise that it won't happen overnight, we can still work at getting it back. Little by little we can build our lives together again. What do you say, love?'

In the firelight he watched her expression soften to reflect her inner joy, and stood up holding out his arms to her. Without a sound Lilian stepped into his embrace laying her cheek thankfully against his shoulder, then with a sigh of content she lifted her face for his kiss.

From her bedroom window Constance looked out over the grounds of Low Shields where the early April sun was shining down on a garden coming alive again. The snowdrops and crocuses were gone now but clusters of daffodils splashed colour from the front of the house right up the drive, and she paused in the act of brushing her hair to study the figure of a man who had appeared, making his way slowly along the straight.

Behind her the maid placed her hot water jug on her wash stand and was about to leave when Constance called her to her side.

'Do you recognise that person, Annie?'

Squinting her eyes into the distance she shook her head.

'No miss. I don't think I've ever seen him before, but he's a bit too far away to be sure.'

Hardly aware of being left by herself again Constance kept watching the man. There was something about his general build and the way he held his head that she suddenly knew meant something important to her, and she dropped her hairbrush onto the bed and pulled on her dress before leaving the room, running down the stairs on an incredulous burst of hope.

Outside in the crisp air she stood for a moment on top of the steps, studying the man in the grey overcoat and scarf, then he waved and called to her.

'Connie!'

She began to run, aware every second that she was reliving her dream of how Ralph would return to her, yet hardly daring to believe that this time she was awake. Her dark hair with its streaks of grey flowed out in the light wind as she ran, but her face had lost its gaunt unhappy look and she was laughing as she reached his side. He held her tightly to him, closing his eyes as he kissed the top of her head, and she babbled incoherently, both laughing and crying in her happiness.

'I just can't believe you're really here. I heard from your family that you were missing in action, and I thought you had surely been killed.'

'I feared the same about you. Thank God you're still alive, Connie! It's taken me so long to find this place when all I had to go on were the things you had told me over four years ago.'

With her arms still around him she rubbed her

cheek against the roughness of his coat. 'Where have you been? I wrote to your sister just before Christmas 1915 and she told me the news about you, but although I didn't give up hope right away I never heard anything else from her.'

'I was taken prisoner and details would be forwarded to Sybil in due time, but they were all killed shortly afterwards in a Zeppelin raid. I found that out when I got back to this country. I'd planned to stay there for a while before travelling north, but ... that was it.'

'Oh Ralph, how awful.'

They began to walk towards the house, arm in arm, and Constance added softly. 'My parents are dead too, but the Spanish Flu did that three months ago. It's been too cruel after everything people have suffered in the war.'

Ralph stopped and hugged her fiercely. 'Poor little Connie. Is there no one else?'

'My sister and brother-in-law.'

'And me if you'll have me. Could you face being a schoolteacher's wife?'

To the side of the dining room curtains Annie and Mrs Evans, the cook, peeped out discreetly at the man and woman standing in the driveway kissing each other again as if their lives depended on it, then Annie pulled the green velvet back across the gap.

'They'll be coming in, Cook! Let's get back to the kitchen before they find us.' She whispered, and they scurried away to prepare breakfast for two.

CHAPTER EIGHTEEN

It was the evening of Gilfell's Fancy Dress Ball, the first event that could be in any way deemed a victory celebration, and in the bedroom that Lilian shared again with Bill she studied her reflection in the wardrobe mirror.

'Do I look like a Moonlight Night?' She asked her husband as he walked in from the landing. 'Tell me the truth.'

Bill smiled. 'You look lovely. Where did you find that white dress to sew the crescent moon and all those silver stars onto? I don't remember seeing it before.'

'Louisa gave it to me. It was her first wedding dress apparently, when she married the obnoxious Terence Marshall. It's a little short for me, but that will help when the children and I walk up to the Assembly Rooms. It was a good idea to allow children to attend, don't you think?'

Spinning round she watched the full skirt billow out like a cloud and gave a nod of complete satisfaction.

'Yes. It will look beautiful when we're dancing. You'll try not to be too late, won't you?'

Wondering wryly just how well Lilian imagined he could dance with his bad leg, Bill was still determined to do the best he could, and gave her a quick kiss before going downstairs to answer the door to Agnes Hall who sat with Marion so often these days when everyone else was out. His mother's deteriorating mental state continued to upset him, especially on the days when she persistently asked where Gilbert was, but George Hatton had assured him that there was nothing more to be done about it except to keep a close watch on her for her own safety.

He had recently suggested to Lilian that they invite the Hattons for dinner one night, but her response had been curiously negative, yet when he later broached the subject of Constance Fairburn and her new fiancé having a meal with them her enthusiasm had been unstinted and they had enjoyed a pleasant evening together.

Ralph Miller had recently been granted the position of Headmaster at Gilfell Village School, following the retirement of Mr Johnson who had held the post for over twenty years, and he and Constance were to be married in a few weeks' time, a piece of news that both Lilian and himself had greeted with unreserved approval. He had always liked Constance, and Lilian, who had reason to be grateful to her, liked her too. She and her Ralph deserved to be happy.

Edward was the only one in the Assembly Rooms that evening not in fancy dress, having steadfastly refused to wear the sailor's outfit that Lilian had hired for him, for he was secretly pretending that the ball was being given for him in honour of his birthday and that he had to stand out from the crowd. With the advent of adolescence his features were beginning to subtly alter in favour of his mother and, wearing his first pair of long trousers, he informed everyone he could that today, 21st May 1919, he was thirteen.

Winifred trotted behind him in her fairy costume, occasionally bobbing up and down so that the carefully made gossamer wings attached to the back of her bodice flapped around as though she were about to fly, then she would giggle and wave her wand, quite unabashed by the fact that there were so many people packed into the room that she performed virtually unnoticed.

Their grandfather, James Rutherford, had also resisted dressing up, but his wife and daughter had bullied him into submission, and tonight, aided by two bed sheets and a headband, he looked like a very well fed sheikh as he sat in a corner drinking home made wine. Beside him, little Marguerite in a ballerina costume sat watching everything, suddenly too tired to run after Helen any more, and he patted the top of her blonde head and smiled at her as she looked up.

'You look funny, Daddy.' She said, and he nodded solemnly.

'Yes. I know.'

A few yards away Edward moved through another crowd of chattering adults towards a pretty fair-haired shepherdess who was standing with one of her stepfather's crooks, polished and beribboned for the occasion.

'Helen!'

She smiled as he reached her side. 'Hello, Edward. Happy birthday. We have a present for you, but you won't get it until tomorrow when you all come to our house for tea.'

He grinned. 'I was only going to tell you about my birthday in case you'd forgotten. I'm thirteen

441

now. Shall we go to the refreshment tables and get something to eat?'

Louisa had been talking to Lilian but now she walked towards her husband and youngest daughter, her simple Grecian outfit charmingly topped by the ends of her upswept hair falling in many tiny ringlets towards her shoulders. She had often wanted to have her hair cut short like Lilian's, but tonight she was pleased she had not. James' expression lightened at the sight of her, and he mused with pleasure on the fact that no women in the village had ever openly slighted Louisa again since she had married him. He had loved Lilian's mother, Emily, and part of him still did, but he loved his second wife too: both women loved differently just as they themselves were different.

Louisa sat down at his side taking Marguerite on her knee, and the little girl's eyes began to close in the comfort of her arms as James said 'You look beautiful. You're by far the loveliest woman here, but I feel a proper pickle done up like this, Louie.'

Louisa laughed. 'You look fine, and it's a wonderful night. It's as though everyone's prepared to move on now and the whole atmosphere's touched by it, don't you agree?'

'It's the first time in over four years that there's been such a feeling and it's good, as you say, but for most families it hides grief that will never go away. You and I are very lucky to be personally untouched by bereavement.'

'That's true.'

A minor commotion at the entrance drew their

attention to the arrival of Ralph Miller with Constance and Bella. The man was dressed as a pirate and on each side of him walked a Fairburn sister, Bella, in a pale green flowing gown festooned with flowers, and Constance in a flounced scarlet flamenco dress and mantilla, explaining to everyone that she was a Spanish lady, Bella the Spirit of Summer, and the gentleman was her fiancé, Ralph Miller, whom they would all soon recognise as the new Headmaster of the village school. A ripple of surprise passed through the surrounding onlookers and Louisa smiled as she watched.

'They look so happy don't they? I wonder where Bella's husband is?'

'I've heard that he lives much more quietly since he had that heart attack at the end of January. Doesn't seem to go anywhere apart from the mines, and that isn't very often. Apparently Constance has taken a leaf out of our Lilian's book and is learning to run the business with the aid of an experienced manager she appointed to act in Johnny's place. She's bought herself a motor car too and drives herself everywhere these days, especially to and from White Court.'

Catching sight of Lilian at the opposite end of the room Louisa waved to the slim figure in her flowing white dress, whilst up on the stage a young man sat down at the piano where once Emma Dallow would have been, and a drummer and fiddler from Dalton took their places beside him ready to start the music for dancing.

Along the rough cart track Bill Robinson, dressed

443

as a highwayman, walked towards the Assembly Rooms, his mask in his hand ready to put on at the door. He had waited until his mother had fallen asleep before leaving her in Agnes' capable care, and he was enjoying his leisurely stroll in the ever deepening dusk along territory that he had once doubted he would ever see again. Mere yards from the party, where he could clearly hear the happy sounds of the villagers of Gilfell and surrounding district celebrating, he stopped beside a five bar gate and leaned his elbows along the top of it for a few moments. From this vantage point it was possible to look down the valley towards Dalton and believe that the events of the last four years had never happened, but they had happened, and taken his brother Gilbert with the thousands of others who would never come home again, while Jenny seemed to be devoting all her free time to organising a monument to the Kenhope area's war dead. He and Lilian had offered to help her, but it seemed as though she needed to achieve this memorial as nearly alone as she could, as her personal tribute to her husband. Afterwards, she explained gently, she would begin to move on in her life.

Tonight everything looked as it always had, and the only noise outside the building was the occasional bleat of a ewe to her lamb. Peaceful. Unchanging. Yet it was all an illusion. Great changes would take place in the next few decades, of that he felt quite certain, and while he could not guess what they would be he knew that the old familiar life of the valley had gone for good.

He and Lilian were now working together building up the garage into a proper bus company, and he smiled to himself thinking of the many arguments they had gone through debating whether or not she would become a permanent driver. Finally succeeding in persuading her to work in the office instead, Bill had admitted that he feared for her safety in managing the newly arrived second bus on the dangerous curves and inclines of the roads during the treacherous conditions of winter, despite the future services of the eagerly awaited snowplough. Their new driver was a man from Dalton returned from active service and happy to be taught how to handle the large vehicles. Things were going well with a healthy profit expected after a while, and soon he and Lilian could discuss buying a third bus; maybe one that would extend their journeys even further afield.

A sudden burst of music from the Assembly Rooms ended Bill's contented reverie, and he took off his tricorn hat and donned the mask before replacing it. Like most of the men present at the Fancy Dress Ball that night he felt more than a little ridiculous, but when he stepped inside the hall he forgot all about it as he spied Lilian just in front of him watching the dancers. Moving to stand behind her he put his arms round her white satin waist, drawing her back against him, and for a moment she closed her eyes savouring the feel of her head against his chest and the faint familiar smell of his shaving soap. His embrace tightened as he drew them both out to join the dancing, smiling as her skirt billowed out gracefully as it had done earlier in their bedroom. Once, in what now seemed like another lifetime, Lilian had been all he needed to be happy and, despite all that had happened since then, that part of him had never really changed. She was still, and always had been, as dear to him as the day they had married.

Putting his head close to hers he whispered in her ear. 'It's your birthday soon, Mrs Robinson. Name anything you want in this world and I promise I'll get it for you.'

The grey eyes looking up into his were gently teasing. 'Thank you, Mr Robinson. I'll have to give some very serious thought to your wonderful offer.'

Gathering her even closer to him, Bill Robinson was aware of a deep sense of peace. He and Lilian had travelled a long rocky road for many years, but now at last all was well between them, and he began again softly.

'About your birthday...'

'It really isn't important.' Her interruption as she pressed her cheek warmly against his almost caused him to break the rhythm of their steps, although neither seemed aware of it. 'Whatever you choose to give me for my birthday will be lovely, Bill, but since you've come back to me, in every possible way, I already have all I could want.'

'And I the same.' He admitted after a moment, his voice gruff with emotion, and they waltzed on, happily oblivious to everything and everyone except themselves.

The publishers hope that this book has given you enjoyable reading. Large Print Books are especially designed to be as easy to see and hold as possible. If you wish a complete list of our books please ask at your local library or write directly to:

Magna Large Print Books
Magna House, Long Preston,
Skipton, North Yorkshire.
BD23 4ND

This Large Print Book for the partially sighted, who cannot read normal print, is published under the auspices of

THE ULVERSCROFT FOUNDATION